"In Elliot's latest gripping novel the mystery and suspense are top-notch, and the romance embedded within will quench love story junkies' thirst, too. The author's eye for detail makes this one play out more like a movie rather than a book. It can easily be read as a standalone but is obviously much better if the prior three are digested first."

—*Romantic Times Book Reviews* on *Targeted*, 4 stars

"Elliot's latest addition to her thrilling, edge-of-your-seat series, Bone Secrets, will scare the crap out of you, yet allow you to swoon over the building romantic setting, which provides quite the picturesque backdrop. Her novel contains thrills, chills, snow and . . . hey, you never know! The surprises and cliffhangers are satisfying, yet edgy enough to keep you feverishly flipping the pages."

—*Romantic Times Book Reviews* on *Known*, 4 stars

"Elliot's best work to date. The author's talent is evident in the characters' wit and smart dialogue . . . One wouldn't necessarily think a psychological thriller and romance would mesh together well, but Elliot knows what she's doing when she turns readers' minds inside out and then softens the blow with an unforgettable love story."

—*Romantic Times Book Reviews* on *Vanished*, 4½ stars, Top Pick

"Kendra Elliot does it again! Filled with twists, turns, and spine-tingling details, *Alone* is an impressive addition to the Bone Secrets series."

—Laura Griffin, *New York Times* bestselling author

"Elliot once again proves to be a genius in the genre with her third heart-pounding novel in the Bone Secrets collection. The author knows romance and suspense, reeling readers in instantaneously and wowing them with an extremely surprising finish . . . Elliot's best by a mile!"
—*Romantic Times Book Reviews* on *Buried*, 4½ stars,
Top Pick (HOT)

"Make room on your keeper shelf! *Hidden* has it all: intricate plotting, engaging characters, a truly twisted villain. I can't wait to see what Kendra Elliot dishes up next!"
—Karen Rose, *New York Times* bestselling author

A
MERCIFUL
DEATH

ALSO BY KENDRA ELLIOT

BONE SECRETS NOVELS

Hidden

Chilled

Buried

Alone

Known

CALLAHAN & MCLANE

PART OF THE BONE SECRETS WORLD

Vanished

Bridged

Spiraled

Targeted

ROGUE RIVER NOVELLAS

On Her Father's Grave

Her Grave Secrets

Dead in Her Tracks

Death and Her Devotion

A
MERCIFUL
DEATH

KENDRA
ELLIOT

Montlake
Romance

Published by Montlake Romance, Seattle

www.apub.com

Amazon, the Amazon logo, and Montlake Romance are trademarks of Amazon.com, Inc., or its affiliates.

ISBN-13: 9781477818268 (hardcover)
ISBN-10: 147781826X (hardcover)

ISBN-13: 9781503939790 (paperback)
ISBN-10: 1503939790 (paperback)

Cover design by Eileen Carey

Printed in the United States of America
First edition

For my mother,
who taught me how to can applesauce and pickles.
For my father,
who taught me how to chop wood. And stack it
perfectly.

ONE

Mercy Kilpatrick wondered whom she'd ticked off at the Portland FBI office.

She stepped out of the car and walked past the two Deschutes County Sheriff SUVs to study the property around the lonely home in the wooded east-side foothills of the Cascade Mountains. Rain plunked on Mercy's hood, and her breath hung in the air. She tucked the ends of her long, dark curls inside her coat, noting the large amount of debris in the home's yard. What would appear to be a series of overgrown hedges and casual piles of junk to anyone else, she immediately identified as a carefully planned funneling system.

"What a mess," said Special Agent Eddie Peterson, who'd been temporarily assigned with her. "Looks like a hoarder lives here."

"Not a mess." She gestured at the thorny hedge and a huge rusted pile of scrap metal. "What direction do those items make you want to go?"

"Not that way," stated Eddie.

"Exactly. The owner deliberately piled all his crap to guide visitors to that open area in front of the house, stopping them from wandering around to the sides and back. Now look up." She pointed at a boarded-up window on the second story with a narrow opening cut into its center. "His junk positions strangers right where he can see them." Eddie nodded, surprise crossing his face.

Ned Fahey's home had been hard to find. The dirt-and-gravel roads weren't labeled, and they'd had to follow precise, mileage-based directions given to them by the county sheriff to find the house hidden deep in the forest. Mercy noted the fireproof metal roof and the sandbags stacked six feet high against the front of the house. The tired-looking cabin was far from any neighbors but close to a natural spring.

Mercy approved.

"What's with the sandbags?" Eddie muttered. "We're at an elevation of four thousand feet."

"Mass. Mass stops bullets and slows the bad guys. And sandbags are cheap."

"So he was nuts."

"He was prepared."

She'd smelled a light odor of decay in the yard, and as she climbed the porch steps to the house, it slapped her full in the face. *He's been dead several days.* A stone-faced Deschutes County deputy held out a log for her and Eddie to sign. Mercy eyed the deputy's simple wedding ring. His spouse would not be happy when he arrived home with corpse scent clinging to his clothes.

Next to her, Eddie breathed heavily through his mouth. "Don't puke," she ordered under her breath as she slipped disposable booties over her rubber rain boots.

He shook his head, but his expression was doubtful. She liked Eddie. He was a sharp agent with a positive attitude, but he was a young city boy and stood out here in the boonies with his hipster haircut and nerdy glasses. His expensive leather shoes with the heavy treads would never be the same after the mud in Ned Fahey's yard.

But they looked good.

Used to look good.

Inside the house, she stopped to examine the front door. It was steel. The door had four hinges and three dead bolts; the additional bolts were positioned near the top and bottom of the door.

Fahey had built an excellent defense. He'd done everything right, but someone had managed to break through his barriers.

That shouldn't have happened.

Mercy heard voices upstairs and followed. Two crime scene techs directed her and Eddie down the hall to a bedroom at the back of the house. An increasing buzzing sound made Mercy's stomach turn over; it was a sound she'd heard about but never experienced for herself. Eddie swore under his breath as they turned into Fahey's bedroom, and the medical examiner glanced up from her inspection of a bloated body on the bed.

Mercy had been right about the source of the noise. The room vibrated with the low roar of flies that had discovered the corpse's orifices. She avoided looking closely at the distended belly that strained the buttons of its clothing. The face was the worst. Unrecognizable behind the black screen of flies.

The medical examiner nodded at the agents as Mercy introduced herself and Eddie. Mercy guessed the medical examiner wasn't much older than she. She was tiny and trim, making Mercy feel abnormally tall.

Dr. Natasha Lockhart introduced herself, peeled off her gloves, and laid them on the body. "I understand he was known to the FBI," she said, lifting a brow.

"He's on the no-fly list," Mercy said. The list was one of a few the FBI used for its terrorism persons to watch. Ned Fahey had been on it for several years. The corpse on the bed had a history of brushes with the federal government. Sovereign citizens and right-wing militia types were his preferred company. From the reports Mercy had read on the long drive from Portland, she gathered that Fahey had talked the talk but had been unable to walk the walk. He'd been arrested several times for minor destruction of federal property, but someone else had always been the ringleader. Fahey's criminal charges had seemed to slide off him as if he were coated in Teflon.

"Well, someone decided they no longer needed Mr. Fahey around," said Dr. Lockhart. "He must have been a sound sleeper to not hear our killer enter his house and place a weapon against his forehead."

"Against?" Mercy asked.

"Yep. Even under all the flies, I can see the tattooing of the gun-powder in the skin around the entry hole. One nice hole in and one out. Through and through. Lots of power behind the round for it to go through that cleanly." Dr. Lockhart grinned at Eddie, who swayed slightly as he stood by Mercy. "The flies brush away easily enough. For a moment."

"Caliber?" Eddie asked in a strangled voice.

Dr. Lockhart shrugged. "Big. Not a puny twenty-two. I'm sure you'll find the bullet burrowed in something below."

Mercy stepped forward and squatted next to the bed, shining a flashlight underneath, intending to see if the round had gone into the floor, but the space under the bed was crammed with plastic storage containers. *Of course it is.*

She glanced around the room, noticing the heavy-duty trunks stacked neatly in each corner. She knew exactly what the closets would look like. Floor-to-ceiling storage neatly labeled and organized. Fahey lived alone, but Mercy knew they'd uncover enough supplies to last a small family through the next decade.

Fahey wasn't a hoarder; he was a prepper. His life centered on being prepared for TEOTWAWKI.

The end of the world as we know it.

And he was the third Deschutes County prepper to be murdered in his own home over the last few weeks.

"Did you handle the first two deaths, Dr. Lockhart?" she asked.

"Call me Natasha," she said. "You mean the other two prepper murders? I responded to the first, and an associate went to the second. I can tell you the first death wasn't nice and neat like this. He fought for his life. Think they're connected?"

Mercy gave a smile that said nothing. "That's what we're here to find out."

"Dr. Lockhart's damned right about that first death," said a new voice in the room.

Mercy and Eddie turned to find a tall, angular man with a sheriff's star studying both of them. His gaze grew puzzled as it lingered on the thick frames of Eddie's black glasses. No doubt the residents of Deschutes County didn't see a lot of hip 1950s throwbacks. Mercy made introductions. Sheriff Ward Rhodes appeared to be in his sixties. Decades of sun exposure had created deep lines and rough patches on his face, but his eyes were clear and keen and probing.

"This room looks like a tea party compared to the scene at the Biggs murder. That place had a dozen bullet holes in the walls, and old man Biggs fought back with a knife."

Mercy knew Jefferson Biggs had been sixty-five and wondered how he'd earned the title of *old man* from this sheriff who was in the same age group.

Probably an indication of Biggs's get-off-my-lawn attitude more than his age.

"But none of the homes—including this one—showed forced entry, correct?" asked Eddie politely.

Sheriff Rhodes nodded. "That's right." He scowled at Eddie. "Anyone ever tell you that you look like James Dean? With glasses?"

"I get that a lot."

Mercy bit her lip. Eddie claimed to be surprised by the comparison, but she knew he liked it. "But if there's no forced entry here, and Ned Fahey was asleep," she said, "then someone knew how to get inside the house or was also sleeping in the house."

"He's wearing pajamas," agreed Dr. Lockhart. "I don't know the time of death yet. The putrefaction is very progressed. I'll know more after lab tests."

"We examined the house," said Sheriff Rhodes. "There's no sign that anyone was sleeping here or of any forced entry. There's another bedroom, but it doesn't look like it's been slept in for a few decades. The sofa downstairs doesn't have any pillows or blankets to indicate that someone else was here." He paused. "Front door was wide open when we got here."

"I take it Ned Fahey was the type to keep his doors locked tight?" Mercy asked half in jest. The short walk through the house had shown her a man who took home defense very seriously. "Who reported his death?"

"Toby Cox. He gives Ned a hand around here. Was supposed to help Ned move some wood this morning. He said the door was open and when he saw the situation he called us. I sent him home a few hours ago. He's not quite right in the head, and this shook him up something fierce."

"You know most of the local residents?" Mercy asked.

The sheriff shrugged. "I know most. But who can know everyone? I know the people I know," he said simply. "This home is far from any city limits, so whenever Ned had an issue, he called us at the county."

"Issue? Who'd Ned have problems with?" Mercy asked. She understood the politics and social behaviors of small towns and rural communities. She'd spent the first eighteen years of her life in a small town. The residents tried to make everyone's business their own. Now she lived in a large, urban condo complex where she knew two of her neighbors' names. First names.

She liked it that way.

"Someone broke into a couple of Ned's outbuildings one time. Stole his quad and a bunch of fuel. He was pretty steamed about that. We never did find it. Other calls have been complaints of people hunting or trespassing on his property. He's got a good ten acres here, and the borders aren't marked very well. Ned posted some **KEEP OUT** signs, but you can only cover so much ground with those. He used to fire a shotgun to scare people off. After that happened a few times, we asked him to call us first. Scared the crap out of a backpacking family one time."

"No dogs?"

"I told him to get a few. He said they eat too much."

Mercy nodded. *Fewer mouths to feed.*

"Income?" she asked.

"Social Security." Sheriff Rhodes twisted his lips.

Mercy understood. It was common for the antigovernment types to raise hell about paying their taxes or buying licenses, but don't *dare* touch their Social Security.

"Anything missing?" asked Eddie. "Is there anyone who would even know what's missing?"

"As far as I know, Toby Cox was the only person to step foot in this house in the last ten years. We can ask him, but I'll warn you he's not the most observant type." Rhodes cleared his throat, a sheepish look on his face. "I can't take it too seriously, but I'll tell you Toby was terrified and rambling that the cave man had killed Ned."

"What?" asked Eddie. "A caveman? Like prehistoric?"

Mercy simply stared at the sheriff. Communities had their rumors and legends, but this was one she'd never heard of.

"No, I gathered from my talk with Toby that it was more like a mountain man. But like I said, he gets confused easily. The boy's not all there. I can't give it any weight."

"Did he see this cave man?" Mercy asked.

"No. My impression was that Ned had told Toby the story to scare the crap out of him. Seemed to work."

"Got it."

"But we do have one interesting thing," said the sheriff. "Someone broke into a storage unit outside. Follow me."

Mercy sucked in deep breaths of fresh air as she followed the sheriff down the porch stairs. He led them through the junk-lined funnel and fifty feet down the dirt road before veering off on a path. She smugly noted her toes were dry in her cheery rain boots. She'd warned Eddie to dress appropriately, but he'd brushed it off. This wasn't rain on concrete sidewalks in downtown Portland; this was a rainstorm in the Cascades. Mud, heavy brush, wandering streams, and more mud. She glanced back and saw Eddie wipe the rain off his forehead, and he gave a wry smile with a pointed look at his mud-caked shoes.

Yep.

They ducked under a yellow ribbon of police tape that surrounded a small shed. "The crime scene techs have already processed the scene," Sheriff Rhodes advised. "But try to watch where you step."

Mercy studied the mess of crisscrossing boot prints and didn't see a clear place to step. The sheriff simply walked through, so she followed. The shed was about fifteen by twenty feet and hidden by tall rhododendrons. From the outside it looked as if a strong wind would flatten the tiny outbuilding, but inside Mercy noticed the walls had been heavily reinforced and the room was lined with sandbags along the dirt floor.

"Chain on the door was cut. I should say all *three* chains on the door were cut," the sheriff corrected himself. He gestured toward a big hole in the ground near the back wall of the shed. The lid to an ancient deep freezer opened out of the hole.

Bodies?

Mercy peered into the buried freezer. Empty. She sniffed the air, catching the minty odor of a weapon lubricant she knew some gun enthusiasts swore by, and a hint of gunpowder smell. Ned had hidden an arsenal in the ground.

"Weapons," she stated flatly. Fahey had had three guns registered in his name. He wouldn't have worked this hard to hide three guns. He could have easily stored a few dozen in the huge freezer. Mercy wondered how Ned had controlled the humidity for the guns. As far as weapons storage went, this wasn't ideal.

"There was one of those little cordless humidifiers in there," Rhodes stated as if he'd read her mind. "But someone had to know where to dig to find the freezer." He gestured at the piles of fresh dirt. "I wonder how well camouflaged the freezer was. This isn't a place I'd come looking for weapons."

"Anyone know how many weapons he actually had?" Mercy asked.

The sheriff shrugged and looked into the freezer. "Lots is my guess."

"You said there were three chains locking the door?" Eddie asked. "To me that screams, 'I've got something valuable in here.'" He pointed at a narrow steel rod on the dirt floor. "If I broke through three sets of locks and chains and found an empty shed, I'd start plunging that into the ground until I hit something."

Sure enough, there were narrow holes in scattered places across the floor of the shed.

"He's a prepper," Mercy stated. "It's expected he'd have a stash of guns somewhere."

"They didn't have to murder him in his bed to steal his guns," Rhodes pointed out.

"They?" asked Mercy, her ears perking up.

The sheriff raised his hands defensively. "No proof. Just going by the amount of work I see here and the number of footprints found in front of this shed. The techs are running a comparison on Fahey's and Toby Cox's boots to see what's left. They'll let us know how many people were here."

"Can't rule out Cox," Eddie pointed out.

Sheriff Rhodes nodded, but Mercy saw the regret in his eyes. She suspected he liked this Toby Cox who wasn't "right in the head."

Mercy mentally placed Toby Cox at the top of her list to interview.

TWO

"I want to see the other two murder sites," Mercy told Eddie as she drove toward Eagle's Nest.

Out of the corner of her eye, she saw him nod as he focused on a file in his lap.

"They're both on the other side of Eagle's Nest," he replied. "I'll pull up the location of the first."

The two agents had driven directly to Ned Fahey's hideaway from Portland after Mercy's office exchanged several phone calls with Bend's supervisory senior resident agent (SSRA). The other two murders had taken place closer to the city of Eagle's Nest, but the locations were still a good half hour from the Bend office. The Bend office needed help, Mercy's supervisor had explained as she told the two of them about their temporary assignment. It had only five agents, a few support staff, and no domestic terrorism agents.

Because of the victims' histories, the large number of missing weapons from all three murders could point to someone preparing for a domestic terrorism event.

Her boss's words rang in her head. Several dozen guns were missing from the first two murder sites, and Ned Fahey had buried a large illegal stash on his property.

An event. A calm way of saying a group might be gearing up to overtake a federal building. Or worse.

The rain clouds had blown off as they left Ned Fahey's home, and now blue sky peeked through as they departed the denser forest, headed for lower altitudes. As they pulled away from the foothills, Mercy spotted the white mountain peaks of the Cascades in her rearview mirror, thrilled she could see several at a time. She'd taken the sight for granted as a kid. In Portland she saw primarily one peak; on a clear day she might see one or two more. But in this part of Central Oregon, where the skies were often blue, multiple peaks gleamed.

The air felt cleaner too.

She headed down a straight stretch of highway, tall pines towering along both sides of the road.

"Hey. The trees changed color," Eddie said as he stared out the window.

"They changed back where we crested the Cascade Range. Those are ponderosa pines and they're a paler green than the firs you're used to on our side of the Cascades. The trunks are redder too."

"What are the silvery, scrubby-looking bushes everywhere?"

"Sagebrush."

"The forest feels different over here," Eddie remarked. "There's still giant green trees everywhere, but the underbrush isn't dense at all like on the west side. Tons of rocks here too."

"The pines will thin out soon. And you'll see acres of ranchland and lava rocks and brush depending on where you go."

Mercy noticed her knuckles were white as she gripped the steering wheel. She drove without thinking, instinctively heading toward the town where she'd spent the first eighteen years of her life.

"Turn at the next left," Eddie instructed.

I know.

"I grew up in Eagle's Nest."

Eddie's head jerked up, and she felt his stare bore into the side of her head. She kept her eyes on the road.

"I don't believe that you remembered that particular fact two seconds ago," Eddie stated. "Why didn't you say something? Does the boss know?"

"She knows. I left home when I was eighteen and haven't been back. Family stuff, you know."

He shifted in his seat to face her. "I hear a good story percolating, Special Agent Kilpatrick. Spill it."

"No story." She refused to look at him.

"Bullshit. You haven't been home since you were eighteen? Did they beat you? Do they belong to a cult?"

She gave a short laugh. "Neither." *Not exactly.*

"Then what? You've talked to them, right? E-mails? Texts? Leaving home means you simply didn't return to the town, right?" He looked out the windshield at the trees. "I haven't seen anything out here to make me want to drive the four hours."

Mercy pressed her lips together, wishing she'd not started the conversation. "There's been no contact at all. Nothing."

"*What?* Do you have siblings?"

"Four."

"*Four?* And you've never called or e-mailed *any* of them?"

She shook her head, unable to speak.

"What's wrong with your family? My mom would fry me if she didn't hear from me at least once a month."

"They're different." *Understatement.* "Can we not discuss this right now?"

"You brought it up."

"I know I did, and I'll tell you about it later." *Maybe.* She took the final turn into Eagle's Nest and drove down the two-lane road she knew would take them through the center of town.

She slowed to the posted twenty-five miles per hour. The lofty name Eagle's Nest implied that the town sat on a hill, grandly overlooking a valley. It lied. Eagle's Nest sat on the flat. The town's elevation was three thousand feet, but so was that of the hundreds of acres surrounding it. She drove past the schools, craning her neck to get a good look. According to the rusting signs, the older building still housed the high school, while the larger "new" building still held K–8. The "new" building had been constructed in the seventies, before she was born. Behind the old building she saw the lights for the football field and stands. New red bleachers stood on one side of the field.

September. *Should be a football game this weekend.*

"Did you go to school there?" Eddie asked.

"Yes."

The road took a sharp turn. On her left the sawmill was still closed. Its roof sagged more than she remembered, and weathered plywood covered all the windows. The familiar sign was gone. The mill had been abandoned when she was quite young, but it'd always had a big sign with a message board out front. In her teens the town had used the tall message board to post event dates in mismatched letters, but for a long time before that it'd simply proclaimed: WE'LL BE BACK.

All that was left now was a jagged, broken metal post, and Mercy felt a small pin stab her heart. It'd been everyone's habit to check the board to keep a finger on the pulse of the community. Senior citizen birthdays. Fairs. Bake sales.

Now they probably post on the city's Facebook page.

Everyone in the community had sworn the lumber mill would reopen. She'd heard it over and over. At one time the city had kept the mill's property free of dumped garbage and replaced the windows broken by stupid kids. *"Someone will buy it. We simply need the right business to come along."*

The missing message board said the town had lost faith.

The mill was a victim of poor economics, federal policies on tree harvests, and increased conservation measures. Now it looked like a good location to create a Halloween haunted house.

She kept driving. Suddenly one- and two-story buildings lined both sides of the street. She scanned their signs. Several were new to her, but some hadn't changed. EAGLE'S NEST POLICE DEPARTMENT, EAGLE'S NEST CITY HALL, GRAND MOVIE THEATER, POST OFFICE, JOHN DEERE DEALERSHIP. She noticed a church had been converted to a senior center. The old Norwood home now called itself "Sandy's Bed & Breakfast."

Eddie pointed at a tiny shop. "Hey, that looks promising. I need caffeine. Pull over."

Mercy pulled into a slanted parking space, remembering how she'd had to learn to parallel park when she moved to Portland. It wasn't a skill needed in tiny towns. The Coffee Café occupied a building where she'd once spent hours as a teen browsing used books. It looked fresh and updated, and the Illy brand coffee sign in the window suggested the owners took their coffee seriously. The store was a small, bright flower in the depressing gray of the streets and tired buildings. She glanced up and down the street. A few trucks drove past, but no one strolled the sidewalks.

The bell jangled as they pulled open the door. Mercy unzipped her jacket, appreciating the rush of heat and coffee scents.

"Hi there." A teenage girl popped out of a doorway behind the counter. "What can I get for you?"

She was cute and smiley, with a perky ponytail. She regarded them with faint curiosity, but she was polite and kept her questions to herself. Mercy studied the chalkboard menu just inside the door as Eddie stepped forward and ordered something with a triple shot. The girl started his espresso, and Eddie looked over his shoulder at Mercy. "She could be you twenty years ago," he said in a low voice, a question in his eyes.

Uh-oh.

Mercy moved to get a better look at their barista. The girl's hair was lighter, but the eyes and the shape of her face were spot-on. *Pearl's daughter? Owen's?* She admired the small gemstone stud in the girl's nose. Whoever she was, she had a rebellious streak. Mercy's parents would have ripped the stud out every time they saw it.

"I'll take an Americano. Do you have heavy cream instead of half-and-half?" Mercy asked as she stepped closer. The barista met her gaze, nodded enthusiastically, and went back to creating heaven in a cup.

Whoever she was, the sight of Mercy meant nothing to her.

Mercy breathed out a sigh of relief.

"Do you live in town?" Eddie asked the barista as Mercy silently cursed him. The agent liked people and enjoyed hearing their stories. He'd start up a conversation while waiting in line at the grocery store.

The girl smiled. "Just outside of town."

"You aren't working here alone, are you?"

At the flash of alarm in the barista's eyes, Mercy punched him in the arm.

"I mean . . . I'm not a weirdo. I'm wondering about your safety," Eddie said lamely.

"Ignore him," Mercy said with a smile meant to calm the startled girl. "He means well and he's harmless."

"My father's in back," she said tentatively. The sunshine drained out of her face, and she eyed Eddie with caution.

"That's good," admitted Eddie. "Didn't mean to freak you out."

The barista held up their cups. Mercy reached for both, and watched the girl's gaze shoot to Mercy's left side under her jacket. "You're law enforcement," the girl said as she nodded toward the weapon.

"Doesn't everyone around here carry?" asked Eddie in a joking tone.

"Usually revolvers, not Glocks." Interest lit up her eyes. "Is this because of the men that were murdered recently? I heard Ned Fahey was found dead this morning."

The gossip chain was in full swing.

"Kaylie? Everything okay?" a tall man asked sharply as he stepped into the doorway behind the barista, his broad shoulders filling the space.

Mercy's heart stopped as she locked eyes with the man. Shock swept his face.

"Holy shit!" he muttered.

"Dad!"

"Sorry, hon."

He was big and dark haired, with a thick beard that hadn't grayed. Mercy had never seen him with a beard, but she recognized her brother instantly. She didn't speak, letting Levi decide what to do. He looked from her to his daughter and then back again, taking in Eddie in the same glance.

"You from out of town to investigate the murders?" he asked Eddie. "I didn't realize the FBI was involved. That seems odd."

Mercy swallowed. Her brother had ignored her. *But* he knew they were FBI. That meant he knew what she did for a living. He hadn't abandoned her completely.

"We come when our help is requested," Eddie replied noncommittally.

"Didn't know anyone had asked," said Levi. He looked at Mercy, all recognition gone from his eyes. "Coffee's on the house today."

"We appreciate it, but we'll pay," said Eddie. He pulled cash out of his wallet and gave Mercy a side-eyed questioning glance. *What the fuck is going on?*

She couldn't move. Or speak. Her fingers had frozen to the hot cups in her hands.

"Have a good day," Kaylie said automatically as she handed Eddie his change.

He dropped it in the tip jar. "You too." He took his cup out of Mercy's hand, his gaze still questioning her.

Mercy took one last lingering look at her niece and then at her brother. Levi turned and vanished without acknowledging her again. She followed Eddie out into the cold and got in their car. She held her coffee with both hands, unable to look at the other agent.

"That guy clearly knew you but didn't say anything," Eddie stated. "And since the barista who looks *exactly* like you is his daughter, I assume he's your brother?" His voice cracked on the final word.

Mercy nodded and sipped her coffee. *Damn.* She'd forgotten to add the heavy cream.

"Who doesn't acknowledge his sister? Not that you said anything either," he muttered. "So I assume whatever the issue is, it goes both ways? Did you know that was his coffee place?"

"No."

Eddie sighed and took a long swig out of his paper cup. "Sorry, Mercy. None of my business." He paused for all of two seconds. "Tell me you knew that was your niece."

"No. I suspected it once you pointed it out, but I didn't know which sibling of mine she belonged to."

"You knew this brother had kids, right?"

"One."

"He didn't wear a wedding ring. Was he married?"

"No. When I left, his girlfriend wouldn't let him visit their one-year-old daughter. I guess that changed." Mercy set down her cup and started the car. "Let's get going to the other crime scene before it's full dark." She backed out of the parking space. Embarrassment with a small spark of fury flushed her face. She hadn't heard a peep out of her family in fifteen years.

What other surprises waited for her in Eagle's Nest?

THREE

Truman Daly swore under his breath.

He'd followed the old Ford pickup for a mile as it weaved and bobbed down the rural highway, the driver pointedly ignoring the swirling lights and sirens from Truman's vehicle. He had to make a quick decision before the Ford entered a populated part of the town. Truman knew the driver and fully expected an earful when he finally got Anders Beebe to the side of the road. An earful he'd already heard a half-dozen times in his six months as Eagle's Nest police chief. The old Ford caught a tire in the soft shoulder and overcorrected into the oncoming lane, then swerved back into its own.

Anders has to be drunk.

Making his decision, Truman accelerated and pulled the department's Tahoe into the other lane, preparing to tap the old-timer's right rear fender and send him into a spin. Instead, before Truman could tap the Ford, a huge cloud of steam burst out from under Anders's hood, and he pulled off the road and rolled to a stop. Truman parked behind him and wished his department could afford a body camera to record the imminent kooky conversation.

With one hand on the butt of his gun, he approached the vehicle. The window was jerkily lowered by a hand crank. "Anders? You okay?" he asked.

"What the *hell* did you do to my truck?" The old-timer's words ran together, and Truman picked up the scent of beer from five feet away. *"How in the Lord's high heaven did you do that?"*

"I didn't do anything to your truck. Something's up with your engine."

"Yes, you did! You police got some new fancy gadget to illegally stop citizens. How much tax money did the government spend on *that?*"

"Can you step out of the vehicle for me?" Truman asked. He knew Anders was generally harmless, but he'd never encountered him drunk, so his reflexes were on high alert.

"I do not consent!" Anders shrieked. Truman stepped close enough to see empty beer cans on the Ford's bench seat.

"How much have you drunk today, Anders?" he asked.

"I do not consent! Codes and statutes aren't laws unless I consent!"

Truman sighed. Even while he was drunk, Anders's sovereign citizen beliefs were in full force.

"Your vehicle's not going any farther today, Anders. Let me give you a ride and you can call someone to look at it."

The man's red-rimmed, pale-blue eyes couldn't hold eye contact with Truman. The lines in Anders's face were deeper than usual, and his gray hair stuck out in all directions from under his hat. "I do not wish to create joinder with you," he stated.

Truman bit his tongue. Sovereign citizens had a whole litany of confusing pseudo-legalese to quote whenever they encountered a government official. The first time one had told Truman he didn't want to create joinder with him, Truman had nearly replied that he wasn't asking for sex. "I don't want to create joinder with you either, Anders, but I will help you back to town. Does that work for you?"

"I'm a freeman on the land," he sang.

"We're all free men, Anders. Why don't you hop out and let's see what's happened under your hood?" At least Anders wasn't yelling at him anymore, but he was swaying nonstop in his seat. Truman doubted he could walk.

Probably why Anders had decided to drive.

The Ford's door creaked open and Anders tried to stand but stumbled forward into Truman's arms.

"Gotcha." Truman turned his face away from the alcohol and body odor fumes. "Let's get you to my vehicle." He guided the man to the back door of his Tahoe, deftly checking him for weapons on the way.

"I don't want to create joinder with you," Anders muttered as Truman's hands ran over his faded denim overalls.

"That makes two of us," Truman replied. Two rifles sat in the rear window gun rack of the Ford's cab, but Anders didn't have anything smaller on his body. Truman cuffed him, put him in the back seat, and went back to check the Ford. He removed the weapons, cranked up the window, grabbed the keys from the ignition, and locked it up.

He returned to his vehicle and found Anders snoring in the back seat.

All the better. Sovereign citizens preferred to do their battles with words. Their statements were a lot of nonsense to Truman's ears, but he knew they fully believed that they could avoid commonplace legal charges by making various oral declarations. They could talk their twisted legalese for hours, and the nonstop confrontations were exhausting.

He considered it a blessing to listen to Anders snore on the drive back to town.

Truman walked Anders through the small police department and was getting him settled in one of the three holding cells when Officer Royce Gibson stuck his head in the room and wrinkled his nose.

"Jesus, what's that smell?"

"The usual cocktail of alcohol and body odor," Truman answered. He stepped out of the cell and locked the door.

"Hey, Anders," said Royce. "When'd you last shower?"

Truman sent him a look, and the young officer had the decency to look abashed.

"I am liberated from the government and not subject to US laws," slurred Anders.

"In that case, consider this a safe place to wait until you can walk without help," offered Truman. The older man nodded, lay down on his cot, and started snoring again.

"No joinder," Truman said in an amused voice.

"I have no idea what the hell he means when he says that," said Royce. "I ignore it."

"He believes it keeps him from being subject to our laws. Something about there not being a legal agreement between him and us." Truman shook his head. "Keep an eye on him. I'm headed home for the evening."

"Wait a minute. I was coming to tell you that the FBI in Bend called; they've got two agents from Portland going to . . . the . . . Biggs murder scene. They want someone to walk them through it since it's over two weeks old . . . and the door is locked."

The steak-and-baked-potato dinner Truman had been thinking about all day suddenly got pushed back an hour. Or two. His stomach grumbled in protest. "Does it have to be tonight?"

"My understanding is they're waiting outside the house already."

Truman gave a short nod and strode toward the door, grabbing the cowboy hat he'd hung up when he arrived with Anders. He shoved it on his head. No one was poking around Jefferson Biggs's home unless he was watching their every move.

◆ ◆ ◆

Five minutes later Truman pulled up behind another black Tahoe in front of the two-week-old murder scene.

Two people stepped out of the vehicle, and he was briefly surprised to see a woman.

Have I been in Eagle's Nest too long? He'd worked with plenty of women at his old law enforcement job and in the army. Six months in this isolated part of the country was turning him into a redneck. He didn't have any women officers on his force, but according to the other guys, none had ever applied.

The man wore glasses and a heavy wool coat. No hat. He strode toward Truman, holding out his hand. "Special Agent Eddie Peterson. We appreciate you letting us in the house." His handshake was strong, his eye contact solid.

The woman stepped forward, and Truman stopped himself from touching the brim of his hat when he realized her hand was out to shake. "Special Agent Mercy Kilpatrick." Her handshake wasn't as strong, but her green eyes were probing and intelligent. Truman felt as if she'd examined him inside and out, and learned all his secrets in one long glance. She was as tall as her partner, but had smartly worn a waterproof coat with a hood. And rubber boots.

"Truman Daly. I'm the police chief of Eagle's Nest. A little more notice next time would be nice." He couldn't stop the small reprimand; they were taking his time, and he was hungry.

"Our apologies," said Special Agent Peterson. "We just left the Fahey scene and wanted to get a look at the previous two scenes while the first was fresh in our minds."

Truman scowled. "I heard Ned Fahey was murdered. You think it's related to this one?" Mentally he swore at Deschutes County's Sheriff Rhodes. The sheriff had kept all the details about Fahey's death under his hat, and now Truman looked like an uninformed idiot. Granted, Fahey's property was on county land, but Truman had considered the odd man an honorary resident of Eagle's Nest since he liked to hang out occasionally at the John Deere dealership and shoot the breeze with the other locals who assembled there at the crack of dawn every weekday morning for bad coffee and gossip.

Special Agent Kilpatrick turned away to look at the house. "It's possible," she said from under her hood. He couldn't see her lips move, just the rain sparkling on a few escaped black curls that wouldn't stay under her coat.

In the last minutes of daylight, the home and outbuildings looked lonely. As if they were waiting for their owner to return. The emptiness settled over Truman and threatened to bury him in memories. Jefferson Biggs would never return to his home. Truman had recently moved to Eagle's Nest to be closer to Uncle Jefferson, and now he was gone. *What's keeping me here?* Truman's roots hadn't grown very deep in six months.

"Is the power still on in the home?" Kilpatrick asked. "It looks dark."

"It is. The house is on city power, but it has a few backup systems in case that fails," answered Truman.

"Good." Her hood bobbed in a nod. "Were you one of the first responders? Did you see the scene before it was investigated?"

"I found him," Truman said shortly. "I let myself in when he didn't show up for coffee."

Kilpatrick faced him, curiosity in her features. "You had a key?"

He wanted to squirm under her green-eyed scrutiny. "He's my uncle."

Sympathy flooded her gaze. "I'm very sorry. How horrible for you. Do you have other family in town?"

Truman felt the invisible walls rise around his heart. They'd been activated numerous times since Uncle Jefferson's death. "No, we were the only two who lived in Oregon."

"You didn't step down from the investigation?" Peterson asked.

"This isn't the big city. I don't have access to a stable of investigators. Besides, I wanted to oversee every step, so I knew it was done right."

Kilpatrick silently studied him for a long second. He held her gaze. She could reprimand him all she wanted; this was his town, and he had the final say.

"Let's take a look," she said. "Lead the way and give us a running commentary on what you found."

Truman gave a stiff nod and led the two outsiders toward the house.

"You don't have any suspects?" Peterson asked as they avoided several lake-size puddles in the dim light.

"None. I lifted dozens of prints. Ninety-nine percent were my uncle's or mine. No hits on the others."

"But his arsenal was emptied," Kilpatrick stated.

"Yes. Every last weapon." Last week Truman had discovered that his uncle had registered only two guns in his name. He'd known his uncle owned at least thirty different weapons.

He paused at the door and pulled the keys out of his coat pocket. His copies of his uncle's keys were on an ancient Pabst Blue Ribbon key chain that Truman had envied during his teen years. He flipped through the keys, slipped one in the lock, and glanced over his shoulder at the agents. "Ready?"

FOUR

Sheriff Rhodes's words flashed through Mercy's mind.

He'd called Ned Fahey's murder site a tea party compared to the Biggs scene.

What are we walking into?

"Nothing's changed since the day I found him," warned Truman.

Mercy nodded at the police chief. "We're ready." Truman paused a second longer and then shoved open the door, leading the way in.

"Booties?" Eddie asked before stepping over the threshold. He and Mercy had put on vinyl gloves as they walked through the yard.

"We vacuumed up every lick of evidence from the floor. Essentially the scene has been released, but I appreciate your gloves." He flicked a light switch, and two lamps lit up in the small living room.

"Essentially it's been released?" Mercy asked.

Pain flashed in the chief's eyes whenever he mentioned his uncle. "Jefferson left everything to me. It's my house now, and I'm not going to clean it up until I figure out who did this."

Mercy imagined the old house gathering dust and cobwebs growing over the crime scene. *How long will he wait?*

Clearly the nephew was still grieving.

Maybe we should ask for someone else to show us the scene.

But one look at the determined jaw of the chief as he scanned the interior of the home told her he was their best source of information about Jefferson Biggs. She had to move past any concern about his feelings.

The house had a strong scent of a tobacco pipe. A smell Mercy remembered from her childhood. Her grandmother had hated the "stinky pipe" and would send her grandfather outside to smoke, but the odor had always clung to his clothes.

The small living room had one old sofa, two chairs, no TV, and several faded prints of elk on the walls. The dark-brown carpet was heavily matted, and in front of a well-used easy chair the carpet was worn down nearly to the mesh backing. There was no sign of a woman's touch.

If the victim left everything to his nephew, does that mean he had no children?

She needed to review the Biggs file.

"He was found back here." Truman turned down a narrow hallway. She and Eddie followed.

A dark, reddish-brown smear zigzagged along one wall and ended in a distinct handprint. Ragged bullet holes surrounded a door frame halfway down the hall. The door was also peppered with holes. Truman pushed it open with one finger and stepped back as he gestured them toward the dark room.

Mercy moved forward and blindly felt around the corner for a light switch in the black space. It was a small bathroom, and the floor was covered with thick, swirling patterns of dried blood. Bullet holes covered the back wall. A few more holes peppered the old linoleum.

It was brutal.

"He took refuge in the bathroom?" Eddie asked behind her.

"Yep. After confronting someone in his kitchen. The blood trail starts out there. I found one of his kitchen knives on the bathroom floor beside him. He was shot eleven times." The chief's voice was a monotone. "Someone else's blood was on the knife, so I know he delivered at least one injury."

Mercy looked back at him. "Your uncle was a fighter."

"Absolutely. He didn't take shit from anyone. I suspect he was very offended that someone was trying to kill him and struck back out of sheer pissed-offedness instead of out of defense."

She smiled at his description, and the air of tension around the chief thinned.

"I suspect he's sitting in heaven all proud that he fought until the end but still pissed that they got the best of him," Truman added.

"He sounds like a real character," said Mercy.

"You'll find this county is packed with characters. I've never experienced such a diverse crowd of people in such a small population."

"Let's look at the kitchen," suggested Eddie. The three of them walked single file back down the narrow hall to the kitchen at the rear of the home.

Mercy spotted dishes in the sink and some blood spattered on the floor and lower cupboards. "He pulled the knife out of that block on the counter?"

"Yes."

She circled the room carefully. "No bullet holes out here?"

"No," said Truman. "They're all in the bathroom area."

"Forced entry?" she asked.

"No signs."

"Is the blood in here your uncle's or more mystery blood?" asked Eddie.

"Both."

"So someone in the kitchen made your uncle start swinging the knife around? That must have been quite the conversation," said Mercy.

"I imagine it was pretty heated, considering the way it ended," Truman said dryly. He didn't look offended, and Mercy was pleased the chief didn't mind a little banter in the face of a raw situation. Humor was an easy coping tool, and cops used it regularly. There was no disrespect, just investigators trying to protect their hearts from horrible sights left by the underbelly of humanity.

"Why is the FBI suddenly interested in my uncle's murder?" Truman asked in a low voice. "It's the missing weapons, isn't it? I know Ned Fahey lived in an armed fortress out in West Bumfuck. Are his weapons gone too?"

Eddie met Mercy's gaze and gave a brief shrug with one shoulder.

"Ned Fahey has a history of antigovernment actions," said Mercy. "That and the combination of a lot of missing weapons got the attention of our domestic terrorism department."

"Ned wasn't a terrorist," stated Truman, anger growing in his gaze. "He was an opinionated old man whose knees gave him debilitating pain every time the weather changed. He wasn't the type to blow up federal buildings."

"How long have you been in Eagle's Nest?" asked Mercy quietly.

"Six months." Truman raised his chin. "But I spent three high school summers right here in this house. I know how this community functions."

Mercy's heart stopped for a brief second. If he'd recognized her, he hadn't said so. She had no recollection of Jefferson Biggs's nephew visiting during the summers. Truman Daly appeared to be a few years older than she . . . probably the age of one of her siblings, so no doubt she would have been beneath his notice.

"As a summer visitor, you'd still be an outsider," she stated. "The town would welcome you, but you wouldn't be privy to their secrets. You'd only see what they wanted you to see."

His brown gaze narrowed on hers. "You think so?" His tone implied she had no idea what she was talking about.

She shrugged. "I grew up in a small town. I know the mentality. It takes a couple of decades and lots of family roots to be allowed into the inner circles."

An odd look flashed across his face, telling her she'd struck a nerve, and she suspected the six-month-old police chief had encountered plenty of barriers to the acceptance he wanted from the town.

"They'll trust you eventually," she added encouragingly. "It simply takes time."

"Give me a big city any day," chimed in Eddie. "If you keep your eyes on the sidewalk then everyone gets along just fine."

Truman didn't reply, and Mercy knew she'd exposed a truth he'd been trying to deny. The police chief had a lot going for him, she admitted. He was direct, had a trustworthy face, and wore his cowboy hat like he'd been born to it. All three were positives in Eagle's Nest. She didn't see a wedding ring, so no doubt he'd shot to the top of the town's available bachelor list. His short, dark hair and brown gaze made him easy on the eyes. Local girls were always looking for a good-looking guy with a solid job.

"Basically, large amounts of weapons have been missing from all three recent deaths." Eddie brought them back to Truman's original question.

"You think one person is stockpiling?" the chief asked.

"We don't know," said Mercy. "We're here to find out why. Were these men murdered for their weapons? Or did someone get lucky three times in a row?"

"I'd think it'd take more than missing weapons for the FBI to send extra agents," commented Truman. "Surely the agents out of Bend could have handled this. What aren't you telling me? It's aliens, isn't it? You're the real Mulder and Scully."

Mercy wished it were the first time she'd heard the joke.

"Trust that we want to get to the bottom of your uncle's death as much as you do," said Eddie in a firm voice.

Truman gave him a look that could have melted steel.

"Since you know someone was stabbed or sliced by your uncle's knife, I assume no one was spotted with a fresh injury in the days after

Jefferson's murder?" Mercy asked, distracting the police chief before he ripped Eddie's glasses from his face for patronizing him.

"I followed up on that. No one went to the emergency room, and I put out the word that I was looking for someone who'd been cut."

Mercy had manned the front desk of the tiny Eagle's Nest hospital one summer in high school. It had seven beds, and the accounts receivable were handwritten ledgers in a single file cabinet. She'd known who in town paid five dollars a month on a thousand-dollar hospital bill. It'd been a lot of people.

"I wouldn't go to the emergency room for an injury I received while killing someone," commented Eddie.

"I also followed up with the vets. But most people around here have basic medical skills. If you get hurt, oftentimes professional help is far away."

Mercy nodded. When she was ten, she'd watched her mother stitch up a deep gash in her father's leg. He'd gripped a bottle of alcohol and held a thick piece of leather in his teeth, occasionally pulling out the leather to take a deep draw on the bottle. He didn't want to pay a doctor when his wife could stitch him up just fine. Her mother had been highly regarded as a midwife and self-taught medic.

"Who do you think did this?" She closely watched the chief's face.

The air in the kitchen shifted slightly, and Eddie looked expectantly at the police chief. Mercy wondered if they'd get a straight answer out of the nephew. It was in his best interest to tell them all he knew or suspected, but outsiders weren't trusted in Eagle's Nest. Yes, Truman Daly was an outsider, but the FBI might as well have it printed in yellow across the backs of their dark jackets.

Truman's jaw shifted slightly to one side, and Mercy could almost see the waves of frustration roll off his shoulders. "I don't know," he admitted quietly. "Believe me, I've been up nights trying to figure it out. I've gone through every piece of paper in this home and checked all his banking records. I can't figure it out. I hate to say it, but I think he simply got into an argument with a friend and it blew up. I think the shooter cleaned out his weapons cache simply because of the value of the guns."

Mercy wanted to believe him. The small edge of desperation in his tone told her he was truly at a loss. And his eyes were honest. She'd interviewed a lot of liars in her six years at the FBI. Some fooled her; some didn't.

For now, she'd accept that he'd told them everything.

"Are the weapons traceable?" Eddie asked.

Truman winced. "Only two were registered."

The clock over the stove showed it was nearly eight o'clock. She and Eddie still needed to check in to their hotel. "I'd like to come back tomorrow when it's daylight and see the rest of the property," she told the chief. "We also need to visit the other scene."

"Just call the department and leave a message. I'll meet you here," Truman offered. His energy had dimmed and resignation dipped his shoulders. The house felt quieter than when they'd first entered.

"Thank you." The tour and its guide had made the case personal. Mercy was now determined to solve Jefferson Biggs's murder for the nephew as much as for the victim.

FIVE

"Here ya go, Chief."

With a wink and a smile, Diane set a beer in front of him and darted off to help another patron before Truman could thank her. He wrapped his fingers around the cold glass and held it below his nose for a few seconds. The stress of the tour of his uncle's home melted away at the smell of hops and citrus. The bar was a dive, but it was the only bar in Eagle's Nest. The wood floor needed serious help and all the tables were uneven, but the service was five star and the burgers beat anything he'd ever eaten in San Jose. After the Deere dealership, it was the main hangout for the men of the town. Opinions were freely expressed with few consequences. There was an occasional brief fistfight, but Truman had yet to lock someone up for fighting at the bar.

It was a good place.

A slap on his back made his beer slosh over his hand, and Mike Bevins slid onto the stool next to him, sporting a wide grin.

"Asshole." Truman grabbed a napkin to wipe off his hand.

"Sorry, didn't see the beer." Mike pushed up on the brim of his Oregon Ducks cap.

"Yes, you did."

Mike caught Diane's attention, pointed at Truman's beer, and held up one finger. She nodded and whipped a glass under the right tap.

Mike had been one of the guys he'd bummed around with during the three high school summers he'd spent in Eagle's Nest. Each summer they'd pick up the friendship as if Truman had never left town. When Truman had accepted the police chief job, Mike had been one of the first to congratulate him and treat him as if he were one of the locals. Their friendship had always been easy and sincere, and he'd smoothed Truman's move to the small town. He was always ready to introduce Truman to a new face or offer his support during the city council meetings.

Truman liked having Mike at his back.

"How's work?" he asked Mike.

"Same shit, different day." Mike nodded his thanks at Diane for his beer. "The old man is pressuring me again."

Truman knew Mike's father wanted him to take more responsibility at the big Bevins ranch. The ranch was a huge machine that used a dozen hands to keep moving. He also knew Mike wanted to get the hell out of Dodge. He had a dream of living in Portland and teaching survival classes to middle-class suburbanites who had money to burn. There was nothing Mike loved better than disappearing into the wilderness for two weeks, living out of his backpack. Truman had thought it was cool when they were eighteen, but now he preferred the comfort of his bed, a hot shower, and fresh coffee.

Mike's father didn't support his dream; he wanted his son to take over his legacy.

Considering Mike was inching close to forty, Truman wondered if he'd ever jump ship.

"What are you going to do?" Truman asked, knowing Mike needed to vent.

"Dunno." Mike focused on downing a third of his beer. "I'll know when the time is right. I heard the FBI shipped in some agents from Portland to work on the murders."

Truman didn't mind the subject change. "They did, and I'm glad. We need all the help we can get on the prepper murders."

"You don't see them as elbowing you out and taking over?"

"Heck no. Do you know how limited my resources are in Eagle's Nest? I rely on Deschutes County and the state police for almost everything. I'm used to playing nicely with others."

Mike looked into his beer. "I'm sorry about Jefferson. I know I've said it before, but I can't imagine how bad it sucks for you."

"Thank you."

A companionable silence stretched for a few seconds. He never felt the need for useless small talk with Mike.

"How many FBI agents?"

"Two."

"That's it?" Mike raised his brows. "Is that really going to make a difference?"

Truman thought of Mercy Kilpatrick and the intense focus he'd seen on her face and heard in her questions. "I think so. It'll be their sole assignment while they're here. I'm constantly pulled in a half-dozen directions, and so is the county sheriff and the Bend FBI office. These two agents' primary assignment is to find the murderers."

"More than one killer?" Mike leaned closer, his eyes narrowing. He smelled of fresh-cut wood, and Truman noticed the faint powder of sawdust on his heavy dark jacket.

"Don't know. Don't quote me on that."

Mike slowly nodded, weighing Truman's words.

"Seriously," Truman said. "We don't know if there's more than one guy."

"I heard there's a shitload of weapons missing from Ned Fahey's place. That sounds like more than one person to me. Were you up there this morning?"

"No. It fell under county jurisdiction, but I'll take a look at some point since they think it's related to Jefferson's death." He heard his voice catch on his uncle's name. *It's so hard to say.*

"That has to be frustrating," said Mike. "Since the last city you worked in was so big, I bet you aren't used to dealing with so many different jurisdictions."

"In a way," admitted Truman. "My boundaries are much more narrow here, but I have a better handle on the people. I don't feel like I'm constantly in a new situation with new faces. The faces here grew familiar over a few months."

"After a while you'll know within minutes who did each crime. People around here aren't very original."

"Can't say I appreciate original crimes," admitted Truman. A memory flashed, and he shut it down as he wiped away the small beads of moisture on his upper lip.

Or is that beer foam?

"I bet you've seen some weird shit."

Under his arms, sweat blossomed. "Not really." He took another big drink of his beer and scrambled for a change of topic. *Sports. Cars. Women.*

"What's the most unusual thing you've come across?" Mike asked before Truman could form a coherent question. "I once read about a cop who found a hand in a suspect's backpack. A whole fucking hand. Rings and everything."

"Nothing like that. Excuse me a moment." Truman headed toward the bathroom, needing space between Mike and himself and the caustic memory that'd barged into his brain. He slammed the heel of his hand against the men's room door and strode in as the memory broke free.

Thick clouds of pale gray smoke billowed from under the hood of the burning abandoned car when Truman discovered it on the dead-end street. Officer Selena Madero pulled up as he called in his arrival. Nearly a dozen people milled around, watching the car burn, some taking videos, some talking on their cell phones.

"Back up!" Truman hollered at the crowd. "Everyone get away from the car. What happened?" he asked the closest woman, who balanced a toddler on one hip. She clutched her daughter with one hand; her other hand gripped an amulet at her neck.

She answered in Spanish too rapid for him to follow, her eyes wide.

"She doesn't know," answered Officer Madero. "She says she heard people yelling and then smelled the smoke."

"Is someone in the car?" Truman asked.

The woman gave him a terrified look and shrugged, shaking her head.

"Does anyone know if someone is in there?" he shouted at the other observers. Flames licked at the wheel wells and burst out of the grille. The voluminous smoke turned black.

No one spoke up. Some held up their hands in an I-don't-know gesture.

"Crap," Truman mumbled. He glanced at Officer Madero. She was young, one of the newest recruits on the force, and she had her focus on him, looking for guidance.

"What do we do?" she asked in a low voice.

"Get everyone farther away from the car. Our priority is to keep everyone safe."

An ear-piercing shriek made him spin around. A gray-haired woman ran full steam at the car, screaming in Spanish. A man grabbed her around the waist as she tore by. She beat him with her fists, but he didn't let go.

"She says her daughter is in the car!" Officer Madero sprinted toward it.

"Madero!" Truman shouted. He took two steps after the other officer and halted, unable to think straight. What can I do? *The flames at the front end of the car had multiplied and the amount of dense black smoke*

stunned him. Fire extinguisher. *Truman dashed to his trunk, hoping he'd made the right decision.*

The crowd let out a series of shouts.

Truman's blood froze as he glanced back.

A young woman in the rear seat leaned her face against the car glass, her mouth wide open, her eyes terrified. Her face was pressed against the glass as if she couldn't support herself, and Truman instantly knew her hands were tied behind her back. The mother's shrieks intensified. The man holding her back met Truman's gaze, questioning if he should let her run toward the car. Truman shook his head.

Madero grabbed the handle of the rear car door and tugged. "It's locked!" she shouted. The black smoke billowed around her head and shoulders, briefly shrouding her.

A few of the crowd rushed forward to check the other doors.

Truman grabbed his extinguisher and glass puncher to break the window. With one in each hand, he tore toward the car. The flames intensified and people backed away, their hands and arms shielding their faces from the heat.

Madero didn't leave. She hammered frantically at the window with her small flashlight. The woman in the car locked eyes with Truman, and he pumped his legs harder.

The car exploded.

An outline of Madero flashed in the blast as a wall of heat and power threw Truman backward.

His head hit the concrete.

Truman rubbed his hands under the icy water in the bathroom and grabbed a paper towel, then doused it under the stream and wiped it across his face.

The shudders stopped.

He stared at his reflection in the mirror. *I should have pulled Madero away instead of getting the fire extinguisher.* He could still see Madero's silhouette in the bright light. And the face of the woman in the car. Over and over and over. His heart pounded in his chest.

Count five things you can touch.

He placed one hand on the cold metal spigot of the sink and let the stream run over his other hand, concentrating on the sensation of running water. Then he ran a wet hand over his spiky hair, touched the rough fabric of his sleeve, and deliberately banged a knee into the white sink, welcoming the small pain.

Count four things you can see.

He focused on the small scar on his chin. *One.* The other injuries to his face had healed and nearly vanished, but he knew where they lurked. A faint line here, a pale divot there. *Two, three, four.* His breathing slowed.

Count three things you can hear.

Scratchy music through the single ceiling speaker. The water in the sink. The murmur of voices from the bar.

Count two things you can smell.

He ended the mental recitation. By the end of the third step out of the five the psychiatrist had taught him for handling panic attacks, his heart rate had slowed and his sweats were gone. He took a quick inventory of his feelings. *All calm; I'm grounded.* He mentally stepped back and took an unemotional look at what else he'd locked away in his memories.

After two days, Officer Selena Madero had died from her burns.

The woman in the car had been tied up by her boyfriend and deliberately left in the burning car because she'd broken up with him. She'd been dead when the paramedics arrived.

Truman had been released from the hospital and had taken medical leave, spending time with the department's psychiatrist. His vest had protected him from most of the flying, burning debris, but he still had two burns on his thighs. After a year they were still sensitive to the touch and itched and burned at random moments.

Constant reminders.

The victim's moments of terror before the explosion ate at his gut and brain and heart.

He couldn't comprehend the mind of a human who'd do that to another person. Especially a woman he'd once claimed to love.

The boyfriend was tried and sentenced. Truman avoided the trial except for his own brief testimony. He couldn't have stomached the statements from the victim's mother, who had pleaded with her daughter not to date the man, or the words from the medical examiner about the condition of her corpse.

If only I'd arrived sooner.

If only I hadn't run for the fire extinguisher first.

Would it have mattered?

The psychiatrist had shown him how to get a handle on the survivor's guilt, and techniques for managing the panic attacks, but he hadn't been able to restore Truman's faith in humankind. He'd been close to leaving law enforcement for good.

Then he'd received the call from Eagle's Nest and his brain had seized the idea, as if someone had thrown him a lifeline. A small town where everyone knew everyone else. A town where people looked out for their neighbors and didn't set their significant others on fire.

It became a beacon of change in his mind. A city where he wouldn't deal with gangs or excessive homelessness.

A town where he could be a person, not a uniform, who helped.

"Shitty people are everywhere," the psychiatrist had told Truman when they'd discussed his job offer. "Small towns, big cities, African villages. You can't run away from it."

Truman had known his doctor was right, but a quick visit to the town of Eagle's Nest, where he'd spent those high school summers, rekindled a fire that had been doused when that car exploded. He'd felt compelled to follow that new energy and hold tight to its source. Since the explosion he'd been lost, drifting through life, searching for something that made him feel alive.

He'd been willing to follow that feeling to Eagle's Nest.

He strode across the creaking floor of the bar. It'd been the right decision. He'd been welcomed to the small town. He felt wanted and he felt needed. No longer an anonymous face with a uniform and a badge, he had friends, he had a purpose, and he slept soundly at night.

But after that panic attack, tonight might be an exception.

SIX

Mercy peered out her motel room doorway and checked the outdoor walkway for Eddie. It appeared he'd settled into his room. She quietly walked past his door and down the iron steps to the parking lot. She opened the rear of the Tahoe, then stretched to yank the blanket off the heavy-duty backpack she'd stowed before they left Portland. Twenty minutes earlier Eddie had helped her lift their suitcases out of the back and accepted a bottled water from the stash she'd stored in the rear of the SUV, but he hadn't asked what was under the blanket.

It's not a big deal. Everyone carries extra supplies when traveling over the Cascade Mountain Range.

Then why hide it? She pulled the jerky, almond butter, and fresh celery out of the backpack, leaving the freeze-dried foods. She hated to leave the pack in the Tahoe overnight. People break in to vehicles. But she didn't want to answer questions from Eddie if he spotted her with it in the morning, and she didn't want to leave it in her motel room. Common sense wouldn't let her drive anywhere without it.

Common sense? Or paranoia?

She ran through a mental list of the contents, deciding what else she needed in the hotel room, and dug in a side pocket for a Leatherman tool. She shoved the pack far into the Tahoe's depth and tossed the blanket back over it.

The backpack kept her sane. If they broke down in the middle of nowhere, she had supplies to last them for several days.

They'd checked in to a pathetic, small motel ten minutes outside Bend. Some sort of conference was going on in the city, and every semidecent room had been booked for months. The FBI administrative assistant in Portland had apologized profusely as she handed them their assignments, promising she'd get them switched to a nicer place close to the Bend FBI office in a few days.

It made no difference to Mercy. Small was good. Less likely to attract attention, and she preferred to see her vehicle from her room. If a situation arose, she could have her backpack in hand and be off the motel grounds in twenty seconds.

Back in her room, she locked the door, slid the bolt, and hooked the chain. The door was a surprisingly heavy wood and blocked all cold drafts. She moved a chair across the room and propped it under the door handle. Then she opened and closed the big sliding window next to the door, checking its weight and lock. It also had been constructed to keep out the temperatures, a necessity in the cold winters of Bend.

Bend was an outdoor enthusiast's paradise. Prime skiing in the mountains, white-water rafting on the rivers, miles of biking and running trails. The high desert climate was usually dry with cool nights, sunny days, and some snow in the winter. Typically Bend had a lovely Indian summer in late September, but she and Eddie had arrived at the tail end of a storm. The forecast was sunny for the rest of the week.

She closed the heavy drapes and then explored every nook and cranny of the room, looking under the bed and checking every drawer. Once she'd seen everything in the tiny room, she sat on the bed with a sigh and opened her almond butter, attacking it with her celery. The salt, crunch, and oil hit her tongue, making her close her eyes in happiness. They'd stopped at a drive-through in Bend, where Eddie had ordered a burger, but she'd claimed not to be hungry. In truth she'd been starving and craving her own *real* food.

While she crunched she opened her laptop and checked the local news websites. Ned Fahey's murder wasn't mentioned. Then she checked national headlines and the stock market's performance, and moved on to international headlines.

Nothing troubling jumped out at her. It was more of the same old, same old, day-to-day rotation of the world.

She could sleep tonight.

She paired her jerky and celery and took a bite, reviewing the day in her mind as she leaned against the headboard.

She'd been gone from Eagle's Nest for fifteen years. During the trip from Portland, she'd mentally steeled herself to run into family, but she hadn't expected it within two minutes of arriving. Levi had aged, but she'd known her brother instantly. His refusal to acknowledge her had cut deep, but she'd emotionally slapped a bandage on it. In the quiet of the hotel room, she slowly peeled back the bandage, waiting for the rush of pain.

It didn't come.

She frowned and tore off a bite of jerky, focusing on the small twinge of loss. Had she matured and gotten a handle on her family's rejection? Levi had been closest to her in age. He'd been the one who'd played hide-and-seek in the barn, built a tree house, and swum in the creek with her. He'd been her primary playmate until he was fourteen and his friends pressured him to leave behind his twelve-year-old sister.

What is Kaylie like?

Levi's daughter had been a one-year-old when Mercy left town. She'd been born outside of marriage, to the delight of all the wagging tongues in town. His girlfriend's parents had supported their daughter's desire to avoid Levi, claiming the young man was a hellion and would never amount to anything. Mercy's parents had also been furious, but their reasons had been different.

Pressing her ear to their bedroom door one night, she'd heard them verbally tear nineteen-year-old Levi apart.

"How do you plan to feed a child when you don't have a steady job?"

"God made birth control for a reason!"

"You are now responsible for the livelihood of a child. Be a man."

They didn't care if the woman didn't want to see Levi, but they expected him to provide for his child. Somehow.

Family first, community second.

Mercy's parents, Karl and Deborah, lived and breathed by that credo and had built a small, tight community circle within the population of Eagle's Nest. Everyone pulled their own weight and brought something useful to the Kilpatrick community. If you were a leech or unreliable, eventually your invitations to barbecues and picnics faded away. Karl surrounded himself with men and families who had a singular purpose: to survive whatever the world threw their way. They believed in preparation, personal health, and learning. Her parents' mantras echoed in her head.

Seek doers, not talkers.

Choose friends wisely.

Be frugal.

Family first.

Except when it comes to me.

He sat in his vehicle outside the roadside motel, watching a skinny beam of light that shone between the curtains in room 232. Two hours ago Mercy Kilpatrick had arrived with the other agent. They'd talked for a few minutes outside her door, and then the male agent had gone to his own room. Mercy had briefly left her room to grab some things out of a bag in her SUV, but he'd seen neither of them since then.

He'd idly wondered if the man would return to her room, but his room's light had turned off an hour ago. An inconsistent faint flicker on the curtains told him the male agent was watching TV.

Eleven o'clock. *Why am I still here?* He shifted in his seat, flexing his toes in his boots, trying to warm them. It was fucking freezing, and he didn't dare turn on his engine to warm up the vehicle.

Mercy's light went off.

He stared at the large window covered by draperies. *Is she going to sleep? Should I leave?*

Then it happened.

Her door opened and she stepped out. Not in pajamas and a robe, ready to knock on her partner's door for a rendezvous. She was dressed in black, with a small bag in hand. She closed her door and stood silently on the outdoor walkway, looking and listening.

He didn't move, feeling as if she could see directly into his vehicle. He'd parked in the shadows, avoiding the hotel parking lot lights.

She can't see me.

But she stared in his direction for a long time. His heart beat faster and small dots of sweat formed on his temples. She finally moved to the stairs and jogged down. He listened closely, but her feet didn't make a sound. She unlocked her Tahoe and the cab light stayed off as she opened the door.

Smart.

She started the vehicle and pulled out of the parking lot. He turned his ignition and kept his headlights off as he followed, unconcerned about being seen by other vehicles. The local area rolled up its sidewalks at eight.

He immediately realized she wasn't headed toward Eagle's Nest. Or Bend. Forty minutes later he was eyeing the level of his gas tank and wondering if he needed to turn around. She'd led him toward the Cascades, following the foothills for a while, and then taking a dizzying course of turns. Her speed hadn't changed the whole time, and he suspected she didn't see him.

Where the fuck is she going?

He took a sharp right turn, expecting to see her taillights up ahead. They weren't there.

"Shit!" He sped up, looking for a road she could have turned down. She'd led him to an unfamiliar and thickly forested area of the foothills that was crisscrossed with logging roads. Of course there were no signs anywhere.

It would be hell to find his way out.

He gambled and took another right turn. No taillights. With a curse he pulled over to the side of the road and stared into the dark.

Now what?

Did she do that on purpose? Did she spot me?

Pissed, he flipped on his headlights and pulled a U-turn. Tonight he wasn't going to discover why she'd returned to Eagle's Nest after fifteen years.

There was always tomorrow night.

SEVEN

The next morning Mercy and Eddie sat in a small but new-smelling meeting room at the Bend FBI office. Across the table sat Supervisory Senior Resident Agent Jeff Garrison and Intelligence Analyst Darby Cowan. The office had a total of five agents along with the intelligence analyst, a staff operations specialist, and an administrative assistant.

No wonder they'd reached out to Portland for support.

Clearly the Bend office had a casual dress code. Jeff was in jeans and Darby wore pants made of some high-tech weather- and tear-resistant material that Mercy had seen in outdoor stores. Darby didn't look like a data cruncher; she looked as if she'd rather be climbing one of the Three Sisters mountains. A loose braid held back her long hair, and she moved with the athleticism of someone who ran marathons every weekend. Mercy guessed she was around forty.

Jeff Garrison appeared to be about Mercy's age and seemed quite mellow for an SSRA. Shouldering the responsibility of the satellite office hadn't given him the strained look Mercy recognized in many supervisors. In fact, he'd made her instantly relax the first time he shook her hand and smiled. Mercy was envious of the gift. He and Eddie had immediately discovered a shared passion for sushi and launched into a detailed conversation after Eddie asked for a restaurant recommendation. Mercy tuned them out, watching Darby deftly pass out papers.

"Since you're from Portland, I've taken the liberty of giving a brief description of some of the *groups* of residents you'll come across on this side of the Cascades. I hesitate to call them factions, because I feel that has a negative connotation and that label doesn't apply to everyone," the tall analyst said. "Then we'll move on to how the victims' associations might have made them targets."

Mercy hadn't informed them that she was from Eagle's Nest and didn't need an education, but she wondered if Jeff knew her background. Regardless, she wanted to hear Darby's description of the *groups*.

"All three victims are well-known preppers," Darby stated. "There's a lot of different types of preppers out there, but basically these people believe in being ready for a natural disaster or a man-caused disaster that creates either a temporary or permanent change in their lives.

"You've seen the shows on TV. Some of these people are slightly nutty, but a lot of them are good, hard-working folks who plan ahead. They focus on food supply, protection, personal health, and finding an ideal location to live. Generally we don't have any problems with this group. They keep to themselves, usually pay their taxes, and don't call attention to their way of life. They like to keep it quiet. They don't want others to know their homes are fully supplied, because they might be overrun when aliens destroy the major cities."

Eddie snorted.

"They're well stocked with weapons, but generally nonviolent," Darby added.

Mercy said nothing, her gaze on her printout.

"Next we have the sovereign citizens." Darby sighed. "Even with all my research, I don't understand the logic of these guys. Just understand that they have a totally different interpretation of our laws and the Constitution. They don't believe they are US citizens, they don't think they're subject to our taxes, and they believe they can't be tried for a lot of crimes. They often call themselves freemen. Some officials think they're dangerous, but mainly they like to file a lot of paperwork to tie up our judicial system. They're great at turning a forty-dollar traffic ticket into two file boxes of paperwork and possibly a couple of nights in jail in contempt of court because they're driving the judge nuts. Generally nonviolent."

"Were any of the victims associated with this group?" Eddie asked.

"Not directly, but Ned Fahey has some distant family members that identify with the group." Darby glanced at her sheet. "Militants are next. There's a large variety of splinter groups that fall under that heading. Philosophies range from minor anti-federal government to gung ho, start-my-own-country crazy. I can't summarize this group very well; they're too diverse in their beliefs and actions. Each one varies in their complaints and level of violence." Darby sat back in her chair. "Those are the CliffsNotes to our area. You'll also encounter a lot of ranchers, Native Americans, and aging hippies."

"No Crips or Bloods or Mafia?" Eddie joked.

"No." A small smile crossed Darby's face.

"What about normal people?" he asked.

"Lots," replied Jeff. "The Bend area is packed with families and retirees who've moved here for the beauty and outdoor lifestyle. They love the diverse seasons and clean air. Out in Eagle's Nest it's more rural, more isolated, and the people who live there tend to have deep roots. New people don't usually move in; It's economically depressed and there's little industry to draw workers." His kind brown gaze met Mercy's. "But you already knew that."

Darby perked up, and looked from Mercy to Jeff. "What? Did I miss something?" Her perceptive gaze settled on Mercy.

"I grew up in Eagle's Nest. But I haven't been back in fifteen years."

Darby's eyebrows rose. "No kidding. How was my population recap?"

"Excellent. Sounds like not much has changed," Mercy said.

"It hasn't," said Jeff. "Bend has had huge population growth over the last thirty years, but Eagle's Nest has stayed stable."

Mercy leaned forward. "You've studied the locals, Darby. Who would attack preppers?"

Darby folded her printout three times, deliberately creasing the edges as she considered Mercy's question. Mercy knew several intelligence analysts who could condense ten thousand facts into a concise summary with brilliant insight. Darby struck her as that sort of data nut.

"I don't know," replied Darby. "The silence after each killing is startling. Usually there is *someone* who talks when crimes like these happen. The guy who shows off his new gun to his friends . . . the guy who brags that so-and-so won't cause them problems anymore. *Something*."

"You believe it's all the same killer?" Mercy asked.

Jeff twisted his lips. "We've got no hard evidence to tie the cases together. As of this morning, we know three different weapons were used—all different calibers. None of the fingerprints or footprints found at the scenes are the same . . . but who knows if the killer even left fingerprints. The common thread is the missing weapons and that the victims were known preppers."

"Is it possible you've missed a victim?"

Darby shook her head. "Our murder rate out here is very low. There're no other unsolved murders this year."

"We just put the pieces together yesterday," said Jeff. "We were aware of two men who'd been killed in Deschutes County, but neither the sheriff nor the police chief had asked for any help. And I understand why: they each believed they had an isolated murder case. The missing weapons from the first murder, Enoch Finch, weren't brought up until later."

"I noticed that," said Mercy. "What happened?"

"Well, no one knew guns were missing because Enoch lived alone and kept to himself. A cousin came to town a week after the death to sort through the effects. He's the one that claims weapons are missing. The county sheriff knew Enoch had one missing registered gun, but the cousin swears Enoch had shown him at least twenty rifles and pistols on his last visit."

"I'm noticing a theme here," said Mercy. "All of these guys had a *lot* more weapons than were registered." She tapped her pen on the table. "Did the thieves know they were stealing illegal weapons?" *A facet to consider.*

"Anything else missing?" Eddie asked.

"The cousin wasn't certain. The rest of the home looked okay to him."

Mercy eyed Darby. "And once you heard of the missing Finch weapons, you started to wonder if the first two cases were related."

Darby nodded. "And when I got word that a cache of weapons was missing from the third murder, I approached Jeff and he decided we needed more agents. This has the potential to blow up into a domestic terrorism nightmare."

"My office is spread too thin," said Jeff. "I don't have a domestic terrorism agent on staff. I rely on Darby to keep us informed, but there's something to be said for DT experience."

"You know I'm originally from cybercrimes, right?" said Eddie. "I've been on temporary loan to DT for only a few weeks."

"So you're saying you might be useless?" Darby asked with a glint in her eye.

"Try me." He grinned back.

Mercy jumped in. "So *back* to my question about a single killer," she said to Darby. "What's your gut tell you? Outside of the hard evidence."

"I don't know. Logic tells me it can't be coincidence that three men were killed within two weeks in a county that usually gets three murders a year, and each time the only thing missing is a large number of weapons," said Darby. She shifted in her seat. "To me, it doesn't sound like the work of one person, simply because of the number of weapons. What's one person going to do with that many weapons?"

"Maybe it's a small group working together," suggested Eddie.

"Where's the chatter?" asked Darby. "Where's the leak? Like I said, someone always talks."

"It's only been two weeks," said Mercy. "Maybe with more time someone will talk."

"I feel like we've dropped the ball by not making the connection between the cases earlier," said Jeff.

"You haven't dropped the ball," said Eddie. "You called us in once you had concerns. We'll investigate from here and keep you in the loop."

The SSRA winced. "I still feel like I'm slacking."

"Slacking?" Darby snapped. "I know how many active cases this office has. Poor Melissa can't keep up. We should have more support staff."

"Not in the budget," Jeff answered.

Supervisors everywhere use that line.

Mercy had worked with seven different supervisors during her time with the FBI. On the basis of her experience, she was positive they rehearsed that line in supervisor class.

"If we're done here, we'll head out to examine the scenes in the daylight," said Mercy. "But first I have an interview scheduled with one of Ned Fahey's neighbors. The sheriff said he'd give him a ride to the Eagle's Nest police department to talk."

Jeff scanned some papers in front of him until he found a name. "Toby Cox? Is that who you're interviewing?"

"Yes, I guess he helped Ned out around the property. As far as the sheriff knows, Toby is the only one who's been in the house in the last ten years."

"This report from the sheriff says Toby Cox is simpleminded." Jeff met Mercy's gaze. "I don't think that's a diagnosis or even a politically correct way to put it, but I get the feeling that the sheriff doubts the quality of this witness's information."

"We'll evaluate what Toby has to say and see if he's credible. Anything else?"

The four of them exchanged glances around the table.

"No? Then we're off." Mercy stood.

Jeff shook her hand, his eyes kind. "Good luck."

EIGHT

Mercy and Eddie parked in front of the tiny Eagle's Nest police station.

It'd sat in the exact same location since Mercy was a kid. Even the outdoor paint was the same dull shade of khaki. She held her breath as she stepped inside, expecting to see white-haired Mrs. Smythe, who'd answered the phone and managed the police station since Mercy was born. Mercy had no doubt that the busybody would instantly recognize her. Instead a very young man the size of an offensive lineman sat at Mrs. Smythe's desk.

A welcoming grin crossed his face as they entered. "Are you with the FBI? The chief is expecting you." The nameplate on his desk said he was Lucas Ingram. His smile was contagious, and Mercy wondered if he was old enough to have finished high school.

Maybe he's the son of an officer.

Eddie held out his hand. "You're Lucas? Do you run the show around here?"

"I am. And welcome to my domain. You need anything, let me know." Lucas stood to shake hands and he towered over Eddie, who wasn't short.

"How old are you?" Eddie blurted.

"Nineteen. I've been working out front here for over a year, and I'm damned good at it." Lucas's wide face grew slightly defensive, and Mercy wondered how often he'd had to defend his holding a job that was typically filled by a woman.

"I can tell," she told the young man. "They're lucky to have you."

"And no, I don't want to be a cop," Lucas said. "That's everyone's next question. I like keeping the station's stuff organized and doing what I can to make their day go easier. I'd much rather sit at this desk, answer the phone, and delegate than ride around in a patrol car."

"You're a born manager," said Mercy.

"Yep." Lucas beamed.

"If you're done managing the FBI, can you get them some coffee and bring it to my office so we can talk?" a familiar voice asked.

Truman Daly had silently appeared in the reception area. "Morning, Agents," he said with a nod to Mercy and Eddie.

"Good morning, Chief," said Eddie as Mercy nodded back.

The chief looked as if he'd barely slept, and Mercy wondered if his uncle's death or the pressures of the job had kept him awake at night. Surely it wasn't too demanding to keep watch over Eagle's Nest.

"Sheriff Rhodes already dropped off Toby Cox. He'll be back in a half hour for him, so I suggest we get started." He turned and headed down a narrow hallway, leaving Mercy and Eddie to follow.

"He's been cranky this morning. Don't let it get to you," Lucas whispered conspiratorially. "How would you like your coffee?" he asked in a louder voice.

"Black," Mercy said in unison with Eddie, bypassing her usual heavy cream in favor of being easy. The two of them followed the chief to his office. The hallway was lined with photos. Mercy wanted to stop and study them, positive she'd recognize some faces, but she kept her gaze on the chief's back. As they moved into his office, another young man waited patiently in a folding chair. He looked up as they entered.

Toby Cox had Down syndrome.

Mercy wondered why Sheriff Rhodes hadn't been more specific in his report, but maybe he didn't know the difference. Some people were ignorant. Or assholes.

"Toby, this is Mercy and Eddie from the FBI. They're the ones with the questions about Ned Fahey."

The boy stood and shook their hands. Close up, Mercy realized he wasn't a boy and wondered how old he was. His grip was tight on her hand.

"Don't I know you?" he asked Mercy, hanging on to her hand.

Her mind raced. She didn't remember a Cox family or a boy with Down syndrome.

"I don't think s-so," she stuttered. "How long have you lived in Eagle's Nest?"

He peered closer at her, ignoring her question. "The coffee shop. You look like Kaylie," he said in satisfaction. "You look like Kaylie *a lot*. Except she's not old," he added triumphantly.

Eddie coughed. Out of the corner of her eye, she saw Truman grin.

"I've lived in Eagle's Nest since I was twenty. We moved here ten years ago," he answered, clearly pleased that he'd solved his mystery. "I knew you looked like someone."

"I see the resemblance too, Toby," Truman answered. "Have a seat, folks."

Mercy abruptly wondered if Toby's parents should be present. She was unclear on his rights. Of course, she had no idea of his mental capacity yet. To her limited knowledge, people with Down syndrome varied widely in their abilities. She looked to Truman, who sat in his chair and watched Toby with confidence. She decided that if he'd felt there was an issue, he wouldn't have allowed the meeting.

"How often did you help Ned Fahey around his place?" Mercy asked, pulling out her pen and small notebook, jumping into the interview. "Do you live close to him?"

"I live a quarter mile from Ned. If he doesn't call and tell me not to come, I go there every Monday and Wednesday to help for three hours." Toby's eye contact was good . . . well, partially good. He was slightly cross-eyed in one eye, but his answers were direct. Mercy smiled, pleased they had a good witness.

"Did you help last Wednesday?" Toby had been the one to find Ned on the following Monday.

"Yes. It was wood-chopping day. Wednesdays is almost always wood-chopping day. He chops, I pick it up and stack it. He didn't call to cancel, so I went back on Monday." He looked down at his clenched hands in his lap.

"That must have been horrible for you," Mercy said gently. "He was a good friend, right?"

"Oh no. Ned was my boss, not a friend. He was very crabby. Even my parents say he was crabby."

Mercy bit her lip at his blunt reply. "Did you like working for Ned?"

"I did. He needed help because his back and knees always hurt. It was the right thing to do."

"Did he pay you?" Eddie asked.

"Yes."

Mercy and Eddie waited to hear how much, but Toby didn't volunteer the information. Mercy wondered if he didn't know or if he'd been raised not to discuss money matters. Her parents had never told her how much money they earned or paid for anything. The only time money had been mentioned was when it wasn't available. Which was often.

"When you got there yesterday, was the front door unlocked?" Eddie asked.

Toby turned to look at him and intently studied his face. "I like your glasses. Those are cool."

"Thank you," said Eddie, blinking rapidly. "Ummm . . . what was my question?"

"You asked if the door was unlocked," said Toby. "It was. I knocked several times first. I always knock, but Ned didn't answer this time. I opened the door and went in." He looked down again. "I hope that was okay."

"You did the right thing, Toby," reassured Mercy.

"I found him dead," he whispered. "He had a hole in his head."

"Then what did you do?" asked Eddie.

"I ran home and told my parents. They called the sheriff." He ducked his head. "Ned told me the cave man would try to get him."

Mercy remembered the rumor Sheriff Rhodes had been embarrassed to bring up. "Did you ever see this cave man?"

"No."

"Did Ned say he'd ever seen him?"

Toby scrunched up his face as he thought. "No. Because I asked what he looked like and Ned said he didn't know. But he thought he was really big and really mean."

"Why did Ned think the cave man would be interested in him?" Eddie asked.

"That's what the cave man does," answered Toby. "He steals other people's hard work and then kills them. He's *lazy*," he said emphatically.

Laziness would be the ultimate sin to a prepper like Ned.

"Did you ever see a lot of guns in Ned's house?" Mercy asked.

"No." Toby paused. "But there were a lot of them out in the shed."

"Which shed?"

"The one that you take the path to. You can't see it from the house. The guns are buried in the ground."

"Did you ever count them?" Mercy asked.

"No, but one time Ned said he had twenty-five. That was a long time ago. He might have sold some since then."

"When was the last time you saw them buried in the ground?" asked Eddie.

Toby ran a hand through his short, straw-colored hair as he thought hard. "Last summer," he finally answered. "I remember it was hot."

Mercy had a thought. "Did Ned have stuff buried anywhere else?"

"Not that I know about. Well, his septic tank is buried in the ground. But that's how everyone's is."

"Did you see any strangers visit Ned?" Mercy asked carefully, wondering if the question was too broad. She'd realized they needed to be very direct in their queries.

Toby shrugged. "People have to drive by our place to get to Ned's. Sometimes I don't recognize the vehicles that go by."

"Toby's parents' house sits a good ways back from the road," Truman clarified. "I assume you couldn't see every car that drives by?"

"That's right. I'd have to be watching outside. From inside the house, I can only hear them."

"Did you hear anyone go by on the weekend?" Mercy asked.

"Yes."

She waited a few moments and then finally asked, "Did you see the vehicles, Toby?"

"No."

Mercy silently sighed and changed her line of questioning. "Did anyone visit Ned when you were helping him with wood chopping last Wednesday?"

His forehead wrinkled in concentration. "No. Not that Wednesday."

"He had a visitor on a different Wednesday?"

"Yes. A few Wednesdays ago. He yelled at someone who'd stopped their truck on the road in front of his house. He told them to 'fucking get lost.'"

"They didn't get out of the vehicle?" Eddie asked.

"No, they took off when he waved the ax and moved closer to their truck." Toby grinned. "It was funny. He was mad."

Mercy raised a brow at Truman, who lifted one shoulder.

"I don't know anything about it," Truman said. "Could have been tourists or even a bill collector." He leaned forward and rested his arms on his desk. "Hey, Toby, who did Ned dislike? Who'd he complain about all the time?"

"Leighton Underwood," Toby said promptly. "And Uncle Sam."

Mercy assumed he meant the Uncle Sam who was her boss, but she wrote it in her notebook beside Underwood's name in case Ned had an actual uncle named Sam.

"Who's Underwood?" she asked Truman.

"I suspect their property lines butt up against each other. I know Leighton lives out in the same general area, but he doesn't come to town as much as Ned did. Someone else could tell you if there was bad blood between the two of them."

"Toby, did Ned have anything else on his property that he was real proud of besides his guns?" Mercy asked.

"He was real proud of his food. He always said he had enough stored away to outlast the commies. He liked his garden too. We spent lots of hours working in his garden and building a tall fence to keep out the critters."

"Those are important," agreed Mercy. "If you were to go back inside Ned's house, do you think you would notice if anything was missing?"

Toby sat up straight in his chair. "I don't want to go back there! He was dead! Don't make me go back in that house!" His fingers blanched as he clenched his hands. "I don't want to see his ghost!"

Truman came out from behind his desk and put one hand on Toby's shoulder in a tight grip. "No one's going to make you go back." He looked Mercy square in the eye, daring her to challenge him.

Mercy wasn't interested in forcing Toby, knowing it would be counterproductive. But she believed he had a good memory and that with the right questions, they could hear more insight into Ned Fahey.

"You know Ned's not there anymore, right, Toby?" she asked. "They took his body away."

Toby wouldn't look up. "Where'd they take him?" he asked slowly.

"They took him to a special doctor who studies dead people. This doctor knows how to look for clues about who killed him," answered Mercy.

"A medical examiner." Toby finally looked at her again. "Like on *CSI*."

"That's right. We want to know who did this to Ned. That's why we're going back to look for clues at his house. But we won't know if the killer stole something. I bet you would notice if something was gone."

Toby had started to shake his head as she talked. "I don't want to go back."

Mercy saw Truman's fingers grip Toby's shoulder a little tighter. "That's fine, Toby. But please consider it. We could really use your help to figure out what happened."

Lucas tapped on the office door and brought in the coffees. "Sheriff Rhodes is back."

"We're almost done," answered Truman. He looked at Eddie and Mercy. "Anything else for Toby?"

"Not now," said Mercy. "If we have more questions, can we talk with you again, Toby?"

"Yes."

Truman walked him out of the office.

Eddie leaned close to Mercy. "What do you think?"

"He's a good witness if we ask the right questions."

"I agree. I don't know if he saw anything helpful, though." Eddie glanced at his notes. "We've got Leighton Underwood to follow up on and a random vehicle that stopped by one day. I think we need to talk with more of Ned's cronies."

"Ned's cronies meet at the John Deere place at five a.m.," said Truman as he reappeared.

"Does Leighton Underwood meet there too?" asked Eddie.

"Occasionally."

Mercy looked at Eddie, trying to weigh priorities. They needed to stay on Ned's case because it was fresh, but they had a lot of catching up to do on the other two deaths. She was torn.

"Where can I rent a car?" Eddie asked Truman. "I think we need another set of wheels so we can split up and cover more ground."

Why didn't I think of that?

"I can have someone run you back to Bend for a rental if you'd like. That'd save some time," suggested Truman. At Eddie's nod he hollered down the hall. "Lucas! Get Gibson back to the station. I've got an errand for him."

Truman looked at Mercy. "What's your plan?"

"I'd like to talk to Leighton Underwood. Now."

NINE

FBI Special Agent Mercy Kilpatrick followed Truman in her black Tahoe as he led the way to Leighton Underwood's home.

Even though Leighton was a neighbor of Ned Fahey's, the route to his home was in a completely different direction. There was no fast way to get there, and Truman suspected Leighton liked it that way.

Remembering Toby Cox's comparison of Mercy to young Kaylie at the coffee shop, Truman told his phone to dial a number and listened to it ring as he drove. As soon as Toby had mentioned Kaylie, Truman realized why he felt as if he'd seen Mercy before. On the basis of looks, the FBI agent could be Kaylie's mother. And since they both were named Kilpatrick, Truman had a strong suspicion that she was. He'd heard Levi Kilpatrick's wife had left him and his baby girl years ago. Now it looked as if she was back in town.

But as an FBI agent?

One woman would know the full story.

"Hello?" Ina Smythe's frail voice sounded in his car.

"Hi, Ina, it's Truman."

"Enunciate clearly, son. It sounds like you're in a tin can."

"Sorry about that, I'm in the car. I only have a minute, Ina, but I wanted to ask you about Levi Kilpatrick. What can you tell me about his wife who left?"

Truman had relied on Ina Smythe to help smooth his way into Eagle's Nest. She'd sat at the front desk in the police station for forty years before retiring six months before Truman was hired. She was the one who'd reached out and told him about the police chief opening. "No one else wants it, Truman. They'll have to consider an outsider, and you know how that could turn out. You're sort of a familiar face around here, you've got the necessary experience, and we know your uncle Jefferson can pull some weight with the town council. What do you think about moving to Eagle's Nest permanently?"

He'd been ready for a change.

Ina coughed three times, and it echoed in his vehicle before she answered his question. "Deirdre? She wasn't his wife. She never married him, although he pushed for it. She took off for southern California somewhere when that little girl was one and left the baby with Levi. Her parents fought to get custody, but the court awarded it to Levi. Darn good decision. Her parents were too full of themselves, and I was glad when they moved not long after that. I don't know if they keep in touch with their granddaughter or not."

The name "Deirdre" made Truman deflate. Had she changed her name? If not, where did Mercy Kilpatrick fit in? She had to be a cousin of some sort; there was no denying her resemblance to Kaylie Kilpatrick. But the Kilpatricks had never mentioned any cousins in his presence.

"Does the name Mercy Kilpatrick mean anything to you?" Truman asked.

"*Mercy? Mercy Kilpatrick?* Where on earth did you hear about her?"

"Then you do know her." His curiosity shot off the charts.

"Of course I know her. Why do you ask? Who's talking about that girl?"

"No one's talking about her. I just met her."

"*She's here?* In town?"

"Yes. Is that a bad thing?"

His vehicle grew silent. "Ina? You there?"

"Yes. I'm thinking . . . I'm trying to remember the whole story . . . but there's pieces missing." She colorfully swore, making Truman grin. "I'm trying to get the tale straight in my head, but my memory isn't what it used to be."

"*Who is she?*"

"Why, she's Karl and Deborah Kilpatrick's youngest girl."

Truman nearly missed his turn. He'd heard about only four Kilpatrick siblings. They were very active in the Eagle's Nest community. No one had breathed a word about a fifth. Mercy wasn't Kaylie's mother; she was her aunt.

"But she hasn't been in town since she finished high school," Ina continued. "I can't remember why she left, but everyone in her family was angry and I suspected something was hushed up . . . dammit. What did that girl do?" Ina made a sputtering noise in the phone. "It was something juicy, I'm certain, but I can't put my finger on it."

"Well, you answered my question. You can get back to me about the gossip."

"What's she doing here?"

"She's an FBI agent out of Portland. She's been assigned to Jefferson's death along with the deaths of Enoch Finch and Ned Fahey. You heard about Ned, right?"

"Of course I did. My memory might not work that great anymore, but my ears work just fine. That old cranky coot probably waved his ax at the wrong person."

Truman wondered if the ax was a habit of Ned's he hadn't heard about.

"But little Mercy Kilpatrick is an FBI agent, you say? That's got to stick in her father's craw. He's not a fan of the federal government."

"I wouldn't call her little." Mercy could nearly look him in the eye. He knew Karl and Deborah ran a small ranch just outside town, and their blind daughter, Rose, lived with them. Their other three adult children were scattered around the county.

And then there was Mercy.

Truman grinned. Mercy hadn't said a word when Toby brought up Kaylie; she'd pretended not to know whom he meant. In other words, she wasn't broadcasting her relationship to the Kilpatrick clan. *Why?*

"And Ina, could you keep it to yourself for a bit? I don't think she wants to advertise that she's in town, but please let me know when you remember what happened. I'd like to hear the story."

Ina huffed but reluctantly agreed. "Is Lucas still doing a good job?" she asked. "Not slacking off yet, I hope. I knew he'd be a good replacement for me when I watched him reorganize all my recipes when he was fifteen. Did I tell you he put them on one of those tablet things? I can make the words nice and big so they're easy for these old eyes to read."

"Your grandson is a good fit," said Truman. "And he likes his job."

"Good." Satisfaction rang in her tone.

"One more thing, Ina. Have you ever heard a rumor of a cave man who lives in the forest around here?"

"A what?" she asked.

"Cave man," Truman repeated, feeling a flush cover his face.

"Can't say I've heard that one mentioned in the last forty years."

"You have heard of him?" Truman's voice shot up an octave.

"I can remember hearing about some old mean man who lived in a cave. He hated children and would kill any who stumbled into his domain," she mused. "Terrified me when I was a kid, and as I got older it kept me from ever venturing too far into the woods alone. But I suspect that was the intention of the story. To scare kids out of stupid behavior."

"Like when a parent tells you to be good or the bogeyman will get you."

"Yes, something like that. Might be originally based in some fact. It wouldn't surprise me to learn that there were a few unsocial types illegally roughing it in the state forest."

Is there a grain of truth to the cave man story?

Could the preppers have been murdered by an angry mountain man who wanted their weapons?

He didn't know what to think.

Truman ended the call with a promise to visit next weekend. He tried to have coffee with Ina Smythe once a month. The woman had been close friends with his uncle Jefferson. Sometimes Truman had wondered *how close*, but neither of them had ever hinted at a romantic relationship. Truman had made teenage assumptions based on looks. Looks exchanged between the two of them during the summers he stayed in Eagle's Nest, and the feeling that permeated the air when the two of them were in the same room. As a teen Truman had twice been hauled into the Eagle's Nest police station for some juvenile prank, and Ina had always stuck up for him and then gotten him released from the holding cell after four hours.

Last month during coffee, he'd asked her why she hadn't gotten him immediately out of the jail cell. She'd cackled and replied, "You deserved those four hours in that cell. Probably more. I figured it was a good place for you to think about the stupid things you'd done."

She'd been right.

He frowned. Ina didn't have memory problems. She never missed a beat when reciting some random incident that'd happened forty years before. Or remembering one of her eighteen great-grandchildren's birthdays.

Why couldn't she remember the reason Mercy Kilpatrick had left town?

Or is she not telling me on purpose?

The thoughts swirled in his brain for a few minutes as he took the last turn to Leighton's home. Special Agent Kilpatrick preferred to keep things to herself. When she'd made the comment last night about being from a small town, why hadn't she mentioned that she was from *his* small town?

If she wants to keep it a secret, I'll let her.

Sooner or later she'd be exposed. This was Eagle's Nest. A poor place to hide secrets.

He pulled onto the soggy road shoulder in front of Underwood's home. Mercy hadn't wanted him to accompany her, but he'd insisted, arguing that Leighton was the type to shoot a stranger and *then* ask their business. It wasn't completely true—although Leighton was known to answer the door with his gun in hand—but Truman wanted to keep his finger in the investigation. If his uncle had been killed by the same person who had shot Ned Fahey, he wanted to know. He planned to keep the two FBI agents as close as possible. He'd offered his little meeting room as home base so they wouldn't have to travel back and forth to Bend, and they'd accepted.

When he'd heard the agents had been put up in the roach motel halfway between Eagle's Nest and Bend, he'd called Sandy's Bed & Breakfast. She had two rooms opening up tomorrow. He'd casually mentioned the B&B to the agents. "She's got a great breakfast buffet for her guests. Eggs, hash browns, amazing bacon," Truman had said to sweeten the deal. Mercy hadn't seemed interested, but Eddie's eyes had lit up at the thought of getting out of the bare-bones motel. They'd agreed to stop by and talk to Sandy later in the day.

He'd do what it took to stay close to the FBI investigation.

He stepped out of his vehicle and walked back to Mercy's Tahoe. The two vehicles matched, except for the department logo on Truman's door. Mercy slammed her door and pulled up her jacket hood. Her heavy coat had a bit of black fake fur trim around the hood that made the green of her eyes pop. Now that he knew she was related to the other Kilpatricks, he recalled that her oldest brother, Owen, had the same intense eyes. Truman decided they looked better on Mercy. The color was wasted on a man. Other than the green, she was all black. Black hair, coat, pants, and boots.

"Looks wet," she commented.

Truman agreed. Leighton had several lake-size puddles lining the mud driveway to his home. Truman hadn't wanted to risk the driveway even in his four-wheel drive. And there was Leighton's gun reputation to consider. Parking on the road had been the wise decision.

The two of them headed down the drive, stepping where the mud didn't threaten to steal their boots.

"Leighton!" Truman cupped his hands and hollered. "You home?"

The roar of a shotgun answered him.

TEN

Mercy was shoved into the mud and lost her breath as Truman's bulk crashed on top of her.

"Leighton! It's Chief Daly! Hold your fire!"

Her right ear rang from his shout. "Get off me," she muttered. She'd landed on her stomach and tasted dirt. She elbowed him in the gut. *"Get off!"*

"Keep your head down," he snapped. "Leighton? It's Chief Daly!" he hollered again.

"Chief?" came a male voice from the house.

Mercy raised her head, trying to find a human to match to the voice.

"That's right. Are you going to fire again?"

"Who's with you?"

"Another officer."

Mercy raised a brow but figured it was close enough to the truth.

"Sorry about that," said the voice from the house. "I shot in the air, you know. Wasn't shootin' *at* you."

"I figured," answered Truman. He got off Mercy's back.

She pushed to her knees and surveyed her clothes. *Shit.* Her knees, her thighs, and the lower half of her jacket were dripping with muddy water. At least the gravel had protected her chest and arms. Truman offered her a hand. She gave him a dark look and accepted. "Did you know he'd fire at us?" she asked as she wiped at her knees with a soaked glove.

"I didn't know he wouldn't."

Same difference.

"And it was just a warning shot."

She stopped swiping and stared at him.

He met her gaze and shrugged. "Different rules out here."

He was right. At one time she'd known the rules. Had she been in the city for too long?

"Sorry about the mud." He pulled a package of tissues out of his coat pocket and handed it to her.

She shook her head at the plastic package on her palm. "I don't think these will cut it."

"We'll get a towel from Leighton. He'll feel bad that you got muddy."

He sounded sincere, and she stole a look at his face to see if he was making fun of her. He wasn't. Concern shone in his brown eyes. She eyed the rest of him. Other than a little mud on his boots, he'd managed to avoid the filthy water.

"Glad I could break your fall," she said.

"I appreciate it." He grinned, and the last grain of her annoyance with him shattered. Police Chief Truman Daly had a smile to stop traffic. *He probably breaks hearts right and left with that smile.* The tall man had been serious and reserved since she'd met him, which was understandable because of his uncle's death. But out here in the rainy woods surrounding Leighton's property, he'd relaxed, even though someone had fired a gun less than a minute ago.

"Chief? You comin' in?" Leighton called.

"On our way."

"You sure he's safe?" Mercy asked.

"He already said he wasn't shooting at us."

She fought the urge to roll her eyes. "I'm trusting you."

"Good idea." They continued their cautious wading to Leighton's home. The house didn't have a front porch. It had a small set of concrete stairs that led up to a larger concrete block in front of the door, which listed to the right. Leighton Underwood stood in the open doorway, his shotgun pointed away and tucked under one arm. It took Mercy a long second to recognize it as a peaceful pose. In Portland, seeing this stance in a doorway would have sent her in the opposite direction.

"My glasses busted." Leighton squinted at them. He was tall and proud looking, with a thick mane of white hair that'd receded several inches from his forehead. As Mercy stopped at the bottom of the stairs, the man studied her from head to toe. His name wasn't familiar to her. Even if he knew her parents, he probably didn't remember her.

"Can we come in, Leighton?" Truman asked.

"Who's this? You said another officer. Unless you hired a woman yesterday, I'm pretty certain there's no women on the Eagle's Nest force." Skepticism filled his lined face.

"I'm with the FBI," Mercy said. "We're investigating the death of your neighbor, Ned Fahey."

Leighton's chin rose. "I heard that asshole got himself killed."

"Now, Leighton—" Truman started.

"Any chance I could borrow a towel?" Mercy asked. "I fell in the mud when your gun went off."

He squinted at her pants. "Of course. Come in. I apologize again for that, but I couldn't see who was here. All I saw was those big black rigs you drove. And you know what *that* means." He stood to the side and waved them into the home. "Don't worry about your muddy boots. Stay on the hard floor and I'll mop it up later."

Mercy stepped inside and was overwhelmed by the odor of ground beef and onions. Her stomach rumbled. She followed the "hard floor" directly to the right and into a kitchen. No food was cooking on the stove. "What did our black vehicles mean to you?"

Leighton bustled past her and set his gun in a corner. He opened a closet door and pulled out a tan towel. She thanked him as he handed it to her. Its nap was nearly gone and it was mostly mesh, but she was grateful.

"You know what those trucks can mean. *The feds*," he whispered. "They all drive around in those big black SUVs. Usually in a caravan of sorts." He cackled. "I guess I was partially right, since you're a fed."

"Call me Mercy, please." She rubbed at her coat, turning the tan towel dark with dirty water. "Why would you expect the federal government to show up at your house? And would you shoot first if it was the government?"

Leighton rubbed at his bristly chin. "Well, I guess shooting first wouldn't be the smartest way to say hello. But I've been on edge lately. I've missed some payments on the mortgage and I've been getting those calls."

"Those would be from your mortgage company, not the government. I don't think the government sees your mortgage as their problem yet."

"How far behind are you?" Truman asked quietly. "Do you need a small loan? Just until things are right again?"

Mercy looked at him in surprise. *Would the police chief open his own pockets?*

"I don't need another loan," snapped Leighton. "Got enough."

"Did you know the town has a short-term emergency fund for problems just like this?" Truman added.

Hope appeared on Leighton's face and then vanished just as rapidly. "I'm not in the city limits."

"I'd call you an honorary resident. You spend money in Eagle's Nest, right? I'll put in a good word with the town treasurer for you."

The older man seemed to shrink. "I don't want to lose my house. Had to pay some medical bills and fell behind."

Truman clapped him on the shoulder. "Happens to everyone. That's why we set up the fund. Now . . . you're one of the closest neighbors to Ned Fahey. Did you notice anything unusual over the weekend?"

Mercy admired the way Truman had addressed Leighton's problem without making a big issue out of it and moved on as if making town loans was a daily part of his job. Maybe it was. She wondered how this mystery emergency fund was paid for.

"I can't see Ned's property from here. It's at least a half mile away. Our properties are divided by a small stream that runs off the Cascades, but during the summer it turns into a dry wash. This fall when it started flowing again, it went a different way. It moved at least a hundred yards into my lower field. Ned said according to the land deeds, that meant he owned half my field. I don't think so." If steam could come out of human ears, a dense cloud would be surrounding Leighton's head.

"That doesn't sound very fair," Mercy sympathized. Land was precious to the residents, and they guarded it fiercely. It didn't excuse Leighton for firing when he'd thought they were government agents coming to seize his property, but it gave her a little more insight into what made him tick. "So you're saying you haven't been close enough to Ned's property—his actual property—to see if anything happened over there."

"Nope."

"Hear any shots recently?" Truman asked.

"I always hear shots. But it could be coming from the McCloud or Hackett places. Hard to tell the direction sometimes."

Mercy studied the older man. Would he kill Ned Fahey to get his hundred yards of property back? He seemed honest enough, but she was reserving judgment.

"Did you order a new pair of glasses?" asked Truman. "I don't want you shooting someone who doesn't deserve it."

"Yep. Went into Bend last week. They should be ready tomorrow."

"Good," said Mercy. She frowned. "Do you have a ride to the eye doctor?"

"What for?" Leighton looked confused.

"Can you see well enough to drive?"

"I've been driving that road to Bend for fifty years. I could do it with my eyes shut."

Mercy decided this wasn't her problem. "I don't suppose you have any ideas about who would hurt Ned Fahey? I assume you know about Jefferson Biggs and Enoch Finch. We're looking for a common denominator in all three deaths."

Leighton scratched one ear. "Ned was always pissing people off. He liked to wave his ax around a little too much. I called him Injun Ned one time and I thought he was going to take my scalp for it."

Mercy bit the inside of her cheek.

"But he was pretty harmless. Kept to himself. He talked about being prepared for the end of the world all the time. I can only handle so much of that, you know. It was like a religion to him. He claimed he could last for months without relying on a grocery store or the county service for his heat." Sorrow crossed his face. "I guess all that work was for nothin' now."

"Did you know how many guns he had?" asked Mercy.

Leighton gave her an odd look. "What's it matter? A man has a right to own all the guns he wants. Never saw the point of owning more than five or so . . . I mean, you can only fire one at a time." Concentration narrowed his brows. "I think I've probably seen him with three different guns over the years. He preferred his ax."

That statement didn't match what Mercy suspected Ned owned. But the ax description was consistent.

She and Truman thanked Leighton for his time, and she handed him the wet towel. "Thank you for the towel."

"I'm sorry I scared you into the mud." He apologized with a small, gentlemanly bow.

Outside she asked Truman his opinion.

The chief walked another ten feet before replying, clearly organizing his thoughts. "I don't know if we learned anything from him or not. The change in property lines because of the creek is interesting, but I don't think it's a motive for murder."

"I agree." Mercy waited for a moment, but he appeared to be done talking. "Is there really a town fund for personal emergencies?"

Truman winced. "Not really. But I'll do what I can to keep him in his home. That's how it starts, you know."

"How what starts?"

"A lot of the antigovernment attitudes. It's like a line of dominoes. Usually the first domino is tipped over by having their home foreclosed on. Something personal happened . . . either they got ill and racked up huge medical bills or they lost their job and couldn't find another. They have to choose whether to feed their kids or pay the mortgage. Guess which is going to come first?"

Mercy knew he was right. She'd seen it happen over and over.

"Suddenly the home that's been in their family for decades is ripped out from under them and their credit rating is destroyed. They need a place to live. They need a job and they need their pride restored. It's a lot easier to stop the dominoes before they start tipping. If all Leighton needs is a bit of cash to tide him over, then we'll make it happen."

"Maybe he's a gambler." Mercy played the devil's advocate. "Maybe he spends all his money on porn."

"You can find every kind of porn for free on the Internet these days," Truman replied dryly. "A guy who pays for it isn't very bright, but I know what you're saying. I'll sit down and talk with Leighton to get an idea of how deep he's in debt and why there's a problem. Ina Smythe used to be the one who handled the logistics of our 'private fund.' I took it over because I didn't think people wanted to talk to nineteen-year-old Lucas about their problems."

"That's very kind of you." Mercy had always been partially terrified of Mrs. Smythe, but she suspected her teenage perspective of the woman as a tyrant hadn't been very accurate. She wondered what else she'd been wrong about.

Truman shrugged. "People are willing to tell me stuff."

Her opinion of the police chief was slowly coming together. He had a strong sense of honor about his residents. He was a listener. He wore his authority well and didn't seem to need to feed his ego. All positive things in Mercy's book. "Eddie is going to the Enoch Finch scene after he picks up the rental," Mercy said. "Can we go back to your uncle's home now? I'd like to see it in the daylight."

The chief looked at his watch. "It's time for lunch. You take time for lunch, don't you?" He looked sideways at her.

Mercy knew the most convenient places to eat would be smack in the center of Eagle's Nest. "I have something in my bag to tide me over. If you want to stop and grab something, I can meet you at the house."

Truman stopped and turned toward her. She halted, meeting the chief's brown gaze. A subtle challenge shone in his eyes. "Now, if you want to find out what's going on around here, one of the best things you can do is be seen. Let people know the FBI is searching for a murderer. And I think it's important for this town to see that the FBI isn't a stiff fed hiding behind a pair of sunglasses and a dark suit. I think putting a personal face on the FBI will go a long way in getting some cooperation. You look approachable. You're polite, and most of the men will think you're harmless."

"Harmless?" Mercy snapped.

"I didn't say they'd be right." Truman flashed another showstopping grin. "I know you wouldn't be here if you weren't the best at what you do, but getting people to lower their defenses can only help us. If you'd rather sit in your vehicle and eat one of those high-protein bars made of powdered meat and daisies, go ahead."

The challenge still glinted in his eyes.

Dammit. He was right.

Who would recognize her next?

ELEVEN

Truman picked the busiest restaurant for lunch.

If Special Agent Kilpatrick wanted to keep secrets from him, he'd make her squirm a bit. Her pride had flashed when he'd said the men in town would see her as harmless, but it was true and it'd work in her favor. He saw her waver for a moment, fighting her need to stay anonymous and wanting to do the best thing for her investigation. He'd known he'd win. In less than a day, he'd learned she was dedicated to her job.

He held open the diner door for her and removed his hat. Mercy stepped in and immediately moved to one side as she scanned the restaurant. Her hood was still up.

The diner was nearly empty.

Disappointment washed over Truman. One of these times someone was going to recognize Mercy Kilpatrick and he wanted to be there when it happened. If only to see her scramble. He grinned. *Why am I so looking forward to it?*

Usually he didn't relish another person's discomfort, but Mercy was playing a game with him, and he was due for a score. She slowly lowered her hood as he pointed at the last booth. "Have a seat. I need to say hello to a few people first." She nodded and strode away. Truman took his time greeting two old-timers who were nursing their bottomless cups of coffee. Neither of them asked about the woman who'd come in with him. He stopped and greeted a mother he didn't recognize with two small children. He gave each of the boys a police badge sticker and learned the mother lived on Oak Street. She was flirty, with big smiles and artificial laughter. He saw her gaze shoot to his left hand. He checked hers. No ring. He silently sighed, tousled the boys' heads, and politely broke away.

Mercy studied the menu, her profile to him as he walked down the aisle. Even though he couldn't see her eyes, she was still quite striking. Her jawline was sharp and her nose turned up the slightest bit. Nothing about her said FBI agent.

Until she turned her questioning stare on you.

Her mind seemed to be constantly analyzing and processing data. She didn't waste words, Truman had happily noted. He hated nothing worse than people who spoke to hear themselves talk or people who tried to cover up that they were slackers by using an avalanche of words. More words did not mean more intelligence.

He slid into the booth. "The burger is excellent. Mushrooms and Swiss."

Mercy nodded, not lifting her gaze from the menu. "Not much of a burger fan, but thanks. How's the enchilada salad?"

"I have no idea."

"How you doing, Chief?" Their waitress appeared.

"Great. Thanks, Sara. Your kids staying out of trouble?"

"So far they've only broken the refrigerator door this week, but we're barely through Tuesday. You want the usual?"

"Yes. Mercy?"

Mercy looked at the waitress. "Coffee with heavy cream and the enchilada salad, please. No cheese."

"The toppings are mostly cheese," said Sara. "You want extra olives and salsa?"

"Sounds great."

Sara vanished, and he swore Mercy exhaled in relief. Or maybe he imagined it. A vibration came from her purse on the booth bench. She grabbed her phone out of her bag and studied the screen. "Autopsy results on Ned Fahey."

"What's it say?" He waited impatiently while she opened the e-mail and scrolled. A narrow groove appeared between her eyebrows as she focused on the tiny print.

"Know that, know that, know that . . . ," she muttered.

"Anything new?"

"Here we go. Time of death is estimated to be between midnight Saturday and six a.m. Sunday." Her face softened. "He had some of the worst arthritis in his back and knees that Dr. Lockhart has ever seen. Poor guy. No wonder everyone said he was crabby. He was in constant pain."

"The gunshot wound is still the cause of death, right?"

"Yes. Have we heard if they found the bullet? The county evidence team was supposed to search."

"No one's told me."

"I'll e-mail Jeff and ask."

"Jeff?"

"The SSRA in Bend."

Her temporary boss.

Mercy looked up from her phone, satisfaction in her gaze. "Now we can focus on that time period. That's a big help."

"Hello, Chief Daly, I hope you're having a good day."

Truman looked up to find Barbara Johnson's round face beaming at him. The retired high school teacher was one of his favorite residents. Probably because she was always positive and upbeat. Being around her always lifted his spirits. "I am, Barbara. Can I intro—"

"Mercy Kilpatrick?" Astonishment rang in Barbara's tone. Mercy was out of her seat and hugging the woman before Truman could blink.

The women pulled apart and stared at each other before laughing and hugging again. Barbara wiped tears from her eyes. "Oh, girl. It's so good to see you! I've thought about you so many times over the years." They pulled apart again and Barbara looked Mercy up and down. "You look fantastic. City life agrees with you."

"Thank you so much, Mrs. Johnson."

"Call me Barbara now. You're not a child anymore." She looked at Truman. "Mercy was one of my star pupils. I always knew she'd go far."

Mercy wiped at her own eyes. "Thank you, Mrs.—Barbara," she said awkwardly. "You don't know how much that means to me. You were a rock I could lean on, and I always could talk to you."

"Where have you been? Why haven't you come back to visit before now?" the woman asked. "I see your parents all the time, but they never talk about you."

Mercy glanced at Truman and guilt flashed in her eyes. "It's a long story. Can we meet at another time to talk? I'm working right now."

"I'm sure the police chief won't—"

"Can we please save it for later, Barbara? I'd love to catch up with you," Mercy said quickly. "We're tight on time." She shot a pleading glance at Truman.

He was tempted to invite the kind woman to join them, simply to see how Mercy reacted. "She's right, Barbara. We need to eat and run."

Disappointment flooded Barbara's face, and Truman's heart twisted at the unfamiliar sight. "All right." She shook a finger at Mercy. "You better not leave town without paying me a visit. I'll hunt you down if you do."

"I promise," Mercy agreed.

The woman left after a few more words, and Mercy slid back into the booth as Sara appeared with their food. Truman silently added ketchup and mustard to his burger, swirling it around on the bun. He put the burger back together and took a bite, slowly chewing. He waited through a full minute of silence while Mercy attacked her salad, her gaze firmly on her food. He finally spoke.

"So . . . Special Agent Kilpatrick. I think you have something to tell me."

◆　◆　◆

Mercy swallowed a large corn chip and it scratched its way down her esophagus. She coughed and grabbed her glass of water. Truman took a bite of burger and calmly watched her as he chewed.

How much does he know?

She mentally raced through explanations, discarding most of them as she poked at her salad.

Stick to the truth. Doesn't have to be the whole truth.

"I grew up in Eagle's Nest, but I haven't lived here since I was eighteen." She risked a look at him, meeting his gaze. Truman showed no surprise. He was proving to have a solid poker face.

He took another bite of burger, and ketchup dripped onto his plate. His gaze didn't leave her eyes. One of his brows rose. *And?*

"I had an argument with my parents." She shrugged. "Teen stuff, you know. Boundaries. Life philosophies. Seeing how far I could push." She stabbed at her salad a few more times, no longer hungry. "Anyway, I haven't had a reason to come back."

"But you've been in touch with your parents."

"No."

"Nothing?"

"Nope."

"E-mail? Christmas cards?"

"None of us have tried anything."

"But you've got four siblings. You talk to them, right?"

Mercy blanched. "You knew?"

"I put it together after Toby Cox said you looked like Kaylie Kilpatrick. I thought maybe you were her mother who took off years ago, but Ina Smythe set me straight."

Mercy set down her fork as a black haze tunneled her vision. "What else did Mrs. Smythe tell you?"

"She couldn't remember why you left town."

Good.

"Why didn't you immediately tell me you were from Eagle's Nest?" His brows narrowed as he took a drink from his soda. "Were you trying to get the job done and get out before anyone noticed you?"

"Something like that." Mercy sat perfectly still, fighting her body's need to dash out the door. "This isn't my favorite place."

Truman nodded, seeming to accept that, but Mercy could tell he knew there was more to the story. He wasn't going to pry it out of her. Yet.

"Your boss know you're from here?"

"My boss in Portland does. She must have told the SSRA in Bend, because he mentioned it."

"Is that why they sent you? They thought you'd have some insight into this community?"

Mercy paused. *Could that be the reason?* "I'd just cleared some cases off my desk. I was due for a new assignment."

"And Peterson? Why'd they send him? There's no way that agent has any roots on this side of the Cascades."

"He worked on one of the cases I just closed. We work well together."

"Anything else I should know?" Truman asked. He dropped his gaze and focused on cleaning up the ketchup with a fry.

"No."

"Good."

Silence hung over the table for a few minutes as Mercy tackled her salad again. For a small-town diner, it served an excellent salsa.

"How you doin', Chief?" A gravelly voice interrupted their meal.

Mercy looked up and caught her breath. *Joziah Bevins.* Her memory of the man merged with the older man in front of her. The lines in his face had tripled, his hair had thinned and whitened, and there was a new stoop to his shoulders. *He's old!*

Has my father aged the same way?

My mother?

Her throat thickened and she blinked rapidly.

"Hey, Joziah. Just catching some lunch," said Truman.

Joziah turned his attention to Mercy, and his smile slowly faded. Recognition fluttered and then faded in his eyes.

"This is Mercy Kilpatrick. She's with the Portland FBI office."

Recognition caught flame. "Well. Mercy Kilpatrick. It's been a long time. I hadn't heard you were with the FBI. You've really outgrown our little town, haven't you?" Curiosity and caution shone in his gaze.

She expected him to pat her on the head and call her a *good little woman.* If he told her to show her pretty smile, she'd stomp on his toes.

He'd said both things to her before, but she'd never had the desire to stomp on his toes. Of course, back then she'd believed that type of comment was acceptable.

Funny how she'd changed.

"Nice to see you again, Joziah." Her mouth felt odd saying his name; he was still Mr. Bevins in her brain. Or "that asshole Bevins." She heard the words in her father's voice.

"Been out to see your parents?" Joziah asked.

Why is that the first thing anyone asks? "Not yet. I just got here."

He nodded, wheels and gears spinning behind his eyes. He glanced at Truman and back at her. "Working on the murders?"

"We've asked the FBI for some support," said Truman. "They have a lot more resources than Eagle's Nest or county."

"I was very sorry to hear about your uncle," Joziah said to Truman. "He was a part of the community for a long time."

"Thank you, Joziah."

Bevins said his farewells and took a seat at the diner's counter, placing his cowboy hat on the seat next to him.

Mercy had held her breath the whole time. When she was a child, Joziah had scared the crap out of her. Nothing had changed.

"Jesus," said Truman. "I thought you were going to puke."

Mercy stared at him. "What?"

"When you first looked at him, you turned slightly green. I take it there's some history there? Not everyone gets a big hug like Barbara Johnson?"

"He and my father don't like each other. I grew up learning to avoid him."

"You're an adult now. I think you can make your own decisions about people. I assume he and your father butted heads over some things?"

"That's putting it mildly."

"Joziah Bevins is a popular man around town. Your father commands respect too."

"It's always been that way."

"Should I have not introduced you?"

"You had to say something."

"I could have left off your last name and the FBI part. That seems disrespectful, though. Would you prefer I do that from here on out?"

Mercy glared at him. "I'm not hiding from anyone."

Truman grinned. "Oh yeah? Coulda fooled me."

TWELVE

Two decades ago

"Dammit, Deborah! I know it was one of Bevins's crew!"

"You don't know that, Karl. You're making assumptions!"

Mercy hid at the top of the stairs, listening to her parents argue. They rarely raised their voices, and shouting was unheard of in their home. But their loud whispers had been enough to wake twelve-year-old Mercy and make her sneak out of the bedroom she shared with Pearl and Rose. The house was dark except for a dim-yellow glow from downstairs. That meant they were arguing in the kitchen, lit by the single bulb in the stove's hood.

"Someone shot that cow. One of my best."

"Accidents happen, Karl."

"That was no accident. Bevins approached me again about joining his circle. He wants me to bring along our entire group. That's not going to happen, and I've told him several times before."

"He's just scared and trying to reinforce his position. You're valuable. His vet doesn't have half the skills you do."

"It's not just me, Deborah. He wants you too."

Her mother was silent. Mercy could imagine her mother's one-shouldered shrug. She wasn't a vain woman, but she knew her midwifery skills were unmatched in the area. All the area women called on her mother throughout their pregnancies. Even the ones who had medical insurance and went to a real doctor in Bend. They still checked in with her mother and asked for second opinions. It made Mercy proud.

"I know the cow was shot intentionally," her father said, losing some steam. "It's no coincidence that yesterday I turned Bevins down again."

"What can we do?" asked Deborah.

The silence was long and Mercy leaned forward, waiting for her father's answer. Joziah Bevins was the one man her father complained about. Karl Kilpatrick never had a bad word to say about anyone, unless it was Mr. Bevins. And even then, Mercy suspected he held back his words a lot of the time.

"Nothing."

Mercy sagged against the stair rail in relief. She didn't want her father to fight Mr. Bevins. Someone would get killed. Her brothers claimed their father wasn't scared of Joziah Bevins, but her father's frustration scared Mercy. Focusing on the care of his family and working on his preparations kept her father occupied, but this one man seemed to get to him.

"We have a plan," said Deborah soothingly. "No one is going to change it. We've surrounded ourselves with good people who will stand by us. He's simply jealous. He's trying to force people to do his will and doesn't understand that doesn't command respect. He sees you getting respect and it eats at him."

Her father said nothing.

"Come back to bed."

The kitchen was silent and Mercy heard a click as the bulb was turned off. The dark swallowed up the house. She crawled on her hands and knees back to her room and felt her way to her bed.

"Are they okay?" Rose whispered in the pitch black. A faint snore came from the bunk above Mercy. Pearl could sleep through anything.

"*Yes. Dad thinks Joziah Bevins shot Daisy.*" Mercy stared into the dark and imagined she was Rose. No sight. Ever. Rose didn't seem to mind it so much, but Mercy thanked God every day that he'd not chosen her to be the blind Kilpatrick sister. She wouldn't have been as accepting as Rose.

"*Mom will calm him down.*"

"*She did.*"

"*Poor Daisy,*" whispered Rose. "*She was good about coming when I called her. She'd always hold still for me.*"

All the animals on the ranch held still for Rose. Mercy swore they were more considerate around her sister, as if they knew Rose couldn't see where they set their big hooves. Mercy had several favorite cows, and Daisy had been one of them. She felt a hot tear roll from the corner of her eye to her pillow. She hadn't cried when her father told her that Daisy was dead. But now, here in the dark, she felt safe expressing her sorrow for the sweet soul.

"*She'll have to be replaced,*" said Mercy, swallowing hard. "*She was important.*"

"*Two of the cows will calve in a few months,*" said Rose. "*We're good.*"

Mercy let the conversation drift away, her brain weighing the loss of the cow to the ranch. Milk, breeder, meat if needed. But cattle also required food, shelter, and health care. It was a fine balance to have the right amount of cows so that their benefit outweighed the cost. Her father had it down to a science for the size of his family. Everything had a value. Heirloom vegetable seeds: high value. A treadle sewing machine: high value. A compact disc player: low value.

Not even as a Christmas present.

Mercy understood. But it didn't mean she liked it.

"I'd like to start with the outbuildings," said Mercy.

She and Truman had arrived at his uncle's home. In the harsh light of the day, it looked sadder than the night before. As if it'd finally accepted that its occupant would never return. She followed Truman across the grassy area in front of the home to the drive that led behind the house. She noted how all the downspouts led to large plastic water barrels. The water wouldn't be good for drinking, but it would work for washing clothes or flushing toilets. Their boots crunched on the gravel. "What do you plan to do with the property?" Mercy asked, needing to fill the silence. Truman hadn't said much since they'd arrived. Tension was hovering around him again.

Mercy liked him better without the dark cloud.

"I haven't decided. There's still some legal paperwork to be handled. Luckily the mortgage was paid off long ago. Now I just have to pay the property taxes on it."

"It should sell for a decent price," Mercy said. "How many acres?"

"Eleven. I can't think about selling yet."

Mercy wondered if the November property tax bill would speed up his decision.

Truman undid the heavy lock and pulled away the chain that bound the two doors to the small barn. The warped and faded wood made the structure look as if it was a month away from collapse. He grabbed the handle of one door and hauled on it with all his weight. The door groaned as it slid open. Mercy wondered how strong his uncle had been to regularly open that door. She stepped inside, letting her eyes adjust to the dim light. Truman flicked a switch.

"Oh!"

The outside of the dilapidated barn was misleading. Inside was a clean concrete floor and pristine paint on the insulated walls. The temperature inside was almost comfortable. "He kept his weapons in here?"

"Yes."

Truman led the way to the back of the barn and opened a wood cabinet to expose a huge gun safe. Its heavy metal door was ajar. Truman opened the door all the way to show Mercy it was empty.

"You know the combination?" she asked.

"I don't. That's why it's still open. I'll have to get an expert out here if I want it to be usable again."

"It was found open?"

"Yes."

"So someone was close enough to your uncle to know the combination."

"Or he opened it for someone."

Mercy thought on that. "I didn't know your uncle, but he sounds like that type that wouldn't do that. Who do you think he'd open it for?"

"No one that I can think of. He trusted no one. Except for maybe Ina Smythe. But she wouldn't be interested in his weapons." Truman paused. "She doesn't get around very well anymore. I can't see her making the short walk from the house to the barn."

Mercy studied the rest of the interior. Simple custom cabinets and deep bins lined the walls. "Mind if I look around?"

Truman waved a hand. "Look all you want. I can't tell if anything else is missing. Everything looks stuffed full to me."

She opened the thin plywood doors of the cabinet next to the one that housed the gun safe.

"Diesel," said Truman.

Mercy nodded, mentally estimating the gallons. Jefferson Biggs had laid in a good store.

"I didn't see any gasoline," he commented.

"Diesel is safer to store and has a longer storage life than gasoline."

She peeked in a few more cabinets on the other side of the structure. Canning supplies, glass jars full of fruit and vegetables, and canned goods crammed the shelves. She lightly touched a laminated chart on the inside of the door that kept track of his rotation system.

"I've never heard of canned butter," Truman remarked. "That can't taste good."

"It tastes like normal butter."

He pointed at a large stack of huge pink salt licks. "My uncle didn't have any cows and there's enough salt here for a city. Who needs that much salt?"

"I suspect he planned to use them to attract game at some point in the future," Mercy said. "It beats hunting. Have the game come to you."

She found several stacks of empty food-grade buckets and more buckets with tight-fitting lids filled with baking supplies. Fishing supplies, medical supplies, tools, every type of battery made. The wealth astounded her.

"I can't believe they only took the guns. Why was all this left behind?" she mumbled.

"It'd be a pain in the butt to move," said Truman.

"But this is years of preparation. *Good* preparation. It's like gold."

"To some people."

She looked at him. "If the electrical grid crashes, you'll be glad you have this."

He didn't say anything.

"Did you know your uncle was a prepper?"

"Of course. I spent a lot of time during the summers helping him out. One of the other sheds is packed full of wood I've chopped over the years." He gave the loaded cabinets a sour look. "Doesn't mean I subscribe to the lifestyle."

"It's more than a lifestyle," Mercy said. "It's a life philosophy. Removing yourself from being dependent on others. Self-reliance."

"No one can completely survive on their own. We need other people."

"Eventually. But if you had to hide out for a month, could you?"

"Sure."

"Can you be ready in ten minutes?"

"No. I'd need to get my stuff together."

"How will you pack food for a month?"

"I'd go to one of the outdoor stores. Load up on those freeze-dried meals."

"In that store you'll be fighting ninety-nine percent of the population, who had the same bright idea." She glanced back at the rows and rows of canned food. "The one thing that surprises me is how exposed this storage is. Anyone could take an ax to that chain on the door and steal his supplies. Usually preppers hide their stores in fear of being swarmed when an emergency happens. Did the rest of the town know your uncle did this?"

"I imagine so. Although he didn't talk about it much."

"Maybe he was relying on the look of the barn to keep people from raiding. I was surprised when you opened the door."

Truman took a hard look at her. "You were raised in this *life philosophy*, weren't you? I've heard the Kilpatricks believe in being prepared."

"Everyone believes in it, but not everyone acts on it. Or knows how to." She looked around. "Your uncle did a good job."

"It doesn't explain how or why his guns were taken."

Mercy realized she'd lost focus on her examination of the property. They were looking for evidence of who'd killed his uncle. The well-stocked larder and supplies had distracted her. "Let me know if you need help figuring out what to do with all of this."

Truman scanned the cabinets. "I imagine there're plenty of people in town who could use some of the food."

She wanted to stop him from handing it out willy-nilly. "Everyone has needs. Give it to someone who will appreciate it for what it is."

He gave her an odd look. "It's food. Basics."

"It could be the difference between life and death."

"Does Special Agent Peterson know you're a hoarder?"

Mercy froze. *He's just pushing my buttons.* "Your uncle wasn't a hoarder. He was smart. I admire someone who thinks ahead."

"I do too. But not if it rules every aspect of their life." He tipped his head toward the door. "Want to see the rest?"

She nodded and followed him out the door.

Truman blew out a breath as they walked to the next little shed.

Jefferson Biggs had been slightly nuts. Truman had dreaded showing Mercy the shrine to his uncle's obsession, but she'd admired it. Instead of shock and surprise, she'd had the same look that his uncle got on his face when he looked at his supplies. Reverence. Pride. He'd always given Truman the impression he was silently counting and calculating as he eyed his handiwork.

Mercy had looked exactly the same.

How does a former prepper from Central Oregon end up working for the federal government as an FBI agent?

The dichotomy between her past and present intrigued him. He studied her from the corner of his eye. She had the town polish of his suburbanite sister, and he wondered if she'd deliberately worked to leave her rural roots behind or if it'd happened naturally over time. So far she'd moved and spoken like someone very comfortable with ranch life, but he suspected she was just as at ease in a modern-art museum.

He unlocked the doors to the shed and stood back. This one wouldn't take very long. It was packed with chopped wood and nothing else. Mercy glanced in and nodded. "Does he have a greenhouse?"

"A small one." He led her around the woodshed to the small glass greenhouse. He'd helped repair two of the glass panes when he was a teen, since his baseball had been at fault. His gaze went straight to those panes; they still looked good.

Mercy stepped inside, inhaled the moist air, and immediately darted to some potted trees. "Lemon trees! And limes!" She couldn't stop smiling. "Dwarf trees. You've got liquid gold here."

Truman raised a brow, unimpressed. The trees she'd exclaimed over were squatty looking, their fruit barely showing. She poked around in the greenhouse for a few moments, examining leaves and muttering to

A Merciful Death

herself. He waited patiently at the door as she looked her fill and then finally stepped out of the glass building with a sigh.

"Your uncle was a smart man. Where are his vehicles? I assume he has more than one? Maybe even a quad or motorcycle of some sort."

She'd surprised him again. "He has a truck in the garage attached to the house. He also has an ancient Jeep that he used to let me drive around the property when I was a teen. And a motorcycle that I wasn't allowed to touch."

"Let's see."

They went back to the house, and Truman stopped to push the automatic garage door opener he'd fastened to the visor in his vehicle. As the double door rolled up, Mercy peered into the garage. It was exactly as he'd said. A truck, an ancient Jeep, and the motorcycle. She walked around the vehicles but wasn't looking at them. He followed her gaze to the multiple generators lining one wall.

"Does he have a well?" she asked.

"Yes. The water tastes like crap."

She smiled. "You shouldn't sell this house. This is a great property. It's a little too close to town for some people, but he's set it up nicely to be self-sufficient."

"I don't want to live here." He sounded like a whiner.

"Do you mind if we go inside?"

He pushed open the door between the house and garage as an answer. She walked past him and he got a whiff of fresh-baked lemon bars. *Her shampoo?* They silently walked the home. Truman had said everything he had to say the night before and didn't feel the need to fill the silence with useless words. He caught her watching him a few times and wondered what she saw on his face.

Pain?

A desire for revenge?

She stopped in the long hallway and pointed at a framed collage of faded pictures. "What goes through your mind when you look at this?"

93

Truman stepped closer to look, even though he knew each picture by heart. They were candid shots of his uncle and his friends. Most of them were from the 1970s. Avoiding her eyes, he pressed his lips together as he considered her question. "I think of my uncle living here alone. I think how much we butted heads, but deep down I always knew he cared. I always wondered if he missed me when I went home for the school year."

"Did you ever consider attending school here?"

"Hell no. This was a good place to blow off some steam during the summer, but I didn't want to live here."

"Did you know kids your own age when you lived here?"

Memories flooded his brain. Some good, some shitty. "Yes."

"What was hanging here?" she outlined a faint rectangle on the wall.

"A mirror. It was in pieces when I got here that morning."

Mercy stared at the white rectangle the old mirror had left by protecting the wall from dirt for decades.

She took a few steps and looked in the bathroom they'd studied last night, but she wasn't looking at the floor this time.

"The gunshots broke the mirror in here, right?"

"Yes." Truman didn't like how her eyes had widened as she'd studied the wall. "Why?"

She turned and strode into his uncle's bedroom, scanning every corner. "Were there any mirrors in here?"

Truman scowled. "Not that I'm aware of."

"Did you find any other broken mirror fragments in the house?" Her voice rose an octave.

He thought. "No. Why are you asking?"

She shook her head as she went back down the hall. She stopped where the broken mirror had hung. "It was knocked off the wall in the scuffle. It's so close to the bathroom. Someone bumped it."

"That's what I assumed. What were you thinking?"

Her green gaze met his. "For a split second it reminded me of another scene."

He didn't know what crime she was talking about, but judging by the horror she was attempting to hide behind her gaze, he knew it'd been a bad one.

"I need to call Eddie."

His antennae rose. "Why?"

"Maybe he noticed something I missed at Ned Fahey's house."

"Like what?"

"Like more broken mirrors."

Mercy paced in the yard in front of Jefferson Biggs's home, swearing at Eddie under her breath.

"Pick up, pick up. Dammit!" It went to voice mail. She left a message for him to call her right back and sent a text requesting the same.

Her heart hadn't slowed since Truman had said a mirror had been broken.

Not the same. It's not the same. That would be impossible.

Or could it be?

No. He's gone.

Her phone rang in her hand and she nearly dropped it. "Eddie?"

"Yeah, what's up?"

"Where are you?" she asked.

"I'm at Enoch Finch's home. Would you believe almost everything has been removed from the house? I guess the family thought they had free rein to come in and help themselves to whatever they wanted." Disgust rang in his tone. "The sheriff told them he'd collected all the evidence and had turned it over to a cousin, but that was only three days ago! It looks like a mob of Christmas bargain hunters plowed through the place."

"Did you notice if the mirror in the bathroom was broken?"

Eddie was silent for a long moment. "It is. Why do you ask? How'd you know that?"

Mercy's knees threatened to give out on her.

"Mercy? *Why* did you ask that?"

"Maybe one of the family members did it," she said. "It sounds like they weren't very careful."

"I can check the official report on the murder," said Eddie. "Or it'd probably be quicker to ask one of the officers who was here. You're not answering my question."

"The bathroom mirror at Jefferson Biggs's home was broken."

"I remember. It was hit by a bullet or two."

"There was another small mirror hanging in the hallway that'd been broken."

"I don't know what you're getting at," Eddie stated, losing his patience. "Mirrors break. Especially when people are shooting or fighting for their lives."

"Did you look in the bathroom at Ned Fahey's home?"

"I didn't."

"We need to find out if his mirrors are intact."

"Jesus Christ, Mercy. *Why?*"

She swallowed hard. "There have been murders in Eagle's Nest before. He always broke all the mirrors."

Eddie was silent.

"I'm not jumping to conclusions, Eddie."

"Did they catch him?"

Mercy swallowed. "No."

THIRTEEN

Truman felt as if he'd had a door slammed in his face.

He tossed a five-dollar bill on the counter at the gas station as the attendant rang up his Doritos.

Back at Jefferson's house, Mercy had made a phone call to her partner and then told him she had to leave. When he'd pressed for more answers, she'd shook her head. "Eddie says the bathroom mirror was broken at Enoch Finch's home, but he didn't notice the mirror when we were at Ned Fahey's the other day, so we're going to check." She'd forced a stiff smile. "I'm sure I'm jumping to conclusions. I don't want to waste your time with what is probably a wild hair. If it turns out to be something important, I'll let you know."

She'd driven off.

Leaving him with a hell of a lot of questions and no answers.

Broken mirrors.

He'd gone back to his office and Googled for crimes with the signature. No luck. He'd started to fill out a ViCAP request and realized "broken mirrors" wasn't enough to create a useful search. More data was needed to narrow the field.

He'd have to sit on his hands until Mercy decided to share her information with him. He could call Sheriff Rhodes and put out some feelers. The man had worked law enforcement in the area for at least two decades and might know what Mercy was talking about.

But maybe it wasn't a local crime she'd been reminded of. It could have been something she'd seen in Portland or during her previous posting.

Shit.

Frustration rolled over him as he dropped his change in the tip jar on the gas station counter.

"Later, Chief."

Truman finally looked the scrawny attendant in the eye. "Sorry, Sid. I'm a bit distracted." He kicked himself. It was a priority that he give his full attention to whoever was in front of him. Everyone deserved his respect. A large part of his job was knowing how and when to listen.

"I was sorry to hear about your uncle," said Sid gruffly, dropping eye contact. His hair fell across his face, further hiding him from Truman's view.

Truman was touched. It was the most personal thing the shy young man had ever said to him.

"Thank you, Sid. Enjoy your day." Truman turned and nearly bumped into Mike Bevins.

"Hey, Truman, how's it going?"

The men shook hands and bantered for a few moments until Mike's sidekick stepped in the store.

Craig Rafferty looked away instead of meeting Truman's gaze.

Asshole.

Some people in this town will never accept me.

He needed to accept that fact. Their reasons ranged from pure stubbornness to dislike of government officials. For some, the simple fact that he hadn't been born on this side of the Cascades was reason enough to permanently view him as an outsider.

He wasn't certain what Craig Rafferty's reasons were, but his attitude toward Truman had been consistent since they'd met when they were teens.

Truman didn't understand why Mike still hung around with Craig, but both men worked for Mike's dad, Joziah Bevins, so Truman assumed Mike was just keeping the peace.

Truman nodded at Mike and headed out to his vehicle, remembering when he'd first learned what Craig was like.

"Go, Truman! Don't be a fucking wuss!"

Truman backed up the steep slope with the rope swing in his hand, watching where he stepped in the dirt and weeds with his bare feet. He tightened his grip and held his breath as he dashed forward and leaped. The rope swung him far out over the fast-moving water, and for a split second he was suspended. He let go.

And fell and fell.

His skin stung as the freezing water slapped his body. Underwater, his lungs begged to suck in a breath, but he kept his mouth clamped shut. Bubbles surrounded his face and he pumped his arms and legs, propelling himself to the surface. He broke and gasped for breath.

Cold!

Cheers came from the guys on the bank. Truman shook the water out of his eyes and started to swim to shore. The current had already moved him far down from his entry point. His arms shook from the strain of fighting the current. Shouts made him look up, and he saw Craig Rafferty swing out over the water. Truman treaded water, enjoying the fear on Craig's face and the huge splash. Cheers went up again, and Mike grabbed the rope as it swung back and worked his way up the bank. Truman took a few more strokes toward shore but kept an eye on Mike, waiting to see if he was going to flip upside down again.

Mike didn't go. His gaze was fixed on the water. More shouts.

Four of the guys were pointing at the water and yelling.

Truman looked where they pointed, experiencing a split second of terror that a deadly river creature had appeared. Instead he saw Craig, facedown in the water, caught in the current and flowing rapidly downstream.

"Truman!" He heard Mike's shout above the others.

He didn't pause. He changed direction, putting himself on a collision course with Craig. His arms had tired and the cold water sucked the strength out of his legs. He pushed on, locking his gaze on Craig's hair.

Lift your head!

Craig vanished below the water and panic lit up Truman's chest. He tracked the course he believed Craig's body would take and swam harder, pumping his arms and legs. Craig's back surfaced and Truman adjusted his interception path.

Almost there.

Truman sucked in a deep breath and went underwater to use his strongest strokes. His fingertips touched skin. He lunged and caught Craig's ankle. He let the current carry them as he worked his way up Craig's body and turned his face out of the water.

"Craig! Craig!" He slapped the teenager.

Nothing.

There was no way to apply chest compressions as they shot down the river. Truman linked an arm around Craig's neck and paddled one-handed toward shore. His progress was slow, the river rushing them farther downstream, but the shoreline eventually came closer.

"Crap!"

Big rocks littered the water where Truman estimated he'd finally reach shore. At the rapid rate they were moving, it would hurt when they hit one. He moved Craig to his other arm and braced his left arm to catch the rock.

The impact knocked the breath out of him, and he went under. He clamped his right arm around Craig's neck, determined not to lose hold. He came up for air, and the rush of the water pinned him against the rock. At least they were no longer moving. His gaze estimated the distance to shore: fifteen feet.

So close.

But his energy was gone. He yelled at Craig and pinched his lips and poked him as hard as he could in the ribs. He welcomed the pressure of the water that held the two of them against the big rock, giving his muscles a small break, but now he had to fight to keep Craig above water. The current continually caught the other boy's legs, trying to drag him past the rock. There was movement on the shore as the other guys arrived. They had cut the rope swing and one of them was tying it around Mike's waist. Mike waded into the water, using the other big rocks to keep from being swept downstream.

"How's it going?" he panted as he reached Truman and Craig.

"He's not breathing," Truman gasped.

"Are you okay to stay here if I pull him in?"

"I'm not going anywhere." He struggled to unfasten his arm from Craig's neck. His arm had frozen in place. Mike grabbed Craig under the arms and turned onto his back.

"Pull me in!" he shouted. The guys on shore towed them away.

Truman watched Craig's still face as they inched toward shore.

Open your eyes!

Two more guys waded into the water and helped pull Craig to shore. They circled around him on the bank, and Craig disappeared from Truman's sight. Bare shoulders moved up and down as chest compressions were applied. Mike looked over his shoulder at Truman.

Truman couldn't move from the rock.

One of the guys anchored the rope as Mike moved back into the water. "You stuck?" he asked as he reached Truman.

"Fuck yes. My legs can't move. They're numb."

"Relax. Turn around." Mike deftly maneuvered him into the same position he'd used to haul Craig to shore. Truman stared up at the blue sky and towering firs along the riverbank as Mike hauled him in.

He felt like a paralyzed baby.

Rocks grazed his butt and he rolled over to his hands and knees in the water. Every muscle shook. He tried to crawl the last few feet out of the water, but several hands grabbed his arms and lifted him to his feet. He stepped carefully, as no feeling was left in his feet from the icy water. He looked over and saw Craig on his side puking river water.

Relief nearly sent him back to his knees.

One of the guys slapped him on the back. "Nice job! You saved his life." The others gathered around. More slaps on his back.

Truman couldn't speak. He kept watching Craig heave and puke.

Mike led Truman to a rock and made him sit. Truman's knees screamed as they bent. "You okay?" Mike asked.

"Yeah."

"Craig's gonna be all right."

"I see that."

"Nice job, hero." Mike's blue eyes crinkled as they smiled at him.

"Not a hero," said Truman. "Any of you guys would have done the same if you'd been in the water first."

"That water was fucking cold," said Mike. "Comes straight off the Cascade snowmelt."

"No shit."

Craig sat up, wiping his mouth, and looked at the guys surrounding him. "What happened?"

"Truman saved your ass. You got knocked out in the water."

Truman sat on his cold rock, feeling the water drip down his back and his lungs wince as he tried to take deep breaths. Craig barely met his gaze and then looked away.

Truman didn't have the energy to speak.

Craig never looked him in the eye again after that. Truman had expected to be fully accepted after he'd risked his own life for Craig's, but instead he'd been treated as an outsider even more than before. Mike tried to call him a hero a few more times that summer, but Truman put a stop to it. "I was in the right place at the right time. That's not a hero."

But now, more than a decade later, he thought about the incident every time he saw Craig Rafferty.

People are going to treat me however they decide. Nothing I can do about it.

He needed to ignore the people who wanted to keep him on the sidelines. There were plenty of good people in town who'd gone out of their way to make him feel welcome.

He was determined that Eagle's Nest would be his home.

FOURTEEN

A jagged star of cracks covered the medicine cabinet mirror at Ned Fahey's.

Mercy stared at it and swallowed the bile in the back of her throat. The home had one bathroom, and she'd made a quick walk of the house looking for more mirrors. There weren't any.

Coincidence?

"For all we know, it's been broken for two years," said Eddie.

Mercy nodded, but every cell in her body screamed that he was wrong.

"I bet Toby Cox could tell us," he continued. "If he was over here as much as he said he was, he had to use the bathroom at some point."

"I believe he lives in the next home down the road," Mercy said slowly.

"I'll drive."

"Let's walk. It's less than a mile. I need some air."

Outside, Mercy sucked in deep breaths as they walked the gravel road. Ned's home sat higher than the rest of Eagle's Nest, and gray, heavy clouds covered the top third of the trees. The rain had stopped, but the dense firs continued to drip, making occasional plunking sounds in the woods. An odor of moist, decaying dirt hung in the air, and a sad wire fence lined one side of the road, wending its way between the firs and brush. The fence didn't look capable of keeping anyone out. Or in.

"You need to bring me up to speed," Eddie finally said. "What's this case remind you of?"

Mercy swallowed. "Two Eagle's Nest women were murdered when I was a senior in high school. Each was killed in their own home during break-ins about two weeks apart. They never figured out who did it, but he broke all the mirrors in the homes. Bathrooms, hand mirrors, all of them."

"How do you know this?"

She shrugged. "Everyone knew. It's a small town. People started to lock their doors at night."

"And the break-ins just stopped?"

"Yes." *Sort of.*

They walked for a few more moments in silence. "Were the women shot?" Eddie asked.

"No. Strangled. And they were raped."

"Evidence?"

"I don't know . . . I was just a teen. I'm sure there's something in a file box somewhere."

Eddie stopped and Mercy did the same, his brown gaze studying her with concern. "I don't see how that relates to our cases. We've got men who've been shot. Weapons missing. That doesn't sound like your past case with a person who is into overpowering women and rape."

He's right. "But the mirrors. *Who* does that?"

"Someone ugly?"

She gave a weak smile. Her stomach hadn't stopped churning since she'd seen the broken glass earlier at Jefferson Biggs's home. There had to be a connection somewhere.

"Let's not jump to conclusions before we talk to Toby Cox," Eddie said. "There's a chance he can clear this right up."

They walked on. Mercy smelled wood smoke as they reached an unmarked drive on their left. "This should be it," she said.

They'd taken three steps down the drive when a voice spoke. "Hello, FBI agents."

Toby Cox stood in the woods, his brown jacket and pants blending with his surroundings.

Mercy's heart rate shot up, and Eddie's hand jerked toward his weapon, inaccessible under his zipped jacket.

"Hey, Toby. We were just coming to see you," Mercy choked out.

"I saw you drive by. I figured you were going to Ned's," said the man. "I was waiting to watch you leave."

Okay. That's a bit creepy.

"Did you think of anything else you wanted to tell us?" Eddie asked.

Toby stared at him for a few seconds. "No." He paused. "The body is gone, right?"

"Yes," said Mercy.

"Did you see any ghosts?" The look on Toby's face was dead serious.

Mercy and Eddie looked at each other. "I didn't. Did you?" she asked Eddie.

"No, no ghosts anywhere," answered Eddie.

"Ned told me he's seen several ghosts on his property. He said they're ghosts of people who were probably murdered in his house."

Mercy hoped Ned was pleased that he'd scared the crap out of Toby. First the cave man story and now ghosts.

"I've looked for them but never seen one," Toby continued. "Ned said they usually came out at night."

"I don't think you need to worry about ghosts," Eddie told him.

"My parents said Ned's too mean to go to heaven, so he's probably a ghost now and will haunt his farm forever."

Mercy lost any desire to meet Toby's parents. "I don't think that's true. If I was a ghost, I'd leave this cold rain and find somewhere sunny. Ghosts can travel wherever they want, right? I wouldn't stay here."

Toby tilted his head as he looked at her, weighing her words.

"We've been in there twice and haven't seen anything," added Eddie.

"Have you ever used the bathroom in Ned's house?" Mercy asked, dropping the ghost topic.

"Sometimes. But if we were working outside, Ned would tell me to not waste water and to use a tree."

Eddie coughed.

"Was the mirror in the bathroom broken?" Mercy asked, ignoring the images being generated in her brain. "Right now it has cracks covering all of it."

Toby thought hard. "I haven't been in there in a while."

"Surely you'd remember. It looks like a huge cobweb on the mirror."

"I don't remember anything like that," he finally said.

The sense of elation Mercy had hoped for fluttered away. Toby wasn't positive; the mirror could have been previously broken.

I'm paranoid. I'm looking for connections that don't exist.

"Thanks, Toby. You've been a big help." She raised an eyebrow at Eddie, who nodded to indicate he was finished too. They turned around and started their trek back to their vehicles. Toby didn't say anything. Mercy looked back after twenty steps and he still stood in the woods, watching them leave.

Is he lonely?

"That wasn't conclusive," stated Eddie. "But we can look into the cases from when you were a teen. It's worth following up."

"It's not necessary," said Mercy. "We have other things to do."

"I'm surprised you remembered those deaths from that long ago."

The women's faces were clear in Mercy's mind. "Not many people are murdered around here. It was a huge shock. And my sister Pearl's best friend was a victim."

"That's horrible."

"With that connection, I probably remember better than most people."

"I bet your sister remembers too. I don't think we should ignore the old cases."

Mercy deliberately stepped in a puddle, testing the waterproofing of her boots. Eddie was right. She would have to talk to Pearl at some point. The thought sent her anxiety skyrocketing. *Why? She's my sister. What's she going to do? Refuse to see me?*

Maybe.

"You're right. The local police records are probably the best place to start," she admitted. "We also need to check in with Darby. She was going to search online to see if anyone is selling the missing weapons."

"It's going to be hard to search if she doesn't know what weapons to look for," said Eddie. "Why do I feel as if the weapons were stolen without any intention to sell?"

"They're the most expensive items in the homes," Mercy countered. "Easy money."

"I think they wanted them for themselves." He scowled. "Darby would be the one to ask about any militia activity, right? Maybe there's been some chatter about people getting together for something."

"Like occupying a wildlife refuge?"

Eddie snorted. "Something bigger. More deadly. We've got a lot of missing weapons. Who's collecting them?"

"And what for?" whispered Mercy. To an outsider Eagle's Nest would look like a wide spot along the highway. Quiet and harmless, a good place to escape the bustle of the city. Maybe a place to retire or raise children to know about the land. Not the center of homegrown terrorist activity.

"Did the local police department handle the murders last time?" Eddie asked. "Or did county?"

"I don't know," said Mercy. "I can remember the police chief questioning Pearl about her friend, but I don't know if the case expanded beyond the city."

"Good thing Chief Daly likes us."

Mercy didn't say anything.

"I'm glad he suggested that bed-and-breakfast in town. I stopped by there earlier and it smells like a bakery." Eddie's tone perked up. "That beats our current shithole's odor of Pine-Sol and old smoke."

"It's not so bad."

"You and I have very different expectations of hotels."

"It serves its purpose."

"Yeah, but it could serve it with fresh coffee, a big-ass shower, and updated decor."

Mercy shrugged. "I just need a bed and a solid locked door."

"Live a little, would ya? The Bureau has paid a lot more for accommodations in the past. We're not burning their money by having standards. One more night and then we can move."

"How long do you think we'll be in Eagle's Nest?" she asked.

Eddie exhaled deeply and watched his breath disappear into the cold air. "As long as it takes."

A headache started at the back of her skull. The sooner she could leave Eagle's Nest, the better.

FIFTEEN

Mercy felt like a thief.

No backbone, hiding in the shadows, waiting for people to leave the house.

She'd taken a gamble that her parents still attended their Tuesday night social club. She'd crossed her fingers it wasn't their turn to host. Hell, she didn't even know if they still participated, but it was the only way she could think of to see Rose on her own.

I could have called.

No doubt she could locate a phone number somewhere, but she didn't want to risk one of her parents being in the room when Rose answered. So she'd resorted to slinking around like a criminal.

At 7:50 her father's old pickup turned out of their drive and sped down the highway. She spotted two people in the front seat.

Some things never change.

Before she lost her resolve, she turned the key in the ignition and guided her vehicle to the driveway. The home was set far back from the highway. Typical of her parents' mind-set, the drive wasn't marked and wound cautiously through a few fields and groves, placing lots of distance between their home and the rest of the world. Maneuvering down the winding drive took forever. She finally parked in front of the familiar house and stared at it for thirty seconds, calming her vibrating nerves.

It looks exactly the same.

Her years in the small white farmhouse built by her father had been good ones. As a kid she'd been too busy to sit around and wish for a different life. Plus she'd been taught to appreciate what she had. It seemed as if today's kids focused on things they didn't have and how to convince their parents to buy them.

I must be getting old.

She had officially become "an older generation" by complaining about the younger one.

Do I want to do this?

She missed Rose dreadfully. For years she'd felt a physical ache when she'd thought of her sister. Only during the last few years had it eased, but it still echoed in her bones like a bad break that had never healed quite right. The longing had grown exponentially since she'd been back in Eagle's Nest. She loved both her sisters, but she *knew* Rose's heart. Four years her senior, her sister had never seemed blind to her. Rose had run and played as hard as the rest of them. Skinned and bruised knees never slowed her down.

Her sister had been happiness personified and had never expressed anger at the fate that made her blind from birth, at least not to Mercy's ears. But Mercy had been angry for her. Many times she'd cried at the unfairness of a world that revolved around sight when her sister would never see a glimpse. She'd beg God to transfer Rose's blindness to her, and then live in fear that one day he would actually do it.

Over and over she'd describe colors to her blind sister, but there was nothing for Rose to correlate the descriptions with. Rose could recite that grass was green and the sky was blue, but she'd never experienced the sights or seen the subtle color changes. To her they were empty descriptions. Grass was soft or pointy or dry or crunchy or silent. The sky was untouchable; it felt and sounded of nothing.

People asked Rose stupid questions. Mercy understood they were curious, but it was the same questions over and over.

"What do you see?"

"How do you match your clothes?"

"What do you see in your dreams?"

Their mother had solved the clothing issue by having Rose wear only jeans or denim shorts during the summer. "Everything goes with denim," she'd say. Rose also had more dresses than the other girls; dresses didn't need to match anything.

Rose claimed her dreams were just like her everyday life. "I taste, hear, and smell in my dreams. There's nothing to see."

Her favorite things were sounds. Thunderstorms, the sizzle of meat on a grill, any musical instrument.

Her siblings watched over Rose like hawks. Heaven protect any stupid kid who thought it'd be funny to hide Rose's cane. They would have four Kilpatrick siblings to answer to.

Mercy took a few steps toward the quiet house, unable to shake the feeling that she was making a huge mistake.

Did Levi warn her that I'm in town?

Levi hadn't contacted Mercy. She half hoped that he would. She was tired of pretending the past had never happened.

She and Levi and Rose shared a secret. One that had stayed silent for fifteen years.

She stepped heavily on the wood steps, wanting Rose to know that someone was coming to the house, even though her sister would be fully aware that a vehicle had stopped in front. The sound of the unfamiliar engine would tell Rose her parents hadn't returned.

Mercy knocked on the door.

A few seconds passed. "Who is it?" came her sister's firm voice through the door.

Mercy closed her eyes as her lungs seized at the familiar sound of her sister.

"Rose. It's Mercy." Her voice cracked.

She waited.

Locks slid and clicked. The door opened to show a shocked Rose. "Mercy?" She held one hand forward at the exact height of Mercy's face, fingers stretching, aching to touch.

"It's me." She took Rose's hand and guided it to her face. Her sister's expression lit up as her hands gently danced across Mercy's features and hair.

"Talk to me," Rose begged. "I need to hear you speak."

"Uh . . . you look great, Rose. You really do. You haven't changed a bit." It was true. Rose's face was unlined and still shone with the peaceful quality Mercy had envied as a teen. Her sister was a few inches shorter than she and looked fit and happy. "I'm working with the FBI now, and I live in Portland."

Rose's fingers stilled as she touched the wetness on Mercy's cheeks.

"I've missed you, Rose."

Rose hugged her. "Oh my God," she said. She inhaled deeply through her nose. "You still smell the same, Mercy."

Mercy laughed, starting a new round of tears. "I don't know how that's possible."

"It is. Trust me. But your hair is longer and you feel thinner."

"Those are true," Mercy agreed.

Rose tugged her into the house. "Come in, come in! Mom and Dad aren't here. They had their meeting tonight."

"I know," Mercy confessed.

Rose turned an inquisitive face toward her sister, her sightless eyes rolling slightly under her lids. She'd never really opened her eyes. Some people who were blind from birth never did. "You purposefully chose this time to come?" she asked softly.

"I did." Mercy studied her sister's beautiful face.

"You don't want to see them."

"I do. But I think they don't want to see me."

Rose grabbed both of Mercy's hands. "You don't know that. We can't let this come between our family any longer. We need to tell them the truth."

Mercy froze. "No. They chose to shut me down. There's no point in digging it back up. Can you imagine how it would affect our lives if it came out? Levi and I could go to prison!"

"I'm sure the police would understand—"

"After we hid it for fifteen years?" Mercy struggled to keep her voice steady. "Every year we've let it go by has only made it worse." Panic surged and sweat started under her arms.

I shouldn't have come.

Rose's nostrils widened the slightest bit. "Calm down. I won't do anything you don't want me to."

Mercy sucked in several deep breaths. This wasn't how she'd pictured their reunion.

"Come in," Rose begged. "I need to hear your voice some more." Mercy followed her to the small eat-in kitchen at the rear of the house. Rose guided her to a chair at the familiar oak table. Mercy blinked rapidly as she saw the curtains were still the same—but faded. Rose hustled about the kitchen, her sure hands finding exactly what she needed to brew a pot of tea. Mercy's insides slowly unwound and she leaned her spine into the back of the chair.

A familiar colander and wood pestle stood on the counter, and the faint, sweet odor of cooked apples and cinnamon reached Mercy's nose. Her gaze automatically went to the stove, where the canning pot still sat. She closed her eyes and inhaled, remembering . . .

"It's your turn to press the apples," twelve-year-old Mercy snapped at her sister. "I've done the last two batches."

Rose took the pestle and calmly circled it around the colander, smashing the pulp of the boiled apples out through the holes, leaving the slick skins and woody seeds behind. Mercy ladled more scoops of the hot apple pieces into the colander, avoiding her sister's hands. They'd both had their fair share of burns from canning applesauce.

"That batch of jars is done," Rose said as Mercy glanced at the clock. Her sister's mental timer was nearly perfect, as usual. Mercy levered the glass jars out of the boiling water in the canning pot and carefully moved each one to the counter to cool. That made four dozen. And they had three more buckets of apples to go.

The occasional plinking sound told her a cooling jar's seal had formed.

She stood back for a moment to admire the pretty rows of yellow-pink jars. Her mother would be pleased. They went through applesauce quicker than any other canned fruit. It was her brothers' and father's favorite. But gosh darn, she hated the long, hot, sticky process.

"Cut up the next batch of apples," Rose ordered.

Grabbing the big knife, Mercy waved it defiantly at the back of her sister's head.

"Accidentally cut me and you'll be pressing all the apples."

Mercy silently stuck out her tongue at her blind sister.

She opened her eyes. "You've been canning."

"As always," Rose replied. Her sister was as graceful as a dancer. She knew how many steps there were from the faucet to the stove and exactly where to set the old kettle without feeling for the burner. As a child, Mercy had tried the same with her eyes shut. She was pretty good, but Rose was the master.

"Milk in your tea?"

"No, thank you," said Mercy. She paused for a long moment, studying her sister. Her long, dark hair was the same, but her face had lost the fresh plumpness. Now Rose looked . . . mature. Her smile was still stunning; her lips were slightly lopsided, which gave it a perky appeal that Mercy had envied. She still did. "How is your life, Rose?"

She immediately regretted her phrasing. "I mean, what has been going on for the last fifteen years?"

Rose smiled. "I knew what you meant. I'm happy. I hold a preschool at the church three days a week for the little kids. Mom helps out a bit with it, but I do most of it on my own."

"That's fabulous." Mercy wasn't surprised. Rose had loved children. She wanted to ask Rose if she'd ever fallen in love. If she'd ever kissed a man. If she ever worried about the future, because one day their parents wouldn't be around.

Who am I fooling? I bet she takes more care of Mom and Dad than they do of her.

Rose had never let her lack of sight stop her independence.

"The chickens are my responsibility. Mom doesn't ride much anymore, so I keep the horses exercised, and I do most of the gardening."

Tasks Mercy had hated as a teen. Except for the riding. "It sounds like things are good for you."

"It's a different world these days, Mercy." Her face lit up. "And do you know what's the best? The technology that's available to make my life easier."

"Dad doesn't have a problem with that?"

Rose laughed. "He reminds me to never rely on it. But I've survived without it, and I can do it again. Watch this. What's your phone number?" She pulled a cell phone out of her pocket and proceeded to dictate and then send Mercy a text. Then she held the phone over a teacup and, using an app, the phone correctly identified it out loud as a red teacup. "It reads e-mail out loud for me, websites, articles, texts, and books."

"That's amazing, Rose." Mercy loved seeing the excitement on her sister's face. She understood her sister's position on the advancing technology. Mercy used every computer tool available to help her do her

A Merciful Death

job as best as possible, but if it all vanished one day, she was mentally prepared to face the dark.

Rose set a plate of homemade cookies on the table. "Do you miss the life?" she asked softly.

"No." The answer was sure on Mercy's lips. "But I miss you all."

"You never called. Or wrote," Rose whispered.

"Dad made his position extremely clear. And Mom backed him up."

"As she should," added Rose.

Mercy froze, wanting to shout that her mother could make decisions of her own. Deborah Kilpatrick didn't have to bend her will to satisfy her husband. Instead Mercy bit into a cookie.

It's not my place to lecture.

"Do you think about that night?" Rose asked in a small voice as she placed tea bags in two cups, her back to Mercy. If the room hadn't been perfectly quiet, Mercy would have missed the question.

"Every day."

Rose turned around, and Mercy noticed her knuckles were white as she gripped the cups. She set the cups down on the table and took a seat. "The water will be another few minutes."

"It's part of the reason I'm here, Rose. You know the FBI is investigating the recent murders of the preppers, right?"

Rose nodded, her hand still clenched around one of the cups.

"Did you know that mirrors were broken in each of their homes?"

Rose jerked, sending her cup sliding across the table. Mercy snatched it before it went off the edge. She took Rose's hand and wrapped her fingers back around the cup. Her hand felt like ice.

"He's dead," Rose whispered.

"One of them is. One got away."

"The three of us swore to never tell anyone what happened."

"And we've all stuck to that promise," Mercy assured her.

"They killed Pearl's friend back then. And that other girl."

"We never knew that for certain."

"Maybe the one man wasn't actually dead." Rose's words tumbled out of her mouth, tripping over one another. "Maybe he was just wounded and now he's come back."

"The second man could have done these recent murders. The man you heard, but we didn't see."

"I'm not positive I recognized the second voice that night."

"Yes, you are," corrected Mercy. "Your hearing was sharp. Back then you *knew* you'd heard the second man's voice somewhere before. Absolutely positive. If you're doubting it now, it's simply because so much time has gone by. But *I remember* your certainty."

Rose seemed to fold in on herself. "I never heard his voice again. I've listened. For fifteen years, I've listened closely to every man I've met, wondering if he was there that night." She shuddered. "I can still hear it in my dreams."

Mercy's heart broke. "Have you asked Levi what he did with the man who died?"

"I tried a few times after you first left. He'd always cut me off. He doesn't like to talk about it."

"None of us do," whispered Mercy.

"All Levi would say is that no one would ever find the body." Rose's clenched cup rattled on the tabletop. "He would have killed us, Mercy. We're both lucky to be alive."

"I know."

"Oh, Mercy. Do you think he could have lived? Could Levi have been wrong? Has the second man been in Eagle's Nest all this time?"

"I think I need to talk to Levi."

Mercy stood and walked over to one of the windows on the east side of the house. She touched the wall, feeling the small area where the texture was suddenly smoother. The paint still matched perfectly.

"Is it still invisible?" Rose asked, not turning her head in Mercy's direction. "Sometimes I worry it shows. I can almost feel it."

"No one can see the hole from the bullet." Mercy studied the floor, remembering the blood she'd had to clean up. She and Rose had worked for hours, terrified the police would find a trace. Every inch of the floor and several of the walls had been scrubbed down that night.

"We did what we had to do, Rose."

"Did we?"

SIXTEEN

Later that night Mercy couldn't sleep, but it wasn't because she had energy to burn and a list of tasks to tackle. Tonight she was drained, so drained she was unable to relax into sleep. The roller coaster of emotions with Rose had burned her out.

It'd been worth it to talk with her sister again.

But now, as she lay in bed and stared at the ceiling, violence haunted the dim corners of her hotel room. She heard every sound in the old building. A flushed toilet. Footsteps walking past her room. The slam of a car door. She tried to tune them out.

Instead a fifteen-year-old flashback erupted to the surface. Bloodshed and fear and guilt.

Mercy yanked the gate closed and double-checked the latch.

In the dark she followed the path to the house, thankful she'd finished her homework at school. Spring was crazy busy on their farm and it would be nearly eleven by the time she got to bed. Jealousy flashed as she thought of the girls at school who lived in town. No animals to tend, no gardens to weed. Plenty of time to watch TV.

A different life. Mercy and her family lived differently for a reason. One she was proud of, but that didn't mean she always liked it.

Those girls would be very sorry when they found themselves without gas for their cars and food for their meals one day.

Life would give them a crash course in gardening.

Her parents were gone for the night. They'd traveled to Portland for their semiannual shopping trip even though her mother had worried about leaving the three siblings alone after Pearl's friend was murdered. Mercy's father had waved off her concern. "No one can take care of themselves better than our kids."

Her mother had reluctantly agreed. Throughout the year her parents would make a list of items they couldn't get on this side of the Cascades. Last night they'd analyzed their list for hours, debating cost versus necessity of an ultracold medical freezer, a microhydro generator, and a half-dozen other items. Mercy had finally tuned them out. She didn't care what they did. She loved her parents, but sometimes they took their TEOTWAWKI preparations a little too seriously. Other families took vacations; hers tucked away every extra penny.

At least Owen and Pearl could do as they pleased. They'd both married and now lived in their own homes in Eagle's Nest, but Owen still spent a lot of time with her father, asking advice on prepping and then recruiting him and Levi to help him install solar panels. Owen was becoming more like her father every day—so serious about life. What happened to her older brother who would drag race and drink beer behind the Wilsons' barn?

She stepped through the back door of her house. "Rose? Is there any pie left?" she yelled. Her stomach growled at the thought of her sister's apple pie. Rose made an incredible pie. Her sense of smell alerted her when a piecrust was perfect; she didn't need to see the color.

Silence greeted her. Mercy kicked off her wet boots in the mudroom and hung up her jacket. In stocking feet, she checked the cupboards for the remains of the pie. Rose had learned to hide baked goods or else Levi would eat everything. Mercy had eaten one small slice when the pie had come out *of the oven, and she steeled herself for the discovery that Levi had finished the rest.*

She wished he'd get married and move out. He'd already fathered a baby girl; he just needed to get things straight with Kaylie's mother.

Thumping and a small crash sounded from her father's den on the other side of the house.

"Rose? You okay?" Mercy kept snooping through the cupboards, wishing she had Rose's sense of smell to find the pie.

"Darn it! Levi!" Opening the dishwasher, she'd discovered the empty glass pie pan.

More thumping sounded. Mercy slammed the dishwasher and went to see what her sister had knocked over. The front door was wide open, and she pushed it closed as she passed by, following the sounds to the den.

She rounded a hall corner and spotted her sister on the den floor. A man straddled her bleeding body. He looked up as Mercy froze and he lunged for her, knocking her to her knees as she spun around to run.

In the hallway his weight landed on her back, crushing the breath out of her lungs. She fought, swinging her arms and kicking her legs with every fiber of her muscles. She flung her head upward and was rewarded with a satisfying chunk as she connected with his nose.

"Fucking bitch!"

He grabbed her hair, yanking her head back, and punched the side of her face with his other hand. A section of hair ripped out of her scalp. Mercy's eyes watered and her neck throbbed where it overextended. She stopped fighting.

He's going to kill me.

Is Rose already dead?

Is this what happened to those other girls?

Is he the killer?

He released her hair and leaned harder on her back, speaking in her ear, his breath hot on her skin. An odor of fear and excitement reached her nose, rancid and oily. Her brain refused to compute his words of terror.

He yanked on the back of her jeans waistband.

Something erupted deep inside her and she arched back, leading with her elbow, determined to find his face. Her elbow connected with his eye socket and he screamed, slapping his hands over his eye. Mercy scrambled out from under him, kicking frantically, wishing she still wore her boots. She tripped and lunged, barely keeping her balance, to get back to the den to Rose.

Her sister was on her hands and knees; blood trickled from her nose and mouth, and her dress was torn down the front. Her bra and stomach were visible. Mercy stopped in shock and then rushed to help her sister. Rose cowered back and rose to her knees, one of their father's handguns in her shaking hand, pointing at Mercy.

"Rose! It's Mercy."

The gun immediately lowered. "Mercy?" Rose's voice wavered.

"Give me that." Mercy snatched the gun from her hand and whirled around to glimpse the back of their attacker as he vanished around a hall corner. "Don't move!" she ordered Rose, and ran after the man, adrenaline pumping through her limbs.

Shoot him, shoot him, shoot him.

The gun settled comfortably in her grip. She'd fired her father's guns hundreds of times.

This is why he made us drill.

She turned a corner in time to see the man abruptly reverse direction. He'd started to run through the kitchen, but nearly fell over as he changed his mind and lurched in the direction of the front of the house. Mercy planted her feet, aimed, and fired once. Two shots sounded.

He collapsed on the floor of their family room.

She held her position, her heart threatening to beat out of her chest and her panting filling her ears.

He didn't move.

"Mercy? Rose?" Levi shouted from the kitchen.

"We're okay!" she answered.

Her brother peeked around the corner from the kitchen and his eyes widened as he saw her gun aimed at the man on the floor. Blood rapidly pooled around the body.

I'll have to scrub that floor.

"God's eyes, Mercy! Did you shoot him too?"

She spotted the raised gun in her brother's hand. No wonder the thug had reversed direction.

"He attacked Rose, he attacked me. Oh my God." She turned her head in the direction of her sister. "Rose? Are you okay?" Mercy couldn't pull her weapon away from its position, trained on the body.

"I'm okay." Rose's voice shook but sounded strong behind Mercy. "Is he dead?"

"I think so." Mercy looked at her brother. "Check him." Her feet were glued to the floor.

"I shot him too," said Levi. "I could hear you screaming from outside."

Mercy didn't realize she'd screamed. "Check him," she repeated in a whisper.

Levi slowly approached the body, his weapon trained on the figure. She wanted to holler at him to hurry up, he moved so slowly. He finally knelt next to the man and placed his fingertips on his neck.

He waited forever.

"He's dead." Levi moved the head to look at the face. He glanced over his shoulder at Mercy. "Do you know him?"

She found the strength to move her feet and crept forward, the gun lowered at her side. She wasn't ready to set it down, but the compulsion to point it at the body was gone; he was no longer a threat. She looked over Levi's shoulder and couldn't put a name to the face. He was young. In his twenties. He wore the dusty jeans and boots of every other man in town and hadn't shaved in several days. The back of his plaid shirt was soaked with blood.

We shot him in the back.

He's unarmed.

Warmth touched her toes and Mercy jumped back. Her sock was red with his blood. She made a strangled sound and bent over to rip off the sock, wiping at her toes. OhmyGodOhmyGod. She rubbed until every speck was gone.

It just appears to be gone. Tests could still find his blood on my skin.

She met Levi's gaze. "What did we do?" she whispered. "Oh my God, Levi. We'll go to prison for this."

"No, you won't," came Rose's voice. "He was going to kill me. He said over and over that he was going to fuck me and then kill me."

Rose's language made her wince, but Mercy was more alarmed by Rose's white face. Shock. Blood still ran from her sister's nose, and it was smeared across her cheek and down her dress.

"He had my dress up around my waist," Rose said matter-of-factly. "He was moments away from raping me." She shuddered and pulled her cardigan tighter over her dress. "Who is it?"

"We don't know," said Mercy.

"Where's the other guy?"

"What?" Mercy and Levi gasped.

"There were two of them," Rose's knuckles whitened on her sweater. "Two of them grabbed me. One let go when he heard Mercy's voice."

An engine and spinning tires sounded in the distance. Levi ran for the window and pushed back the curtain. He watched for a few seconds and then turned back. "All I could see was a dust cloud."

"They're going to get the police." Mercy's teeth clattered together. "He'll tell them we killed someone."

Levi took three large steps and grabbed her by the shoulders, looking her in the eye. "No, he won't. How will he explain that they were both attacking Rose and you? He won't do that. He's a coward. He's running away. I bet these are the guys who killed Jennifer and Gwen."

Mercy stared at him, desperately wanting to believe. "We killed someone. They'll lock us up."

Levi turned his head to study the man on the floor. "No, they won't. No one will know."

"What?" said Rose. "Levi, are you crazy? We killed someone!"

He gripped Mercy's shoulders tighter, his gaze boring into hers. "Can you clean this up? If I take care of the body, can you and Rose get rid of the blood?"

She blinked. "Yes. Where—"

"Don't ask."

She nodded, not wanting to know.

"Levi, you can't do this," argued Rose. "We need to call the police."

"Why? So they can arrest Mercy and me? Do you want to testify in court about what you just went through?"

"But they need to stop the other guy before he hurts another woman."

Levi's laugh was empty. "He's long gone. They'll never find him. We shook him up. I bet he doesn't try it again."

"But I've heard the other guy's voice before," Rose insisted.

Mercy spun around. "Where?"

Rose's pale face went a shade paler. "At the Bevinses' ranch."

Mercy couldn't breathe. "Rose, are you sure? How do you know?"

"I just know," she said, but her face was uncertain.

"Who is it?" Levi asked. "One of the family? One of the hands?"

"I don't know," Rose cried. "I just know I heard it when we were there for the Saint Patrick's Day barbecue two weeks ago."

"So it could have been anyone," Mercy said. "Nearly the entire town was there for that party."

Rose's face crumpled. "I'm no help."

Mercy pulled off her plaid overshirt as she moved to her sister, and used it to wipe the blood and tears off her sister's face. "You're shook up. That would rattle anyone."

"But I know what I heard," Rose insisted. Mercy exchanged a look with Levi.

"We can't tell Mom and Dad," said Levi slowly. "We especially can't tell them that you heard the voice at the Bevinses' ranch. Dad will declare war."

Mercy stared at him as Rose sucked in a breath. "We have to tell them."

"No. No, we don't," said Levi.

Mercy's mind raced through the possibilities. Dad would stop at nothing until he found who'd attacked his girls. If he thought that person was from the Bevinses' ranch, the town would be more divided than it already was. The police would know she and Levi had shot an unarmed man in the back.

The bare walls of a prison cell flashed in her head. "Levi's right. We clean it up and don't tell anyone."

"I'm getting a tarp." Levi dashed out the back door.

"We can't let him hide that we killed someone, Mercy." Rose's fingers went to Mercy's shoulders and then gently touched her sister's jawline and cheeks. A gesture that meant she needed comfort. Mercy put her hands over Rose's, pressing them into her face, also needing to feel her touch.

"I think it's for the best," Mercy whispered. "I can clean this up. Levi's right. Who's going to come back and accuse us of murder while they were trying to kill us first? He doesn't know this guy is dead. He'd already left."

"But I'm sure he heard the shots."

"Probably, but he can't assume his friend is dead. Most likely he'll think he got away. What exactly happened?"

Rose took a deep breath. "I was cleaning in the den when someone came in through the front door, and I assumed it was Levi because of the heavy boot tread, but I realized there were two sets of boots. Then I heard the mirror in the powder room shatter."

"What?" Mercy dashed to the half bath near the front door. Rose was right. Someone had pulled the small mirror off the wall and thrown it to the floor. "Why?"

"I don't know," Rose answered from right behind her. "One of them laughed as it happened. That's when I got scared. I tried to shut the door to the den, but they beat me to it."

Rose started to shake, and Mercy guided her back to the living room and into a chair. She wrapped her big overshirt over Rose's cardigan. "I'll get you something hot to drink. And then I'll tackle this mess." A small dark circle caught her eye. "Crap. There's a bullet hole in the wall."

"We can patch it," Rose said firmly.

Determination washed over Mercy. "Yes, we can."

In her bed in the dark motel room, tears washed over her cheeks. *Is he back? Did we let a killer go free back then and now he's killing again?*

How could she tell Truman her suspicions without implicating herself?

I could lose my job.

She shuddered. Her job was her life, her pride, her proof that she'd been born for more than living on a ranch and waiting for the world to go to hell.

Did we screw up?

SEVENTEEN

"The broken mirrors at my uncle's made you think of these old murder cases?" Truman asked the next morning.

Mercy raised her chin, feeling slightly ridiculous after telling Truman about the two old Eagle's Nest cases. Her chair in Truman's office was quite low, and he stood with his arms crossed, looking down at her. His expression was bland, but his tone said he was struggling to process the connection between the cases she'd shared and their newly murdered preppers. She was exhausted, operating on three hours of sleep, but she wasn't about to let the chief know it. "Yes. The broken mirrors stuck with me. The second victim was my sister Pearl's best friend."

"What year was it?"

Mercy told him, and he called Lucas into his office. The cheery young man immediately appeared at the door. "Whatcha need, boss?"

"I need the file on two cases from fifteen years ago. I assume nothing was computerized back then?"

Lucas shook his head. "No, but everything should be neatly boxed up back in the storage room. If you give me a name, I can find the file number easy enough. That part's computerized."

Truman looked at Mercy.

"Jennifer Sanders."

Lucas nodded and vanished.

"I don't know a Sanders family in town yet. Do they still live here?" Truman asked.

Mercy raised a brow at him.

"Oh, right. You haven't been around lately. We'll know soon enough. Lucas doesn't know the entire town the way Ina did, but he's trying hard to catch up."

A man knocked lightly on the jamb of Truman's open door. "Hey, Chief, you got a minute?"

Mercy looked over her shoulder. Her gaze landed on the man's clerical collar and then climbed to his face. He wore a heavy leather jacket and faded jeans with a sports cap pulled low on his face. Her brain couldn't connect the collar with the face. Something was off.

"What can I do for you, David?"

David nodded at Mercy with a polite smile and then turned to Truman. "I was looking—"

He stopped, and his gaze shot back to Mercy. Confusion raced over his features, and Mercy silently sighed. *This is getting old.* She stood and held out her hand. "Mercy Kilpatrick."

David's mouth opened, but no noise came out as he shook her hand.

Then she recognized him. David Aguirre had been a close buddy of her brother Owen. No wonder her brain wouldn't connect the collar with the face; David had been a wild hell-raiser in his youth. She was stunned that he now worked behind a pulpit instead of living behind bars.

"Mercy? Holy cow. I haven't seen you in ages." A wide grin crossed his face.

"Nice to see you, David." She nodded at his collar. "I see you've left behind your hellfire ways."

"Absolutely. God got a hold of me before I dug my own grave." A pious look crossed his face and his tone lowered, his gaze becoming concerned. "And how are you?"

Her faith was no business of his. To Mercy he'd always be the asshole who'd shot BBs at her chickens and landed her brother in jail for underage drinking. She didn't care who he was now.

"Very well, thank you. You were about to ask the chief something?"

"Uh . . . yeah . . . did you find out who keeps ticketing the cars parked on the south side of the church?"

"I did. And I looked it over, David. The sign at the far end of the block clearly says no parking. You'll need to tell people not to park by the yellow curb. Even on Sundays. No exceptions. It's a safety issue."

Annoyance flashed in David's eyes, triggering several memories for Mercy. He'd had a quick temper in the past, often striking out with his fists before thinking. Apparently he still had the temper but had learned a semblance of control.

Praise God.

"Got it," David said. He looked back to Mercy. "You in town for long?" His enthusiasm at seeing her had waned. Mercy wondered if he'd remembered the time she'd kicked him in the groin for fighting with her brother.

"Not long. Good seeing you."

He touched the brim of his cap and vanished.

She turned to find Truman looking expectantly at her. "He was best friends with Owen," she said.

"Still is, I believe. You know more people in town than I do." His brown eyes studied her, curiosity hovering.

"The files?" she reminded him.

Lucas appeared and held out a sticky note. "Here's the case number, the box number, and which shelf you'll find it on. I saw Jennifer Sanders was cross-referenced with another woman's name, Gwen Vargas. Her file is in the same box if you need it."

"Perfect. Thanks, Lucas." She took the note.

Truman came around to the front of the desk and deftly plucked the yellow piece of paper from her fingers. "Let's take a look."

Truman immediately noticed that someone had cleaned up the records and evidence storage room. *Lucas.* He made a mental note to buy him a latte. Ina Smythe had always kept the room well organized, but someone had swept out all the dust bunnies and spiderwebs that'd formed. His department didn't collect a lot of evidence; mostly they handed out tickets and took the role of a cool head in disputes. Truman figured he hadn't set foot in the evidence and file room in over a month. The file box was exactly where Lucas had indicated it would be. The large room was packed with rows of ceiling-to-floor shelves stuffed full with boxes and evidence. They found the box in the second-to-last row, right at eye level. Truman grabbed the entire box. Mercy stopped him with a hand on his arm, eyeing the label on the front.

"According to this, there are six different cases assigned to this single box."

Truman looked. "And?"

"Two of these are murder cases and that's *all* the evidence and case notes?"

"Maybe the other cases are shoplifting. Skinny files. We store the bulky evidence somewhere else. There could be a reference inside the box to other storage."

Mercy looked resigned. "Maybe."

Truman understood. Two women had been murdered. A person would expect to find tons of evidence and notes on the case. Something that showed the police had exhausted every lead. A single box that held six cases didn't give confidence.

He directed her down a hall to the small room he'd offered for their investigation. Neither she nor Special Agent Peterson had made use of the room yet, and Truman figured it was time. He'd already learned that Jennifer Sanders's and Gwen Vargas's murders had been handled solely by the Eagle's Nest PD. Truman was slightly stunned. *Why didn't the chief ask the state or county for help?*

Truman's department resources were pretty small, leading him to assume that fifteen years ago they had been even smaller. What had made the chief confident his department could handle two murders? And the cases were still unsolved. Where was the follow-up?

That chief had passed away ten years ago. Truman wished Ben Cooley was back from Mexico. Cooley had been a cop in Eagle's Nest for thirty years but was currently in Puerto Vallarta for his fiftieth wedding anniversary. He wouldn't be back on the job until next week. Truman hoped he'd gotten an international calling plan for his cell phone. He might need to call the older officer.

He set the box on the table and lifted the lid. Inside, the six cases were individually sealed. He'd been right that the other four cases were represented by small files. They barely took up two inches of space. The other two cases had multiple notebooks and manila envelopes in their sealed plastic covers. He grabbed the largest one, which matched the case number on Lucas's sticky note, unsealed it, and handed it to Mercy. "Nothing leaves this room."

"Of course not." She pulled out a chair and immediately started flipping through the biggest notebook. It was the Jennifer Sanders murder book. Autopsy report, evidence reports, all officer notes, photos. A copy of every piece of the paper trail from the case was in the notebook or referenced. Truman read over Mercy's shoulder for a few moments. Long enough to learn that Jennifer had died a horrible death. A senior school photo was in the front of the book. Jennifer had had long, dark hair and an incredible smile. It was a startling contrast to the images of her dead body, with its swollen face and purple lividity on the bare limbs.

He saw Mercy pause at a candid photo of Jennifer with three other laughing girls. Mercy slipped it out of its plastic envelope, flipped it over, scanned the names written on the back, and looked at the photo again. Truman read fast enough to know that the second girl was Mercy's sister Pearl. He leaned closer. The Pearl he knew today no longer looked like that vibrant teenager.

What is Mercy thinking?

He pulled the second fat case out of the box, checked the remaining cases to be certain they were still sealed, and ran his fingertips along the bottom of the box to check for any loose papers. All clean. He set the lid on the box and pushed it away, then sat down to open the second packet, placing plenty of space between himself and Mercy. Every piece of paper should be labeled with a case number, but he wasn't taking any chances on mixing things up between the two.

Gwen Vargas had been twenty-two. Truman skimmed through her book, noting that Mercy had been right that she'd been strangled and raped. Photos of the scene showed a broken hand mirror on a small table in Gwen's bedroom, and shattered mirrors in her bathroom and her parents' bathroom.

Why?

According to the officer's notes, Gwen had been home alone. Her father and mother found her when they returned home late that night from a rodeo. Her boyfriend had been at the same rodeo and was alibied by several witnesses. The officer had written that the boyfriend's grief appeared sincere. Truman looked at the officer's signature and smiled. Ben Cooley. At least he had one person he could ask about the investigation. He flipped through the book. Interviews. Pictures. Outside of the boyfriend, there didn't seem to be any suspects.

No other suspects?

"Anything jump out at you?" Mercy asked, her gaze still on Jennifer's murder book.

"Not yet. Where was Jennifer killed?"

"Her apartment. Her roommate had moved out two weeks before."

"How many broken mirrors?" he asked.

Mercy flipped a few pages. "Four. Two bathrooms and two other small mirrors in the apartment."

"What'd he strangle her with?"

"His hands," Mercy said shortly.

"Same happened with this one. Left naked?"

"Yes."

Truman took some time to carefully read the fingerprint report. "This fingerprint report is no help. And It's been noted that there's no crossover with Jennifer's case. Both murders had several unidentifiable prints, but they weren't present at both scenes."

Mercy nodded. "But so much else is the same. It must have been done by the same person. This autopsy report says there was no semen to examine from the rape. He must have worn a condom."

"I saw the same results in Gwen's report. Someone came prepared. I wonder if the police looked into other rapes or attempted rapes in the surrounding areas."

Mercy looked up, her green eyes wide. "Lord, I hope they did. That seems like a basic step."

"I'm sure that's noted in here somewhere. I spotted the signature of one of my men in this book. He's out of town right now, but I can call him if we have questions. He's pretty sharp for seventy. I have no doubt he remembers these cases."

"I suspect everyone in town remembers these cases," said Mercy. "Nothing rocked the community like these girls' deaths did."

"And still unsolved after all these years. I assume there are no obvious suspects in your notes?" Truman asked quietly.

Mercy shook her head.

He flipped to the back of Gwen's book. "I don't see any follow-up records. How about yours?"

Mercy scanned through her book. "None. No one did anything? That's unheard of. Someone should have talked to the people involved every few years to see if they remembered anything new. What about the families? Surely they hounded the police to not give up!" She gave Truman a stricken look, and he was surprised by the dark circles under her eyes. "Why? Why no follow-up?"

Defensiveness rose in his chest. A need to stick up for his department even though he'd been in charge only six months. Instead he shrugged. "Few man-hours. Other investigations. Turnover."

"Unacceptable," muttered Mercy, looking back at the senior picture of Jennifer Sanders. "Someone should be fired."

"Ben Cooley is the only one left from that era. Hell if I'm firing him. He's been invaluable to me." An image of the older officer's kind smile popped into Truman's head. "He's not one to take initiative, but he's incredibly solid and excellent at following orders. Very thorough."

"The first thing we need to do is follow up with the people who were close to these girls," stated Mercy.

"You're here to focus on the three current murders," Truman pointed out. "Outside of the broken mirrors, I don't see anything to connect these to your current cases." His internal fire to solve his uncle's murder was driving him to keep the FBI on track. So far Mercy appeared to be a solid investigator, but she was getting distracted by history.

Maybe I should be dealing with her partner.

He studied the woman at the table. Was she too close to the old cases? She'd been here two days and already looked exhausted. Had the FBI sent the right person to help solve these crimes?

"I know," she said. "Eddie is going over the Enoch Finch case with Deschutes County today. I'm currently waiting to hear more from the medical examiner about Ned Fahey, and one of our analysts is searching places where the stolen weapons might have been sold."

Truman didn't tell her he'd already gone through the Finch investigation with a fine-tooth comb. Once he'd seen the connection between his uncle and Enoch Finch, he'd immediately contacted Deschutes County to share notes. He hadn't spotted any new leads or possible avenues that the county investigators had missed. Hopefully, Special Agent Peterson would spot something new.

"Are the two of you moving into the bed-and-breakfast?" he asked.

"Yes. We need to be out of the motel before eleven." She didn't look up from her pages.

"That motel is horrible."

"It's not so bad."

He raised one brow. His sister and mother wouldn't have spent one night in that place. Granted, his sister was a diva and insisted everything she owned be the best available, but even a woman with lower standards should show some interest in leaving the slum. Maybe Mercy didn't need comforts. He remembered Mercy's awe at his uncle's supplies. What he'd seen as an embarrassment, she'd admired.

The Kilpatricks are preppers.

But Mercy lived in Portland and had a high-status job with the federal government. In law enforcement.

Clearly she'd left her heritage behind.

Has she?

Roots can run deep. She might imply she was estranged from her family, but he'd glimpsed her face as she'd studied the old photo of her sister. Pain. Longing. Regret. She'd shown them all.

When Joziah Bevins had stopped by their table, fear had flashed across her face. It'd vanished immediately, replaced by confidence. Real confidence? Forced? Truman mulled it over. Joziah was intimidating, and Truman knew he avoided Karl, the Kilpatrick patriarch, and suspected there was old bad blood there. Did it extend to the daughter?

None of my business.

As long as they didn't start shooting at each other.

"Truman, look at this." Mercy slid over her notebook and tapped a page with one finger.

He took the notebook, reading the header on the page: "Items missing from the Sanders home."

A box of inexpensive jewelry.

Two rifles and a handgun.

$550 in cash.

Holding his breath, Truman flipped the pages of Gwen Vargas's murder book.

Missing items: jewelry, cash, photo album, two handguns.

Truman looked up, meeting Mercy's gaze. "The weapons?"

"Yes. It's not the big hauls from the recent murders, but it's something."

"They—or he—took the easiest items to sell for the most money," he argued.

"I know."

"The Vargas murder included a photo album."

Her brows came together. "That's odd. I haven't seen anything personal taken in the other cases."

"We don't know what else could be missing from the recent cases. There was no one to ask."

"Men who live alone and are isolated. Easy pickings."

"Nothing about my uncle was easy," corrected Truman.

"You're right. And from what I saw at Ned Fahey's house, he made everything as difficult as possible."

"I'm not sure these old cases can be connected," Truman said slowly. "The motivations appear totally different."

"They're fifteen years apart," said Mercy. "Motivations change. I'll get some searches going through ViCAP and see if anything similar has happened in the Pacific Northwest. Maybe he hasn't been inactive all this time."

Truman nodded.

Or has someone been biding their time in Eagle's Nest?

EIGHTEEN

Mercy hauled her small suitcase up the wooden stairs of Sandy's Bed & Breakfast. No ADA ramp in sight. To Mercy this would always be the old Norwood house. A house she'd avoided while growing up because old man Norwood and his wife were seriously creepy. The huge house had been straight out of a horror film with its three stories, turrets, peeling paint, and failing gingerbread trim. Now it shone with cheerful colors in the style of a Victorian painted lady, and the architectural details had been lovingly restored.

Someone had sunk a lot of money and elbow grease into the house.

Eddie opened the door with the oval lead glass and Mercy followed, feeling slightly grumpy.

Bed-and-breakfasts weren't her thing. Too personal. She'd prefer an anonymous hotel with four plain walls where the staff didn't know her name and she didn't have to share a breakfast table with strangers.

"Smell that?" Eddie whispered. "Now I'm hungry again."

She inhaled, and the odor of fresh-baked cookies flooded her senses. Her stomach rumbled.

Dammit.

"Hello, hello! I'm so glad you're here!" A tall, slender woman with long, red hair came through a swinging door behind a small reception desk. She wiped her hands on her white apron and gave them a genuine smile. Flour dusted her T-shirt. She reminded Mercy of a hostess on a TV cooking show. "Nice to see you again, Agent Peterson." She nodded at Eddie. "I have your rooms ready for you." She held out a hand to Mercy.

Mercy took it. "I'm Mercy." The cookie odor hovered around the woman, and Mercy couldn't help but return her smile.

"You don't know how relieved we are to be here," said Eddie. "Do I smell cookies?" he asked hopefully.

"I'm always happy to have law enforcement staying in my place," Sandy said. "It always feels a little safer. And the cookies have just a few more minutes. Once you're settled into your rooms, you'll find a plate of cookies right over there on that table. They'll be there every afternoon. And there's always fresh coffee."

"I'm in heaven," Eddie muttered. "Are you single?"

"No," Sandy said firmly with a flash of dimples. "You're young enough to be my son."

"Adoption works too."

"You're going to be trouble, aren't you?" she asked.

"No, ma'am."

Mercy fought to control her eye roll. "It smells great. Which way to the rooms?"

Sandy led her upstairs to a pleasant room with an attached bath. Mercy peeked in the bathroom. Eddie was right: it had a newly tiled big-ass shower. As Sandy took Eddie to his room, Mercy jogged back downstairs and out the door to get her water and food stash out of the back of the Tahoe. She slammed the rear door of the Tahoe shut, and a white pickup caught her eye as it parked at the post office across the street. A man stepped out and walked around the back of the truck, his profile to her.

She caught her breath.

She knew the walk and the tilt of his head. Even the style of cap was familiar.

His jeans were faded and loose, and heavy work boots were on his feet. *Dad.*

He walked in the door of the post office and vanished.

Mercy couldn't move, her bag gripped in her hand.

Does he know I'm in town?

No doubt. Gossip travels fast, and she'd bumped into too many familiar faces.

He looked older. His hair was white instead of salt and pepper. His shoulders were more stooped. He was still thin. No aging beer paunch for him. He took his health too seriously to allow it.

She took two steps in the direction of the ancient Ford truck, unsurprised that her father had kept it running all these years. He didn't buy anything new. He'd drive the truck until it could no longer be repaired.

What will I say to him?

She stopped. Unable to take another step as fear coiled in her stomach.

Hey, Dad. Remember me?

What if he didn't acknowledge her? Like Levi hadn't?

I can't deal with this right now.

She turned around and blindly walked up the steps to Sandy's, barely able to lift her feet, drowning in a need to connect with the rest of her family.

Pearl.

Pearl would talk to her. And Mercy could ask her about Jennifer Sanders. A work interview.

Yes, that's what it will be.

Eddie had offered to come with her, but Mercy turned him down. Concern had flashed in his eyes when he realized she was headed to see a sister she hadn't spoken with in fifteen years.

She didn't want his pity. She didn't want him to smooth the way for her.

It was something she had to do on her own.

She'd thought about asking Truman Daly to meet her there. The Sanders case belonged to his department, and he had the right to know that Mercy was contacting a witness. But she talked herself out of calling him, knowing she'd update him later. She didn't want any observers if Pearl slammed the door in her face.

Those brown eyes of his saw too much.

She knew Truman was trying to figure her out, and she wasn't ready for it. Eddie and her coworkers saw what she wanted them to see. A hard-working but slightly unsocial agent. But Truman had seen her reaction to his uncle's home and her encounters with Joziah Bevins and David Aguirre.

She wasn't ready to let him see more. Especially a reunion with her estranged sister.

The driveway to her sister's small ranch home was long. Mercy had checked to see if the home was still owned by Rick Turner, Pearl's husband, and wasn't surprised to see that Pearl's name wasn't on the public record as a co-owner. It was the mind-set she expected from her family. Men own the property; women lean on the men.

As they work their fingers off to take care of their home and family.

Pearl had been her first sibling to get married. Mercy had been awestruck by her sister in her white wedding dress. Pearl and Rick had seemed mature and worldly to Mercy's twelve-year-old eyes. Now, knowing her sister had been only eighteen when she married made Mercy want to cry. Pearl had gotten pregnant immediately.

At thirty-three Mercy still didn't feel ready for kids.

The outside of the home was well kept. But as she stepped out of the car, she was hit by the recognizable stench of pigs. Mercy had raised a few pigs while growing up, but apparently Rick had *a lot*. The barn and pens were set far back from the home, but even with the lack of wind, the odor spread. What was it like during the summer heat?

Does Pearl know her home stinks?

As a teen Pearl had been fascinated with fashion and makeup. Knowing that she was now married to a pig farmer made Mercy's heart hurt. But someone had to raise pigs. Pigs were an important source of protein and fat and great for barter. Her father would view the pigs as riches. If meat was no longer available at the grocery store, Rick would be a wealthy and popular man.

Mercy would have preferred sheep.

She spotted a high fence around a garden to one side of the home. Judging by the amount of lush greens growing, the fence did its job to keep out the deer. She couldn't see any neighboring farms and remembered that Rick's father had gifted the couple ten acres of his land when they'd married. Pearl had been ecstatic over planning and decorating the home they'd built. At one time Mercy had been wildly jealous of her sister's independence; now she saw a prison. Did her sister have any regrets?

Mercy swallowed, studying the small front porch. A good-size corn husker sat in one corner. Memories waxed and waned. Aching arms from turning the wheel as Rose fed the dried ears of corn into the machine. Watching the empty husks fly to one side. The smell of dried corn kernels slowly filling the bucket below.

A craving for parched corn made her mouth water. Her mother would sauté it with a bit of brown sugar and salt. A favorite snack.

Did Pearl's kids run the old-fashioned machine?

She knocked and waited to see her sister.

A shadow passed behind the peephole and Mercy held her breath. Would Pearl speak to her?

The door flew open and her sister stared, her mouth hanging open. "Mercy?" she whispered.

Tears formed in Mercy's eyes and her throat swelled. She nodded. Pearl looked older. The glamorous young woman Mercy remembered had been replaced by a mother who now kept her hair in a simple ponytail and wore a faded top Mercy recognized from fifteen years ago. Pearl looked much older than her nearly forty years.

Pearl lunged at her, wrapping her arms around Mercy in a tight squeeze. "It's been so long!" Pearl pulled back, her gaze scanning Mercy from head to toe, and then hugged her again. Mercy still couldn't talk. Her arms wrapped themselves around her sister and gripped tightly.

Pearl pulled back again and wiped at her eyes. "Oh Lord. Oh Lord, Mercy. I think of you every day."

Mercy felt like a twelve-year-old again. Unable to speak and worried about saying something utterly stupid. She wiped her eyes and continued nodding, feeling as if her skin had been ripped off and her sensitive nerve endings left raw.

"I'm sorry, Pearl," she finally sputtered.

"Come in, come in!" Pearl grabbed her arm and pulled her inside the home.

The pig smell vanished and was replaced by a wonderful cooking smell. Stew or steak or meat pie.

It smelled like home.

Pearl stopped and stared at her again. She reached out and brushed a clump of hair out of Mercy's eyes, a gesture she'd made a million times in their past. Mercy forced an awkward smile. "Hi, Pearl."

"I can't believe it. What are you doing here?"

Mercy finally saw some of the eagerness fade from Pearl's eyes. She'd remembered that Mercy was no longer considered one of the family. All contact had been ordered to cease.

"Levi didn't tell you I was in town?"

"No, you saw him already?" A faint hurt flashed in Pearl's eyes.

"I *saw* him at the coffee shop," Mercy admitted. "He wouldn't speak to me. I assumed he'd tell everyone I was here."

Pearl nodded, and Mercy wondered if she regretted letting her in her home and was now the sibling who'd broken her father's rule.

"Are you just visiting?" Pearl asked cautiously. "Have you seen Mom and Dad?"

Mercy took a deep breath. "I'm working. I'm investigating the recent murders. And no, I haven't seen our parents." She studied Pearl's face, hoping for a hint of what her reception from her parents would be. Pearl wore a poker face, and Mercy interpreted it as meaning Pearl believed she wouldn't be welcome.

"You mean Jefferson Biggs? And the other two men? I know another was found on Monday."

"Yes."

"I'd heard you worked for the FBI."

"I've been there six years. Right now I work out of the Portland office in domestic terrorism, but I've been assigned to help out the Bend office with these murders."

"Domestic terrorism," Pearl repeated. "They think these murdered men were domestic terrorists?"

"Not really," assured Mercy. "What caught our eye was all the weapons that have been stolen, along with the murders. And what that stockpile of weapons could mean in the hands of one person or a group of persons."

Pearl nodded, her face still carefully blank.

"Why would someone do that, Pearl?"

"I don't know."

The silence stretched for three long seconds as they tried to read each other's faces. Pearl knew as well as Mercy did that the area was littered with people who were angry with the government for good reasons and for lousy reasons. People who felt their rights, their land, or their wealth had been stripped away because of unfair laws. When weapons and anger and distrust were mixed with the right personality, it could become a volatile situation. One Mercy hoped to prevent.

Mercy smiled. "It's good to see you," she whispered. No matter the situation that had broken their family apart, Pearl was her sister. "How are your kids?"

"One's married and the other is a junior in high school," Pearl said proudly. "Are you married?"

"No. It's never happened for me."

Pity flashed in Pearl's eyes.

"I love my job," Mercy felt the need to state. "Part of the reason I'm here is because we're also looking into Jennifer Sanders's death. I discovered there's been no follow-up since the first investigation."

Pearl looked away. "I try not to think about that anymore. Would you like something to drink?"

Mercy agreed and followed Pearl into the kitchen. The atmosphere had changed, and the excitement of their seeing each other had been replaced by caution and curiosity. And walls. Walls had gone up in Pearl's eyes at the mention of Jennifer. Did Pearl think Mercy had visited only because she had official questions?

It was partially true.

"I wanted to see you," Mercy said as she watched Pearl make two cups of tea. The faint scent of licorice filled the room, and Mercy smiled. It'd been their mother's favorite tea. Mercy still bought it. "I'm not here solely for work."

Pearl gave her a knowing look. "So you're saying you would have stopped by at some point or another?"

Mercy had no answer.

"It's okay, Mercy. I understand. It's a two-way street. I could have reached out to you."

But you never would. Not since our father ordered everyone not to associate with me.

It was stupid. They were adults abiding by their father's ancient demands.

Some habits were hard to break.

Especially if you believed Dad was absolutely right.

Pearl set a mug of tea in front of her and sat in the chair across the table. A decorative sign above the sink said: USE IT UP. WEAR IT OUT. MAKE DO OR DO WITHOUT.

How many times did I hear my father say that?

Mercy wouldn't have chosen those words to decorate her kitchen. "Can we talk about Jennifer?" she asked.

Pearl took a sip of tea and nodded, her gaze on the tablecloth. Mercy drew a notepad out of her bag and her sister frowned at it.

"I feel like I've done something wrong," she said.

"Only if you're the one who killed Jennifer."

Pearl dropped her mug a half inch onto the tabletop and sloshed hot tea on the table. She swore and wiped it up with a napkin from a stack in the center of the table. "Of course I didn't kill her! What kind of question is that?"

"The type of question that points out that you have nothing to feel guilty about."

The annoyance on Pearl's face was reminiscent of their childhood squabbles.

Her sister sighed, propped up an arm, and leaned her chin on one hand, gazing at Mercy. "You're right. What do you want to know?"

"You were interviewed by an Eagle's Nest officer after the murders. Do you remember that?" Mercy didn't mention she'd already read the officer's notes on the interview.

"Of course. I was horrified at what'd happened. The officer was nice and respectful, and wanted to know when I'd talked to her last and if I knew of anyone who'd want to hurt Jennifer."

"Did you?"

"No. Everyone liked Jennifer."

"Was she dating anyone?"

Pearl moved her gaze to stare out the window. "Not right then. She didn't have a steady boyfriend."

"I didn't say steady. Did she date anyone? Even just casual get-togethers?"

"She dated Owen for a while before he married Sheila."

"What? Really?" Mercy straightened in her chair. "I had no idea she dated our brother."

"It didn't last. She dated several of the guys in his circle. David Aguirre, Mike Bevins. Jamie Palmer. Nothing was ever serious, and of course none of them could have been involved in her death . . . *that* was done by someone crazy. Probably someone who was passing through town."

Mercy pressed her lips together. *Crazy* was often discovered in plain sight.

"I've thought and thought about that day," said Pearl. "I could never think of anyone who could be a suspect." She wiped her eyes. "Sometimes I wonder if our daughters would have been best friends like Jennifer and I were."

Sadness overwhelmed Mercy. She'd never had that sort of friendship with another female. Her sisters had been her closest friends. Until they no longer were.

"Levi's daughter is close in age to your son, right?"

"Yes, Kaylie is in the same grade as him." A mothering look entered her eyes. "Kaylie is a bit wild. Levi does his best, but he gives her a lot of leeway that our dad never did."

Mercy remembered the small stud in Kaylie's nose at the coffee shop and silently agreed. And cheered.

"Levi raised her alone?"

"Yes." Pearl hesitated. "He's never been quite the same since Kaylie's mother left. He really cut down on his involvement with the family.

Dad and Owen have just about given up on him. I don't think he pulls his weight. I don't think he wants to anymore."

A chill shot through Mercy at the thought of Levi being cut from the family's circle.

Why does that bother me? I was cut.

She hated the thought of anyone being on their own. She'd learned to pave her own way, and it hadn't been easy. Every day she was fully aware that she didn't have her own community to lean on. When she'd first left, it'd been freeing, but it'd also been terrifying. Walking a tight-rope without a net.

She'd compensated by working her ass off. Staying prepared.

"I caught a glimpse of Dad earlier in town," she said slowly. "He looks the same, but older."

Pearl tipped her head. "You look older too." Her gaze seemed to probe, searching for Mercy's vulnerable spots. "Mom hasn't changed. More gray. Hell, even I've got plenty of gray now."

Mercy met the gaze, wondering if she was looking at herself in six years. She knew that between her and Rose, she had the strongest resemblance to Pearl. *But I haven't raised two kids and lived on a farm with pigs.*

She had an overwhelming need to break her sister out of her prison. She leaned forward and lowered her voice. "Are you happy, Pearl? Is Rick good to you? Is there something else you want to do with your life?"

Shock crossed her sister's face. Then anger. "Of course I'm happy! I'm doing exactly what I wanted to do, and I'm married to the best husband in the world. We have a good life here, Mercy. We don't need to live in the big city and buy the latest iPhones and designer handbags," she snapped. "Don't pity me because I still live in Eagle's Nest. It's a good place to live a simple life."

Mercy saw the lies in Pearl's eyes; she didn't challenge them. "I was just catching up on the last fifteen years. I'm not judging you." The lie soured on her tongue.

She looked down at her blank notepad and calmed her brain, focusing on the second reason for visiting her sister. "Did you know weapons were stolen from Jennifer's apartment that night?"

"No." Surprise infused Pearl's tone. "I knew she had a few guns. Everyone does. Is that important?"

"We're not sure. Weapons were missing from Gwen Vargas's home too."

Pearl sat back in her chair. "Huh." She was quiet for a moment. "Easy to sell."

"Yes," agreed Mercy. "A photo album was missing from Gwen's home, but nothing like that was reported from Jennifer's. Do you know if anything personal was stolen? Maybe something her parents mentioned later?"

"I don't recall," said Pearl. "I didn't talk to her parents except at her funeral."

"Did the officers ever show you pictures of the crime scene?"

"No. *And I don't want to see them.*"

"What if I got you some pictures of Jennifer's room? Would you be able to tell if anything was missing?"

Pearl thought for a moment. "I honestly don't know."

"You practically lived there."

A sad smile crossed her sister's face. "That's true. I could look—as long as they're not pictures of . . . the body—but it's been a long time to remember small details."

"I'll keep that option in mind. Do you remember what happened to the mirrors in the crime scenes?"

Pearl covered her mouth with one hand. "I'd forgotten about that. They were all broken. It was odd."

"Have you heard of anything else like that happening around here?"

She thought hard for a moment and slowly shook her head, her gaze unfocused. "I think I'd remember if something like that happened again. So many rumors were going around after their deaths . . . they said the killer was disfigured and couldn't look at himself in the mirror. Or it was actually a woman who hated both Gwen and Jennifer because they were attractive."

"They were raped."

"Rumors don't follow logic, and there are other methods of rape, you know."

Mercy froze. Had penetration with a foreign object been considered? There'd been no semen. She needed to read the police reports again.

Pearl made a good point.

But I know a woman wasn't there when Rose and I were attacked.

Doubt flooded through her. Mental images clashing with logic.

A woman could have been there. Or instigated the crimes.

She took several deep breaths, trying to rationally process the new possibility her sister had raised.

Could a woman have recently killed the three men? And stolen their weapons?

She kicked herself for allowing a sexual bias to cloud her thinking. *Don't discount women.* They were capable of having done any of the crimes. The odds stated their killer or killers were male, but that didn't mean they shouldn't consider a woman.

"Was there someone *that* jealous of Jennifer?"

Her sister took a deep breath. "I don't know."

"You don't know or won't say?" Mercy asked carefully.

"Just because someone is a bitch, it doesn't mean they're capable of murder."

"Very true. But if you have suspicions, you should speak up."

"I didn't have suspicions. There's no way she would have done something like that."

"Who?"

"Teresa Cooley. But just because she fought with Jennifer doesn't mean she'd kill her. Or Gwen."

Mercy couldn't put a face with the name. It was slightly familiar. She scribbled it on her notepad, feeling as if she'd read the name recently. Perhaps in the police reports. Pearl might not have suggested the name years ago, but possibly someone else had.

Was a woman behind the attacks back then?

A small door to her memories tried to burst open. She mentally leaned against it, refusing to let its contents send her hiding under her covers. The memory of the attack didn't need to resurface again. Once after her visit with Rose had been enough.

"Teresa went to school with you and Jennifer?"

"And Gwen, who was two years behind us, but we didn't know her that well. But seriously, Mercy. It was high school mean-girl stuff between Jennifer and Teresa. Jennifer grew out of it, but Teresa never did. I was married, for gosh sakes, and Teresa acted like I wanted to steal her boyfriend. We were twenty-four, but Teresa seemed to have gotten stuck on age eighteen." Pearl tapped the table. "I'll say it again: that doesn't mean she killed anyone."

"I know," agreed Mercy. Exhaustion swamped her. She was operating on little sleep, and her conversation with her sister had taken emotional turns she hadn't expected.

Mercy ran out of questions, but she wasn't ready to leave. Something inside her made her want to linger. She wanted to see pictures of Pearl's children—all twelve years of school photos—and hear what activities her kids loved to do. She wanted to enjoy her cup of tea and simply gossip, the way they used to.

She didn't deserve it.

Mercy stood and put away her notepad. "That's all I have. I need to get back to work."

Pearl stood but didn't say anything. Mercy avoided her gaze.

They walked to the front door, and Mercy finally looked at her sister. "I'm staying at Sandy's Bed & Breakfast if you remember something about Jennifer that might be helpful."

"How long are you staying in town?"

"Shouldn't be long. Just until we get some answers." She fiddled with her bag, unable to hold eye contact for longer than a few seconds. She sensed an opportunity rapidly fading, never to be offered again.

Then she was caught up in Pearl's arms again. "Don't be a stranger, Mercy. You're welcome here." Scents of home and family overwhelmed her, and she leaned into her sister's embrace.

Mercy struggled to see the road as she drove back to town.

NINETEEN

Mercy parked in front of the Coffee Café.

Is this a bad idea?

Her conversation with Rose had made her certain she needed to talk to Levi. She needed to know that the man who'd attacked her and Rose was dead.

The image of the man's bleeding body on her parents' kitchen floor clogged her mind. She shuddered. The murder had always clung to her like a bad scent she couldn't wash away. She knew no one else could smell it, but it always felt acutely evident. Some days it faded. She'd spend a few weeks without stress, and life would plod forward. She got up, she went to work, she came home.

But she still felt its stain.

Especially at work when her coworkers searched for a killer.

She was a killer.

Bile burned in the back of her throat. She climbed out of her vehicle, putting all thoughts of that night out of her head, and strode toward the cheery building. She hoped Levi was covering the shop and not Kaylie. If he wasn't alone, she'd order a coffee and leave. She'd managed to talk to Rose and Pearl; she could handle Levi.

She entered, not surprised to find the coffee shop empty in the middle of the afternoon. Mornings were the time for refueling.

Levi stepped out of the back room at the sound of her footsteps and froze as he spotted her.

"Are we alone?" she asked before he could tell her to get lost.

"No." Levi looked over his shoulder. "Hey, Owen?"

Mercy wanted to dash back out the door. She'd been mentally prepared for one brother, not two.

Owen appeared in the doorway, his eyebrows raised in question. "Yeah, Levi . . ." His voice trailed off as he focused on Mercy.

Her oldest brother looked like her old recollections of her dad. Lean, but ready to explode with power when provoked. She met his gaze, startled to see her own eyes in someone else's face. Even though she'd lived with him for most of her childhood, today it felt brand new.

"Crap," her oldest brother said. He looked from her to Levi. "You two look like you have something to talk about. I don't want any part of it." He ducked back through the doorway and then reappeared with his hat in his hand. He strode around the counter, his attention focused on the front door, his boot steps ringing with determination.

"Owen," Mercy started.

"Don't talk to me, Mercy. You nearly ripped this family apart. I hope you're not back to finish the job." He shoved his hat on his head without a glance in her direction. The door slammed behind him.

She wanted to melt into the floor. She looked at Levi, prepared to see condemnation. Instead there was sympathy.

"Ignore him."

She grasped the thin olive branch. "I don't have a choice."

"I mean don't let his words and actions affect you."

"Easier said than done," she whispered. "Was what I did that bad? Seriously? After fifteen years, no one is ready to forgive me for making a personal choice?"

Levi didn't answer. He picked up a cloth and started to wipe down the espresso machine, averting his eyes. "It's water under the bridge. For me."

"Then why wouldn't you talk to me on Monday? You acted like you'd never met me."

His hand halted midwipe and his gaze flew to hers. "I was following your lead. You didn't say a word when I appeared. I didn't know who you were with or what he knew about you. When you didn't acknowledge me, I figured it was for a good reason."

Mercy pressed a hand against her forehead. "Oh shit. I was following *your* lead. I assumed you didn't want Kaylie to know who I was. Plus I was floored to find you in here. We only stopped because we wanted coffee."

Levi snorted. "I guess we both screwed up."

She blew out a huge breath and summoned her courage. "Can we start over? Levi, I'm so happy to see you." She stared at him, leaving the ball in his court, her heart in his hands. *Will he shoot me down?*

He tossed the cloth on the counter and came out from behind the coffee bar. Before she could move, he'd wrapped both his arms around her and lifted her off the ground, spinning in a circle. "Baby Mercy, you don't know how much I've missed you."

"Don't call me baby," she choked out. Her heart felt like the Grinch's as it expanded to three times its size and relief shot through her.

In a way, reconnecting with Levi was better than with her sisters. Part of her had always known her sisters would take her back. But men were a different story.

He set her down and his eyes glistened.

"What about Owen?" she whispered.

"Fuck him. If he wants to hold a grudge the rest of his life, let him. He can grow old and sour like Dad." He paused. "It's the only way he knows how to behave."

She knew that. Owen had always been a follower, unable to make his own decisions. He was more comfortable doing what other people dictated, and apparently nothing had changed.

"We need to talk about that night," she said in a low voice.

He took a half step back and looked her in the eye. "Why? It's in the past. It's over."

She bit her lip as she wondered how much to share with him. "He's dead, right?"

Levi stared at her. "Why are you asking that now?"

"Because something's come up that's made me question it."

"He's dead."

"How do you know?"

He seemed to shrink in front of her eyes. "Because I've checked," he said quietly. "Three times I've gone back to see if he'd been found. No one has disturbed him."

"Where is he?"

His face drained. "I think it's best only I know that information. You need to take my word for it. I found a good place to stash the body. It's just bones now."

Some of her stress drained away, and she swayed slightly in her boots.

One down. What about the second man?

Levi scowled. "You need coffee." He directed her to a tall stool at a close table. "What can I make you?"

"Americano. Heavy cream."

He clanked some things behind the counter, and the machine started to hiss as the water was pressed through the grounds. "I need to know why you're asking if he's dead," he said without looking up from his task.

"Remember the mirrors?"

His gaze shot to hers. "Yes."

"They're happening again. Here."

"Women?"

"No, older men. The preppers."

He frowned as he worked on her drink. "It's a coincidence. It's clearly different."

"It is and it isn't. That's why I had to ask if he was still dead."

Levi brought her the drink in a bright-turquoise cup with matching saucer. He settled himself on a stool next to her. "He wasn't alone that night."

Mercy's anxiety came back. "Rose is having doubts about whether she heard a second voice that night."

"Well, no one came looking for the dead man and no one reported the shooting at our place. I expected the police to show up the next day. And then when that didn't happen, I expected it every day after," said Levi. Stress lined his face, and he appeared older than when she'd first entered the shop.

"I remember. For years I've waited for someone to tap me on the shoulder and say they know what happened that night."

They sat in silence for a moment as Mercy sipped at her drink.

"How come no one ever came looking for him?" she whispered. "People don't disappear without questions being asked."

Levi took a deep breath and blew it out. "I didn't recognize him. None of us did. I don't think he was from around here."

"And the second person didn't report it—"

"Because he knew he was just as guilty. It would have been like calling the police to complain that your heroin was stolen."

The two of them and Rose had often repeated this logic to calm their nerves when stress and guilt from the murder threatened to overtake their lives.

"We ended the cycle of attacks back then," Levi pointed out, leaning toward her across the table. "You or Rose were going to be next. We stopped him."

"Did we? Because someone is breaking mirrors and killing again." Mercy stared at him.

"They aren't after young women. It has to be someone different."

"I think it's the second guy. The one who got away," she whispered.

"You're jumping to conclusions."

"Did you know weapons were stolen in the Sanders and Vargas murders? It didn't stand out back then, but it seems relevant now with the weapons missing from the current three murders."

Levi rubbed at his beard. "Anyone would have stolen the weapons back then. Have you traced sales of the current weapons?"

"No." Her shoulders sagged. "We have an analyst working on it. It's hard when the weapons were probably bought illegally to start with. And I bet some of the purchases go back forty years."

"Back then it was no big deal to sell a rifle to your neighbor. No one cared. So we're back to the same question we've asked for fifteen years. *Who's the second guy?*"

The background music of the café filled the silence between her and Levi. Nancy Wilson's powerful voice asked in song if she was so afraid of one who was so afraid of her.

"We don't know how to find him, and he's afraid of being found." She stated the obvious.

"Did Rose say more about who she thinks it was?" Levi asked.

"Not when I talked with her yesterday. Most of the town was at the Bevins barbecue the day she thought she heard the voice for the first time. There's no guarantee she's remembering that part correctly." Mercy's brain started to spin. "She could have heard it in a store . . . or maybe even mixed it up with something on TV . . . we don't know that was where she heard it." Anxiety started as a small bud in her chest and quickly bloomed. Rose's early certainty about where she'd heard the second voice was the catalyst that'd pitted Mercy against her father.

She'd defended her sister's belief and wanted to go to the Bevins ranch and find the source of the voice. They'd made up a lie, telling her father that Rose had heard a man outside their home and thought someone was about to break in, never revealing to him or the rest of the family that someone had broken in and attacked his daughters.

Her father had declared Rose was mistaken about the voice and refused to allow Mercy to rock his fragile relationship with the powerful rancher. He'd told Mercy to stay silent. When she'd rebelled against the silence, it'd enhanced the problems she already had with her father's views on the roles of women. At home. In public. For the future. Mercy knew she couldn't live in the shadow of a man for the rest of her life. Their fights came to a head, and he told her to accept his ways or leave for good.

The family had supported his decision, leaving Mercy ostracized and standing alone with her beliefs.

She made the difficult choice and left Eagle's Nest, her family, and the only way of life she'd ever known, but her attacker was never far from her thoughts. Memories of him persisted.

His smell.

His hands.

His hot breath. And sharp nails. And stinging punches. And—

She shut it down.

Not now.

Mercy had felt abandoned.

She'd been nearly raped and murdered and had kept it a secret.

And her family had stood up against her.

"How did you get your job?" Levi abruptly asked.

She embraced the change of subject and directed her brain back from the edge of an abyss. She knew Levi wasn't asking about her educational requirements. He wanted to know how she could have killed someone and become an FBI agent. "Lies of omission. It was easy for me to say I've never been convicted of a crime. And I passed all their psychological testing without problems."

"That's because it was justified," Levi said firmly. "In your heart you know you did what was right. We both did. Do you like your job?"

"I love it," she admitted. "My brain is engaged every day. I spend a lot of time staring at a computer screen, but I love assembling the puzzle pieces once I find them."

"Sounds dull," said Levi. "But you were always the one asking questions and looking deeper into stuff. I can remember you digging in the dirt for hours, fascinated with every layer you uncovered."

"It changed colors and textures. I wanted to know why." It was true. She would pick apart a piece of nature, break it into the smallest elements she could see, and then pester her siblings with her questions.

"I always figured you for some sort of scientist," he said gruffly.

"I like what I'm doing better."

"You're lucky you left."

His tone stabbed her heart. "You can't mean that." His gaze focused on her coffee, and she wished he'd look at her.

"For a long time I didn't think you were lucky. I was pissed at you and I was glad that the fighting in the family stopped once you left, but then I resented you for escaping."

If he'd slapped her, she couldn't have been more shocked. "Nothing's keeping you here. Why resent *me*?"

"I was stuck. I had Kaylie and her mom to deal with. I didn't have the open road that you did."

"Open road?" Anger flew up her throat. "I was shoved out the door and told to not come back. My father told me I was wrong. My choice was to live under his rules or leave. That's no fucking open road!"

He cringed, but he looked her in the eye. "I know that. I can see it now. But back then I just wanted out too. This isn't how I pictured my life."

Mercy scanned the coffee shop. "It looks like a pretty damned fine life to me. You've got a beautiful daughter and a great business supplying crack to your buyers." She met his gaze. "It appears peaceful."

Levi looked at the room with pride. "Kaylie did most of it. She's got a knack for making something sort of awesome out of a pile of junk." He glanced at Mercy. "She's a lot like you."

Mercy didn't know what to say. *She's obsessive? She can't turn her brain off?*

"Dad was wrong to put you in such a hard place." His Adam's apple moved up and down. "I told him he'd fucked up. But I told him too late. You were long gone. He has his pride. He'll never admit he made a mistake."

Mercy sat silently. It was probably the closest she'd ever feel to being vindicated.

It felt empty. Pointless.

For years she'd wanted to tell her family, "You're making a mistake," and Levi had just admitted it.

It didn't heal her soul-deep ache.

She sipped her drink, not tasting it, dumbfounded that Levi's words hadn't healed her years of guilt.

Nothing's changed.

I'm still estranged from half my family. I've lost years I'll never get back.

"It's a delicate balance here, Mercy," Levi said. He rubbed a cuticle with his thumbnail and she noticed all his cuticles were red and swollen. "Everything is about status and power. The fact that Dad and Joziah Bevins can exist in the same town is due to a lot of hard work and careful words."

She thought of Daisy the cow.

Levi didn't look her in the eye as he picked at the cuticle. The ugly undercurrents that she'd felt as a teenager in Eagle's Nest were still here. Nothing had changed. People cared only about protecting their own asses.

Bells jingled and she felt a rush of cool air from outdoors hit her back. She tensed, realizing her back was exposed to whoever had walked in, but Levi stood and instantly transformed into Happy Coffee Dude. "Hey, guys, how's it going?"

He glanced at Mercy and raised a questioning brow.

She didn't know what her brother wanted. He headed behind the coffee bar, asking the men who'd entered what they would like to drink. Four men in heavy boots plodded past her, their coats dotted with misting rain. The smells of wet dirt and fresh air followed in their wake. Mercy studied their backs and listened to her brother's patter. He called them all by name. Craig, Mike, Ray, Chuck. Between coffee orders, Levi continued to shoot her the same questioning look.

One of the men turned and gazed at her over his shoulder. It took her a full two seconds to recognize him.

Mike Bevins.

Levi was asking if I want them to know who I am.

Mike broke off from the group and strode toward her with his hand outstretched. "You're one of the FBI agents in town, aren't you? We appreciate you taking a look into these murders. Our whole town has been rattled." She stood and shook his hand.

No recognition in his eyes.

Relief flowed through her, along with a bit of annoyance. Mike had hung out with Owen in his youth. Apparently the youngest Kilpatrick sibling had been beneath his notice.

She gave an automatic smile. "We're doing what we can." Behind him she saw the other three men turn to note the exchange. She recognized Craig Rafferty but couldn't place the other two men.

The one named Chuck strolled over with his huge coffee cup. His dark eyes studied her over the lid as he took a sip. "Cops in coffee shops. How's that for a stereotype?"

She wanted to kick him in the side of the kneecap. Hard.

"Just like ranch hands in Wranglers and boots," she replied. She touched her upper lip. "You've got foam on your moustache. I guess you ranching guys don't drink your coffee black anymore." She winked at him with a sly grin. "I like hazelnut syrup too." *Gag.*

Mike grinned and elbowed the other man. "Watch out, Chuck. She's onto you."

Anger flashed in Chuck's eyes and he turned his back.

"Ignore him." Mike Bevins was still smiling.

"I will." She sat back down and sipped her own drink, hoping he'd see she was done with the encounter. Mike Bevins reminded her too much of his father, Joziah. Same build, same eyes. At least Mike felt genuinely friendly. Joziah's attitude had always felt forced.

"If you need someone to show you around town, I'm more than happy to." His blue eyes shone with speculation.

Uh-oh.

"Thank you. I'm good. GPS, you know."

"That doesn't tell you where to find a great dinner," he pressed. He leaned closer and rested a booted foot on a stool. "I liked the way you handled Chuck."

She wanted to sigh. "Thank you. But really . . . I'm good." She could be polite for only so long.

He held her gaze for another long moment, a puzzled look crossing his face.

Not used to being turned down?

She forced a smile to take out the sting, showing her teeth. *Why can't women simply say no and men leave it at that?* "I'm working," she added, kicking herself for feeling the need to let him down easy and protect his ego.

Mike nodded. "As you wish. Enjoy Eagle's Nest." He turned and went back to where the last of the guys was paying for his drink. The men tromped out, giving her polite nods or touching their hat brims. Chuck looked straight ahead.

Levi sank back into the seat across from her. "Mike recognized you?"

"Nope. He knew I was one of the agents in town, so I assume that much has made the gossip rounds. My name will eventually follow." *How will he feel when he realizes he hit on Owen's little sister?*

"I didn't know if you wanted me to introduce you."

"Not yet."

"What'd you say to Chuck?"

"I complimented his drink."

"He's an ass. Hasn't been in town that long."

"I recognized Craig Rafferty. I had a bit of a crush on him way back when."

"No way! You were a *child*."

"Old enough to be interested in my brother's cute friends. I liked them tall and moody."

"He's gone nowhere in fifteen years. Has worked at the same job all this time. Good thing you didn't hook up back then, because you'd be the wife of a ranch hand. How's that sound, Special Agent Kilpatrick?"

"Some days that sounds good."

"I don't believe that. That coat you're wearing probably costs two weeks of his salary."

Her coat was an investment. A quality that'd last forever. "Your fashion knowledge has greatly expanded."

"I have a teenage daughter."

"Touché."

Studying her sibling, Mercy finally relaxed. A bridge had spanned their fifteen years of silence, and the enormity of the long years faded away. His face was again familiar; the crinkles at the corners of his eyes felt normal. He was her brother.

Optimism filled her. She wanted to know everything about her brother and Kaylie.

His teeth flashed in a big grin. "What are you thinking?" he asked.

"For the first time, I'm glad I'm back."

TWENTY

Truman sat at his desk, looking at the broken-mirrors photos from Ned Fahey's and Enoch Finch's homes. He'd memorized the photos from Uncle Jefferson's home. Now he stared at the others, searching for something in common and wondering if he could figure out what had been used to break the mirrors.

Bullets had destroyed the mirrors in Jefferson's home. Just as they'd destroyed his uncle.

But no bullets had been found behind the mirrors in the other two homes.

Why hadn't anyone else connected the mirrors from the old cases yet? Surely there was a police officer or county deputy who recalled that detail. Why had it been pointed out by someone who'd been a teenager at the time?

Coincidence?

If Mercy Kilpatrick hadn't been assigned to the murders, would those two old cases still be sitting in the file room? Waiting for Lucas to run a duster over their box?

Truman didn't believe in coincidences. Not yet, anyway.

He laid out all the broken-mirror pictures on his desk. Five different cases. Fourteen different pictures. The glass of each small accessory mirror had fallen out of its frame, but the bathroom mirrors had stayed glued in place. Except for in one of the Vargas bathrooms, where the mirror had been a medicine cabinet door and it'd crumbled to pieces across the counter.

Did the same person cause all this destruction?

Why?

Truman wanted to bang his head on his desk. It would be as helpful as staring at pictures.

"Chief?" Royce Gibson stepped into his office. "You wanted an update on the agents?"

A pang of guilt struck Truman's chest. "Sure."

"Special Agent Peterson headed in the direction of Bend. I assume he's going to the FBI office. Special Agent Kilpatrick headed out on Route Eighty-Two this morning. I didn't follow either of them outside the city limits."

Truman thought for a minute. "Rick Turner lives off Eighty-Two, right?"

"Yes, sir."

Mercy had been headed toward her sister's house. Truman wondered if she was nervous. She hadn't said much about her sister that morning, but Truman had put enough pieces together to know it wasn't going to be an easy visit.

"Thanks, Royce."

The cop lingered in the doorway, shifting from one foot to another and letting his gaze roam about the room.

"Is there something else?" Suspicion prickled at the back of Truman's neck.

"It might be stupid."

"Let me be the judge of that."

Royce fidgeted some more. "There're rumors going about. Not a lot, but I've heard it three times now. And everyone says they don't know if it's true."

"What is it, Royce?" Eagle's Nest thrived on rumor. Truman got some of his best information from the gossip chain. Along with a lot of garbage.

"Ever hear of the cave man?" he asked in a wavering voice.

Truman raised a brow. *Ina's cave man?*

Royce's face turned red and he studied his shoes. "You said to tell you everything."

"Spit it out."

The cop managed to look him in the eye. "I heard some hunters spotted weapons near a cave along with signs of someone living there. They left quickly, afraid they'd stumbled onto personal property."

"When? What hunters?" Truman barked.

"Don't know. The hunters were from the other side of the Cascades. They mentioned it in passing somewhere in town, asking if anyone lived in a cave around here. With all the talk about the weapons stolen lately, I thought it might be important."

Truman sat silently. *Hunters? Telling stories in the bar?* "Anyone else ever mention a cave man?"

Royce looked at his shoes again.

Truman waited.

"There were always stories passed around. Someone would say they'd seen some creepy guy who lived in the forest. No one ever claimed he had a bunch of weapons. But they always said he'd shoot at you."

"Stories? Like rumors you tell in high school?"

"Yeah, something like that."

Truman counted to ten. "Can you be more specific, Royce? Can you remember the name of someone who actually saw this cave man or his weapons?"

Royce looked miserable. "Like I said, it's just rumors. But I thought the hunters saying they'd seen the same thing added some credibility."

"Is the hunter story recent?"

"Yeah."

"Shit." He eyed the young cop. "Can you try to track down the story? Start with the bartenders and waiters. Maybe Sandy at the B&B. Try to find someone who remembers hearing it from the hunters' actual mouths . . . not their drinking buddies. Try to pinpoint some sort of location too. Surely you guys who went to high school together know one section of the forest that everyone avoids, right? Sometimes rumors evolve from facts. Let's figure out what's what."

The cop nodded eagerly. "I'll get right on it." He gave a minisalute and strode down the hallway with a sense of purpose.

Did I just send an officer to chase a figment of an alcohol-fueled imagination?

It didn't matter. Any bit of information needed to be taken seriously, and this wasn't the first time he'd heard of the cave man. Truman wasn't above following up on rumors of a cave man with a cache of weapons.

His phone rang.

"Truman Daly."

"Chief? This is Natasha Lockhart from the ME's office."

Truman pictured the petite medical examiner. His uncle's death had been his first encounter with her. She'd come across as highly competent and driven. Good qualities to have in her job.

"Yes, Dr. Lockhart, what can I do for you?"

"I've sent you an e-mail along with the FBI and Deschutes County, but I wanted to talk to you because I know this is personal."

His stomach-acid level suddenly tripled.

"Some of the lab work on Enoch Finch and your uncle came back. You know certain tests can take a few weeks, right? I analyze some tissues at our office, but I typically send out for more in-depth testing."

"Right." *Get on with it.*

"Enoch Finch had traces of Rohypnol in his blood work. Your uncle had the same in his system."

Truman was silent. Jefferson Biggs had preached against all prescription medications. He believed the pharmaceutical companies brainwashed people to believe they needed chemicals. A conspiracy to take Americans' money and keep them addicted to their products. Had his uncle lied to him? Preached against medications while popping pills in his bathroom? He wouldn't be the first hypocrite Truman had encountered.

But this was his uncle. He firmly believed the man had never lied to him.

"Truman?"

"I'm here. You're checking Ned Fahey for the same medication?"

"I am." She paused. "Your uncle's meds actually turned up in his stomach contents. He'd just taken it."

Truman remembered the two glasses on his uncle's kitchen counter. He knew there'd been Scotch in both glasses, an indication Jefferson had shared a drink with someone that evening. The glasses had been printed, but only his uncle's prints had been found. One of the glasses had no prints.

Had the killer been close enough to Jefferson to share a drink first? And then coolly wipe down his glass before he left?

"I have an idea of how the drug might have gotten in his system," Truman said slowly. "He wasn't one to take medication."

"Wherever it came from, it's odd that both men had it."

"Agreed." Truman chatted with the ME for another minute and then ended the call. He headed down the hall to the evidence locker, to the stack of evidence boxes from his uncle's murder. After a few moments of searching, he found the bag with the two glasses. He slipped on a pair of vinyl gloves and broke the seal to examine the glasses. Fine black fingerprint powder still coated them.

He held one to his nose and sniffed. The odor of Scotch still lingered.

Could they find the medication in the dried residue on the glasses?

It was worth a shot.

His uncle wasn't a liar. Someone would have had to trick him to get drugs into his body.

Someone he was willing to share a drink with.

TWENTY-ONE

Mercy zipped up her black jacket and shoved her gloves in her pockets as she looked longingly at the B&B's comfy bed. Exhaustion and nerves made her want to crawl under the covers, but she knew she'd never get to sleep. Only one thing helped her calm her nerves when she was stressed. Her late-night jaunt from the hotel two nights ago had soothed her brain and made her feel as if she wasn't spinning her wheels. She needed that sense of accomplishment before she had the right to relax.

Someone knocked on her door.

Eddie? She'd told him good night an hour ago, at nine o'clock.

She looked through the peephole and caught her breath.

Kaylie Kilpatrick. Her niece.

The hall light made the teen's nose stud sparkle as she glanced to the right and left. Impatience crossed her face and she knocked again.

Does she know who I am?

Why would she be here if she didn't?

Mercy realized she wouldn't be leaving the B&B tonight. She flipped both the locks and opened the door.

Kaylie stood still, studying Mercy's face. Mercy let her stare as she did her own examination.

Mercy had a good four inches on the teen, and Kaylie's hair was lighter, but the eyes were the same.

"You're my aunt," the girl stated.

"Yes."

"My name's Kaylie."

"I know," said Mercy, unable to think of a better reply.

Kaylie glanced to the right and left again. "Can I come in for a minute? I'd like to talk to you."

Against her better judgment, Mercy stepped back and let her enter. Kaylie glanced around the room and then sat on the chair by a tiny desk. Her eyes widened as she focused on Mercy's jacket. "Oh. Were you leaving?"

"It's nothing that can't wait." Mercy closed the door, slipped off her jacket, and sat on the bed with a silent sigh, facing the teen. "Did your dad tell you who I am?"

"Yes." Kaylie's gaze still tracked Mercy from head to toe. "After you guys left with your coffee on Monday, I asked him why he was being weird. I hounded him until he told me this afternoon." Her brows narrowed as she stared. "I can see a resemblance. People always say I look like Aunt Pearl, but I think I look more like you. Dad said you were kicked out of the family, but he won't tell me why." She looked at Mercy expectantly.

"I think if your father didn't share that story, then he has a good reason. I'm not ready to talk about it."

Disappointment covered Kaylie's face. "I thought you'd say that."

"Why are you here, Kaylie?"

The girl looked down at her clenched hands. "I want to leave town when I graduate from high school."

Mercy waited.

"My father doesn't want me to."

Mercy didn't know what the girl expected from her, the estranged aunt. "What about your mother?"

"My dad has full custody. My mom remarried. She has another family now."

The pang in the girl's voice made Mercy's heart break. "I'm sorry, Kaylie."

The girl waved her hand, brushing all thoughts of her mother to the side. "I'm over it. But you left town after high school, right?"

Caution flooded Mercy. "That's right."

"You went to college and now you're doing your own thing. *I want that!* Dad wants me to attend the community college in Bend."

"That's not a bad idea—"

"*But I want to get away!* I can't live here. I want to see stuff and travel and meet new people!" Her eyes pleaded with Mercy.

She took a deep breath. "Kaylie, I'm not sure this is any of my business. Your family and I—"

"I know. *I know.* You haven't spoken in forever. But could you help me figure out how to pay for a college that's farther away? I want to do what you did . . . leave this crappy town behind and learn about different things. I don't want to be a mom, grow a garden, store food, and raise a crop of kids. I want to *do things.*"

"I'm not sure you should be talking to me—"

"I don't care if you're shunned by the family."

Mercy held up a hand. "That's not what I meant. You should be talking to your counselor at school. It's their job to help you find the best route to college. There's financial aid and scholarships. Stay in state and you can probably afford it. How are your grades?"

"Mostly As."

"That's a good start. You're a junior, right? Keep the grades up and start doing your scholarship research."

"I've talked to my counselor about college. He always asks what my dad wants me to do."

Mercy took a strong dislike to Kaylie's counselor. "Then lie."

Kaylie stared at Mercy for a long moment. "Why will no one talk about you? There are no pictures of you at Grandma and Grandpa's house. I've looked."

Mercy couldn't speak.

No photos. As if I don't exist.

Kaylie looked down. "I'm sorry. I didn't mean to upset you. I assumed you were over it."

Mercy blinked a few times, wondering what the teen had seen in her expression. "It's a long story. It's complicated."

Annoyance crossed Kaylie's face as she met Mercy's gaze. "You're definitely related to Dad. That's exactly what he said." She studied Mercy intently. "Do you have kids? Are you married?"

"No and no."

"How did you come to work for the FBI?" Kaylie tipped her head in concentration. A movement reminiscent of Rose when she was listening closely.

"I applied a few years after college," Mercy said. "I'd studied criminal justice believing I wanted to be a crime scene investigator. Then the FBI caught my eye."

Kaylie nodded, her brows still together. Mercy knew she was memorizing every word she said and felt the heavy weight of giving life advice to her niece. "Do something you love," she told the teen.

The teen's posture relaxed. "I love food," she said in a dreamy voice, gazing into the distance. "I love to cook, but I especially love to bake. I make all the pastries at the coffee shop. I'd be happy doing that all day long." She straightened. "But I don't want to do it in Eagle's Nest. I want to do it where it's busy and the atmosphere is electric. I see the same people over and over here."

"Obviously you don't need a college education to follow that dream, but I'd recommend getting a degree first anyway. College would be your opportunity to expand your horizons and see more of the world. Then you can figure out where you want to pursue your passion."

"But how did *you* do it? How did you pay for all that?"

Images from her college years flashed and faded, reminders of how meager her resources had been. "Money was tight, but that was nothing new to me. What was new was learning to hustle. I learned how to ask questions, dig for answers, and swallow my pride. I knew if I wanted to make it on my own, I had to learn how to make things happen. No one was going to hand me anything . . . I had to go get it. Before I went to college I worked three different jobs, lived in an apartment with three other people, and ate a lot of ramen noodles. I haunted my financial aid advisor's office and constantly searched for ways to get the most value for my dollar. It was definitely a new world for me. It wasn't Eagle's Nest."

Kaylie nodded. "Everyone around here tells me to focus on being ready for the future, but they mean staying put in Eagle's Nest to wait for our government to collapse." She wrinkled her nose. "I think my dad has second thoughts about that ever happening."

"How is that?"

She gave a teenage shrug. "Even though he preaches to me about how ideal Eagle's Nest is, he doesn't go help Grandpa the way he used to. They had a big fight about a year ago—I don't know what it was about, but he's stepped back from Grandpa's community since then. I've seen him avoid phone calls and meetings."

"I assume he still visits with his friends?" Mercy had a million questions, but she held back. She didn't want to pull Kaylie into the divide between her and the rest of her family. She'd made good progress with three of her siblings, but knew she needed to take it slow.

Even though Kaylie had taken the first step when she knocked on her door.

"Some of them. But he's been short tempered lately. I heard him tell David Aguirre to go to hell."

"The minister?"

"Yeah, Dad hasn't ever really liked him. Says he's a liar and shouldn't be preaching to others."

Levi and I agree on that.

"I think David was always more of Owen's friend, not your dad's," said Mercy. "At least that's how it used to be."

"It's still that way. David is part of Grandpa's circle," added Kaylie.

Mercy nodded. Her father had always surrounded himself with people he believed would have his back in an uncertain future. Mercy wondered if it had been Owen's doing to include David in that tight-knit circle. Did he have other skills besides preaching? Engineering skills? Livestock? Botany? Maybe her father thought it was prudent to have one of God's servants on his side.

She didn't snort out loud.

"I don't think society is going to fall apart," Kaylie said softly. "How can my life revolve around preparing for something that I don't think will ever happen?" She turned pleading eyes to her aunt.

Mercy understood. She'd had the same thought a million times and struggled with the conflict it'd created in her soul. She'd watched her parents systematically prepare for an uncertain future, but at the same time watched the rest of the world moving on as normal. A foreign market would crash, her parents would tense, convinced it was the first step, and nothing would happen. Americans still went to school, went to work, bought groceries, and rode their bikes.

Are they living a lie?

"I know how you feel," Mercy started. She paused, knowing it wasn't her place to tell the girl what to do. "All I can tell you is how I've dealt with those feelings. The preparing and looking ahead has been ingrained in your life from birth, right?"

Kaylie nodded.

"But if you step away, you'll feel worried, insecure . . . like you're walking on a tightrope. No matter how badly I wanted to relax and enjoy a normal life, the doubt crept up and I wondered if I was foolish for not doing simple things like storing extra food or maintaining an alternative power supply. Do you worry that if you leave for college and start a new life that you'll find out your dad was right to prepare for an uncertain future? And that you'll suffer for it?"

"Yes! Every day." Kaylie was hanging on every word.

"Then how can you do both at the same time?"

Her niece's eyes widened. "Do both? How?"

Mercy saw the wheels start to turn.

"Is that what you do?" Kaylie's voice rose an octave. "You haven't fully given it up? But what about a community? Who will you rely on to help you?"

"I rely on myself," Mercy whispered, feeling as if her entire obsessive-compulsive soul was on display for her niece.

"How?"

"Make a plan. It's possible, but it's not the same as having a circle of like-minded people to rely on," Mercy admitted. "My plan has some holes, but I feel better knowing I've done something. When I start to feel uncertain, I do more and it helps me relax."

"Where—?"

"That's not important. What you need to know is that you're a strong person and you can do whatever the hell you feel like, as long as you're not hurting anyone else. If you don't like the way something makes you feel, then change it."

Kaylie sat silently for a few moments, processing the information. Mercy hoped the girl could see some different possibilities now. When she'd been a teen, she'd been shown over and over the same path as Kaylie. Mercy had been okay with it, accepting that it was the smart way to live. Then she'd started to have doubts, and before she could come to terms with her doubts, her world exploded and she was shoved out the door, forced to fly on her own.

Shunned.

After that she completely rejected her family's lifestyle.

Until she couldn't live without it. Anxiety attacked within six months of her leaving, and she discovered that for her own peace of mind she had to prepare. All her life she'd been told that the power grid could collapse; she couldn't blow off that possibility. So she started. It was small changes at first. Storing food. Batteries. Cash. Gold. She hid her compulsion from her roommates.

Then it'd gotten bigger.

And she still hid it. Hiding it was easier than answering questions.

After fifteen years, Kaylie was the first family member she'd discussed it with. Talking about it out loud was a relief. The girl wouldn't judge her; she understood what it was like to grow up with preppers. A subtle bond flowed between her and the teen. A bond she hadn't felt since she left home. *Someone to talk to.*

"Is it so bad living here, Kaylie?"

Kaylie gave her a sour look.

A tiny part of Mercy wanted to tell the girl to embrace the people around her and accept the way of life. A larger part wanted to scream at the teen and tell her to run away as fast as possible.

It wasn't her place to tell the girl what to do.

But she sympathized. Her siblings had seen the prepping lifestyle as one of community and smart planning. She remembered how Pearl had shuddered as Mercy wondered out loud what it would be like to work and live in New York City: "I wouldn't want to be in that city when the power and food supplies are cut off. There'll be riots. People will attack each other. That's crazy talk, Mercy."

"But what if it never happens? How can we reject something on a what-if scenario?"

"It's best to be away from the big cities when it happens. A few private acres. Room to grow and raise what you need." Those were her parents' words in Pearl's mouth.

Had all the kids been brainwashed?

Or simply taught to plan ahead?

"Look into college, Kaylie. Figure out how to pay for it and go. Do what you need to do to stay prepared." Mercy swallowed the lump in her throat. "Your father will always be waiting here for you when you come back."

"Then why aren't your parents waiting for you?"

TWENTY-TWO

Jane Beebe struggled to see beyond her headlights in the darkness of the insane morning hour.

"Goddamned old coot. Why in the hell do you insist on living in the middle of nowhere?"

Her brother, Anders, should have bought a condo in her building in Bend—as she'd suggested a dozen times—instead of living on five acres away from society. He'd laughed at the idea. "Where will I keep all my stuff?"

"You don't need all that junk."

"You don't know that. One day you might be real thankful I kept it."

"Oh yeah? What am I going to do with a hundred rusting cars that don't run?"

She leaned closer to her steering wheel and blinked, staring hard at the road. Out here there were no lines on the roads, no streetlights, and the turns occurred without warning. She was determined to be careful; her eyes didn't see as well at night as they used to. When Anders had *finally* agreed to visit the oncologist in Portland, she'd signed him up for the first appointment available. She glanced at the clock on her dashboard. They had five hours until his appointment time.

He better be ready.

If he'd changed his mind without telling her, she was going to hit him over the head with one of his two dozen cast-iron frying pans and drag him into the car. She'd wanted to drive to Portland yesterday and stay overnight in a hotel so they wouldn't be in a rush and worried about making his appointment on time. Anders had refused to spend the money.

But doesn't think twice about making me get up before the ass-crack of dawn to drive.

He'd lost his license a few years ago, refusing to pay for the renewal. "Why does a freeman have to pay for the right to drive on free roads?"

"They aren't free," Jane had pointed out. "Your taxes pay for them."

"Even more reason why I have the right to drive on them."

Multiple tickets for driving without a license had put a damper on his enthusiasm for driving as a freeman. He'd filed paperwork on top of paperwork to protest the tickets. When an exasperated judge was about to send him to jail for a few days for being such a pain in the ass, Jane had caught wind of it and paid the tickets.

Anders had argued bitterly. "They don't have the right to ticket me for traveling about this country. They're just making laws to collect more of our money."

Jane had refused to engage in the everyday argument.

She slammed on her brakes and took a sharp turn into Anders's driveway. The pine-lined road had widened the slightest bit, and she'd nearly missed the opening on the right. No signs. No indication whatsoever that her brother lived a half mile down the dirt drive.

She swore as her car bounced through a rut, slamming her shoulder into the driver's door.

Why do I bother?

Because someone has to.

Her older sister had died, and she felt obligated to look out for Anders. Even if he was a bit cracked in the skull. Family was family.

She weaved her way down the dirt road among the sea of abandoned autos that her brother was so fond of collecting.

Maybe it's a good thing he refused to move to my building. What would my neighbors think of him?

Shame washed over her at her thoughts, but it wasn't the first time she'd had them. There were a few reasons she hadn't pressed *really hard* on the issue, one of them being what her neighbors would think of *her*. She handled her guilt by checking in on her brother a few times a year. He seemed to thrive on his own.

Although one of these days he would be locked up for his unlicensed driving. All the cops in the area knew Anders, but someone was going to get fed up with his behavior.

At least he acknowledged that it wasn't a good idea to drive to Portland on his own.

Light shone from the windows of his house. *Thank goodness he's up.*

She parked and stepped carefully across the muddy, empty space to his home. She'd lifted a hand to knock when she saw the door had been left open a crack for her. She pushed it in. "Anders?"

Silence greeted her.

"Are you ready to go? We've got a long drive."

She wiped her feet on the worn mat and stepped in the home. "Anders!"

Maybe he stepped outside for something. That's why the door was open.

She headed toward the kitchen, smelling coffee and planning to pour herself a quick cup to enjoy until her brother was ready to go.

The odor of urine and worse stopped her at the kitchen doorway.

Anders was faceup on the kitchen floor in a pool of blood.

Jane dropped her purse and dived to her knees next to her brother. *"Anders!"* She grabbed his face, turning it toward her, but his eyes were blank. She pressed a shaking hand against his warm neck, searching for a pulse. She held her breath as she tried to find a vein beating in his neck.

Nothing.

She clawed at his blood-soaked shirt and saw the seeping holes in his chest.

Sitting back on her heels, she knelt silently with one hand resting gently on his chest. No heartbeat. No breaths.

She waited longer.

Nothing.

"Oh, Anders. I thought your mutterings about the cave man were a bunch of bull."

Regret and shame flooded through her for not taking her brother more seriously.

One of his hands clenched a revolver. She looked over her shoulder and saw bullet holes in the wall near where she'd entered the kitchen.

"I hope you got the asshole."

TWENTY-THREE

Truman was tired of seeing murdered old men.

Three days ago he'd hauled Anders Beebe into a holding cell for driving drunk.

Today he was dead.

He stood in the kitchen doorway of Anders's home and kept his anger in check as the county's crime tech photographed every element of the scene. Across the room, Mercy and Eddie watched the photographer move about the area. A county deputy had called Truman at six this morning, and he'd immediately called Mercy to share the news of the Beebe murder.

Her voice had been full of sleep when she answered her cell phone. But she'd come to her senses instantly. "Why are you calling us, Truman? This sounds like it's a county case."

"It is. Let's just say the sheriff is a little slow to see the connection to your other cases, so he hasn't called the FBI yet. Consider my phone call a favor to him."

"Eddie and I will be there in thirty minutes."

Sheriff Ward Rhodes had covered his ass as the agents showed up at the Beebe home, telling Mercy and Eddie he was just about to call them. He was on the phone and waved his hand at the house. "Take a look." And went back to his phone call.

Mercy had smiled to the sheriff's face, but rolled her eyes behind his back. Eddie had spotted it and poked her in the ribs. She'd batted his hand away.

Their casual closeness made Truman envious. *When was the last time I had someone to banter with like that?*

Mercy had caught him watching them and winked.

His breath caught.

Special Agent Kilpatrick had amazing eyes.

She's rather amazing all around. Sharp. Driven. Intelligent.

Yesterday she'd shown an emotional side that'd raised his concerns, but he still believed she was as motivated as he to find the killer.

Someone who'd now killed four men within a few weeks.

Anders Beebe had been shot several times in the chest. His blood covered the floor of the kitchen, and faint spray coated several cabinets.

"This scene seems different than the other scenes," said Mercy. "It feels rushed. Like he didn't find what he expected when he entered the house. No one else was shot to death in their kitchen. Even with Jefferson Biggs, it appeared they had a drink before he became suspicious."

"I agree," said Eddie. "Especially since Anders fired a weapon at our suspect. Our guy was the aggressor in our other scenes. What went wrong this time?"

"Come look back here." Truman gestured for the agents to follow him. They trailed him down a long hallway to a small room at the back of the house. In the closet a gun safe stood wide open. And full of guns.

"He didn't take the weapons." Mercy looked stunned. "Was he scared off?"

"Anders Beebe's sister showed up at five this morning to drive him to Portland for a doctor's visit later this morning."

"All the way in Portland?" asked Eddie.

"A cancer specialist."

Kendra Elliot

"Oh." Agent Peterson pushed on the nose of his glasses. "So it's possible she interrupted something."

"She said her brother was warm when she found him, but she didn't hear anyone else or see anyone leave."

"How about another vehicle?"

Truman shook his head. "Did you see the number of cars out front? Most of them look like they haven't run in thirty years." Anders Beebe had liked to tinker with vehicles, and he'd never turned away a car that someone wanted to simply drop off and forget. The front acre of his property was a vehicle graveyard. "His sister said it was dark, and she didn't even look at the other vehicles. She's used to driving around several dozen cars to make her way to his home."

"Perfect camouflage to park his car," muttered Mercy. "Is anything missing from the home?"

"The sister said she doesn't know. She comes to Anders's home about once every other month, and she claims it's always a mess." Truman looked around the room and agreed. Boxes and bins were haphazardly stacked along every wall. Mercy flipped open the lid of the one closest to her and glanced inside.

"Towels," she said. "I guess no one wants to run out of towels. *Ugh.* They stink." She closed the lid. Distaste crossed her face.

Truman understood why her reaction to Anders Beebe's prepping was completely different from her reaction to his uncle's. His uncle had been neat and organized and clean. This house was a fire hazard of piles and emitted a bad, sour smell. As if damp things hadn't dried out in a few years. His uncle's home was a palace compared to this.

"Where's the bathroom?" Mercy asked.

Truman had been waiting for her to ask. He was surprised it hadn't been the first thing she'd asked when she arrived, and suspected she'd simply been biding her time. He pointed across the hall, and she and Eddie crossed out of the room. That familiar lemon scent reached

188

Truman as the agents passed him. A spot of sunshine in the gloomy home.

No way is that Agent Peterson's scent.

The two agents stared at the broken bathroom mirror for several seconds. "Are there any more?" Mercy asked, her green gaze meeting his.

"That's the only bathroom. I haven't found any other small mirrors."

"This is different too," Eddie added. "It's barely cracked. The other mirrors were *destroyed*."

Mercy stared at the mirror. "Is it because he was interrupted? Or his heart wasn't in it? What if it's been cracked for decades?"

"Could someone else have done it?" Truman finally asked what he'd been thinking since he first walked the scene. "Do we have a copycat? Nothing is quite what we expected."

Mercy and Eddie exchanged a glance. Both gave small shrugs. They appeared as stumped as he was.

"We'll treat it as being connected," said Eddie. "But we can't rule out that any of these crimes were done by more than one person."

"Is the sister still here?" Mercy asked.

"I think so. One of the county deputies was walking the property outside with her, looking for anything missing or odd." He led the agents out of the house and paused on the front porch, looking for Jane Beebe.

"What a bunch of junk," Eddie said, looking over the sea of vehicles. "I understand liking to tinker with cars and even collecting cars, but this is hoarding. Just like inside. These cars are a bunch of crap. Probably a half-dozen environmental laws are being broken too."

Truman silently agreed. Most of the vehicles were covered in rust. Windshields and wheels missing.

"Another man's treasure," said Mercy.

"He's lucky he doesn't have close neighbors and that the vehicles aren't visible from the road," Eddie added. "I don't envy the people who have to clean this up."

"Maybe they'll find a trunk full of gold," suggested Mercy.

"Good luck," said her partner.

"That's Jane," said Truman, spotting the woman and a deputy as they came through a gate to the back of the property. The woman was tall and slender, and she moved with an effortless confidence even though the knees of her jeans were dark with blood. She spotted the group watching her and moved their way.

"What have you found out?" Her voice was as confident as her posture. Her gaze swept over the FBI agents.

Truman made introductions.

"I'm very sorry for your loss," Mercy said as she shook the older woman's hand. "I understand you don't come out to the property that often?"

Truman couldn't help but compare the two women as they stood face-to-face on the porch. Both were tall, with stubborn chins and a very direct manner. Jane seemed to recognize a kindred soul in Agent Kilpatrick and directed her words to her.

"That's correct. Anders was getting up there in years and took decent care of himself. I don't think he ate or bathed as often as he should, but he didn't like me coming around and nagging him . . . as he put it. So I kept my visits to a minimum. He wasn't a very social old coot."

Truman agreed. His encounters with Anders Beebe had been full of suspicion on the old man's part. He'd spent most of his time with the police chief arguing random bits of law in a way that made Truman's head hurt.

"Was Anders having problems with anyone? Had he argued with a neighbor?" Eddie asked.

Jane stared at him. "A neighbor? Isn't this clearly the work of the same murderer as those other three preppers in the last few weeks? Why are you asking about neighbors when you should be looking for who killed those other men?"

Truman hid a grin. Jane wasn't a pushover.

Eddie backpedaled. "We're doing that. But we always ask in case this isn't what it appears to be at first glance. If you told me a neighbor had come over with a rifle and threatened Anders yesterday, we'd follow that lead first, no matter how similar it was to the other crimes." His smile looked forced.

"No fights that I've heard of." Jane sniffed. "Anders would need to leave the house to make enemies. He didn't leave very often. He liked being alone."

"Nothing wrong with that," added Mercy. "Did you notice anything missing from the property during your walk with the deputy?"

Jane sighed. "I noticed that my brother was letting things rot to shit."

Mercy smiled at the woman's language. "That doesn't sound like someone who strives to be prepared."

"He was a damned prepper. No need to use soft language around me." Jane gestured at the acre of cars. "He was also a hoarder and believed in every conspiracy theory under the sun. A glorious trifecta. Thank the Lord he wasn't on social media. It would have filled his mind with a million other theories. He was convinced his cancer came from his smallpox vaccination because the government worried the country was getting too crowded and that was a good way to thin it out."

"That's an awfully long-term plan," said Eddie.

Jane turned faded-blue eyes his way. "He was nuts, but I found most of his theories quite entertaining."

"I understand you didn't see anyone leave when you arrived this morning," said Mercy. "We think you might have scared him away."

"You'd think Anders's shooting at him would have scared him away," said Jane. "I was happy to see he got off a few shots at his killer. Did you find any blood that didn't belong to my brother? I hope the shooter's bleeding out in the forest somewhere."

"That would help us greatly," agreed Mercy. "They'll examine all the blood spatter, but I didn't see a trail that left the kitchen. If the killer bled from a gunshot, it didn't happen in the house."

"He was expecting him, you know," Jane said matter-of-factly, looking at Truman.

Truman stilled. "What do you mean?"

"When I talked to Anders yesterday about his appointment, he said he was expecting someone to try to come kill him in his sleep like the other preppers. He said, 'I'm old, I'm alone, I prep, and I have a lot of guns. He's probably already sniffing around my land.'"

Truman didn't know what to say. "Did he have any evidence he was being watched? Was there something that led him to believe he was a target?"

"He fits the description of the other victims," said Jane. "That was enough for him. They talk, you know . . . all these old guys with nothing better to do. Get a bunch of them together and they're a bunch of hens. The latest rumor Anders told me was that there was a cave man who lived in the forest and targeted them, wanting their supplies." Guilt crossed her face. "I told him no one wanted his crap. What would a cave man do with all his old cars?"

"Cave man," Truman repeated. *That's three times I've heard that rumor this week. From three very different sources.*

"Someone else mentioned a cave man in regard to another case," Mercy said. "Had Anders ever mentioned it before yesterday?"

"Not a cave man. Little green men, yes. G-men in black suits with dark glasses, yes. You see why I don't take his concerns too seriously."

"Were there any other reasons Anders believed he'd be targeted by this cave man? Any strange encounters?" asked Eddie.

"He didn't believe he would be specifically targeted," Jane said in a schoolteacher voice. "He was being *prepared*. It's what he does," she added simply. "Just as he was prepared for the water supply to be poisoned. He was also prepared for a personal home-invasion-type attack."

The agents looked at Truman. Anders's preparation hadn't been enough.

"Are there dozens of men in our area waiting for someone to break into their home?" Truman asked softly. *Waiting on a cave man to attack?*

"Wouldn't you be?" Mercy asked. "If three women who lived my lifestyle had been targeted in my area, I'd be looking over my shoulder. I think that's expected behavior."

"We're going to end up with a rash of people getting shot in the middle of the night," muttered Truman.

"If someone's breaking into my home in the middle of nowhere, they have it coming," said Eddie.

The agent had a point.

TWENTY-FOUR

"A woman called in and says teens are racing up and down Old Foster Road again," Lucas reported over the phone.

Truman was glad for the diversion. He'd spent a frustrating morning at Anders's murder scene, and cracking a few teenage boys' skulls together sounded good. "She recognize any of the cars?"

"No. But she says there are at least three of them. One of them plowed over a **SLOW DOWN** sign she'd posted a few weeks ago."

Kids.

Old Foster Road was great for racing. It had wide-open, straight stretches of pavement and little traffic. But the few residents who owned property along the road were tired of the noise, the danger, and the occasional accidents on one sharp curve.

"I'm two minutes away. I'll check it out."

Thursday. High school kids *should* be in school. But high schoolers weren't the only ones who liked to race along the road. Truman suspected he'd find a few twentysomethings without regular jobs. Maybe even some thirtysomethings.

He took the next left and pressed on the accelerator, enjoying the rush of the souped-up engine under the vehicle's hood. His morning hadn't gotten off to the best start. On Monday, Anders had been sleeping off a drink in the back seat of a police vehicle. Now he was dead and penciled in on a murdered list that included Truman's uncle.

Who was killing the preppers?

Will there be more?

The thought made Truman's stomach turn. The population of Eagle's Nest wasn't very big. What percentage of his town would die before they figured out the identity of the killer?

The FBI had sent some of the evidence collected in the other three cases to its own lab. The county had processed most of it without any good leads, but the FBI felt it could find some solid answers.

Truman didn't care who did the work as long as it got done. The more eyes on the evidence the better. As a small-town police chief, he relied on the county and Oregon state police labs to handle any evidence he needed tested. Often their wait times were lengthy, but murders were usually pushed to the front of the priority line.

He turned onto Old Foster Road, driving slowly and prepared to pull onto the shoulder if he spotted racers headed his way.

The road was quiet.

Crap.

He spent a few minutes driving up and down the length of the road. It was a beautiful, clear day. The storm from earlier in the week had blown through, and now it looked as if Central Oregon could enjoy its Indian summer. Blue skies, hints of summer heat, but cool evenings. The last hurrah before cold temperatures kicked in for the winter.

Still no racers. He sighed, disappointed he wouldn't have any kids to chew out. He called Lucas.

"Everyone's split," he told his dispatcher.

"Yeah, she called back and said it'd gotten quiet. I was hoping you'd spot them as they were leaving."

"I didn't see anyone."

"Hey, Royce wants to talk to you." There was a crackling sound as the line was handed off.

"Hey, Chief."

"What's up, Royce?"

"I talked to a bunch of people about the cave man rumors." Royce cleared his throat. "According to Henry at Henry's Meats, he had a couple of hunters bring in a buck, and they mentioned seeing a few weapons outside a cave not far from Owlie Lake. Henry didn't keep any paperwork with their names on it, so I don't think we can find them, but he said they also asked him about the cave man rumors."

"Had Henry heard of that before?"

"No. He's never heard of a cave man." Royce said something unintelligible to Lucas. "Hang on, boss." More unintelligible words.

Truman pulled onto the shoulder of Old Foster Road and waited, hoping the racers would return.

"Lucas has heard of the cave man." Surprise filled Royce's voice. "He says kids talk about it in high school."

From Truman's perspective, Royce wasn't that much older than Lucas. Maybe five years? If Royce had heard about it in high school, it made sense that Lucas would have too.

"He said kids claim the cave man's been seen at Owlie Lake."

Truman had been to Owlie Lake a few times. Plenty of tourists stopped there to swim or hike. He could picture where the forest sloped back and up steep hills from the lake. A possible place to find caves.

"Sounds like it's worth checking out." He glanced at the time. He had a few hours before lunch. Plenty of time to take a casual walk around the lake. "Lucas, I'll be out at Owlie Lake for a bit."

He debated calling Special Agent Kilpatrick to see if she wanted to go with him.

What would he say? *I heard another rumor about the cave man and a bunch of guns out near Owlie Lake? Shall we go see if we can find our murder suspect?*

The corniness of it nearly kept him from reaching out to her until he remembered that she had grown up in Eagle's Nest. How long ago had the cave man rumors started?

Mercy Kilpatrick had said she'd never heard of a cave man when Jane Beebe mentioned it that morning. But maybe she had a hunch where to find this cave.

Mercy slammed her vehicle door and waved a hand at the figure who sat on a rock and looked over the lake.

Police Chief Daly could have been posing for an outdoors magazine. She'd noticed he rarely wore a uniform, preferring jeans and work shirts with his badge. He was a good cop, she'd decided. He clearly cared about the people in his town and had an alert mind that didn't miss much.

Unfamiliar self-consciousness rolled over her as she picked her way along the slick trail to his rock seat. Usually she didn't give a crap about what other people thought of her, but suddenly she cared what Truman Daly thought.

He wouldn't have asked me out here if he didn't have some faith in my skills.

Or else he simply wanted a former resident's opinion.

She twisted her lips at the thought. He could have asked anyone.

But I'm the only FBI agent who's lived here.

She drew closer, choosing careful foot placement on the rocky lake shore. "Hey, Truman. Looks like we've gotten rid of the rain."

He grinned, the corners of his eyes crinkling. *Wow. He's really good looking when he smiles.* She couldn't help but smile back.

"I was hoping you'd take another ten or fifteen minutes," he told her. "I'm enjoying the sun. It's pretty rare that I can sit and do nothing."

"I thought Eagle's Nest was a sleepy town with little crime. I'd guess you spend a lot of time with your feet up on your desk." She spotted a faint scar on his chin. A fight? He'd skipped shaving that morning and the slight growth made it stand out.

How does the other guy look?

"I wish. There's always something. And it's never simple, you know? Nothing can ever be fixed with a web search or a quick phone call. Usually it involves me showing up in person and talking with someone for two hours. The people around here like to talk. A lot."

"It's a lost skill back in Portland. I must answer a hundred e-mails a day. It doesn't leave time for casual talk, except in the elevator."

"So you're saying this is a vacation for you."

Her brows rose. "Not quite."

"Did you see your family yet?"

"Some of them." She looked out over the lake. "I haven't been to this lake in ages."

His raised eyebrow indicated he'd noticed she had changed the subject. "When I called, you said you'd never heard of the cave man when you were growing up." He didn't get off his rock, so Mercy picked another large rock to sit on. If he wanted ten more minutes of sunshine before they started their search, he could have it.

"Nope. That was a new one to me, but I've always loved this water. I swam here dozens of times as a teen. It was a bit of a teen hangout during the summer."

The blue sky reflected off the water. It was quiet. No car sounds, no phones ringing, no useless chatter.

"It is wonderful," Truman agreed.

She took a deep breath and settled on the rock, closing her eyes for a brief second, inhaling the scent of sun-toasted rocks and murky lake water. Tension melted out of her.

"I think that's the first time I've seen you let your guard down, Special Agent Kilpatrick."

She turned to glare at him, but his gaze was relaxed and happy. For a split second Mercy lost herself in his eyes' brown depths.

She swallowed.

No. Not for you. Unprofessional.

The thoughts stung.

He stood and held out a hand. "Let's take a look around."

She took his hand as her feet wobbled on the rounded surfaces of the big rocks. *Time to get back to work.*

Truman didn't want the hours by the lake to end.

He and Mercy had walked the entire circumference of the small lake. No cave man. No weapons. Now they headed away from the lake and to the west, where the land sloped up several hundred feet to a dust-colored table-rock formation. She'd seemed as pleased with the sun as he was. She'd pulled her long, dark hair into a ponytail, and her step grew lighter.

He didn't want to go back to the office.

Mercy was easy to be around. She didn't take herself too seriously and had even cracked a half smile at some of his lame jokes. She'd shared bits and pieces of growing up in Eagle's Nest, and he'd identified with a lot of her observations, as they'd correlated with his high school summer experiences.

"That must have been the worst for you, having to live here while all your friends were having fun back home," she said.

"I hated the first few weeks of the first summer I lived here. But once I found some friends, it was sorta fun. Teens around here make their own entertainment. Get four guys together with one dirt bike and an empty field, and your entire week is set. Back home I had to search for things to do."

"Where were you from?"

"San Jose."

"That's quite different from Eagle's Nest."

"But Eagle's Nest isn't bad. I've seen places a lot worse."

"Like what?"

Truman glanced at her, wondering if she was just making idle conversation, but her gaze was focused on him with her brows raised, waiting for an answer.

"I did a couple of tours in Africa. I've never seen poverty like that."

"Army?"

"Yes."

"What did you do when you got out?" Curiosity filled her tone.

"I joined the city's police force back home. I'd done that for several years when I got word of the job up here. I was ready for a change." *That's putting it mildly.* He kept his tone even, making it sound as if he'd taken the Eagle's Nest job on a whim, while he tightened the lock on his memories.

"This town is definitely a change. Do you have siblings?"

"One sister. She lives in Bellevue, Washington, and is married to a—"

"Microsoft executive?"

He laughed. "Yes. Too stereotypical? She shops and seems to spend a lot of time in the gym."

"Does she have kids?"

"No. Not sure there will be."

"Do you want to go back to California?" she asked. "How can you handle such a different way of life?"

Truman thought for a long time before answering. "I feel good here. Like I'm making a difference. Back home there were too many people. I rarely saw the same people every week unless they were career criminals. In Eagle's Nest it isn't crime that brings me in touch with the residents. It's usually some sort of need, and I like the challenge of meeting those needs."

"I imagine there isn't that much real crime," said Mercy.

"But I'm always busy. Whether it's arbitrating arguments or pulling a truck out of a ditch. Every night when I go home, I ask myself what I could have done better. I look for more that can be done. I have more freedom here to make good things happen. I don't have to fill out a form in triplicate to make a request. In Eagle's Nest I can just do it."

Her smile was wide. "You've impressed me, Chief Daly."

Her words touched him. "I'm not trying to impress anyone. I'm simply trying to do a job I love and leave things a little better behind me. The only bureaucracy is me and the city council. But Ina Smythe has them firmly under her thumb. And she likes me," he added with a grin.

"I remember being scared of her when I was younger."

"That's understandable. She still intimidates me a bit."

"It's been interesting running into people I never thought I'd see again," Mercy said slowly. "Inside I suddenly go back to being eighteen years old. It's like the last fifteen years never happened. It's a bit disconcerting." Her mouth snapped shut, and she turned her head away from him, as if she'd revealed something highly personal.

Her sun-inspired happiness had evaporated. Whatever had driven Mercy Kilpatrick from town still affected her. Vulnerability had disrupted the FBI agent's composed surface again in his presence. But it never lasted; it vanished within seconds.

Something was buried under her layers.

He was determined to keep digging. Gently. But he knew it was time to back off for the moment.

She moved behind him as the trail narrowed. It wasn't really a trail, more of a faint, continuous flattening of the dirt. He inhaled the scent of sunbaked soil and junipers. It was a distinctively Central Oregon scent that he associated with his teenage summers. The path steepened and he worked his legs to maneuver around the lava rocks and pines. Their conversation drifted off, their concentration on their foot placement.

"Do you know this area very well?" Mercy was slightly out of breath.

"No. You?"

"Yes. We're going to come out on a wide ridge about halfway up this peak in a few minutes."

He wanted to ask her what she'd done in the area as a teenager, but he needed his breath for the climb. Ten minutes later the trail flattened and widened, revealing a beautiful view to the east. Truman stopped to take in the sights. "That's incredible." Acres of treetops covered the land in every direction. Owlie Lake was no longer visible. The land seemed to stretch out forever, revealing rolling tan fields beyond the trees.

"Kids came up here to smoke. And do other things," Mercy said. She studied the area around them. "I don't see any garbage left behind. I guess this area has fallen out of favor with the teenagers too. Maybe no one wants to hike these days."

"I hadn't heard it was a popular spot," said Truman.

"Where are the hot spots these days?"

"Behind the Ralston barn. Along Milne Creek about a mile past the state campground."

Mercy nodded. "Much easier to get to."

"But easier for the cops to check out too. This would have been my choice of place if I was fooling around. None of my patrol officers would willingly make that hike to bust some kids." Truman studied the face of the solid rock embankment behind them. It shot straight up for about fifty feet. The path appeared to continue to the north, veering away from the rock.

"Maybe the rumors of the cave man kept them away," suggested Mercy. "Perhaps it's not just generational laziness."

"Maybe." Truman still hadn't made up his mind about the rumor. "Do you remember any caves around here?"

Mercy wrinkled her nose in thought. "There should be a hollowed-out area that's a few dozen feet off the path not far from here. I wouldn't call it a cave. Just a dip in the rock."

"Let's look." He waved her ahead of him, and she followed the path to the north. A few minutes later, she broke off from the path and wound through some brush and rocks back to the rock face. They found Mercy's hollow in the rock. It was quite deep.

"This is a lot deeper than I remember," Mercy said. She stepped into the opening and moved her face close to the rock, running her fingertips along its rough surface. "It looks as if it's been chiseled out more."

"That'd take decades. I'd say it's been blasted out."

"That sounds dangerous."

"I agree." Truman pointed at an area of ash and charred logs near one wall. "Someone's stayed here long enough to build a fire." He kicked at a few burned logs. "Remnants of tin cans and beer caps." He stepped back out of the cave and spotted a lazy pile of dried branches. "I guess that's their woodpile." If he stared hard enough he could make out a flattened spot on the cave floor where someone *might* have spread a sleeping bag.

Truman stepped deeper into the cave. The ceiling abruptly dropped and he squatted, peering into the darkness. He pulled out a small flashlight and shone it into the darkness. He couldn't see the end of the cave. "It's deep. Crazy low, though. I'd have to crawl to see how deep it goes. I don't think this part was blasted. I think the blasting revealed this deeper crevice."

Mercy bent over and peered over his shoulder. The odor of baked lemon bars distracted him. "Holy shit. It is deep. Are you claustrophobic at all?"

He didn't like the eagerness in her tone. "A bit."

"Then I'll take a look. Get out of the way."

Truman awkwardly backed out of the opening until he could stand without whacking his head. "Are you sure?"

"Absolutely. The curiosity is killing me." Her eyes shone.

He handed her his flashlight as the acid in his stomach protested. "Be careful. Don't get stuck."

She grinned and dropped to her hands and knees to crawl in the hole. "I trust you'll haul me out if I'm stuck."

"Depends how deep you've gone."

She crawled a few feet and dropped to her stomach, scooting forward. Her boots dragged behind her.

Jesus Christ. Watching her belly-crawl into the narrow opening made him light headed. *How far will she go?*

"It's wider back here." Her voice didn't echo through the tunnel; it sounded muffled by the rocks and dirt.

He knelt and looked in the hole. A faint glow from the flashlight in her hand outlined her head and shoulders. Her boots were swallowed up in the dark.

"Be careful," he repeated. *Fuck. What if we're suddenly hit by the once-in-a-lifetime earthquake they've been predicting for the last fifty years?*

"Maybe you should come out now." His voice cracked.

She didn't answer.

"Mercy?" He estimated she was a good fifteen feet down the tunnel. *What if there's not enough oxygen? Can I crawl in and pull her out?*

He didn't know.

"Mercy," he said firmly. "That's far enough."

"Coming."

Relief rocked through him.

It took a lifetime for her to back out of the tunnel. Once her boots were within his reach, he grabbed one firmly. He didn't pull, but he kept a solid hand on the leather because it calmed his gut. Her calves were

A Merciful Death

covered in fine rock and dust. She awkwardly backed out the rest of the way, her dark ponytail covered with the same debris.

Truman backed up to where he could stand, his heart racing. *I'm not letting her do that again.*

She twisted around to a sitting position, and triumphantly slid a rifle out of the tunnel. Her eyes gleamed in her dirty face. "There's got to be fifty weapons in there. All stashed in big garbage bags."

TWENTY-FIVE

Mercy's feet had started to ache an hour ago.

Truman, Eddie, several evidence technicians, and SSRA Jeff Garrison and Intelligence Analyst Darby Cowan from the Bend FBI office had converged on the hill behind Owlie Lake, and they'd all been standing around for too many hours. Amazingly, Mercy had been able to call the Bend office from the beautiful, remote location. Jeff Garrison's excitement over the weapons cache had made her day. She wished she could have been present to see him tell Darby. The FBI analyst's eyes had glowed as she watched the weapons being removed from the narrow tunnel in the mountain.

More data to mine.

Mercy knew Darby had been up to her neck in weapons research as she tried to make progress on the missing weapons from the prepper murders. According to a quick conversation Mercy had with Jeff, Darby had been supremely frustrated. "She's been consulting with the ATF, and they're keeping a close eye on these cases, but they haven't uncovered any new leads either." Jeff gave Mercy an admiring smile. "This is the biggest lead yet."

"Truman's the one who suggested we investigate the area," Mercy pointed out.

"But he didn't know where to look, right?"

"You're lucky I remembered an old make-out spot."

Jeff's brows rose. "Is that what it was? You came here often?"

She snorted. "More like I followed my brothers. They were the ones who got in trouble."

"I can't believe you crawled in there."

Mercy would have done it again. Small spaces didn't bother her, and she didn't understand why some people reacted so strongly to them. *If you can get in, you can get out, right?*

The first two evidence technicians on the scene had refused to enter the tunnel. One woman had dissolved in tears after she gave it a half-hearted attempt. Mercy had offered to retrieve the rest of the weapons, but Jeff Garrison had refused. He wanted an experienced team to process the scene and the removal. They'd waited another hour for a tech who claimed he wasn't claustrophobic. When the tech finally huffed and puffed his way up the path, Mercy had wondered if the large man would fit in the tunnel, but he'd scooted in with ease.

Mercy didn't know how evidence could be handled correctly in the tunnel. It was full of rock and dust, and even though the weapons were bagged, they were covered with debris. Whoever had chosen this place to hide them wasn't a weapons lover. The guns would have slowly become useless.

Her father would have been furious at the improper storage.

Even Mercy was annoyed by it.

Truman joined her and Jeff. He'd been talking with Darby and Eddie, and Mercy had overheard Darby recommend hiking trails and a kayaking site. She'd seen Truman make some notes on his phone as Darby talked. Eddie had appeared politely interested, but Mercy didn't think his interests extended to kayaking. A big yacht on a smooth lake, maybe.

Getting out on the water sounded good to Mercy. She hadn't kayaked in years. A smooth bit of river. The damp scent of waterlogged moss. Towering pines. The sound of water over the rocks. Nothing between her and nature but a paddle and the kayak.

Yes, I could do that.

Would Truman be interested?

She yanked her meandering thoughts back to the present. Murder. Guns. *Focus.*

Truman was looking at her with a puzzled gaze. She glanced at Jeff, who was giving her the same look. "What?" she asked.

"Jeff asked you if you're sure the cave had deepened since you were last here," Truman said.

"Absolutely. Before, it could barely keep a few people dry from the rain. Now it's much bigger."

"Are you sure it's the same one?" Jeff asked.

"I checked the area," said Mercy. "I couldn't find another."

"She walked right to this one," added Truman. "I had no doubt she knew where she was going."

"We need to figure out when it was deepened," said Jeff. "Was it done deliberately to hide the weapons? Or did someone stumble on it by chance?"

"The tunnel part felt natural to me," said Mercy. "Someone got lucky finding that as a hidden storage space. Did anyone check with the Forest Service to ask if they were aware of any blasting in the area?" She knew it was a long shot. It could have happened anytime in the last fifteen years.

"I had Darby call. They have no records of anything like that."

"Could be as simple as a couple of high school kids fooling around with explosives they'd found," said Truman. "What about reported injuries from explosives?"

"I could ask Levi," said Mercy. "He would probably remember if something like that had happened. Word travels fast when someone nearly blows their hand off."

"Ina Smythe too," Truman said as he pulled out his phone. "I'll give her a call." He stepped away and Mercy did the same thing as she dialed Levi.

It felt foreign to call her brother. They'd exchanged numbers yesterday, and at the time she'd wondered if she'd ever use his. She and Levi weren't at the stage where she could text him a casual "Hey, what's up?" or a selfie.

How many times over the years have I wished I had his number in my phone?

She'd wanted someone to share her successes with. Her college graduation. Her FBI acceptance. Her posting in Portland. She'd celebrated with friends, but she'd always been painfully aware her family was out of reach. Now her brother was available at the touch of a button. Rose and Pearl too.

Slowly she was making progress.

"Mercy?" her brother answered.

"Yes, it's me. I have a question for you." There was no coffee bar noise in the background, and she wondered where he was.

"What's up?"

"Do you remember the spot up behind Owlie Lake where you guys used to drink and bring girls?"

"The lookout? The one you have to hike up to?"

"Yes. Do you remember the cave that was off the path?"

"Why are you asking?" His voice was cautious.

"Because I'm up here right now and it doesn't look like I remember. The cave is pretty deep, and there's a low tunnel that runs even deeper from the back."

"That's not right. You must be somewhere else. It wasn't deep at all."

"I'm positive I'm in the right spot. I don't know of any other caves up here, do you?"

"Mercy, what's going on?" Levi sounded deadly serious.

"I'm trying to figure out when someone made this cave deeper."

"Why are you poking around up there?"

Frustration rolled over her. Why did her brother care—

She gripped her phone tighter. "What is up here, Levi?"

He was silent.

"Oh God. Are you saying you . . . is this where . . ." She couldn't breathe. She took several more steps to put more distance between her and the group of investigators.

"Mercy, where exactly are you?"

Her mind spun. *Did Levi stash a corpse up here? Is the crime scene team about to find a pile of bones?*

"At the lookout. The flat area where you can see forever."

He exhaled loudly over the phone.

"Levi, we found a bunch of guns stashed in that cave. I *know* it's the same cave; someone made it bigger."

"Are you saying that area is crawling with FBI now?" His voice rose an octave.

"Something like that. But just near the cave for now."

"Have they gone down the steep slope off the trail at all?"

"No." Mercy wondered if they would. It had sharp drops in several areas. A wrongly placed foot could send someone sliding through rocks and shrubs for a good fifty feet. "Why would you pick such a popular spot?" she hissed into the phone.

Oh my God.

"I panicked. I didn't know where to go where no one would see me, and I knew I didn't have time to dig a hole." His words tumbled out of his mouth. "And only part of that trail was popular back then. No one goes down the slope; it's too dangerous. People stay on the trails."

"What if someone had been here that night? Levi, how were you going to explain a *dead body*?" Adrenaline pooled in her stomach. How had her brother managed to get a corpse up the hill? He'd been a big, strong twenty-year-old back then . . . *but still.*

"Nothing happened. It was a pain in the ass, but I got it done."

"What if they find something *now*? I'm supposed to pretend I don't know what happened?"

"Yes."

"Dammit." She wiped the sweat off her temples. The sun had long gone behind the ridge, and there was no reason for her to be sweating. She felt as if she had a huge sign on her back for every investigator to read: **MURDERER.**

"Everything's going to be fine. No one is going to think you have anything to do with an ancient murder victim."

"Is it buried?"

"Sort of. The rain keeps washing the dirt away because it's on a slope. The last time I was up there I managed to cover it with rocks pretty well. Someone would have to be paying very close attention to spot it."

Or have a dog with them.

The sweat started again as she wondered if Jeff would request a dog to search the area.

"Look," she said. "You don't know anything about the cave being blasted somehow to make it deeper, right?"

"Right. I haven't checked the cave since we were kids. I remember it as pretty shallow."

"Do you remember hearing of anyone who'd been hurt by explosives? A prank gone awry? An idiot playing with fireworks and got hurt? Something like that?"

Levi was silent for a long moment. "No. I can't remember anything like that."

Mercy closed her eyes. Her world had tilted the slightest bit. As if it hadn't been off kilter enough. *He's right. No one can connect a dead body up here with me. Or him.*

Unless Levi accidentally left something behind.

"We don't have any idea who he was, right?" she whispered.

"No. He didn't have a wallet." He paused. "I've paid attention over the years, and no missing person reports have sounded like him. He wasn't from around here. Or else no one around here gave a rip about him."

"I need to go," she said softly. People were waiting. This wasn't the phone call she'd expected to have.

"Be careful, Mercy." Levi told her. "And call me . . . if . . . you know."

If they find a body.

"I will." She ended the call, composed her face, and walked back to the others. Truman was already there.

"Ina doesn't remember hearing of someone hurt in some sort of explosion," he said.

"Levi doesn't either. And he remembers the cave being shallow the way I did. He said he hasn't been back up here or at least checked out the cave since he was twenty." Her voice sounded normal.

Jeff twisted his lips. "Hopefully we can find some evidence with all those weapons that'll give us a direction to investigate." He looked at the scenery around him. "I want to expand the search area. Not just outside the cave. Go at least twenty meters in each direction from the cave. And I want the parking area at the lake searched too."

"What about the path?" Truman asked. "It's at least a half mile from the parking area to up here."

"Five feet off each side of the path."

Mercy's knees went fluid. Surely Levi had stashed the body a lot farther off the path than five feet. But someone could still stumble across something to make them look farther.

"You feeling okay, Mercy?" Jeff asked. "You look exhausted."

"I missed lunch," she said, wondering how pale she looked. "And I've been staying up later than I should."

Jeff checked the time. "Go eat. This is going to take hours. I'll keep Eddie here for a while longer. There's no point in all of us standing around to watch." He looked from Truman to Mercy. "What's next on our agenda?"

Mercy tried to remember; her brain felt like mush. "It's too early for lab results on Anders Beebe. I'd like to talk to the parents of Jennifer Sanders or Gwen Vargas."

"I'm going to call Ben Cooley," said Truman. "He was one of the investigators on the Jennifer Sanders case. He still works for me, but he's out of town."

"Cooley?" Mercy asked. The name rang a bell, and she searched for where she'd recently heard it.

Pearl. Pearl talked about Teresa Cooley having a problem with Jennifer.

"Does he have a daughter, Teresa?" she asked.

"I think he has a daughter. I don't remember her name."

"Pearl told me yesterday that a Teresa Cooley had a problem with Jennifer Sanders in the weeks before she was murdered."

"What kind of problem?" Truman asked.

"Pearl described it as mean-girl stuff. Boyfriend jealousy or something like that." Mercy drew a breath, still trying to calm her nerves from Levi's words. "I don't believe it's a woman who's done all this."

"Based on what?" Jeff asked. "I don't want to hear gut feelings; I need facts."

It was a man who attacked me back then.

"It's a gut feeling," she admitted. *I can't tell them what happened back then without turning my life, Levi's, and Rose's upside down.* Guilt cramped her stomach. *Am I slowing down the investigation by not admitting what I know?*

Between the shock from Levi and the guilt, she wanted to go crawl in bed.

Telling them a man attacked me offers no insight on the murders of today. He's dead. His partner might be alive, but I know nothing helpful about him.

Truman's stare seemed to penetrate her brain and read her thoughts. She focused on the rock mountain behind him.

"I'll walk out with you," he said. "I'd like to come when you talk to Jennifer Sanders's parents. I checked and they now live in Bend."

Mercy nodded, wanting desperately to be alone, but her spongy brain couldn't come up with a reasonable refusal.

"Let's go."

TWENTY-SIX

Mercy had promised to meet him at the Eagle's Nest police station at six.

Truman glanced at the clock on the wall for the tenth time. He still had ten minutes, so he shuffled the papers on his desk again, prioritizing what he'd tackle in the morning. He'd sent Lucas on an errand a minute ago and hoped he'd be back before Mercy appeared.

When they'd left the lookout an hour ago, she'd refused Truman's offer of a bite to eat together, stating she needed to make some phone calls and do some computer work before they interviewed Jennifer Sanders's parents.

She'd barely looked him in the eye.

The entire walk back to the Owlie Lake parking lot had been silent. The companionable atmosphere from earlier in the day had vanished. She seemed preoccupied and tired and couldn't keep her focus on the path. She kept scanning the woods and slopes as if expecting the cave man to appear. Truman had wanted to make a joke about it, but she didn't seem to be in a joking mood, so he kept his mouth shut. Instead he got a number for Jennifer's parents and set up a meeting.

Mercy had been ecstatic after she found the rifles, and she'd still been energized when law enforcement had joined them on the lookout. Her attitude had deflated after she talked to her brother.

Was Levi angry with her? Had they fought?

He knew she was estranged from her family and had been mildly surprised when she offered to call her brother, but it appeared the call hadn't gone well.

It was on his mental to-do list: find out what the hell had happened between Mercy and the rest of the Kilpatricks.

It shouldn't be on any list of mine.

He should be concerned solely with finding out who'd killed his uncle. If he learned that, he'd also know who'd killed the other preppers. Guilt poked at him for putting his uncle first, but he wasn't neglecting the other deaths. Jefferson Biggs's death occupied a huge part of his heart; it made him work harder on every case.

Speaking of which . . .

He called Ben Cooley, hoping his older officer had returned from his vacation. He was on the schedule for Monday morning.

"Hello, Truman!" Ben's voice boomed through the line. He didn't yell in person, but he'd somehow gotten it in his head that he needed to yell when he talked on his cell phone. Truman was thankful he didn't yell on the office phone at the police department.

"Are you back in town, Ben?" He fought the urge to yell back.

"Just got in around noon. You need some help? I'd be happy to let Sharon handle the unpacking if you need me to come in for something." The hopefulness in his voice made Truman smile.

"No. You give your wife a hand. I just have some questions about a case that occurred before my time."

"Which one?" Ben hollered.

"Gwen Vargas."

The line was silent for a moment. "What do you want to know about that girl?" His volume dropped. "I can tell you right now, that case has stuck with me for a long time. Not many pretty young things end up murdered in Eagle's Nest, thank the Lord."

"I reviewed the file, since it's never been solved," hedged Truman. "Were there really no other suspects?"

"Well, we looked at the boyfriend first. His alibi was backed up by a half-dozen people, and I'm telling you, he was an absolute wreck. He'd been planning to propose as soon as he saved up enough money for a ring. I thought his interview was honest. Parents checked out clean too."

"But no other suspects?" Truman repeated.

"The evidence didn't give us any new leads to follow. The interviews of her friends and family didn't turn up any leads either. The case went cold really fast. You saw it was tied to the Jennifer Sanders death too, right? Lots of similarities that made us sure it was the same person. Both went cold."

"What do *you* think happened, Ben?"

The line was silent for so long, Truman glanced at the phone screen to see if he was still connected.

"Dunno," Ben finally said. "I think someone was passing through town and kept going. Those attacks were about two weeks apart, and then nothin'. People who do that sort of thing don't just give it up, you know."

"I agree." Truman took a deep breath. "We think there's a possibility that Jefferson's death might be related to these two cold cases. The other three preppers too. You heard we found another one today?"

"I heard," Ben said gruffly. "Anders Beebe knew how to try my patience, but it doesn't mean I wanted him dead."

"Same here."

"How are some old preppers tied to the two girls' cases?"

"Broken mirrors."

A hiss sounded in Truman's ear as Ben sucked in his breath. "Holy Bruce Almighty. I'd totally forgotten about that part. You got broken mirrors in all of the recent cases?"

"Every mirror."

"I'll be goddamned. I can't believe it."

"Were the broken mirrors big news back then? Could someone have heard about it and decided to copy?"

"Well now, I don't know. I seem to remember we kept it to ourselves, since it was one of the things we used to tie the cases together. But you know how hard it is to keep things quiet in this kind of town."

"I do."

"Don't seem possible to be the same person all these years later," Ben muttered. "It doesn't fit."

"I agree. But the mirrors are making us take another look."

"Well, I'll think on it," Ben said. "Maybe I'll come in and read over my notes on the case. That might kick something loose in my brain."

"I'd appreciate it," said Truman. He ended the call with Ben and checked the clock.

Mercy should arrive any moment, and he couldn't sit still. He felt like a middle school student waiting for his crush to enter the classroom.

Shit. Not cool. He was growing more and more attracted to the FBI agent.

Fucking bad timing. Plus she doesn't even live near here.

As if location were the biggest hurdle. *How about working on the same case?*

Green eyes and dark hair popped into his mind. She was stubborn and nearly impossible to get to talk about herself. Maybe it was the air of mystery about her that'd hooked him. He'd always been interested in the unobtainable. He remembered how her face had lit up at his uncle's home as she gazed at the results of his uncle's obsession.

He wanted her to look like that at him. Not at a bunch of baking supplies.

The door out front opened and shut.

Please be Lucas. He strode down the hall and spotted Mercy in a light jacket. She turned and smiled at him and he swore his heart skipped a beat.

Get over yourself. It's not happening.

She seemed to have perked up since they parted an hour ago. Maybe she simply didn't function well on an empty stomach.

"Ready to go?" she asked. "Did you call Cooley?"

"Yes and yes," Truman said. "I was—"

The door flung open again and Lucas stepped in with a cardboard coffee tray and three covered cups. "Here you go, boss."

Reading the sides of the cups, Truman handed one to a surprised Mercy and took one for himself. "Thank you, Lucas."

"Thanks." Mercy took a sip and raised her eyebrows as her eyes widened.

"Is that right?" Truman asked. He'd sent Lucas to get her an Americano with heavy cream. Caffeine was a cure-all for him, and he'd taken a chance it'd help her too.

"It is. I was expecting black coffee."

"That's in my cup."

"Thank you." Her cheeks pinked as she lowered her gaze and took another sip.

Score.

Little things. His mom and sister had always appreciated the little things. His dad had taught him how to listen for them, and it'd never let him down.

Just what am I trying to achieve?

He didn't want to admit his answer.

Mercy studied the profile of the police chief as he drove toward Bend.

It's just a cup of coffee.

But how many times has Eddie bought me coffee? He always grabs me a regular black cup of coffee.

It means nothing.

It meant he was observant. A fact she was already aware of, and a trait that made her nervous. Around Truman Daly she consistently felt slightly exposed, as if he could see she was simply a small-town girl pretending to be an FBI agent. In four days he'd learned more about her than anyone she'd worked with in the last five years.

She didn't like it.

Or do I?

The intensity of his focus on her after her brother's call had unnerved her. She'd expected him to say she'd lied about the conversation. And she probably would have confessed the truth. Her protective shield had been painfully thin at that moment, and her secrets had felt like soda in a shaken bottle. Ready to explode when someone twisted the cap.

Truman appeared to be a good cap twister.

He made light conversation as they drove to Bend, relaying his phone call with Ben Cooley. Mercy listened and tried to remember the old cop from her years in town. She couldn't do it. She also couldn't put a face to his daughter, Teresa Cooley, whom Pearl had talked about.

"Did you ask him if his daughter had a problem with Jennifer Sanders?" Mercy asked.

"I didn't. I'll bring it up next time in person."

"It could have sounded accusatory on the phone."

"I thought so." He glanced over at her, his eyes hidden in the dark. "The caffeine help? You looked ready for sleep after our find at the lookout today."

"I was. Bed had crossed my mind at one point."

"Not sleeping well?"

"I stay up later than I should." Her nighttime activities were taking a toll. She should cut back.

"That's easy enough to fix."

"You'd think so," agreed Mercy. "I should be more disciplined."

Even though it was dark, she felt the disbelief in his look. "I have a hard time believing you're not disciplined, Special Agent Kilpatrick."

"What do you know about Jennifer Sanders's parents?" She changed the subject.

"Nothing. I know they're in their sixties and agreed to meet with us."

"Should be interesting. Fifteen years since their daughter was murdered and no results."

"I hope we can find some answers for them," Truman said quietly. "Parents shouldn't have to suffer like that."

Mercy agreed.

◆ ◆ ◆

John and Arleen Sanders appeared to be in their eighties, not sixties.

Mercy's heart cracked at the permanent pain in Arleen's eyes. Jennifer had been their only child.

"I used to call the police department every few months to find out if anything new had been discovered," said Arleen. "I finally stopped. I would be depressed for days after each call." John patted her limp hand.

Now you're permanently depressed.

The couple lived in a small condo in a retirement village. Mercy had spotted the wing for advanced care across the greenway between the buildings. She believed the constant visual reminder of a possible difficult future would be depressing. She suspected it was supposed to be comforting to see you wouldn't move far if you could no longer live alone. No one believed in planning ahead more than Mercy, but seeing that wing every day wouldn't work for her.

I'd rather have a heart attack while chopping wood.

Arleen was dreadfully thin and frail. Her hair was like a wispy dandelion going to seed. John appeared sturdier, but the tissues around his eyes were red, and age spots dotted his bare scalp. The hope in his gaze as he'd answered the door had driven a spike through Mercy's chest.

She wished she had good news for them.

Arleen had stared curiously at her as they made introductions. "You're one of the Kilpatrick girls."

"Yes."

"Pearl was good friends with our Jennifer. You look a lot like your mother did at your age."

"Pearl still speaks highly of Jennifer," Mercy answered, uncertain how to address the comment about her mother.

Truman took charge of the interview and Mercy was grateful. He was tactful and caring and sounded dedicated to helping the couple. Both parents hung on his every word. He was sincere, impressing Mercy. He wasn't a slick salesman. Truman was exactly what he'd told her he wanted to be: a guy in a position to help people.

Even if he couldn't tell the Sanderses who'd killed their daughter, he let them know it mattered to him. Mercy knew they'd spent years believing no one cared. It'd broken them. Truman offered the first comfort they'd had in ages.

She listened as Truman gently guided them through the few weeks before Jennifer was murdered. They learned Jennifer had been frantically searching to find a roommate, worried she'd have to move back home with her folks. The rent was simply too much for her to handle on her own.

"Was she only considering female roommates? Did she advertise for a roommate?" Mercy asked.

"She didn't advertise," said Arleen. "She was asking everyone in town for leads, but she'd *never* live with a male."

Mercy wondered if Jennifer would refuse to live with a man, imagining them knocking on her door after hearing the attractive woman was looking for a roommate.

"No special man in her life at that time, right?" asked Truman. Both he and Mercy knew this was true on the basis of reports and Mercy's talk with Pearl.

"Not that we knew of," said John.

"She would have told me if she was dating anyone," Arleen said firmly.

Because mothers and daughters share everything.

Mercy's lungs contracted at the thought of the mother she hadn't spoken with in fifteen years.

Arleen hasn't spoken with her daughter in the same amount of time. Look what it's done to her.

She wondered if her mother's eyes looked half as haunted as Arleen's.

I'm not dead. A big difference.

"Was Jennifer friends with Teresa Cooley?" Truman asked, and Mercy straightened a fraction, interested to hear the Sanderses' opinion of Teresa.

The couple looked at each other. "I don't remember that name, do you?" Arleen said to John. He shook his head. "Is she a suspect?" Arleen asked Truman.

"No. Just a woman who had a relationship with your daughter we're trying to understand. If you don't remember her, then their friendship must have been casual."

"I knew all of Jennifer's friends," Arleen stated.

Mercy wondered if Arleen truly believed that. "Did you notice anything missing from Jennifer's things after the murder? I know there was money and weapons missing. Did you discover anything later?"

The couple looked at each other, frowning as they tried to remember. "You said you couldn't find that photo of Jennifer in her prom dress," John finally prompted Arleen.

She turned back to the investigators. "That's right. Jennifer's prom photo was missing. She'd kept it on her dresser for years. It was a lovely picture. She told me she liked it because she looked skinny." She leaned forward to Mercy and said in a hushed voice, "She put on some weight after high school."

Mercy didn't know how to answer that and simply nodded.

"Who was her prom date?" asked Truman.

"She didn't have one. She and several girlfriends—your sister included—went in a group with some boys. I thought it was a good way to do it."

"The picture was of the whole group?" clarified Mercy.

Arleen nodded, staring off into the distance. "I remember your sister Pearl and Gwen Vargas were there, even though Gwen was younger. They allowed all high school grades to go to the prom, not just seniors. I can't remember any of the boys who went."

And Gwen Vargas had a photo album missing. I wonder if it included the same photo.

"Was anything else missing?" Truman asked. Mercy had felt his intensity increase when John mentioned the photo.

The couple gazed at each other again and finally shook their heads. "The prom photo could have simply gotten lost before she was killed," said Arleen. "Or maybe the frame broke or it got ruined somehow. I don't know why anyone would take it."

Truman and Mercy asked a few more questions. They simultaneously came to the conclusion that the Sanderses had provided all the information they could. They said their good-byes, gave more condolences, and left their cards behind.

Mercy checked her e-mail as they got in Truman's vehicle. "Eddie spent the evening talking to some of Enoch Finch's relatives. Remember how they cleaned out his house after his death? Eddie doesn't think he got any useful information. None of these relatives had spoken with Enoch in over six months."

"But they were quick to claim his belongings. Or sell them."

Mercy snorted. "In this e-mail, Eddie calls them scavengers."

"What did you think of the Sanderses?" Truman asked as he focused on the road.

"They make me sad. How awful to only have pictures of your daughter for memories. The missing prom picture was interesting, but like she said, it could have been destroyed and disposed of before the murder."

"My sister kept her prom picture for at least ten years," said Truman. "How about you?"

"I didn't go. I'm surprised Pearl got to go. Our parents kept a pretty tight handle on us girls."

"Not on your brothers?"

"No. They were *men* . . . able to defend themselves."

"That's old-fashioned."

"Tell me about it."

Silence filled the vehicle, pressing on Mercy's lungs, making her wish she were anywhere else than next to this overly observant man.

"That was a gorgeous view out at the lake today," said Truman. "It does me good to see sights like that. Makes me thankful for where I live."

The pressure on her chest vanished. "It was."

"We'll have to get up there again before you go back to Portland."

"No doubt we'll have to go up to the cave for some reason," Mercy replied, checking her phone again. They rode on in silence.

It wasn't until after Truman dropped her off that his words echoed in her head.

Was he referring to work when he said, "get up there again"?

She froze with one foot in the air as she changed into heavy-duty hiking boots.

Of course he was.

His simple statement haunted her for the next hour.

TWENTY-SEVEN

"Why is your sister in town?"

Levi's hand tightened on the coffee shop's phone as he glanced at Kaylie. She giggled as she chatted with a customer. "Why the fuck are you calling me?" he asked in a low voice. He immediately knew who it was, although the only conversation they'd exchanged in years was about what he wanted in his coffee.

"You know why. Now tell me . . . why is she here?"

"It's her job. She didn't request to be sent here. In fact, she's not happy about it."

"I heard she's nosing around in the old murders."

"I don't know anything about that," Levi lied. "The dead preppers are her assignment." Sweat started under his arms. *Why is the past being dug up now?*

"As long as our agreement still stands."

Levi paused. "It does."

"Good. I wouldn't want anything to happen to that pretty daughter of yours. She looks good in pink."

Levi choked back vomit as he stared at the back of Kaylie's pink sweater, her hair curling in long waves down her back. His gaze flew to

A Merciful Death

every corner of the coffee shop, acid rushing into his stomach, anger racing through his veins. *Where is he?* "Mercy knows nothing. And it will stay that way."

"I'll hold you to that." Levi slowly set down the phone, his fingers ice cold. He closed his eyes and lowered his head, his hands braced on the counter, trying to slow the pounding of his heart.

Hurt my daughter and I'll kill you myself. I won't give a fuck about prison.

TWENTY-EIGHT

Truman pulled over down the street from Sandy's Bed & Breakfast, where he could see Mercy's parked Tahoe.

Twenty minutes. I won't wait longer than that.

Mercy had been so distracted when he dropped her off, he'd had a feeling she wouldn't sit still in her room. Sure enough, ten minutes later Mercy emerged from the old house and dashed to her vehicle.

Determined, Truman started his own and followed her out of town. He didn't know what secrets the FBI agent had, but he would get some answers tonight. If she was holding back information that affected his uncle's murder case, he wanted to know about it.

In the morning I can ask her where she went.

So she can ask why I followed her?

He had a good excuse ready. He would simply say he'd been headed home after a quick stop at the police department when he saw her pull out and followed out of curiosity.

I'm going to feel really stupid if she's shacking up with someone.

It wasn't that; he knew it wasn't. She didn't give off the contented vibe of a woman in love.

Her vibe was edgy. On alert. Focused. Determined.

He wanted to know what made her tick. Because whatever it was, his interest constantly kept her in the forefront of his thoughts. He was spending more and more time wondering what she was doing when they weren't in the same room.

It was a huge risk to follow her. It could make her furious and destroy any trust between the two of them.

He nearly hit the brakes to turn around. He wanted her to trust him. Tonight's interview with the Sanderses had gone as smoothly as if they'd worked together for a decade. He wanted their easy partnership to continue.

She'll go back to Portland as soon as this is over.

The thought bothered him. Mercy gone, with no reason for her to come back. Hell. If he floored it, he could drive to Portland from Eagle's Nest in a few short hours. People had made relationships work over much longer distances.

I'm getting ahead of myself. He was working out the logistics of a long-distance relationship before he'd even expressed his interest to her. But something about Mercy Kilpatrick made him want to push forward.

What does she want? Had she considered the possibility of something between them the way he had a dozen times?

He could be totally off base.

But he'd seen her light blush as she tasted her coffee. *She knows.*

Her taillights flashed as she went around a curve. He followed, swearing she wouldn't lose him. Thick clouds blocked all light from the moon and stars, rendering him nearly invisible. No lights lit the rural country highways, and he kept his headlights off, feeling sleazy about the covert move. The only way she'd spot him was if an oncoming car's lights flashed over him. He prayed it wouldn't happen.

A half hour passed as she took several twisting turns through the forested acres. He inched closer, adrenaline making his nerves jangle as he tried to keep his distance and not lose her. The GPS in his dashboard had given up several minutes ago. According to it, he was driving where no roads existed. He had only a general idea of where he was.

He stuck with her until he saw her turn down a narrow unpaved road. Her Tahoe rocked as it maneuvered through ruts.

There's no way that leads to another road. Her final destination is down there.

He pulled over to the nearly nonexistent shoulder and paused. Should he go on foot? He'd seen evidence of a few homes within the last few miles, but not many. The road she'd picked had no visible signage or markers. He was stunned that she'd spotted it in the pitch dark.

He decided to go on foot, praying she hadn't gone far. He moved his Tahoe farther off the road, concerned someone would clip the vehicle in the dark. The SUV lurched into a shallow ditch, and he parked at a steep angle, shoving hard to open his door against gravity.

I should let someone know where I am.

I don't know where the fuck I am.

He set off down the dirt road, cursing at himself. Being reckless wasn't his thing. He thought things through before taking action, but for some reason his brain was slightly disconnected from his actions tonight.

His mother would call it testosterone poisoning.

Fifteen minutes later the forest parted and Truman entered a good-size clearing. He'd kept his flashlight covered with a glove, using the faintest hint of light to keep himself from tripping and falling on his face. Mercy's Tahoe was parked in front of a small A-frame house. Two thin cracks of light shone at the edges of a window, its shade keeping 99 percent of the glow inside.

Am I going to get shot?

He crouched down and listened for a few minutes. He could hear the soft rush of a small stream nearby, but no noise came from the house. He didn't see any other vehicles, but that didn't mean she was alone. He could see the faint outline of a large barn about fifty yards behind the house that could easily hide a few vehicles.

Now what? Go knock?

He doubted every decision he'd made in the last hour. He'd been stupid to spy on her and stupid to follow her. He'd sneaked through the woods on foot like a stalker. Hell, every move he'd made in the last hour had mimicked that of a stalker.

Go home.

But why was she here? Was this related to the cases?

He knew it wasn't a relative's home. He knew where all her family lived.

Stalker.

Possibly it was a good friend whom she'd turned to for comfort after a trying day. A *very* good friend. Images of a naked Mercy rolling in bed with some mountain man made his stomach twist.

A powerful light came on at the back of the house, and he jumped. It lit up the grounds behind the home all the way to the barn, but not to the front where he hid in the dark like a freak. A loud crack shattered the darkness and he ducked. He heard two faint thumps from the direction of the home and raised his head. The crack sounded again, but this time he held still.

Not a gunshot. He knew that sound.

He inched his way around the edge of the clearing, keeping to the safety of the pines. More cracks, thumps, and tearing noises sounded. He moved faster, confident of the origin of the noise. He was probably a good fifty yards from the house when he found a position that showed him the source of the sounds.

Mercy was chopping wood.

Kendra Elliot

She'd shed her coat and wore a tank top that showed every defined muscle in her shoulders as she swung the ax. Her hair was pulled back into a ponytail, and she'd changed into jeans and boots. She'd come prepared to work.

At eleven o'clock at night?

Who does that?

And she complains about not getting enough sleep. He wondered how many nights a week she fled to the forest.

Her ax jammed in a piece of wood and she maneuvered it from side to side. The piece split open and tumbled off the wide stump of a chopping block. She centered another piece and swung.

She had a singular focus. A drive. Truman wondered at the demons that drove her to chop wood in the middle of the night. Her family? Her background of prepping? Was she preparing for a disaster? He glanced at the home and barn again.

Away from everyone. A stream. Woods for hiding, but around the home it's cleared in case of forest fire.

She couldn't leave the prepping life behind.

This was her dirty little secret. Mercy Kilpatrick couldn't separate from the lifestyle. He didn't think she commuted to Portland from the location. She must stay here when she could and spend every minute prepping for a disaster.

He didn't know whether to feel sorry for her or to admire her.

He stepped out of the pitch black and walked until he was at the edge of the light thrown by the powerful bulb on the back of her house. He waited until she'd finished a swing.

"Mercy."

She spun toward him, her ax gripped like a weapon, ready to fight.

"It's Truman." He held perfectly still, knowing she could see his features.

Her chest heaved as she whirled away and buried her ax in the chopping block.

232

Truman wondered if she'd like to do that to his head.

"What are you doing here, Truman?" Her voice was steady as she turned to face him, but she was slightly out of breath. He took a few steps closer, locking his gaze with hers. Her eyes were defensive, her posture stiff. Anger radiated from her.

"Why did you follow me?"

"It wasn't intentional," he lied. "I was headed home after stopping at the police department and saw you leave Sandy's place."

"And wondered where I was going."

"I did. Especially since you'd implied that you were headed to bed. The farther you got away from town, the more curious I got."

Her forehead wrinkled. "Did you follow me out here on Monday night?"

"No."

She nodded, but her eyes didn't accept his answer.

"I didn't. This is the first night and it was purely a coincidence."

"You didn't follow me for nearly thirty miles on a coincidence."

"You're right. I know that sounds disturbing. Even I can see that," he admitted.

"That's stating it mildly. You *fucking followed me*. What did you expect to find?" Fury straightened her spine and shoulders.

"Not this," he told her. "I don't know what I expected. Something to do with the cases, I guess."

"No. This is *my* space and *my* time. I come here to be alone." She turned away and yanked her ax out of the stump with a quick downward jerk. "Go home, Truman."

"No wonder you're tired during the day. How late do you stay?"

"Until I'm done."

He looked around. "Are you ever done? Isn't this an ongoing thing? A lifestyle?" He said the last word cautiously.

She looked over her shoulder at him, her chin in a headstrong position he knew all too well. "So you think I'm crazy like your uncle."

"I didn't say that."

"Did you know that two percent of the American population grows food for the other ninety-eight percent? Did you ever stop to think what would happen if we suddenly lost our food distribution?"

He had. His uncle had preached the same thing. "No."

She opened her mouth and abruptly closed it, pressing her lips together. She was fighting to keep herself from launching into full lecture mode.

"Can you show me what you've done around your place?" he asked. He didn't want to get into an argument with her. He wanted to understand her better.

She stared at him in surprise.

"How often do you come here?" he asked softly. Her rigid body language had faded and he knew the next few minutes would determine if she opened up or sent him scrambling back down the road in the dark.

"Some weekends. All my vacation time."

"Being assigned to Eagle's Nest put you in a handy location to get some things done up here."

"Yes," she agreed. "I couldn't pass up the opportunity. Even if it meant coming at night."

"I understand." He really did.

The desire to sink her ax in Truman's skull had faded.

When she realized who'd said her name, she'd wanted to melt into the ground. Embarrassment, fright, and vulnerability had swamped her. She'd verbally lashed at him, hoping to drive him away. But he'd stood his ground.

Her ground. Her property and home.

Her second-biggest secret.

She'd felt like a wounded wild animal as he'd approached, but he'd come slowly, his voice kind and his gestures quiet to keep her from fleeing.

Truman's voice had a way of calming her. The same way he'd gentled the Sanderses earlier that evening. He'd spoken to her, and she suddenly didn't want to push him away. In fact, he'd asked about her work, and she wanted to show it to him.

She'd never shown anyone her hideout.

The only people who knew about it were the couple down the road and the man who'd sold it to her. It was her center of peace in her hectic life. It grounded her and kept her sane.

"I don't think you can understand," she said slowly. "You don't know what it's like to be raised as I was. From day one, preparing for a disaster has been hammered into my head. I can't get away from it. Even though I don't want to believe it can happen, I *must* have this spot ready in case it does."

"I heard it from my uncle," Truman said. "Not as much as you did, but enough to see the logic in his plans. I admired him for what he did, but he let it run his life. I don't think you do that."

"I don't," she agreed. "My place in Portland has a small supply, but this is where I put my big plans in motion."

"I'd like to see it."

"What for?" *If he sees the inside, he'll know too much about me.* It made her twitchy. She'd been on her own for too long.

"I want to see what you've done. Make me understand."

"Why?" she whispered. She had a sensation of standing at the edge of a giant sinkhole. She needed to step back, but she couldn't move. Truman moved closer, one of his hands held out as if he were approaching a skittish horse.

It was an apt analogy.

"Because I want to know more about you." He stopped walking. He was close enough for her to see the stubble on his jaw and the sincerity in his eyes.

"Are you handling me like the Sanders parents?" She held his gaze.

"I didn't handle them. I meant every word I said. And I mean it now. You make me want to know more."

He's telling the truth.

She broke eye contact. "I have a lot to do tonight."

"I'll help you get it done faster. Maybe you can get some decent sleep."

Her gaze met his again, and she knew she wasn't getting rid of him tonight. She was both relieved and disturbed by the thought.

"Show me the inside."

She nodded, unable to speak, worried she was about to burst into tears. She wanted him close *and* she wanted him gone, and her emotions were about to rip her in two.

Just accept it for tonight.

She turned away. "Follow me." She snatched a light sweater from the railing as she went up the few steps to the deck at the back of her small house. She struggled to get her arms in the twisted garment, and he grabbed the neck and a sleeve, allowing her to slip them in. His warm hands left a tingling spot where he'd touched her shoulder. The sensation persisted as she led him into her home.

"Welcome to my craziness," she said, waving an arm with a flourish.

Mercy's hideaway was small but well laid out. The two-story home had a wood stove in a giant rock fireplace, but the interior was cold. He wondered if she had another source of heat. Clearly she wouldn't bother to heat it when she popped in for only a few hours each night. The walls were wood but well insulated. He knew she'd made the home as weatherproof as possible by the change in the acoustics of their voices as they entered. It was incredibly solid. Blackout shades covered every window.

I'm impressed.

She caught him looking at the shades. "Keeps anyone from seeing the interior lights at night."

"You open them during the day, right?" The cabin had high ceilings and large windows, and a small loft for the second level. The sun and warmth streaming through the big windows must be heavenly.

"When I'm here. Most of the time I keep everything closed up. I don't want people looking in the windows when I'm not around."

"I doubt anyone can find this place."

"You never know."

"Do you have a security system?"

"I do. If it's breached, it sends me a notice on my phone. But there's not a lot I can do from Portland if a break-in happens. I have neighbors who watch things a bit, but they're elderly."

"Call me. I'll come check." He meant it.

She looked stunned. "Thank you."

He scowled at her surprise. "You have friends here. Why don't you use them?" The thought of her in the cabin alone rubbed him the wrong way. *No doubt she could handle an emergency much better than I could.*

She swallowed hard. "I didn't have friends here until this week," she whispered.

"Your family doesn't know about this place?"

"No."

"But isn't one of the cornerstones of prepping to surround yourself with people who can help you? And you offer help in return? My uncle didn't really subscribe to that belief; he tended to piss people off instead of make friends."

"Some people prefer to just be on their own. Rely on themselves. Your uncle might have been one of them."

"Are you?"

She paused. "I don't have much choice."

"You have every choice. There's a town full of people not far from here who are learning that you're mildly awesome. Family too, I believe." *Am I trying to convince her to spend more time here?*

"I won't divide them."

"Divide your family? How can you do that?"

"I nearly did it once. It's not hard." Her jaw snapped closed, and he knew she'd said more than she liked.

He stopped prodding and took another moment to look around her home. "Is that a sewing machine?" It looked like a simple small table with some drawers, but it had a cast-iron foot pedal that reminded him of his grandmother's machine. On top of it a laptop was open, a weather forecasting site on its screen.

"Yes. The machine hides inside the unit. Doesn't need power. You pump the treadle with your feet."

"A relic."

"A useful one."

"I feel like I've stepped into the nineteenth century. Do you have a washboard too?"

Her eyebrows slanted together. "No." Her voice was icy.

He enjoyed her snarky reaction, and his fascination was piqued. Mercy wasn't crazy; she was smart. And resourceful.

"Canning equipment?"

"Of course. And before you ask, I have solar panels, surgery instruments, a gravity-fed water system, and a greenhouse."

"Weapons?"

"Of course. Anything else you want to know?"

Yes. "I'm good for now. What do you need help with tonight?"

"I don't need help."

"Well, I want you coherent for tomorrow. What can I do to get you out of here faster?" He planted his feet and crossed his arms. If chopping wood was what it took to spend time with her, he'd do it.

She stiffened. A split second later she lunged for a light switch, killing the inside and outside lights, drowning them in darkness. He heard her dash across the room, and then a soft snap sounded.

Truman couldn't move. The low light from the laptop screen was too faint for him to maneuver by. "Mercy?"

"Shhhh." Her voice was closer than he'd expected and he saw her silhouette stop at the laptop. With a few keystrokes she pulled up four grainy camera views on the screen. He spotted her barn, the drive out front, and two views of her home. All sensations of being in the nineteenth century vanished.

"What happened?" he whispered.

"I heard a vehicle. I turned on the outdoor infrared floodlights."

Nice.

She enlarged the view of the drive, and he realized that during the seconds in the pitch dark she'd also picked up a rifle.

"See anything?" He removed his gun from his shoulder holster.

"Put your weapon away," she ordered.

"You first."

She was silent. Her figure was tense and alert as she watched the screen. "He backed up. I think he spotted the house and decided to back away."

"I didn't see anything. You saw a vehicle?"

"The quickest flash of a grille as I pulled up the driveway view."

"He might have turned down the wrong road. Or didn't expect to find a house here."

"Or he found exactly what he wanted," she said grimly. "I swear someone followed me Monday night. I managed to shake them. I didn't notice you tonight, but I was thinking about other things. I bet he followed you."

Unease crept into Truman's muscles at the thought that he'd led someone directly to Mercy's home. "Who would follow you? Why?"

Silence.

"The cases?" Truman asked.

"Maybe."

"What else?" he pressed. "Why would someone in this remote area be interested in an FBI agent from Portland?"

Maybe they're interested in the former teenager from Eagle's Nest.

"I think it's time you told me everything, Mercy."

She shuddered.

TWENTY-NINE

He'd nearly lost them.

Then he'd spotted the chief's Tahoe in a ditch. For a moment he'd thought the SUV had run off the road, but it'd simply stopped in an awkward parking spot.

He'd hesitated to drive down the lane, but he hadn't wanted to risk it on foot. Clearly the chief had gone in on foot, and he'd rather not meet the man in the dark. He felt safer in his vehicle. He waited for twenty minutes, debating his options, and then headed down the dirt road. He'd just spotted the haze of light behind an A-frame house when it suddenly went dark and he'd thrown his vehicle into reverse.

Steering awkwardly and stomping on the accelerator, he backed up the curving lane to the main road. Going after the police chief had worked in his favor. He'd been waiting to tail Mercy when he spotted the chief doing the same thing. When the chief had taken off after the agent with his lights off, he couldn't help but follow.

Why was the chief hiding from Mercy Kilpatrick?

Sweating, he put his truck into drive on the main road and floored it.

I know where she goes now. But why?

He didn't know and it didn't matter.

What mattered was that she'd returned. He'd spent fifteen years sliding around in the shadows, purposefully not rocking the boat, and biding his time, playing nice with everyone. He'd forced himself to stay out of trouble, having seen what it did to his friend. But now Mercy had stirred up all sorts of memories and ruined his plans for the weapons.

The weapons.

His golden ticket.

He hadn't planned on killing the preppers, but once he'd loaded up the weapons from the first, he'd realized that the old man would know exactly who had taken his bounty. Frustration had angered him; he hadn't thought his plan through clearly enough. Teachers and friends had always gotten on his case, claiming he couldn't see two hours into the future and needed to plan better.

But the preppers had been simple to fix. One shot. It'd been easy enough, and he'd known he'd have to do the same to cleanly steal the other weapons. The second time hadn't gone as expected, but he'd never experienced anything like the rush of adrenaline from the fight with Jefferson Biggs.

He'd felt invincible.

The rush happened again with Anders Beebe, but then he'd heard the car outside. Furious at being interrupted, he'd left the weapons behind.

And now it was irrelevant. The feds had taken his weapons. *All that work . . .*

Mercy would regret her interference. His fingers tapped on the steering wheel as he remembered a night fifteen years ago. He hadn't gotten what he truly wanted that night. Anger flushed his face as he thought about his stolen weapons.

Maybe it was time. He deserved it.

THIRTY

Truman insisted they immediately leave her cabin. She agreed, activated her security system, locked up, and drove him to his truck out on the road. They briefly argued about their next step. She wanted them to go to their respective places, but he put his foot down and insisted that their discussion wasn't done.

"I'm not waiting until tomorrow when you can brush it off and avoid me," he stated, holding her gaze.

Which had been her exact plan.

He plugged his address into her GPS and followed her out of the forest. After the drive she was surprised when she stopped in front of a tiny, newish home on a crowded street of identical homes in Eagle's Nest. Nothing about the house said that Truman Daly lived there. She'd expected something more manly and rugged. Not the cookie-cutter starter home.

"I rented it," he replied when she asked. "It felt safer than buying."

Had he believed the police chief job might not work out?

He told her to wait in the living room while he did a quick walk of the home and checked the small, fenced yard. While she waited, a gorgeous black cat strolled into the room and leaped onto the arm of the couch to stare at her. Her golden eyes fixed on Mercy, and the tip of her tail flicked as she waited for Mercy to explain herself.

By the time Truman returned, the cat was on her lap, looking extremely pleased. Truman raised a brow at the sight. "That's Simon."

"It's a female."

"I know. I let the little neighbor kid name her. She showed up about a week after I moved in. No one claimed her, so I let her stay."

A golden gaze slowly blinked at Mercy. *That's what he thinks.* Clearly the cat had chosen where she wanted to live.

"I need a beer. What can I get you?" he asked.

"I don't drink."

"Sure you do." He stared at her.

"Vodka and orange juice," she admitted. She could use some vitamin C, and she didn't want to argue with him. The next hour was going to be difficult enough.

He grabbed a chair from the dining set and set it directly in front of her, handing her the drink. He sat down with a sigh and took a long drink from his beer. The citrusy smell of hops wafted across the space between them and tickled her nose.

Exhaustion settled into every muscle and her brain, and she took the tiniest sip of her drink. It wasn't strong. Whatever Truman had in mind, it wasn't to get her drunk and make her spill her guts. His brown gaze fixed on her over the rim of his glass, and an unease stirred her stomach. *What does he want?*

"I have two questions," he said softly. "The first is why do you think someone would follow you, and the second is what happened fifteen years ago that made you leave town? I've looked. There are no police reports involving your family around that time. Little happened that year except for the murders of Jennifer Sanders and Gwen Vargas. But you've already said they were friends of your sister's, not yours."

She nodded and took another minuscule sip. "I don't think either question is any business of yours." *I won't tell him.*

His gaze narrowed. "It is if I think it's affecting your performance on this investigation. You're not getting enough sleep and it shows. You're consistently distracted, and I think you spend more time trying to avoid people in town than investigating."

She jerked and Simon launched from her lap, her claws skittering on the hardwood as she raced out of the room. "I take this investigation very seriously! I am *not* a slacker! I'm doing the best I can." Fury narrowed her vision. *How dare he?* "Who found those weapons today?"

"We did."

"Bullshit. I crawled on my belly into that space after leading you to the cave. If anyone is compromised on this case, it's you with your focus on your uncle. There've been three other victims, you know," she snapped. He didn't spend too much time focused on his uncle, but if he was going to poke her, she would strike back. "You walk around this town like you're the only person seeking justice. We're all working our asses off."

He sat very still. She'd found a wound. "I'm not on some noble crusade for justice," he said. "I want payback for my uncle. Someone out there thinks they're smarter than I am, and I'm going to prove them wrong. Very wrong."

The absolute evenness of his tone disturbed her. Truman Daly was fully in control, or else he was a split second away from snapping. She didn't know which.

"We both want the same thing," said Mercy.

"Then you need to come clean. Something hangs over your head. I see it emerge when you run into people from your past. But it doesn't happen with every person. Just some of them. Why does Joziah Bevins rattle you so bad?"

"There's a history there. Our families were at odds."

"Explain."

She shrugged. "Dad said he shot one of our cows."

Truman leaned back in his chair, surprise on his face. "A cow? That's it?" He blinked. "I mean, that's horrible, but that's not worth years—"

"It was done as a message to my parents. They'd refused to join the Bevinses' community. Again."

"Community? I don't under—"

"Remember how you said earlier that the preppers are often about community? And asked why I was preparing my cabin alone?"

"Yes."

"Some of those communities take themselves very seriously. They're practically micro-towns of specialists. They need doctors and vets and mechanics. They always have a very strong leader."

She saw the comprehension dawn.

"And people declare allegiance to the group?" he asked. "You promise to help a circle of people when disaster strikes? That's the history of the turbulence between your father and Joziah Bevins?"

"Yes. My father has a quiet draw. People trust him and want to be involved with him. Joziah is forceful and demands allegiance and then rules with an iron fist. My father didn't want anything to do with him."

"Your mother's a midwife," Truman stated. "Everyone in town swears by her."

"And my father is skilled with animals. Very important trades."

Truman scratched his head. "Okay. So now I think I get it, but what does that have to do with you leaving?"

"It's a long story."

"I've got all night—at least half the night is left. Start talking."

She wanted to tell him everything. No one had gotten under her skin the way Truman had. She *liked* him.

I like him a lot. More than I should.

Her secrets had festered in her heart and mind for too long. What was the risk?

Her job.

Her family. Levi's family.

Prison?

"You're shaking." Alarm and concern widened his eyes.

"You don't know what you're asking me." He was right; her legs shook as if she were freezing. With a trembling hand, she set her drink on the end table.

"Jesus Christ. How bad is it?"

"I could go to prison," she whispered, her mind spinning out of control. "My brother too. He has a daughter. I don't have anyone, so it's not that big of a deal—"

He leaned closer. "Are you hurting anyone by not talking about it?"

"I don't think so. Believe me, I've asked that a million times." *I'm so cold.* She zipped up her coat, suddenly wanting hot tea, hot chocolate, hot coffee. Something comforting.

He scooted his chair closer, set his beer next to her drink, and took her hands. His were incredibly warm, and she relaxed into the heat.

"Did you kill someone, Mercy?"

She held his gaze, but saw the giant bottomless pit near her feet. *Can I trust him?* She teetered on the edge for a long second and then took a step. "I think so."

He didn't blink. "Why do you only think so?"

"Because Levi shot too. We both did." *No turning back now.* Icy spasms shook her chest and flew down her arms to her hands. He clutched them tighter.

"Who did you shoot?"

"We don't know who it was. We didn't know him."

"Was he hurting you?" he asked carefully.

"Rose. He attacked Rose. And then me," she added softly.

"Then you were justified." He lowered his head and let out a sigh.

"But we hid him. We've hidden it for fifteen years. And didn't tell anyone. We can never tell anyone we killed him." She was babbling. All the words she'd buried deep inside flowed out of her.

"I'm not going to push you to tell anyone—wait a minute." He gripped her hands. "Was this the same person who killed Jennifer and Gwen?"

"We think so."

◆ ◆ ◆

Mercy looked ready to dissolve into a puddle of stressed-out-special-agent goo. Her hands felt like ice and quivered constantly. *What is it like to hide a huge secret for fifteen years?* He ached to take away her stress. Her secret didn't surprise him. The vulnerable glimpses he'd seen from her had warned him she was hiding something big.

She told me she killed someone. And it doesn't change how I feel about her.

Color him surprised.

Her shooting sounded justified to him, but had she stalled the other murder investigations by not coming forward? How would the FBI handle her old story? Had she messed up the current investigations by not revealing what she suspected about the old murders?

Truman doubted she would go to prison for murder, but she would be in life-altering hot water for a slew of other things.

What's my role here? Cop or friend?

He shoved the question aside for the moment, unwilling to explore the answer. Mercy had confided in him. She'd taken a huge risk and he'd pushed her to do it. Guilt was bitter on his tongue.

"Did your father know? Is that why you left?"

She shook her head, her gaze on the floor. "No one knows except Levi and Rose. And now you. We didn't tell my parents the whole truth. We told them that someone had tried to break in . . . and that Rose recognized his voice as someone she associated with the Bevins ranch, but she didn't know who. I wanted my father to confront Joziah and let Rose listen to his workers' voices because the man could have been the one who murdered Jennifer and Gwen. My father refused."

"Wait. You said the attacker was dead. Who would Rose be listening for?"

"There was a second man. She heard him speak that night and knew she'd heard him before but couldn't place the voice. He got away before Levi or I could see him. We heard his truck leave the property."

Two men?

"He left his friend behind? Dead?"

"Yes."

"He never came back searching or asking for his accomplice?"

"No. We expected him to, but it was like the dead man belonged to no one. No one came looking for him. No one was reported missing."

Mercy's story was growing odder by the moment. *Who doesn't report their missing friend?*

A murder accomplice.

"The man who escaped knew the other had been shot?"

"We heard the engine a few moments after the shots. I have no doubt the guns scared him off, but he had no way of knowing if his friend had been hit."

"So you're wrong that I'm the third person to know what happened. One other person knows—the guy you scared off."

Mercy nodded.

"Start from the beginning."

Mercy haltingly told him a story that made his hair stand on end. A break-in. An attack. First Rose and then herself. Gunfire. He'd seen the brutal pictures of Jennifer Sanders and Gwen Vargas. Mercy and Rose had come close to joining them.

Truman was silent as he absorbed the weight of what she'd told him. "Where's the dead man?" he finally asked.

She seemed to crumble. "Levi hid the body."

"Ah, jeez." Truman stood and paced in a circle, running his hands through his hair. Another crime she and Levi could be tried for. "Where the fuck did he hide it?"

She didn't say anything.

"Come on, Mercy."

Her ponytail fell over her shoulder as she shook her head, her eyes distant. "It's Levi's burden. I won't make it worse."

No body, no proof.

She's drawn the line. Her story is just a story unless a body supports it.

He sat back down and took her hands again. She tried to tug them away, but he held on. "I'm here to support you. We'll figure out a way through all this."

"No. *No one can know.*"

"I'm not going to tell anyone."

He wasn't. He'd decided on his role in her story.

It'd been a simple decision that surprised him. He should have mentally and emotionally struggled with the decision, but he'd looked in his heart and immediately known the answer.

Mercy was an honest person. If her shooting hadn't been justified, she would have admitted it.

Damned if I'll let her get hurt by this old crime.

It might be the wrong decision, but it was his decision and he'd stand by it.

People screw up, and she and Levi were guilty of some bad choices, but no one could deny that they had been within their rights to fire, since Mercy and Rose had been attacked.

Have I violated my own ethics?

He'd crossed a line he'd never thought he'd cross. As a member of law enforcement, he had a duty to report that he knew of a death and cover-up. As a decent member of the human race, he had the same obligation. But at the moment it seemed insignificant in light of the stress of the woman in front of him.

Can I live with my decision?

Definitely.

"Your father didn't want to rock the boat any further with Joziah Bevins? Is that why he refused to talk to him?"

Mercy nodded as if her head weighed fifty pounds. "When I pointed out that the person who tried to break in might have murdered those other girls, he brushed it aside. I told him we were putting other women at risk by not looking into what we suspected. When he refused again, I knew I couldn't live under his roof anymore."

"What was his reasoning?" Truman had a hunch about her father's attitude.

"He said other women weren't our responsibility. We only focus on our own."

His hunch was right.

"That didn't sit well with you?"

The sour look she gave pleased him. It was the first sign of the old Mercy.

"I guess it's a philosophical difference." She shrugged. "If you see a nail in the road, you pick it up so it won't lodge in someone else's tire, right? Why on earth would you not do something about a possible murderer?"

"You were eighteen, right? And Levi was even older. You could have gone to the police," he pointed out. "You didn't need to wait for your father."

She laughed. "We didn't view the police as an authority back then. Police were the guys who handed out traffic tickets. The authority and enforcement in town was Joziah Bevins. If we wanted answers and action, Joziah is who we'd talk to."

Truman started to contradict her and then closed his mouth. How many times had he heard the mayor and even Ina suggest they get input from Joziah Bevins before taking a new step? Truman had assumed it was because the man sat on the town council. Not because everyone was scared shitless of him.

Has Joziah influenced some of my decisions?

No. He could say that with confidence. He hadn't crossed swords with Joziah Bevins. Yet.

I'm more of an outsider than I realized. No one had told him about Joziah. Was he expected to fall in line with the rest of the community? They'd be in for a surprise. Truman had no problem standing up for what he thought was right.

Does Mike know how powerful his father is?

Of course he does. It must be one of the reasons he wants to leave. "You think the second man at your house that night was one of Joziah's men."

A reluctant nod. "Exactly. Rose wasn't positive about where she'd heard his voice before. It wasn't enough for Levi and me to confront Bevins on our own. But our father could have done it."

"Your father didn't want anything to do with it."

"And then Levi took his side," Mercy said bitterly. "There's a strong patriarchal core in my family. Levi stood against me when I threatened to go tell on my own. My father said I'd destroy the family if I went to Joziah with accusations of a possible attacker working on his ranch. And my father was right. Every male in my family begged me to let it go and then turned their backs on me when I said I couldn't. And the women stuck with them."

"You couldn't see your family every day and forget about it."

"No. And I couldn't live with such outdated rules. Levi may have been part of the 'protect our wimminfolk' philosophy back then, but now he's over it, thank goodness. I can't say the same for Owen. He still won't talk to me. I think my sisters have gotten past most of it."

"Essentially your father's refusal to do something that might have protected other women from being killed was the last straw for you," Truman said. "But Mercy, if you felt so strongly, why didn't you go report it yourself?" he asked again.

"I was also afraid what I said would reveal that a man had died. I didn't want the police to come investigate a possible attack and discover evidence that Levi and I had shot someone," she whispered.

"Understandable. But hard to live with."

"Yes. I was ashamed when I left town, and I watched the news for months afterward, expecting to hear of more women murdered, but nothing happened, and I was relieved. Maybe the death of the first attacker was enough to stop all the attacks."

"That's possible," said Truman.

"I'd been toying with the idea of leaving Eagle's Nest for a while. After the attacks my father cracked down on me, told me to forget any plans for college. He told me to find a husband and even made a few suggestions of men he thought would take good care of me."

Truman snorted. *If there ever was a woman who didn't need taking care of . . .*

"Right?" Her mouth curved up on one side.

"Didn't your father know you at all?"

"I'm not the same person I was back then. I was a good girl for a long time. I did what they wanted and followed their rules. But then I started to see what was outside of the tight circle I was raised in. I wanted to make my own decisions."

"Leads you to hell every time."

"My family feared so."

"Are you sorry you told me?" Truman asked. Guilt still weighed on him for pressuring her to bare her secret.

She considered him for a long moment. "No. I feel relieved."

"You think the second person who was at your attack might be the one who followed you—possibly twice this week."

Her shoulders tensed again. "It's a possibility, but it seems like a slim one. On the other hand, I don't have any enemies in town that I know of. But I can't imagine that someone involved in those murders would stick around Eagle's Nest for fifteen years."

"It's a town that few people seem to leave." Truman glanced at the clock on the fireplace mantel. It was nearly two a.m. "Crap. I need to get up in three hours."

Mercy didn't move. He'd expected her to make a beeline for the door, but he noticed her green eyes were calm for the first time in several hours. "I don't want to go back to my room right now . . . ," she said slowly. "I can't be alone. Do you care if I sleep on your couch for a few hours?"

His mind shot to several places, but he heard himself say, "No problem. It makes sense considering you might have been followed tonight—by someone other than me. You sure that's what you want?"

She relaxed and smiled. "Yes. Give me a blanket and I'll be asleep in two minutes."

He got her a blanket and showed her the guest bath. If he'd purchased a bed for his guest room, she could have slept there. But it held a treadmill and a weight bench. The couch was all he had to offer.

He handed her a pillow. "Need anything else?"

"No. I'm so tired, I could sleep standing up. I guess confession is exhausting."

"You've been carrying that around for a long time by yourself." He couldn't imagine.

"I got used to it, but it's been worse since I came back here. There are visual reminders everywhere. Back in Portland, I can forget. Mostly."

He told her good night.

As he crawled into his own bed minutes later, he wondered if he'd be able to sleep knowing Mercy Kilpatrick was asleep under his roof. He spent ten minutes reviewing his day and thinking on her dilemma.

She'd dumped a lot of information on him in the last few hours, and none of it changed his perspective of her. Mercy was still a fiercely independent woman and an experienced, sharp agent. If anything, he admired her more.

He wanted to help her; it was what he did. But his goal felt different this time. It wasn't solely about helping her; he had an additional motive.

He wanted to be with her.

THIRTY-ONE

"What the hell?" Mercy circled her vehicle again. Sure enough. All four tires were flat.

Who?

Truman stepped out of his house and locked the door, and she glanced up in time to see a big smile on his face. He'd been grinning since he'd discovered her in his kitchen with a spoon in his peanut butter. She'd woken up starving.

"What the fuck?" He came to a halt and his grin vanished as his gaze went from her face to her tires. "All of them?" he asked in a grim tone.

"Yep. Cameras?"

"No." He glanced across the street. "None of my neighbors have them either."

She sighed.

"I'll drive you to the police station and call the garage. He'll get you fixed up in no time."

Mercy pressed the palms of her hands against her eyes. "How am I going to explain this?"

"Why do you have to explain flat tires? It's clearly vandalism."

She removed her hands and glared at him.

"Oh." His grin came back. "This does look bad."

He was enjoying her discomfort too much. Her phone vibrated with a text, and she pulled it out of her pocket. Eddie.

Where are you?

It'd begun. She replied that she was at the Eagle's Nest police station. "Let's go," she told Truman. "I just told Eddie I'm already at the station. Maybe he won't notice that my vehicle isn't."

She was silent on the short ride to the police station, her brain spinning as she tried to come up with a way to explain why her vehicle was at Truman's. She wasn't ready to tell anyone about her cabin or the attack fifteen years ago, so she couldn't tell anyone that she'd been followed and had stayed at Truman's because it'd been a draining day of confession.

"You're overthinking," Truman stated, keeping his gaze on the road to town.

"I'm not ready to blab the private parts of my life to everyone," Mercy admitted. "You were the first, and I think telling one person is enough for this month. Probably enough for the year."

"Who do you think slashed your tires?"

"Two possibilities: it was random or it was deliberate. If it was deliberate, my money is on whoever was at the cabin last night. He must have seen your department vehicle parked out on the main road. Checking out your house seems a logical thing to do."

She saw a muscle in his jaw twitch and his eyebrows lower.

"I don't like the thought of that," he mumbled.

"You're not the only one."

"I wonder if they checked Sandy's Bed & Breakfast first. And when they saw your vehicle wasn't there, they went to my house."

"Or it was random. High school jerks or someone who simply has a problem with law enforcement."

He looked at her. His gaze said he didn't believe it had been random. Her gut didn't believe it either.

"Someone's definitely following you," he said. "But to me, the slashed tires say he's petty and immature. Angry. Probably has a bad temper. He strikes out at your vehicle instead of you."

"Or he's scared of me," Mercy added.

"What do you mean?"

"Something I've done has scared him and he's trying to stop me. Why would someone be afraid of *me*? The only thing I can come up with is that we're possibly getting close to uncovering who killed your uncle and the other preppers."

"Or they fear that you saw them fifteen years ago."

"I would have gone to the police back then if I'd known *exactly* who it was," she stated.

"Something you've done recently has lit a fire under someone."

"We did find a big cache of weapons yesterday," she added. "Maybe we're closer than we realize."

He drove in silence for a moment. "Are you nervous?"

Disbelief filled her. "Because someone slashed my tires? Hell no. I'm *pissed*."

"Be cautious."

"I'm always careful."

"I don't know how the security is at Sandy's," Truman added.

"She's got heavy doors and good locks. Believe me, I checked."

They parked behind the station. "Cooley's here," Truman said in surprise. "I guess he meant immediately when he said he'd review the files from the old murders."

Mercy was relieved they'd beaten Eddie to the station. She wasn't ready to answer his questions. Inside she met Ben Cooley, a big, jolly man with a perpetual smile, and she couldn't help but like him. Truman lit up when he saw the officer, and vigorously shook his hand.

"You look good with a tan, Ben."

"I was bored out of my mind." He winked at Mercy. "I can't stand sitting in a beach chair all day or standing in museums staring at art. Give my brain something to do, please."

She understood. She could sit still for only a short time too.

Her phone rang, and she excused herself from the two men. Her caller was Natasha Lockhart, who came directly to the point.

"Anders Beebe had Rohypnol in his system. Same as the other three murdered men."

Mercy wasn't surprised.

"I heard Jefferson Biggs still had it in his stomach. Was Anders like that?"

"No. It was well into his system. I'd estimate he'd taken it within twelve hours."

So he possibly had an evening visitor who drugged him.

But when that visitor returned, Anders was up and getting ready for his early day. Mercy wondered how strongly the drug had affected him. She knew he'd managed to get dressed, make coffee, and fire at the intruder. Maybe he hadn't gotten as strong a dose as the other victims.

The ME didn't have any other new information for her, and they ended the call.

She joined Truman and Ben and discovered Lucas had shown up, along with Eddie. They both had coffee in their hands and appeared to have walked over from her brother's shop together. She updated them on Natasha's call.

"I got a call from Darby Cowan this morning," Eddie told her and Truman. "All the *registered* weapons that were missing from our preppers' homes were in that bunch you found yesterday. Along with a lot of weapons that have been reported stolen over the years."

Truman grinned and held up a palm to Mercy. She slapped it. "Yes!" she said. "I knew it."

"It's an amazing find," said Eddie. "The Bend office is all over the weapons. Hopefully they can find some consistent fingerprints on them. That'll help us nail someone."

"I have no idea what you're talking about," Ben Cooley said, looking from one agent to the other. Truman brought him up to date. "Well, I'll be damned," said Ben. "I haven't made that hike in a few decades. Someone had to be really committed to haul all those weapons up there."

Mercy agreed. "What about the stolen weapons from the fifteen-year-old cases?"

"Not there," said Eddie.

Mercy twisted her lips, wishing they'd been included. She liked things to fit neatly. But when cases were fifteen years apart, there were going to be differences.

"I was able to look through the Sanders and Vargas case files this morning," said Ben. "I'm really sorry, but I don't have anything to add. The notes were as I remembered, and they didn't trigger any memories that weren't already written down."

Truman's shoulders slumped a bit, and he slapped Ben on the back. "I appreciate you taking a look."

"Ben, do you have a daughter named Teresa?" Mercy asked bluntly.

His thick white brows rose. "I do. How'd you know that?"

"Pearl Kilpatrick is my sister," Mercy said. "I think she went to high school with Teresa. Jennifer Sanders was Pearl's best friend."

He nodded thoughtfully, studying Mercy. "Could be."

"Did Teresa know Jennifer or Gwen very well?"

Ben nodded. "I remember she was shook up real good when they died."

"Do you think she'd agree to be interviewed to get some insight into the girls' lives back then?"

Truman's lips twitched at her tactful, nonthreatening way of suggesting they interview Teresa.

The old cop shoved his hands in his pockets. "Well, that might help, but you'll have to do it by phone. She's got a one-month-old baby, and they live in Florida now."

That certainly crosses out any involvement from Teresa in the current crimes. But not in the old.

"We'll keep it in mind," she said with a smile. "Thanks for the help."

"Anytime." Ben looked to Truman and said in a lower voice, "What's this I hear about Joziah's health?"

Mercy's ears perked up. She and Truman exchanged a look.

"I haven't heard anything, Ben. What did you hear?"

Ben looked flustered. "Now, I don't hold with rumors, but I heard it from my wife who heard it from Ina's son that Joziah's cancer is back something fierce."

Truman winced. "I'm sorry to hear that, but let's not spread that around until we hear it from Joziah himself."

"They're saying Mike doesn't want to take over the business." Clearly Ben wasn't done with not spreading rumors.

"Mike might have his own plans for his life," said Truman.

"Joziah's death would create a giant hole in this community," Ben continued.

"I agree."

Mercy's brain spun. If Mike didn't want to take over the business, did that mean Joziah's community of preppers would be without a leader? Or would someone step up to fill the void?

Or was she getting caught up in gossip and rumor that had no basis in fact?

"Hey, boss?" Lucas called from his desk. "Tom from the garage says he's at your house. He's loaded Mercy's Tahoe up on his truck and he's taking it to the shop right now."

Every set of eyes in the office looked at Mercy.

She met Eddie's curious gaze. "It's not what you're thinking."

"I'm just wondering what happened to your truck," answered Eddie. A devilish light came into his eyes.

"Flat tire."

Eddie grinned at Truman. "Her tire went flat at your place?"

"It did. All four of them, actually."

"What?" Ben and Eddie spoke together.

Mercy threw up her hands. "You tell them," she ordered Truman as she marched to the small room he'd loaned to her and Eddie.

Eddie had silently turned to Truman for an explanation after Lucas made his announcement about Mercy's Tahoe.

He'd explained Mercy had stayed at his house after late working hours and exhaustion on her part. Without being specific, he said she'd suspected someone had been following her. He could tell Eddie knew he was holding back, but the FBI agent wouldn't press with questions in front of Ben and Lucas.

Truman had later told her that the other men knew her virtue was still intact, and he'd received a sour look in return.

Four hours later Mercy's restlessness was driving Truman crazy.

They'd been poring over the files of the four recent murders and occasionally dipping into the files of the women when something caught their eye. So far he felt as if they'd been spinning their wheels. Mercy was quiet but kept tapping her fingers, and he'd noticed the small half-moons her nails had left in her palms from clenching her fists.

He understood. They both felt as if they were incredibly close to their killer, and that the answer was right in front of them but they couldn't see it.

Mercy didn't look like a woman who'd slept in unexpected quarters last night. She looked refreshed and ready to work. He hadn't been surprised when she grabbed a duffel bag containing clean clothes from her Tahoe last night. The woman was always prepared.

He liked that. He liked a lot of things about Mercy Kilpatrick.

Tell her.

He couldn't. It would break every professional code he knew. He'd wanted to say something last night in his house, but it seemed wrong to bring it up when she was thoroughly rattled. He'd have to stick it out until this case was over.

Then she'll leave.

Maybe she'll work at the Bend office.

In his mind she was packing up, transferring jobs, and moving to Bend because he was interested in her.

And he hadn't said a word.

Idiot.

He slammed Enoch Finch's notebook shut. Mercy jumped and did a double take at the expression on his face, and he wondered what she saw. Determination? Infatuation?

"What is it?" She sat straight in her chair, her hands immobile on the papers she'd been flipping through. "Is everything okay?" Concern flooded her gaze.

Apparently I look sick, not determined.

He looked into her green eyes and chickened out. "We need to step away for an hour. It's lunchtime and I've read the same page three times and still can't tell you what it said."

"I can always eat."

"Let's go. I need a change of scenery."

Thirty minutes later Truman pulled into an angled parking space in front of a restaurant in Bend's Old Mill District. The area was beautiful. Shops, restaurants, clean walkways, and footbridges over the Deschutes River. The district had been overhauled during the last few decades to provide a heart to the city and charm the tourists. Two women jogged by with strollers, couples roamed with cups of coffee, and Truman spotted exactly what he'd been craving. An outdoor table with a view of the water, right next to a heat lamp. The sky was clear blue, but there was a chill in the air. Mercy had protested when they drove out of Eagle's Nest for food, but he'd noticed she relaxed into her seat and focused on the sights as he drove.

She'd gasped when he pulled into the Old Mill District. "This has completely changed since I left. It wasn't like this at all."

"It's one of my favorite places," Truman admitted. Even though it was geared toward tourists with the nearby hotels, wine tasting, and trendy shops, he felt his stress unwind whenever he visited. He wanted that for Mercy.

Her smile indicated he was on the right track.

They got a table on the patio and ordered food and coffee. She slipped on her sunglasses, leaned back in her chair, and turned her face to the sun. They sat in companionable silence for a few minutes, and he wished he could order a beer. The stress of their cases vanished, and he felt like a normal human without any responsibilities. The rain from the beginning of the week was a faint memory, and the latest forecast was full of sun for the next two weeks. As it should be. He was happy.

"Better?" he asked.

"Absolutely."

"I was going a bit crazy in that small room."

Mercy nodded. "I get sucked in. When I'm on a case, I feel like any moment I'm not working on it is wasted time. But I know everyone works better when they step away for a break."

"And you're not getting enough sleep."

She lifted a shoulder. "I sleep." The waiter set their food down and vanished.

Truman attacked his burger.

"Do you think about when this case is finished?" he asked a few minutes later.

She looked down at her salad and moved her sunglasses to the top of her head. "All the time. I want to get it solved."

He scooted his chair forward an inch. "That's not what I mean."

Her green gaze met his. He was lost in their color and her thick black lashes.

The sight stole his breath.

"What do you mean?" She wouldn't make it easy on him.

"I want to ask you out when this is done." Blunt.

She went perfectly still, her gaze still locked on his. "That's not appropriate," she stated.

"I don't see a problem once we're done."

The conversations of the people on the river footpath suddenly seemed very loud.

"I live in Portland," she finally said, looking away.

"So?"

Her gaze flew back to his. "You don't see that as a problem?"

"Sure it's a hurdle. But if that's the first thing you're bringing up, I take it you don't have an objection. I'm trying to find out if you're willing to try this, Mercy. Can I get a straight answer so I can start sleeping better at night?"

Wide eyes looked at him. "You're serious."

"Damned right. You're not seeing anyone, are you?"

"No."

"Good." He leaned forward the slightest bit. "You make me slightly crazy, Mercy. I don't know what it is, but I find I want more of it. Let's get this damned case wrapped up so I can take you out for a good steak dinner."

She glanced at his burger and her salad. "Okay." She blinked. "But—"

"No buts. We'll address any problems as they come. We won't know if we don't try." Something about her had become very necessary to him over the last few days, and he didn't want it to end. A vein in her neck pulsed, and he fought the urge to gently touch it. *Not yet.* He had no idea what he needed, but he knew he couldn't let her simply walk out of his life after closing the case.

"You don't care that I've killed someone and covered it up." Her eyes were cautious.

Is this a test?

"You've never asked me if I've killed anyone."

Compassion filled her face. She didn't speak.

"You aren't the only one who carries a burden," he said quietly.

"You're right. I'm sorry."

"There's nothing to be sorry about. I understand how overwhelming your own problems can be, but hearing that other people have baggage sometimes makes yours a little easier to bear. You're not alone, Mercy. And I'm definitely not perfect."

"I don't know how to do this," she said slowly.

"Then we'll both figure it out as we go along."

"I haven't dated in ages," she admitted. "It's incredibly hard with my job. Men hear what I do and they immediately start acting odd."

"I think it takes someone in law enforcement to understand."

"They're hard to date because of their egos." Her lips twisted.

"Understandable. I think we're both pretty low on the ego scale. So do you accept my offer of dinner?"

Her smile widened. "I do. Will that be here or in Portland?"

A weight lifted from his chest.

His phone rang. Lucas. He tried to ignore it, but Mercy's phone started to ring at the same time. Dread settled over him, and concern flooded her face. "It's Eddie," she said.

Holding her gaze, they both answered their phones. "Someone broke into the Kilpatricks'," Lucas yelled through Truman's phone. "Their daughter Rose is missing."

Her phone at her ear, Mercy's face turned white as she listened to Eddie.

THIRTY-TWO

Her heart racing, Mercy jumped out of Truman's truck and jogged up the driveway to her parents' house.

Déjà vu.

Three days ago she'd approached this house in trepidation, nervous about seeing a sister she hadn't spoken with in fifteen years. Now she was racked with fear for her sister's life. Royce and Eddie had arrived at the home moments before and were talking with her parents. Eddie had an arm around her mother.

Her mother's hair was shot with gray, but she still wore most of it pulled back in a single wide barrette at the back of her head. Nostalgia stabbed Mercy in the heart as she recognized her mother's ancient sweatshirt, and she had an overwhelming need to be the one with an arm around her. Her father's shoulders were stooped, but his head was up in an intractable pose she knew too well.

She met Eddie's gaze, which was full of sympathy and concern, as everyone turned to see who approached.

Mercy's steps slowed and she held her breath, her gaze skimming from face to face.

Will they shut me out?

I can't take the rejection right now.

Her mother's mouth dropped open, and she stepped out from under Eddie's arm. Mercy's vision tunneled on her mother's green eyes, and she walked straight into her open arms.

Acceptance.

Everything was familiar. Same shape, same smell, same embrace. Mercy closed her eyes, pushing aside all thoughts.

"We'll find her, Mom."

Her mother pulled back from their embrace and placed her hands on Mercy's cheeks as tears streamed down her own. Her face had aged. More wrinkles, more folds, a new softness. "I'm so glad to see you, Mercy."

Words Mercy would never forget.

She touched her forehead to her mother's, remembering how her mother had done it each morning before she left for school. Her mother hugged her again.

Truman looked pleased and raised one eyebrow at her.

She nodded at him. All was good. At this split second in time all was good.

Rose.

She moved back, gripping her mother's shoulders. "What happened, Mom?"

Her mother sucked in a deep, wavering breath, but her father answered first. "We just got home. The front door was open, and I can tell there was a struggle in the kitchen."

"There's blood on the kitchen floor," her mother whispered. "Broken glass, a mess everywhere." Her face crumpled. "She's gone. Her phone's on the kitchen counter. She'd never go anywhere without her phone."

Mercy looked at her father. He hadn't made a move toward her, and she stood just as still.

"Dad."

He nodded. "Mercy." His eyebrows were low, his eyes ice cold.

Is that it?

Strengthened by her mother's embrace, Mercy felt her father's rejection roll off her shoulders. *I can handle him.*

"We'd like to take a look in the house," Truman said, breaking the silence.

"Who's been inside?" Mercy asked her mother.

"Just us. We didn't touch anything. As soon as we saw the open door, we knew something was wrong. And when we went in . . ."

"Did you see any vehicles leaving as you arrived? Anything unusual left behind?" Royce asked.

Her mother's hands wouldn't hold still. She touched her bag, her belt, and her sleeves as she looked to her husband, who shook his head. "We didn't notice anything."

"Let's take a look." Truman handed booties and gloves to everyone. As she slipped them on, Mercy studied the heavy door and its multiple locks. Nothing was busted or bent. Rose must have left the door unlocked even though she was home alone. Mercy knew a lot of rural home owners didn't lock their doors, but her father had insisted they keep it locked. Especially after the murders of Jennifer and Gwen.

Mistake number one.

Or did you open it to someone you knew?

The house appeared pristine except for the kitchen. Russet potatoes were strewn about the floor. Some peeled, some not. A glass bowl lay in shatters among the potatoes. Mercy glanced in the sink, where peelings covered the bottom. A vegetable peeler was abandoned in the brown mess.

How many times did I peel potatoes in this kitchen?

She glanced at her parents, who'd stayed out of the way of the officers, and was pleased to see her father holding her mother's hand.

Some good things haven't changed.

Taking care where she stepped, she walked the tile floor. Smears of blood showed where a struggle had occurred. She squatted to get a closer look and spotted a small paring knife on the floor nearly under the stove. She pointed and Royce nodded, aiming his camera at the knife. The officer had been taking photos since they entered, and Mercy couldn't find fault with his thoroughness.

The blood smears led toward the front of the house, but quickly vanished, giving no clue where the bleeder had gone. Mercy wandered down the hall, using her small flashlight to study the floor and walls, searching for more blood. She shone her light in the powder room near the front door and froze as her heart fell through the floor. "Mom?"

Her mother appeared with Truman, Eddie, and her father right behind her.

"Was the bathroom mirror already broken?"

Her mother automatically reached to flip on the switch, but Mercy grabbed her hand. "Don't touch." Mercy stepped back so her mother could see clearly into the room and aimed her flashlight. A small empty frame hung over a sink filled with mirror shards.

"*Noooo.* Rose!"

Mercy grabbed her mother's arm as her knees buckled. Her father pushed his way into the small powder room, took his wife in his arms, and clenched his jaw as he silently stared at the mess in the sink.

They remembered.

Truman swore under his breath. "We need to check the grounds of the ranch. *Royce?*" The other officer appeared. "Call Lucas. We need more help out here. Tell him to contact Jeff Garrison at the Bend FBI office and tell him we've got a case related to the prepper murders."

An hour later, a search of the ranch hadn't revealed Rose.

Nausea had pressed at the back of Mercy's throat since she'd arrived at the house, and twice Truman had asked if she needed to leave. When she'd first studied the blood in the kitchen, the thought that Rose had been taken by the prepper killer had tried to swamp her brain; she'd set it aside, wanting proof. Once she saw the broken mirror, reality had swept in and drowned her doubts.

He has her.

Who is he?

He'd followed Mercy to her cabin. At least twice, maybe more. He'd slashed her tires. Why?

She had no proof, but she was capable of putting two and two together. But *why Rose?*

Truman had rapidly pulled together the investigative team. Deschutes County had sent some deputies to walk the entire property, and Jeff from the Bend office had arrived with another agent.

They weren't short on help.

Mercy sat with her parents in her father's study. The furniture had been rearranged and the rug had been replaced since the night she and Rose were assaulted, but she still felt echoes of the attack. Or maybe they were fresh from today.

"Has anyone been hanging around the ranch?" she asked her parents. *Focus on asking the right questions.*

She couldn't relax while sitting across from her parents. Emotions boiled and cooled inside her.

Concentrate.

"No one new," answered her father. "We have a lot of people come and go, but no one unexpected."

"Can you write up a list of everyone who's been here in the past week, Karl?" Truman asked her father.

He nodded and pulled a sheet of paper from a pile on his desk, then started his list.

"Has Rose complained of anything unusual?" Mercy asked. "Has she felt like she's been watched?"

She felt Truman's gaze on her.

Her parents exchanged a glance and shook their heads. "She did ask me to take her over to the Bevinses' ranch on Wednesday. I thought that was odd," Karl added.

"What did she do there?" Tension climbed up Mercy's spine.

"Nothing. I refused to take her," he stated, a familiar inflexible look in his eyes. "She wanted to talk to some of the hands about putting their kids in her preschool. I told her I wouldn't drive her to go begging on *his* property."

Deborah Kilpatrick touched her husband's leg. "It wasn't begging. She was genuinely concerned that they get a boost before kindergarten like the other children around here."

Sounds like Rose. But why now?

"So she didn't go," Mercy repeated.

Deborah looked at her lap.

"Mom?"

She cast a quick glance at her husband. "I didn't take her, but I know she went over there on Thursday."

Mercy hated the small ducking action of her mother's head as she looked at her husband. "Who took her?" Mercy asked.

Deborah looked straight at her. "David Aguirre. He's the pastor of our church, where Rose teaches preschool."

Karl blew out a breath and folded his arms. His wife ignored him.

Truman tapped Mercy on the shoulder. "Can I talk to you outside?"

She nodded and followed. Truman closed the den door and led her to stand on the porch. County deputies were still working the scene under Eddie and Jeff's directions.

"You think Rose went to the Bevins ranch because of your conversation Tuesday night?" Truman asked in a low voice.

"I do. I think she was trying to listen for the second voice from that night."

"Do you think she found him?"

"*Something* happened." Mercy gestured at the inside of the home.

"Okay. I know David Aguirre pretty well. I'm going to head to his place and ask about Rose's behavior at the ranch and see if he knows exactly who she talked to. I'll let you know what I hear." He gave her arm a parting squeeze and a we'll-find-her smile.

Mercy watched him jog down the steps of her parents' home, placing his hat on his head, an unfamiliar longing in her chest.

Once all this is over . . .

Oh, Rose. Did I get you in trouble?

She walked back inside and put her hand on the doorknob to the den, keenly feeling Truman's absence. She'd grown used to having him beside her. Now she had to face her parents on her own. Crying sounded from the den, and she pushed open the door, Truman immediately gone from her thoughts. Her mother was in tears, her father angry.

All her life she'd known her father would never strike her mother. He might be old-fashioned about some things, but he'd taught her brothers that the moment a man strikes a woman, he stops being a man.

Her mother was frightened for Rose.

"She's my baby," she said to Mercy with a tear-filled face. "I know she's not the youngest, but I knew she'd always be with us. Now she's gone." A sucking breath. "Possibly with a killer. Oh, Karl! What's happening to her right now?"

Her father directed his anger at Mercy. "You stirred this up. This is *your fault.* We'd lived in calm for fifteen years since you left and the first week you're back, Rose goes running off with old ideas. We'd convinced her to *let it go! What did you say to her?* Because you might have gotten her killed!"

Mercy bit her tongue and felt her hands curl into fists.

Reply as a professional, not as their daughter.

"I need to know what she's said about anyone at the Bevins ranch recently." She hated the high pitch of her voice.

"She doesn't associate with anyone over there!" her father roared. "None of us do!"

"I saw Levi talking with a whole crew from there in his coffee shop," Mercy snapped. "And Joziah Bevins greeted me pleasantly this week. You're holding a one-sided grudge!"

"I never threatened his family," her father hissed. "And his daughter isn't *missing!*"

Mercy froze. "When did Joziah threaten our family?"

Karl looked away. "Ages ago."

"What did he say?" she asked sharply.

Her mother's hand was pressed against her mouth as her gaze darted between Mercy and her husband.

"It was implied," Karl said.

"Jesus Christ!" Mercy wanted to strangle him. "I remember when our cow was shot. You had us convinced that Joziah Bevins was second-in-command to Satan. Did he or did he not threaten *physical harm* to us?"

Her father looked away.

Mercy counted to ten and looked to her mother. "Did he directly threaten your children?"

"Not exactly. He wanted our skills and connections," Deborah whispered. "He'd approached me several times in town, trying to get me to convince Karl to join him."

"We stay away from him," her father said solemnly. "When the time comes, we know who our friends will be."

Her energy drained away. "There's more to life than preparing for the end of the world, Dad."

Disappointment clouded his eyes. "Of course there is. But peace of mind is important too. I'd never forgive myself if I let an opportunity to prepare for the future pass because I was lazy."

"No one can accuse you of being lazy," she muttered.

"And I know you haven't left it behind," he added.

Mercy looked at him, keeping her face carefully blank.

"I know about your cabin. Did you think the sale would escape my attention? You've done a good job up there." He nodded approvingly.

She wanted the floor to swallow her up.

"What?" asked her mother, confusion wrinkling her forehead.

He kept my secret.

THIRTY-THREE

Truman found David Aguirre at home.

The church pastor lived in a small double-wide that had belonged to the previous minister until he died and left it to his church. The yard was well tended and Truman knew the paint was fresh because the congregation had gotten together and painted the home last summer as a surprise for their pastor. David answered the door and immediately let Truman in. Part of Truman had hoped to find him drinking a beer and watching football, but instead the sight of a Bible, open notebooks, and a laptop on the dining room table suggested he'd been working.

Something about David had always rubbed him the wrong way. Truman could never put his finger on it, but Mercy's blatant distrust of the man had added to Truman's unease.

David had always been pleasant to Truman; he had no basis for his disquiet.

"I'm glad to see you," David said as he gestured for Truman to take a seat at the kitchen table. "My phone has been ringing off the hook. Coffee?"

"Please. Who's been calling?"

David gave him a side glance as he poured coffee in a huge mug. "Who hasn't? A ton of police crawling all over Karl Kilpatrick's farm? Everyone wants to know what happened. I don't know why they think I would have answers."

"Rose Kilpatrick is missing."

David's hand jerked and coffee slopped on the counter. *"Rose?"*

"You took her to the Bevins place yesterday?" Truman asked, watching David's every reaction.

"I did. She called Wednesday night saying she wanted to talk to his hands about enrolling their young kids in her preschool. She said her father wouldn't take her."

"That surprise you?"

"The fact that her father wouldn't go? Heck no. Everyone knows the heads of the Kilpatrick and Bevins families don't mix."

"Not true for the younger generation, though, right?"

David nodded. "The youngers are always more forgiving. As evidenced by Rose wanting to go over there. And Levi and Owen don't seem to mind hanging out with Mike Bevins. I figured it was a personal thing between the two older men. That's just how it's always been." He raised a brow at Truman. "As a newcomer, how do you see it?"

"The same. What exactly did Rose do over there?"

David set a mug in front of Truman. "You think that trip is related to her disappearance?" Disbelief filled his tone.

"I'm just following up on her last movements."

"Everyone likes Rose. She took chocolate chip scones to the ranch and handed them out. She knows how to get men to listen to her: target their stomachs."

"So nothing weird happened? Do you remember exactly who she talked to? Did you see Joziah?"

David sat in the chair across from Truman and leaned forward, his brown eyes concerned. "You can't believe that anyone over there would do anything to that woman."

"Do *you* know every man on that ranch?" Truman asked. "There has to be some turnover in the hands."

The pastor looked lost in thought. "I saw new faces yesterday, and I let her do all the talking. I didn't want anyone to feel pressured that I was there to ask them to church. I made it clear it was Rose's idea to come talk to them."

Truman's stomach churned.

"What did she do?"

"Well, she wanted to talk to everyone. Said she didn't want any kids passed over. Even when I knew a man was single she insisted on giving him a scone and asking if he knew of any young children who could use some learning time." David rubbed at the stubble on his chin. "I was with her the whole time. She likes to hold your arm when she walks somewhere unfamiliar, you know."

"Were the men polite?"

"Definitely. It was a good-looking woman with home-baked goods. They were more than polite."

"Did she act odd at any point?" Truman was starting to wonder if he was on a ghost chase. "Did she seem surprised or stunned by anyone she talked to?"

David thought and shook his head.

"Did anyone avoid talking to her?"

"Not that I noticed."

Truman's mind spun. *Now what?*

Rose had run her fingertips over every square inch of the room, thankful he'd tied her hands at her front.

Her wrists and ankles were bound, but she'd always had excellent balance. It took some maneuvering, but now she had a good mental map of the room in her head. It was small. Nothing on the walls. One bed.

The wood floors were rough and needed to be refinished. A throw rug in the center of the room was made of the sort of knotted fabric scrap she and her sisters had made rugs from when they were younger. It was crushed nearly flat and had holes in several places. *Old.* She'd woken up on the rug, a smell of dust and chemicals in her nose. She'd called out a few times, but had known immediately that either she was alone in the house or *he* was ignoring her.

She'd felt her way to the room's door, its ancient metal knob and lower keyhole confirming what her nose had decided.

A very old home.

The presence of a bed cemented her belief that she was locked in a home. The sheets and bedding smelled sour and unwashed. Her hands had lightly skimmed the mattress and quilt as her nose picked up clues about its former occupant.

Male.

Old. Or else ill.

She was rarely wrong. More than three decades of smelling people had taught her to identify when people were sick or taking medication, and how often they bathed. All her life she'd been around men who worked outdoors. The previous resident of this bedroom had definitely spent time outside.

The room didn't have a window, but there was a small closet door with an identical knob and keyhole. It was also locked. She'd felt along the frames of both doors, searching for an opening, a weakness, a way to escape. Her tied hands couldn't stretch as high as she wanted, and twice she fell, having forgotten her feet were bound.

She pressed her ear against the wall opposite the door. A faint sound of water. Not water in the pipes, but an actual river or stream close by. But the sound was never consistent, and she wondered if her brain had created it. She tried the other three walls. Silence.

The slam of a far-off door had first woken her, and there'd been no human sounds since then. *Did he leave?*

It'd been a man who'd entered her parents' home. She'd left the back door unlocked, intending to dispose of the potato peelings once she'd finished peeling. She'd felt his presence before she'd heard the closing click of the door and had spun around, the small paring knife in her hand. He hadn't said a word as he took three steps into the kitchen and grabbed her. She'd slashed and thrust with the knife, earning grunts of pain from her attacker. Her bowl of potatoes had spilled and she'd tripped, taking her attacker down with her. He'd sat on her stomach, his hands around her throat, cutting off her windpipe, and she imagined her parents returning home to find her dead among the spilled potatoes. A blow to her jaw created explosions of light behind her eyelids and she had a brief moment of wonder at the sight before the pain registered.

Then she'd woken up here.

Not raped. Not dead.

She had no problem counting her blessings.

I need a weapon. Something small and sharp. Unexpected.

She knelt on the floor, searching for a splinter of wood from the old boards. Fragments of old varnish slid under her fingernails and instantly crumbled. The bed frame was her next target, but it was made from dense hardwood. After she'd felt every board, she perched on the edge of the bed and thought hard. There was nothing to pick up in the room except for the bedding. Either everything had been removed or not much had been there in the first place.

Maybe pictures hung on the walls at one time?

Could a nail have been left behind?

She started skimming the walls again, moving slower. Her first search had been quick, feeling for bigger items. Her pinkies kept growing numb from her raising her hands, and she'd let them dangle for a few minutes before tackling the wall again.

I should be terrified.

She wasn't. Her heart occasionally pounded as if she'd been running on a treadmill, but mainly she was focused and calm. She'd been waiting fifteen years for him to come back. Her brain had rehearsed every possible encounter, and long ago she'd given up being scared.

I know it's him.

Had her visit to the Bevins ranch triggered his retaliation?

She hadn't heard the second voice again. Not yesterday. Not ever.

Has he been living in Eagle's Nest all this time and managed to avoid me?

Or has he just now come back?

Her fingers caught on the edge of the peeling wallpaper and she yanked in frustration, appreciating the sound of the tear. No nails.

A board creaked, and she froze.

He's back.

The sound came from below, as if she was on a second level in the home. Or it could have come from a basement.

Do I yell? Let him know I'm conscious? Is it better to be silent? Her indecision sent sweat dripping down the center of her back. *What if it's not him?*

Another creak came from below.

"Help me." She coughed, surprised by her weak voice and the rawness of her throat. *He nearly choked me.* "Help me!" The second time she sounded like a sick kitten.

Steps sounded. Fast steps.

"Help me!" she squawked, her mouth pressed against the door frame. "Noooo!" she screeched as the steps grew fainter. Someone was running *away*.

She slid down the wall to the floor.

Maybe he's going to get help.

He'll call the police. Mercy must know by now that I'm missing.

Please hurry.

THIRTY-FOUR

Later that evening Truman stepped out on the front porch of the Kilpatrick home and sucked in a deep breath. The tension in the house made him crave a shot of hard alcohol. Or five. Mercy's siblings had arrived over the afternoon. All in various stages of grief and panic over Rose's abduction. Truman had offered comfort when needed, but mostly he'd stood back and observed the interactions between Mercy and her family.

Firmly on the pro-Mercy team were Levi and her mother. Against Mercy were Owen and her father. Pearl floated between the two camps, and Truman understood. She didn't want to pick a side; she wanted to keep everyone happy.

A peacemaker.

Two Bend FBI agents, along with Eddie, were working with Deschutes County on the investigation. Mercy had been firmly set aside from the investigation because of her relation to the victim, and she resented it. She alternated between looking ready to wilt and looking ready to plant her foot in someone's ass. Truman knew she understood, but he'd worried she'd throw the potato salad at Sheriff Ward Rhodes after he patted her shoulder.

Food was everywhere.

Royce was posted out front of the Kilpatrick home to keep the parade of well-intentioned neighbors at a distance. Every ten minutes he brought a casserole or dessert to the front door. Pearl would take the offering and add it to the food already on the kitchen table. She paced between her parents and the kitchen, refilling drinks, getting more spoons, and making countless pots of coffee.

It was a vigil, waiting for the phone to ring.

The FBI agents questioned Deborah and Karl Kilpatrick for well over an hour. Then they talked to Mercy and brought in David Aguirre to question him about Rose's trip to the Bevins ranch. Truman had watched Mercy carefully, waiting to see if she'd tell about her attack fifteen years ago. She'd stayed quiet. He noticed how Levi had casually leaned against the wall, listening to Mercy's interview, his gaze sharply on her face.

He's wondering too.

Guilt flooded Truman. Mercy's story floated through his head for the hundredth time. He still couldn't see a benefit to sharing her story: *A second person at an attack fifteen years ago. The witness who heard his voice is missing.*

What could police do with that information?

Truman couldn't see any leads. But if something suddenly came up so that the information was pertinent, he was going to twist Mercy's arm until she told.

What if we could get a lead from the body Levi hid?

Who knew how many months that could take? And a fifteen-year-old corpse wouldn't point to where Rose Kilpatrick was right now.

Or would it?

Indecision made his stomach hurt. But he was following Mercy's lead on this one. She would know if her story could help the investigation. Judging by the strain on her face, she'd thought about nothing else. When he couldn't watch anymore, he'd gone outside.

Royce came up the porch steps with a basket. The odor of fresh cinnamon rolls reached Truman's nose.

"Take a break," he told Royce. "Get something to eat. I'll watch out front."

"I'm stuffed," Royce muttered. "Seems wrong to be eating at this time."

"Then go for a walk."

The officer nodded and took the newest offering inside. Truman walked out to Royce's vehicle, which blocked the Kilpatricks' drive, and leaned against the driver's door, watching down the lane. The sun had set a few minutes ago, but the sky was still light. He stared up at the darkening sky and asked again for Rose to be released.

Headlights came up the Kilpatricks' drive. Truman straightened as the car pulled closer and parked. He recognized the young woman at the wheel but couldn't remember her name. One of the back windows rolled down, and he spotted two young boys in car seats. The mom stepped out of the vehicle, a covered dish in her hand.

"Evening, Rachel," Truman said as her name miraculously popped into his head.

"Any word, Chief?" she asked as she handed him the warm dish.

"No."

She glanced back at her boys. "Both my kids are in her preschool class. They absolutely love Miss Rose."

"Do they know?" Truman asked quietly. *How do you explain this to a four-year-old?*

Rachel shook her head, tears filling her eyes. "I can't tell them, and I really don't know how I'll handle it . . . if . . ."

Truman gripped the dish. *If she turns up dead.*

"Give my best to her parents." Rachel's shoulders sagged as she walked back to her car. The boys stared solemnly at Truman.

They know something is wrong.

The whole community suffered when something happened to one of its own. Judging by the outpouring of food and well-wishes, Rose Kilpatrick had touched everyone.

A king-cab pickup pulled off the single-lane driveway to let Rachel's vehicle pass. Truman recognized one of the Bevins ranch trucks. Mike Bevins was at the wheel, and Truman could make out other men in the truck. He wondered if one of them was Joziah.

Three hands accompanied Mike. Truman spotted Craig Rafferty's big bulk with a gallon of juice in his hand. The other men carried covered dishes.

Would I ever have seen this on my old job? No. He'd seen mourning families and church services for victims, but he'd never seen anything like the turnout for Rose Kilpatrick. The caring of the community made his throat tighten.

This is why I live here.

He nodded at the four men. "Any word on Rose?" Mike asked.

Truman shook his head. "Appreciate you stopping by."

"Can we give our regards to her parents?" one of the hands asked.

"Not now. They're overwhelmed and talking with the FBI." Truman realized he still held Rachel's warm dish. "Just set your stuff on the steps. I'll take it in."

"Is there anything we can do?" Mike asked as he placed his food on the porch. He shoved his hands in the front pockets of his jeans, looking earnestly at Truman. "I've got a bunch of men ready to volunteer to search. You just say where."

"They don't have any leads on a location yet, but if you notice anything suspicious, let us know. You could ask your guys if any of them happened to be passing by here and saw a vehicle leaving."

Mike raised a brow at his three men. They all shook their heads. "I'll ask the rest when I get back to the ranch."

The Kilpatricks' door opened and Mercy stepped out. Truman thought she looked pale and thinner than usual, but it could be the darkening evening.

"I'm sorry about your sister, Mercy," Mike said, taking off his hat. Nods and "Sorry" came from the other three.

"Thank you. And thank you for the food. That'll be a big help."

Silence filled the air as the men shuffled their feet in the gravel. They said their good-byes and drove off. Mercy let out a giant sigh as she and Truman watched the dust from the truck's tires.

"Everything okay in there?" Truman asked. Mercy stood with her arms wrapped around her, her expression pained.

"As okay as it can be." Her voice shook.

"Hey." Truman stepped in front of her and placed his hands on her shoulders. A faint tremor shook her body, but she looked into his eyes, and he recognized the gaze of a person at the end of her rope. She put up a good front; she behaved as if she were taking everything in stride, but he suspected she was seconds away from collapse.

Every word he wanted to tell her sounded patronizing and empty. He didn't want to give her useless encouragement when her world had been rattled to its core.

Following instinct, he pulled her close, wrapping his arms around her back. She was nearly as tall as he, and her chin rested on his shoulder for a brief second before she ducked her head and pressed her face against his neck. Her entire body shook as she took a gasping breath.

"I wish I'd never come back to Eagle's Nest."

"You're here for a reason."

"The FBI should have sent someone else." Another deep, raspy breath. Her arms were still wrapped around her stomach as if she was scared to let go of herself. He tightened his grip, her hair catching on his chin. She smelled of coffee and cinnamon rolls and pain.

"You're the best person they could have sent. No one knows what makes these people tick like you do."

"I've been gone too long. Everything's changed."

"Still. You have more insight than any other agent."

"All I've done is disrupt. Rose would be home right now if I hadn't brought up the old attacks. She would have never started searching for that voice again."

Truman could say nothing that would change her mind right now.

"I couldn't stay in there anymore. Every time my father looks in my direction, I feel his hatred."

"He doesn't hate you." *Empty words.*

She shuddered. "He blames me. If I'd only been the quiet, obedient daughter he wanted, none of this would have happened."

Truman stepped back to look her in the eye. "Four men would still be dead. Two women would still be dead. And because of you, we're very close to finding a killer."

"But my sister," she whispered. Her tears finally spilled. "I should have reached out before. I've wasted fifteen years because of my pride. We could have—"

"Stop it," Truman ordered, squeezing her shoulders to emphasize his words. "I need you focused if we're going to catch the guy who took your sister."

"Dammit, Truman. This has been a fucked-up day." She wiped her eyes. "And of course Jeff ordered me off Rose's case. He's promised to keep me informed, and I can sit in on any interviews, but outside of my parents and David Aguirre, no one else has seen her."

"You're still on the prepper cases. Any progress we make there is a step forward for Rose."

"True." She straightened her back, took a long, deep breath, and lifted her chin, looking him in the eye. "I won't fall apart like that again."

"Mercy, if anyone has the right to fall apart right now, it's you."

He hugged her again, and this time her hands tentatively went around his waist.

"Thank you," she whispered. "You're the only person I feel like I can lean on."

The heat of her body seeped through his shirt, and he was surprised at how thin she felt under his hands. He knew he'd have a hard time letting go.

"Anytime."

THIRTY-FIVE

Footsteps returned.

Rose sat up, immediately aware of the floor's hard surface. She'd fallen asleep on the rug, preferring it to the dirty bed. She was cold, but not cold enough to use the strong-smelling blankets. Not until she had to.

It was late. Or else very early. Her internal clock said she still had a few hours before her usual wake time. For a second she missed her phone, slightly ashamed at how reliant she'd become on it for its alarm and time. Her father would say, "I told you so." He used technology to get the best out of his small ranch, but he never relied on it. He made certain everything would run as close to normally as possible without power.

And here she was feeling helpless without her phone.

The footsteps in the hallway stopped outside her door. They were different from the running steps she'd heard hours earlier. These were heavier, more confident. A loud pounding sounded on the door and she jumped.

"You awake?"

There was the voice. Finally. After fifteen years of waiting, she knew unequivocally that this was the second man who'd attacked her that night. He pounded on the door again.

"Wake up!"

"I'm awake," she answered before she could decide if it was best to stay silent.

"Get back from the door," he ordered. "On the bed."

Without thinking, Rose scrambled onto the old bed, stale fumes rising as she positioned herself against the headboard.

Then her brain kicked in: *Is he going to rape me?*

Terror froze her muscles as her mind shot down that avenue. Sweat started under her arms and bile churned in her stomach. She grabbed the thin pillow and gripped it across her abdomen. *As if that would stop him.*

She knew of everything in the room; there was nothing to use as a weapon.

I have my hands and feet. My head.

She would fight back with every ounce of her being. She had nothing to lose.

He cautiously opened the door, letting the light from the hallway into the room. While preparing the room for his prisoner, he'd removed the lamp and everything else. He'd considered removing the bed but had decided it might be useful.

The light spilled across Rose Kilpatrick's face, but she didn't flinch. *Does she see no light at all?*

She was on the bed as ordered, looking like a cornered animal, ready to bite if he came too close. He'd always thought of her as a kitten. A helpless, tiny animal that needed someone to take care of it and protect it. For years he'd fantasized about that type of relationship with Rose.

He'd taken her because he deserved it. He'd played by the rules for over a decade and as of yesterday had nothing to show for it. Mercy and her snooping had made certain of that.

Fury over his stolen weapons had driven him to act. With one maneuver he'd punished the woman who'd screwed up his plan and grabbed the reward he'd let slip through his fingers fifteen years ago.

Rose.

He'd silently watched Rose since that night, wondering what her life was like. He got glimpses here and there. Rose walking through a store with one hand on her mother's arm. Rose talking to her preschoolers as they sat in a circle at her feet. He didn't understand how she read them a book and knew when to turn the pages, but the children had watched and listened with rapt attention.

Now she faced him. Her eyes were closed as usual, but her hands clasped a pillow in front of her.

Like a pillow can stop me. But first he needed an answer.

"Who opened the door?" he asked her.

"W-what?"

"*Who opened the front door?* The front door was wide open when I got here."

"I don't know! I've been locked in this room!"

He studied her face but saw only confusion. If she had heard someone come in the house, surely she would have yelled for help. *Could I have left it open?* It didn't matter; she was still here.

"Do you remember me, Rose?" he asked in a low, smooth voice.

"Yes." She looked ready to rip out his throat.

He smiled. Her defiance triggered a pleasing warmth in his belly. "Say my name."

"I only know your voice."

A big weight fell from his shoulders. For a long time, he'd wondered if Rose could identify him—he'd heard blind people had amazing hearing recognition. The few times he did have to greet or thank her, he'd lowered his voice, praying she didn't recognize it, as he fought a need to possess her wholly.

As he stared at her on the bed, that need vibrated inside him. *Patience.*

"Do you know what happened to Kenny that night?"

She said nothing.

"Answer me, Rose. It'll make things easier on you later."

Her lips pressed together.

"I heard the shots. You killed him, didn't you?"

A slight tremor shook her body. It was a powerful feeling to be able to stare at a person without her seeing you. And even better was that she had no idea who was talking to her. He looked his fill, appreciating the beauty of the blind woman.

"I knew he was dead," he said. "I got rid of his shit and told the boss he'd taken off for a different city. He'd only been working there a few weeks and had a hot temper. No one was sorry when they heard he'd split." He hadn't cared that Kenny was gone. He'd always known the man was dangerous. He'd been the driving force behind the attacks on all the women. He'd followed Kenny's lead, loving and hating the simultaneous rush of power and danger.

He'd known it couldn't last.

But he'd learned something from his adventures with Kenny. He liked having a woman subject herself to his demands. The power was exhilarating. One day he'd realized that Rose was the perfect woman for him. She *needed* a man in a way no other woman did.

But once Kenny was gone he'd been scared straight for years. He'd tried to walk the straight and narrow. He'd had a few long-term relationships with women but always found himself jumping to meet their needs, not the other way around. They'd managed to hold the power in the relationship. Not him.

Not the way he *wanted* it to be.

With Rose he knew it would be different. He'd waited for her for a long time.

And now she's mine.

"Do you know where Kenny's body is?" he asked.

She gave him a stubborn look.

Satisfaction rolled through him. "I don't think anyone will stumble across his bones anytime soon." He leaned against the door frame, crossing his arms on his chest, remembering how he'd lived in fear for weeks that someone would knock on his door, asking if he knew anything about an attack at the Kilpatrick place.

Instead there'd been nothing. No rumors had circulated. No cops had knocked on his door.

No one had talked of an attack.

The Kilpatricks had kept it to themselves.

Just as he'd been promised they would.

Karl Kilpatrick was a take-care-of-our-own type of guy who didn't like outside interference in his family. He'd often imagined the patriarch crushing all mention of the attack on his daughters, not wanting the cops nosing around his home, especially if one of the attackers had been killed on the premises.

A thought struck him. "Your father does know what happened that night, right?"

Her fingers tightened on the pillow, but she kept quiet.

"*He doesn't know?* You girls didn't tell your father?" Shock rolled through him and he laughed. "Holy shit. I'm impressed."

Rose held perfectly still.

Something like admiration warmed his chest. "That's part of the reason Mercy left town way back then, isn't it? She needed to get away from your family full of liars. If you only knew how many liars have the last name Kilpatrick. Killing someone is a big secret to live with, and I admit I was surprised to see her return as an FBI agent. I wonder if the Bureau knows they hired a murderer?"

This time Rose caught her breath, filling him with glee that he'd triggered a reaction. "I wonder what would happen if they got an anonymous tip about the background of one of their agents."

Her brows narrowed. "They'd immediately be led to you. I'd tell them of your involvement."

A big grin split his face. "How are you going to do that when you can't identify me?"

She tilted her head, a small smile on her lips. "That's where you're mistaken, Craig Rafferty."

◆ ◆ ◆

It'd been a process of elimination.

Rose had originally heard the mystery voice at the Bevins ranch fifteen years ago. A minute ago when he said he'd told his boss that Kenny took off, she figured the pair of attackers were probably ranch employees. The job was known for its high turnover, and Bevins often hired hands who simply showed up looking for jobs. If this speaker was able to erase all signs of Kenny by simply disposing of his belongings, then Kenny had been one of the hands who traveled until they found a ranch where they fit in comfortably.

There were only a few men who'd been employed at that ranch all this time.

She could easily recognize the voices of Mike Bevins, Chuck, Tim, Randy, and Les.

Craig Rafferty had typically been a silent shadow when she encountered a group of the hands. One whose presence she always felt; he'd emanated the aura of a large, silent man. She'd assumed he was shy or tongue-tied around women.

When she'd delivered scones to the ranch on Thursday, she'd listened closely. Craig Rafferty hadn't been around, and most of the men she'd met were too young. It wasn't until she was locked in this room that she'd realized Craig was one of the men who hadn't been present.

Had he purposefully avoided her?

His heavy steps told her the kidnapper was a large man.

He'd spoken to her as if he knew her, which he did.

Every name but one had been crossed off her list.

She'd been ready to pretend she didn't know his name until he'd threatened her sister. No one threatened her family.

What did I do?

Her legs began to shake.

She'd instinctively defended her sister, and now Craig had a witness who could identify him.

For the first time, she was truly terrified.

The pillow against her stomach wasn't going to stop him.

THIRTY-SIX

"Mercy?"

It took her a moment to realize the whispered voice wasn't part of her dream. As she woke, she was surprised to find that she'd fallen asleep. Nervous energy had kept her pacing her parents' home past two in the morning. Her parents had gone to bed and Pearl had crashed in a spare room while the FBI and county sheriff maintained a quiet vigil in the kitchen.

Truman had ordered her to sit on the couch at one point and sat beside her, threatening to hold her down if she didn't stop pacing. "Give me your hand," he commanded.

She'd given him an odd look but held out a hand. "Now lean your head back, close your eyes, and . . . count pieces of wood as you imagine swinging your ax." She'd snorted. He'd grabbed her mother's hand lotion from the end table, squeezed some into his hand, and started to massage her fingers and palm.

Mercy instantly melted. "Holy crap. Where'd you learn that?"

"Close your eyes."

"Done." His fingers were brutal as they stroked and rubbed.

"Swinging your ax?"

"Yes," she muttered. "Don't stop." It was nearly painful. Every joint she'd abused with swing after swing of the ax was melting into a pool of butter.

"My mother used to do this for me when I worked for the Highway Department in high school. I used a shovel all summer. My hands would cramp every night."

Mercy couldn't think of an answer.

Then a low voice was calling her name, and she woke with her head on Truman's shoulder as they lay on the sofa. Actually she was glued to his side from the hip up. She sat up, feeling the cold as she left his body heat. "Levi?" she whispered. Faint light illuminated a silhouette squatting in front of her.

"I need to talk to you. Outside."

"What happened?" Shock jolted her fully awake. "Did they find Rose? Is she okay?"

"No word on Rose," he whispered.

She deflated.

"Come with me." He took her hand and pulled.

Mercy stood and yawned. "What time is it?"

"Almost five."

"Mercy?" Truman spoke behind her. "What's going on?"

"Nothing," she said. "They haven't found Rose. I'm going to talk with Levi."

"Shouldn't I hear this too, Levi?" Truman asked.

Mercy froze at the suspicion in his voice. She met Levi's gaze. Even in the dim light she could see the anguish and pain.

And guilt.

"Levi?" Her voice cracked. "What's going on?" Apprehension raced through her muscles.

He tightened his grip on her hand. "We need to talk." He sounded next to tears.

"I'm coming too." Truman stood. "Outside. Now."

Mercy glanced toward the kitchen, hearing the faint murmur of voices. *What did Levi do?*

Outside she slipped on a jacket, zipped it up to her chin, and buried her hands in the pockets. With the sun gone, the chill reminded her that winter weather was coming fast. Warm days would soon be a faint memory. She sniffed, inhaling the fresh crispness that hinted at snow and ice.

Levi looked sick. His eyes were bloodshot and his shoulders stooped. He wouldn't make eye contact. Truman stood silently beside her, and she wondered what'd made him insist on listening to their conversation.

"I might have an idea of who took Rose," Levi started.

White-hot shock raced through Mercy. *"Who? Tell the police. Now!"*

Levi held up his hands. "Hear me out first. I could be wrong."

"No! If you have an idea, we need to get on it *now*!"

"Give me sixty seconds, Mercy!"

"I suspect you've already wasted half a day," Truman shot back. "Start talking, Levi. Fast."

Levi seemed to crumble beneath his coat. "Remember how I told you I disposed of . . . that thing by myself?"

Mercy couldn't speak.

"Jesus Christ," said Truman. "Someone helped you get rid of the body?"

"He *knows*?" Levi hissed.

"He knows some," Mercy stated, her mind spinning. "He knows we shot our attacker and you took care of it."

"Oh Lord." Levi turned away, pressing his hands against his eyes. "I'm going to prison."

"I told Mercy I'd keep her story quiet until I saw a need for the truth to come out. I didn't think it was hurting anyone, but it sounds like that might have changed?" Truman asked. "Who was it?"

"Craig Rafferty."

Truman sucked air in between his teeth. "He helped you get rid of the body?"

"Yeah." Levi still couldn't look either of them in the eye. "I didn't know who else to call that night." He cleared his throat. "The guy's name was Kenny."

"The one who died?" Mercy said faintly.

Levi nodded. "He and Craig were the men there that night."

"What? You've known all along it was Craig Rafferty who attacked us?" Mercy's knees shook as Truman swore at Levi. He took a step toward her brother and she grabbed his jacket, holding him back.

Levi knew it was Craig? And did nothing?

She struggled to breathe. The boards under her feet seemed to rock as if she were on a boat, and she swayed, holding fast to Truman's coat for balance.

"Wait! Hear me out. It's not what you think," Levi pleaded.

"You'd better start talking faster," Truman threatened. Mercy was falling to pieces with every sentence, but Truman seemed to get bigger, taller, more looming. Quiet waves of anger floated around him.

"You saw Craig's vehicle out the window," Mercy stated. "At the time you said you couldn't see who it was."

"I saw a flash of it. So I was pretty certain Craig had been there too, but I couldn't believe he'd hurt my sisters."

"And that's who you called to help you get rid of the body?" asked Truman. "The accomplice? What the hell made you do that?"

"I figured he'd have a good reason to keep his mouth shut," said Levi. "I loaded Kenny into the back of my truck and went to Craig's. He was shocked as hell to see me and was totally rattled by Kenny's death. He said Kenny and he were just stopping by when Kenny attacked Rose. Craig freaked out and ran. He was scared shitless and I trusted what he said. Then he told me he thought Kenny might have killed those other two women."

"Craig claimed he wasn't with Kenny at Jennifer's and Gwen's?" Mercy asked. "Liar."

"I believed him at the time. I told him I'd keep my mouth shut about his involvement at our home if he'd help me get rid of the body. He wanted assurance that you and Rose hadn't seen him and wouldn't tell anyone. I told him Rose had heard a second voice, but we'd already agreed to keep it quiet."

"Wait." Mercy's spinning brain locked on to one thought. "How did you assure him Rose and I wouldn't go to the police?"

Levi's face crumpled. "I told him I'd make certain Dad wouldn't let you. That you'd do whatever Dad decreed."

"I had to leave town because of my arguments with Dad!" Truman's hand caught her elbow as she fell back a step. Her vision tunneled; the only thing she could see was Levi's guilt-stricken face. *How could he promise such a thing? Were Rose and I simply pawns to him?* "You took Dad's side! But you were just protecting your own ass!"

"I was protecting yours too! Who knows what would have happened if you'd gone to the police? We both could have ended up in prison. Or what if Rose had identified Craig's voice at the Bevins ranch? That could have ratcheted up the conflict between Dad and Joziah to who knows what level. A full-out war."

"OhmyGodOhmyGodOhmyGod." Mercy turned away from Levi. The brother she'd always trusted . . . his betrayal had stripped her bare, and she strove to keep from falling to her knees. Leaving home had been the hardest thing she'd ever done. Learning Levi had helped push her out the door rubbed salt in her old wound. "Damn you, Levi," she whispered. She wanted to vomit.

How did he do this to me? To Rose and me?

"You've got to believe me that I thought the killer was dead when Kenny died. I didn't believe Craig had anything to do with the attacks," Levi said earnestly. He touched her arm and she shook it off, unable to look at him. "It wasn't until you mentioned the mirrors that I started to have doubts."

"Why didn't you say something then?" Truman sounded ready to rip off her brother's head.

"The cases were too different! Women were raped and murdered back then. Not old men shot in the head! Craig told me that Kenny was some sort of sexual pervert and I thought we were doing the right thing by keeping his death quiet."

"I bet Craig was with him the whole time," Mercy stated quietly.

"I don't know," Levi said. "But he might have been."

A thought struck her. "Could Craig have been the one who stole the prom photos, since he actually knew both women? I don't see Kenny stealing them, as the women were strangers to him." She looked at Levi. "Does mom still have Pearl's old prom photos?"

Levi thought for a moment. "There are some old albums in Dad's office. Our high school stuff. Hang on." He jogged up the porch stairs.

"Pearl was at the same prom as Jennifer and Gwen, correct?" Truman asked.

"Right. It was a big deal in our house. Dad was firmly against Pearl going, but Mom convinced him since Pearl was going with a group of girls, not with a date."

"What are you hoping to see in the pictures?"

"A very tall young man named Craig."

"It won't prove anything."

"I agree," said Mercy. "But it's one common thread that might tighten things up."

Levi came outside, flipping through a fat album. "Here." He tapped an open page and showed the two of them a few candid shots of Pearl in her prom dress, standing in front of her parents' wood stove. Another shot showed her and Jennifer in the same spot.

Mercy blinked, stunned that the dresses and hairstyles were so dated. That night she'd believed her sister was movie-star fashionable. She turned a page and found a formal group picture shot by the prom photographer.

A Night in Italy. The group stood in front of an image of an Italian palace.

Craig Rafferty stood in the back row. Five girls. Three guys.

They all looked incredibly happy.

"Think this is the picture that's missing from both scenes?" Truman asked.

"I do," said Mercy. "I wonder why he took them."

"Souvenirs," mumbled Levi.

What drove the nice young man in this picture to kill women he knew? I'm jumping to conclusions.

"So Craig said he and Kenny were coming for a social call the night they attacked us?" Mercy spit the words as she shut the album.

"He said they were stopping by to see me and he didn't know what Kenny was going to do until he suddenly attacked."

"*Bullshit.* Rose said two men attacked her."

"I didn't know what to think!" Levi pleaded. "My main concern was hiding the body and keeping you and Rose safe."

"Rose isn't safe now," said Truman. "Are you done with your story, Levi? Because we need to tell the FBI to go find Craig Rafferty." He turned away and strode back to the house.

"When did you know?" Mercy whispered. "When did you know Craig had Rose?" A fine, frail thread connected her and her brother. A thread she'd repaired this week. Now it was close to breaking again.

"I don't know that he has her," Levi admitted. "I didn't tell you right away because I wasn't sure. I'm still not sure. I'm just guessing."

"You're lying. Where did you go at midnight?" The look on Levi's face told her he'd suspected all along that Craig had been involved. *Why didn't he say something immediately?*

Because it made him look bad.

Another hole ripped through her heart.

I can never trust him again.

His shoulders slumped. "I went to Craig's to look. There's no one there."

"*Damn you, Levi,*" Mercy swore again, tears flooding her eyes, that thread stretching dangerously tight. "If Rose is dead, this is on *you.*"

Her brother started to cry.

THIRTY-SEVEN

Two hours later every available law enforcement officer had been mobilized, and Craig Rafferty was nowhere to be found.

After Levi's confession, Truman had approached Jeff Garrison, Eddie, and Sheriff Ward Rhodes in the Kilpatrick kitchen. Speaking carefully to protect Mercy's story, he told them that Rose had recently told Levi that she suspected Craig Rafferty had tried to break into their house fifteen years ago. Karl Kilpatrick had been sitting with the officers and chimed in that Rose had heard a voice that night but had never known who'd been outside their home. Sheriff Ward asked if Karl had reported the disturbance back then and Karl had said, "Why would I? Nothing happened."

It was the strongest lead they had, and the officers had thrown everything they had into finding Craig Rafferty's whereabouts.

Craig's house was empty. His vehicle missing. Mike Bevins hadn't seen him since they stopped by the Kilpatrick home last night to offer help. No one at the Bevins ranch had seen him after that. Jeff filed a request for his cell phone records, and officers continued patrols searching for his vehicle.

His disappearance encouraged them that they were on the right track.

Eddie had given Truman an odd look, asking why Levi hadn't mentioned Craig earlier. Truman had shrugged and lied, saying Rose hadn't been positive about the identification and Levi hadn't wanted to send the investigation in the wrong direction. Eddie had nodded, holding Truman's gaze, and Truman suspected he knew he was bending the truth.

The other officers had jumped on the lead, not caring about its source.

And it was looking solid.

But no one could find Craig Rafferty.

Jeff Garrison scribbled on a pad of paper. "Who are his friends? Where's he hang out? Does he own any other properties? Does he go fishing or hunting and use someone's cabin? If he's got a hostage, he needs a place to hold her without any prying eyes."

"That describes nearly every place around here," Truman muttered.

"Get his boss over here," Garrison continued. "I want to talk to the guys he works with. We need to know what he likes to do."

"This is the first time he's taken anyone," Eddie pointed out. "Before, someone was always killed in their home. Why is he changing it up?"

"We thought the most recent kills were for the weapons," Sheriff Rhodes stated. "Taking Rose Kilpatrick doesn't have anything to do with weapons, does it?" He looked to Karl, who shook his head.

"I don't have more than a dozen guns," her father said. "And they're all intact. I checked."

"So he's returned to killing and raping women after a fifteen-year hiatus?" the sheriff muttered.

Karl turned white.

"We don't know that," Truman interjected. "Taking Rose indicates a totally different goal." He wanted to kick the sheriff in the ass for speaking like that in front of her father.

"What's that goal?" Garrison asked, looking at the other men. "That will help us find her."

The other men exchanged glances.

"After Rose visited the Bevins ranch yesterday," Truman said slowly, "he might have decided she was fishing around to identify his voice from all those years ago. Since the prepper murders, we've been taking a hard look at the Jennifer Sanders and Gwen Vargas cases. He could be nervous that he's about to be caught for those. So he eliminates the witness."

"But taking Rose increases the heat," countered Eddie.

"I didn't say he was the sharpest tool in the shed," said Truman.

"Rose and I talked about that attempted break-in the other day," Mercy said.

Truman hadn't heard her enter the room. Her eyes were red and wet. Dark shadows were smudged under them.

"She's wondered for a long time whose voice she heard that night," said Mercy. "I think me being in town and looking into the old murders has stirred things up."

"You flushed out a killer?" Jeff asked.

Mercy held his gaze. "Possibly."

Truman held his breath, wondering if she was about to tell the full story of the attacks. "You said Rose heard someone outside the house that night, right? And the two of you managed to scare him off?"

She looked at him. Indecision in her eyes. Would she tell the truth or use the old story she'd told her parents?

"Yes," she said.

"Shoulda told the police back then," Rhodes muttered. "Maybe we could have caught who murdered those girls."

"Wasn't any of our business," Karl Kilpatrick snapped at Rhodes. "I didn't need the police poking around in my home when nothing happened."

"I bet you want our help now," Rhodes shot back.

Karl leaped to his feet, sending his chair screeching across the kitchen.

Jeff slammed his hands on the table. "Knock it off! Arguing about what someone didn't do fifteen years ago isn't helping. Sit down!" He pointed at Karl. The man glared back but took his seat.

"We'll find your daughter," Jeff said in a calm voice to Karl.

Mercy's father slumped in his chair.

Mercy stared at her father for a few seconds and walked out of the room. Truman followed her out the front door to where she leaned on the rail of the front porch. "It's warm in there," she said.

Truman agreed. "Where's Levi?" he asked.

"He went home. He wanted to be there when Kaylie left for school. I think he'll come back after that." She turned her head toward him, a question in her eyes. "How did you know Levi was hiding something?"

"I didn't."

"You told him you needed to hear what he had to say when he woke me up this morning. Why?"

Truman sat on the rail next to her. "I watched everyone last night. Pearl. Your dad. Levi. He couldn't hold still. Which isn't cause for alarm, but something in his eyes every time he looked at your mother seemed off. He looked crushed . . . but in a guilty sort of way. I chalked it up to the stress of the situation. But when I saw him as he woke you this morning, that was the face of a man with a burden to share."

"So you didn't know what he'd done."

"No. I just knew it could be ugly."

"I have a hard time believing Craig Rafferty is a killer," Mercy said. "I've known him most of my life. He's friends with my brothers."

"I don't know if Levi would call him a friend. Their relationship is based on mutual fear of each other." *What if I hadn't saved Craig that day at the river? Would those girls have died? Would any of this be happening?*

He looked at Mercy beside him. *Would I have met her?*

He would have. At some point their paths would have crossed—somehow. He knew it as firmly as he'd realized his life had changed the day he gave two FBI agents a tour of his uncle's home.

Sometimes you meet a person you're destined to have in your life forever.

She might not know it yet, but he did.

In the middle of murders and mourning one good thing had appeared.

Did you send her to me, Uncle Jefferson?

He'd been angry and depressed since his uncle's death, but looking back, he saw how it'd turned around when she arrived in town. Every day he woke up and looked forward to seeing her again.

Does she feel the same?

"I can't just stand around here," Mercy said, pushing herself off the rail. She started to stride across the porch, as she had paced the night before. "I need to *do something.*"

"Garrison won't let you be involved."

"Then he won't care if we go for a drive. We can at least look for Craig's truck. Maybe he went back to the cave at Owlie Lake."

"The one picked apart by evidence teams?"

She stopped and looked at him, her hands on her hips. "Get me out of here, Truman."

"Yes, ma'am."

An hour later Mercy stared out her window, unable to get something Truman had said yesterday out of her mind. They'd driven down every street in Eagle's Nest, stopped for coffee, and argued over which highway to search next. Truman had won, and they drove, checking every passing truck to see if it was Craig's Chevy.

"Whose death did you cause?" she kept her voice low, her face to the window, but she saw his reflection stiffen.

"Another cop. I hesitated when I should have acted. And then I made the wrong choice when I did act. A woman—maybe two—died because I hesitated."

He haltingly told a story of a burning car that made her want to cry.

"I think you made the right decision in a very stressful moment. The fire extinguisher might have put out the fire."

He didn't say anything.

"I'm sure you've relived it with dozens of different scenarios."

"Knowing that my lack of action led to someone's death put me out of commission for a while. I believed I was done with law enforcement. I'd entered the field wanting to help people and I'd done the opposite—"

"Truman—"

"Let me get this out." He kept his eyes on the road. "This job in Eagle's Nest opened a door that I believed had been slammed firmly shut. Now I pray every day that I make the right decision if that type of situation ever arises again."

"I'm sorry, Truman," she whispered. Survivor's guilt. Doubting his decisions. She understood.

Am I doing the right thing by keeping my secret?

His phone rang through the speakers of the Tahoe. He hit a button on his steering wheel. "Daly."

"Chief Daly?"

"Yes. You're on speaker and I have Special Agent Mercy Kilpatrick with me. Who is this?"

"This is Sharon Cox. I'm Toby's mom."

Mercy came to attention at the name of the witness she'd interviewed days ago.

"Yes, Sharon. Is everything okay with Toby?" Truman asked with concern.

"Well, not really. He's been up all night and is extremely upset. I've never seen him like this." She paused. "He insisted I phone you. He's been pacing and crying and I can't get him to relax. I'm only calling because I need him to settle down and—"

"What's he want you to tell me?" Truman said sharply.

The woman's deep breath sounded over the speakers. "This is going to sound ridiculous, but he says he saw a ghost at Ned Fahey's home yesterday."

Mercy smiled, remembering Toby's fear of ghosts. But Truman scowled and abruptly pulled the Tahoe over onto the red gravel lining the highway. Mercy grabbed her door handle to keep her balance.

Truman stared intently at his dashboard as if he could see Sharon Cox. "Can Toby describe this ghost? Can I talk to Toby?"

"Well," Sharon said reluctantly. "I guess so. If you don't mind. I really didn't want him to bother you, but he's really getting on my—"

"Put him on the phone," Truman ordered.

They heard Sharon holler for Toby.

"You think someone's been in Ned's house," Mercy whispered. *Would Craig take Rose there?*

"I think Toby saw something. He wouldn't be so upset if he hadn't. Could be nothing, but it's worth taking a look." He checked both directions on the two-lane highway and pulled a U-turn.

"Chief Daly?" Toby's voice boomed through the speakers, and Truman turned down the volume.

"Yes, Toby. Mercy from the FBI can hear you too. What's going on?"

"I heard Ned's ghost! You were wrong that his ghost left!"

"Where did you hear it, Toby?"

"I went in his house," Toby said slowly. "I know I'm not supposed to, but I wanted to see if his body was really gone."

"It's gone. Mercy and I told you that. What did you see in there?"

"I didn't make it to his bedroom. I heard his voice—he sounded like he was hurt!"

"Did you look for him?" Truman asked. He pushed the Tahoe up to seventy-five, heading in Ned Fahey's direction.

"No! I got out of there as fast as I could!"

"Could you make out any words?" Mercy spoke up.

"I think he asked me to help him." Toby's voice dissolved into hiccups. "Should I have helped him? I was so scared. I just had to get out of there."

"You did the right thing," Truman reassured him. "Toby, wasn't the house locked up? Do you have a key?"

"I don't have a key. Ned would never give out his keys to anyone." His voice wavered. "He's going to be so mad at me."

"Toby," Mercy said firmly. "How'd you get in the house?"

"I used the tunnel," he whispered.

Mercy and Truman exchanged a look. "The tunnel?" she asked. "Where is that?"

"It starts in the woodshed. You have to move a small stack of wood near the back, but I left it open," he wailed. "Ned always told me to be certain that it was covered back up with cut wood so no one could find it."

A tunnel. Mercy was impressed.

"Why'd he have a tunnel?" Truman asked.

"So he could escape when the feds came for him," Toby answered.

Mercy wondered what the old prepper would have thought of her, a fed, trying to solve his murder.

"I ran out the front door," Toby moaned. "I left that open too. I don't want to go back and close it. But Ned's going to be so mad that I left it *open*."

"Ned's dead," Mercy said gently. "He's not angry with you."

"He's in there," Toby insisted. "He said he'd haunt me and now he's doing it. What if the ghost got out and followed me home? What if it's in my house right now?" he wailed.

"Toby, Mercy and I are on our way. Do you trust us to take care of the ghost?"

Wet hiccups sounded from the speakers.

"We'll go to Ned's and then we'll stop by your house and tell you what we found. I don't believe Ned's ghost would be interested in haunting you. He'd be more interested in playing pranks on Leighton Underwood, right? Why would he want to upset you when you helped him out around his place for so long?"

"True . . ."

"We'll be there soon. Let me talk to your mom again."

Sharon came on the phone.

"I'm going to stop by the Fahey house," Truman told her. "Have you noticed any activity going on there?"

"I haven't seen any ghosts," she snapped. "Toby gets a thought in his head and he won't let go of it and upsets the peace of everyone around him."

"We'll talk to him after we check out the house. We're ten minutes away," Truman said. He ended the call.

"What a horrible woman," Mercy muttered. "Poor Toby. Do you think he really heard a voice?"

"I believe he heard someone ask for help." He looked at Mercy. "I hope that person turns out to be your sister."

"But it was last night," she whispered, her mouth drying up. "A lot can happen in twelve hours." Her brain spun with possibilities. Did she really hear a human? *Could Rose be there?*

Truman's answer was to press on the accelerator.

She picked up her phone, her mind racing, her hope building. *Please let it be Rose.* She latched on to the new information and felt a positive energy grow in her chest. For the first time since Levi's confession, she felt hope. "I'll let Eddie know where we're going. He'll inform the rest."

Hang on, Rose.

THIRTY-EIGHT

Rose took another sip from the bottle of water. It was her last one. She'd used the other bottle to bathe. It seemed wasteful to use drinking water for something as unimportant as cleanliness, but she'd been desperate to remove the essence of Craig Rafferty from her body.

Now she was clean, but the burn between her thighs and the pain around her neck reminded her of what he'd done.

I'm still alive. That's more than Jennifer and Gwen.

He'd left her two bottles of water, a bucket, a towel, and a chocolate muffin.

She counted her blessings.

As she removed the plastic wrap on the muffin, she recognized its scent from the Coffee Café. *Kaylie made it.* The thought of her niece nearly brought her to tears, but none came because Rose didn't have any tears left. Craig had ripped them out of her over the course of several hours during the night. The room stank of him. The bed stank of him. Her hair stank of him.

I'm still alive.

He'd told her in great detail what he and Kenny had done to Jennifer Sanders and Gwen Vargas. Words she could never unhear. Then he'd strangled her, whispering that her life was over as he tightened his grip around her neck, a loud buzz overtaking her brain. But just as she lost consciousness, he removed his hands and her hearing returned. Then he did it again. And again.

She lost count of how many times he took her near death.

"I hold your life in my hands," he crooned with his fingertips on her neck, his lips near her ear. "Literally, your life is *mine*."

He'd played stupid games, asking how many fingers he was holding up, what expression was on his face, or if he was the best-looking man she'd ever seen. She'd been slapped for not answering so she'd answered, throwing out random numbers and stroking his ego. He'd forced her to compliment him over and over. To her surprise, her words made him as happy as real compliments. He'd turn joyful after she'd told him how strong he was, thank her for noticing, and then talk about the men he'd fought.

His brain wasn't right. It was twisted, distorted. She imagined it smelled gangrenous and felt spongy.

When he'd told her Levi had hidden what he'd known about the women's murders, she'd instantly struck at him with her fists, screaming that it wasn't true. To her surprise he'd backed off, assuring her that what Levi had believed wasn't true. "What do you mean?" she'd asked.

"Levi believes that Kenny killed Jennifer and Gwen by himself. He thinks I was clueless that Kenny intended to attack you that night," he explained. "We both know that's not true, don't we?" The slime in his voice turned her stomach. "It's always been about you, Rose," he whispered. "We didn't know your sister was home that night. You're so innocent, moving around town with the confidence that no one will hurt you or refuse you anything. But I bet you're not as innocent as you seem. Have you ever had two men at once, Rose?"

She'd refused to answer and been punched in the stomach, bringing a fresh round of tears. He'd immediately apologized.

"Why did you break the mirrors?" she whispered.

He was silent for a long time before answering. "You'd have to know my father. Mirrors meant vanity to him, and vanity was something you had to beat out of your kids. There were no mirrors in our house when I grew up. I can remember him breaking a tiny mirror of my mother's he'd found in her purse. It was prideful, sinful. She only should be looking at him. When he broke her mirror . . . the look on her face." His voice took on a dreamy tone. "That was power. The way she looked at him in awe and fear. Those women—Jennifer and Gwen—they were vain. They needed to know that the world didn't revolve around how they looked." His finger moved along her cheek. "You've never needed a mirror. You are the absence of vanity. You're as a woman should be."

"Let me go," she whispered.

He stroked her hair. "In time."

The wistful tone in his voice told her she'd be dead before he let her go.

When he tired of using her body, he lay beside her in the filthy bed, positioning her head on his chest, and continued to play with her hair as he talked. And talked.

"I'm going to be important in Eagle's Nest," he promised. "I've waited a long time. I've put in the hours and I deserve it. Joziah Bevins can't last much longer."

She'd stiffened at the name and he felt it.

"You think Mike will be the heir to Joziah's kingdom? Mike doesn't want anything to do with it. Joziah's going to pick the man he thinks is most qualified, and that's going to be me."

"How?" she asked, unable to stop the question. *What makes you so special?*

"Well, I was going to gift him enough weapons to arm an army. I was already on that track when I got a look at the arsenal Enoch Finch owned. What does one old prepper need with so many weapons? Joziah wouldn't have been able to ignore me after that. We've got to be prepared for anything, you know. What if the government comes in and decides to take our land? But your sister ruined my plan. Now I'll just have to convince him I'm the most qualified."

"You knew Enoch?"

He laughed. "I knew them all. I carefully cultivated those old men, feeling them out to see who was hoarding weapons. They're lonely. They say they hate people, but get a little alcohol in them and they talk and talk. I spent many evenings in their homes with a bottle of booze, talking about the society that we should have, and them showing me their preparations. Their arsenals. It was easy enough to slip something stronger in their drinks so I could load up their weapons. But I couldn't let them wake back up.

"It was perfect. No one suspected me. I'd been a part of this community for decades." His hand ran over her long hair. "Your hair is so beautiful. You're the type of woman we'll need after TEOTWAWKI happens, Rose. You're skilled. You listen to your man and do what you're told. We'll need women for support positions. A bunch of men living together makes a huge mess, you know? Tempers get hot too. Women know how to cool us down."

Is that what I've been raised to do?

"Women like your sister—well, they just cause trouble. There's a reason God gave men the strength and women the ability to bear children." He caressed her stomach and she froze. "I don't understand how your father could let her run off and become an enforcer for the government. That's wrong on so many levels. Your father must be humiliated.

"She stole my guns," he muttered. "Those were my property. My ticket to impressing Joziah. She's not a real woman. She's pretending to be a man. Probably can't get laid."

Through her cheek, she felt the muscles of his stomach harden. She cringed. *Not again.*

THIRTY-NINE

The area around Ned's house felt different from when Mercy had first visited last Monday. Today it was sunny; no clouds anywhere. The puddles had dried, and leaves rustled in the light breeze. A far cry from the wet, dreary weather that'd been present on her first day.

Stepping out of Truman's Tahoe, she had a moment of anger with the perfect weather. The world had the nerve to move on as usual. Sunshine, birds, warmth. *Doesn't it know Rose could be dead?*

The sun highlighted the disrepair of Ned's home. Warped boards, curling shingles, weeds. But Mercy knew its looks were deceiving. It was a fortress, designed to project an image of disarray and poverty: *Move along, there's nothing of value here.*

Mercy studied the familiar front yard of junk piles and hedges, remembering how she'd corrected Eddie's comment about its seemingly chaotic structure. The house was quiet, and she wondered if Toby's ghost had been a feral cat.

"The front door is closed," Truman pointed out as he walked around to the passenger side. "Toby said he left it open when he ran out."

True. The hair on her arms lifted, her senses shifting to a higher level of alertness. "Let's stay on this side of the vehicle for now."

Truman cupped his hands around his mouth. "Hello! Anyone home?"

Silence.

"Your thoughts?" she asked.

"I think Toby may have been hearing things," he admitted. "He hasn't gotten over finding Ned's body."

He yelled at the house again with no results.

"Let's try the front door," Mercy suggested.

Truman paused, and she could see him weighing the idea. "I'll let Lucas know we've arrived and are going in."

"If we can get in," she added as he made the call. "Ned had an impressive number of locks on a very heavy door."

He led the way, his hand near the weapon at his side. Mercy followed, unzipping her thin jacket for access to hers. "I feel like I'm being herded to slaughter," Truman muttered as they rounded the second pile of junk along the path.

Mercy kept a careful eye on the windows of the home, searching for any sign of movement.

Something shifted at an upper boarded-up window, and Truman jerked backward, crying out.

Then she heard the crack of the shot.

Truman dropped and Mercy dived behind a pile of rusting metal. Her training took over and she stretched out, dragging Truman through the dirt to cover, and then spun around to aim at the window where she'd seen the movement, her vision laser-focused on locating the threat. *Where'd he go?*

Nothing.

Her heartbeat pounded in her ears and sweat ran down her back as she scanned the house. Behind her, Truman gasped for breath, swearing like an angry redneck. She whirled back to him, ripping off her jacket, ready to apply pressure where he was bleeding. *Oh shit! Oh shit! Oh shit!*

His head was tilted back, his heels digging into the ground, his teeth clenched in pain.

She couldn't see blood. *"Where is it?"* Her hands scrambled across his chest and neck, searching for the bullet hole.

I won't let him die.

He ripped open his buttoned-up shirt, exposing his vest, and dug at its right side with frantic fingers, struggling to catch his breath.

Mercy spotted the flattened slug and elation ripped through her.

"Your vest caught it!"

"I know," he spit out, and then sucked in a deep, ragged breath. *"But holy fuck that hurts!"*

"You're going to hurt like a son of a bitch for a few days, but you'll be okay." Tears blurred her eyes as the violence of the last twenty seconds rushed through her. *Thank goodness I'm already on the ground.* "I'm calling for backup." Her fingers shook as she dialed.

"Looks like we found Craig," Truman gasped.

He was right. In her bones, Mercy knew Craig had taken the shot.

Eddie answered her call. Mercy relayed their location and Truman's situation. "Sit tight," Eddie ordered. "We'll get a county car over there ASAP, but we're all on our way."

She ended the call as Truman struggled to sit up, leaning against a rusted fender cemented to a pile of bricks. Relief swept over her as he moved on his own.

"Fuck me," he muttered, wiping his forehead. "I don't ever want to do that again."

"I've never heard you swear so much, Chief Daly."

He laughed and then moaned at the stab of pain in his chest. "I try to keep it clean. Did you see him?"

"No." Mercy took another glance at the house. "But it's got to be Craig. I saw something move at that boarded-up window. Exactly where I'd shown Eddie how a person had a perfect view if a stranger walked up to this house," she admitted. The conversation seemed ancient. "We're lucky he only took one shot." She'd put on a vest before starting their hunt for Craig Rafferty. It was heavy and uncomfortable, something she rarely wore in her job, but searching for a killer had dictated it be worn.

She'd noticed Truman almost always wore one under his shirt.

This could have ended in a very different situation.

"Now what?" she asked. *Can he walk out of here?*

"Wait for the cavalry," Truman said. "Is this as good of cover as we can get?"

"I'd say so. I'd rather be on the other side of the Tahoe, but no one shooting from the house can get us here." She scanned the pile of junk behind them. "It's mostly bricks and car parts, but it's something. How are you feeling?"

"Like my chest is on fire," he said. "Probably broke some ribs."

"Can you run if we have to?"

"If we have to."

◆ ◆ ◆

The gunshot woke Rose.

I'm still alive.

Loud footsteps pounded down the hallway, and she scooted to the far corner of the bed, as far away from the door as possible. Locks slid and the door flung open. *"Get up!"*

"What's happening?" she shrieked. *Who'd he shoot?* The smell of the fired gun reached her nose.

"Get up!" Craig grabbed her upper arm and lifted her completely off the bed. Her legs scrambled for purchase, and she flung out her arms to keep her balance. He hurled her through the doorway and she fell to her knees.

The air in the hallway smelled heavenly compared to the bedroom.

He hauled her to her feet and dragged her down the hall, her bare feet feeling warped wood floors. They turned into another room and he shoved her against the far wall. "On your knees."

She collapsed against the wall, feeling old plaster and rough boards under her fingertips. She knelt, her forehead pressed against the plaster. One of his legs was firm against her back, but his attention was higher. Metal scraped against wood and he cursed. "Where'd they go?" he muttered.

Who?

Nervous energy rolled off him, and the odor of his sweat filled the room. A second scent emanated from him: her.

Her stomach turned over.

Then she felt his blade press against her cheek.

Truman breathed shallowly, the pain from the shot stabbing him with every inhalation.

At least I'm still breathing.

"Think Rose is in there?" Mercy whispered as they crouched behind their temporary cover.

Truman's gut told him she was. *But is Rose alive?*

A woman's screams sounded from the house and Mercy jumped to her feet. Truman lunged and grabbed her elbow before she dashed to the house. "Sit down!" he ordered as blinding pain radiated from his chest.

Mercy whirled on him, her eyes wide and her chest heaving. *"That's Rose!"*

The screams intensified.

Mercy dropped to her knees and crushed her hands over her ears, pressing her gun against her temple. "He's killing her," she whispered.

Truman grabbed her other arm, holding her down, knowing she was seconds away from bolting toward the house again.

"We can't wait," she hissed, staring him in the eyes. "We've got to go in. I'll go in."

He shifted up to one knee with a low moan and gritted his teeth against the pain. "No one's going in there."

"If we wait for the others, it'll be too late! Craig has to know we called for reinforcements."

"We can't go through the front door," Truman said between clenched teeth. "He'll kill us before we get there. Where's the tunnel?"

With Mercy's help, Truman made it to the Tahoe and backed it up the driveway to the road, out of sight of the house, hoping the shooter would think they'd left. Then they cut back through the woods on foot to where Mercy remembered Ned's woodshed stood. Every step shook Truman's chest, creating shooting pains that radiated up to his brain. Mercy glanced at him with concern a few times, but kept her mouth shut. He'd push on until it was physically impossible, and she knew it. A hundred feet of ground stood between the back door of the home and the woodshed. The woodshed's door was out of view of any windows.

"Think Craig knows about the tunnel?" Truman asked as Mercy peered inside the shed.

"I think he would have locked this door," she replied. She pulled out a tiny flashlight and lit up the space. Chopped wood was stacked from the concrete floor almost to the ceiling. Maneuvering room was tight. She squeezed through a narrow aisle, the wood catching her jacket and hair.

Spiders.

Mercy didn't seem to care, so Truman firmly put all thoughts of hairy spider legs out of his brain and followed. A piece of wood jabbed his chest and he winced, catching his breath.

"I found it!"

He squeezed between a few more feet of wood and found her kneeling in a wider area, peering down into a large hole. A ladder stuck up out of the opening and vanished down into the darkness.

Good Lord. Pushing between the woodpiles had been claustrophobic enough. The sight of the black tunnel made him light-headed, and he looked away.

She shone her flashlight in the hole and cocked her head, listening carefully. "It's quiet. I doubt he knows it exists."

"Where do you think it opens up in the house?"

"I'll guess in the basement. I can't believe none of the crime scene techs or deputies reported a tunnel. It must be hidden well." She tucked her flashlight under her arm and started down the ladder. She dropped the last two feet and squatted, pointing her flashlight down the shaft. "I'm impressed," she said. "He's supported it with wood beams. I'll have to crawl, but it's not the crumbling mess I expected."

She eagerly looked up at Truman, but then her eyebrows narrowed. "You look ready to vomit."

I feel ready to vomit.

"I'll go," she said, looking down the shaft again. "You can wait for backup. Let them know what we're doing. You won't be able to crawl if you've got broken ribs."

"I'm coming."

FORTY

Truman called in their plan as he dueled with his mental monsters. Close spaces had never been his friend.

But he wasn't about to let her enter that house on her own. Rose's screams peaked and waned and repeated; Mercy cringed each time.

He wasn't going to hesitate this time. *Keep moving.*

Rose wasn't going to die with him feet away, unable to make a decision.

He backed down the ladder, cursing that he'd left his flashlight in the SUV. His feet hit dirt, and he crouched to look down the passageway. Mercy was a few feet into the tunnel, her flashlight exposing the boards and dirt.

Every cell in his body screamed for him to get out.

He breathed deeply and focused on her. She was silhouetted by her light, but he saw the concern on her face.

"Are you sure about this? You don't—"

"Stop talking about it." He swallowed hard. "Seriously. Don't talk about it. Makes it worse. Just push on." He clamped his lips together.

She hesitated and then nodded. Turning, she started to crawl, holding her small flashlight in one hand.

Truman followed.

Odors of nature's decomposition and wet dirt assaulted him, constant reminders that he was *underground*. He crawled, keeping his eyes on Mercy's feet. *Think of nothing, think of nothing.* His head bumped the top of the tunnel and dirt showered him.

Visions of a tunnel cave-in filled his brain.

He stopped and lowered his head to his hands, sucking in deep breaths.

Collapse. Suffocation.

"Truman? You okay?"

"Yes," he forced out. "Coming." He lifted his head and pushed forward, focusing on the soles of her boots. The lack of echo and background noise messed with his brain, making the walls feel closer than the eighteen inches on each side of him. The air pressure seemed to increase, and his lungs struggled to function. Sweat dripped on his hands.

Five things you can touch.

Dirt, rocks, my clothes, my face, a board.

Four things you can see.

He squinted in the dark. Her boots. Her ass. The outline of her head. The light.

He kept crawling.

Every time he moved his hand it felt as if a knife sliced through his ribs. He focused on the pain, welcoming the distraction. *Broken ribs?* Probably. Didn't matter. All a doctor would do was tape him up and tell him to take it easy.

His left hand landed in squishy mud, and he recoiled. The rib pain sent an iron spike through his nerves and directly into his brain. He gasped.

"Truman?"

"Keep going." *Don't talk about it.*

She moved on. He pictured the space between the house and the shed above ground. A hundred feet at the most. *How far have we come?* Seeking a diversion, he counted his hand movements, visualizing the numbers in his brain. His head whacked a board and stars lit up his vision.

"The ceiling's lower here," Mercy said.

No shit. His back scraped along the ceiling and he flexed his arms, dropping his upper body a few inches. The back of his belt caught on the same board, and a wave of panic rolled through him. He lowered to his stomach, inching forward on his elbows. *How long can I do this?*

Can I back out?

What if the end is barricaded?

How will we turn around?

He needed to stand; he needed to stretch his arms out to the sides; he needed to *breathe.* He took deeper breaths, his lungs fighting for oxygen. Every breath was insufficient. *I'm suffocating.*

"Truman! Get moving!"

He opened his eyes. Mercy had moved forward a good ten feet and lay on her side, looking back at him, her flashlight aimed at his eyes. "I can't breathe." He squeezed his eyes shut. *Five things . . . dirt.*

All I can feel is dirt. Don't think. Don't think. Get out! Now!

He pushed to his hands and knees and his back slammed against the ceiling.

I need to stand up!

He tried to push off with his hands, but there was nowhere for his body to go. He dropped back to his stomach, his eyes still closed, and dug his elbows into the walls of the tunnel.

Pain shot through his hand and he opened his eyes to the glaring light of her flashlight two feet from his face. She'd brought her boot heel down on his hand.

"*Crawl.* Now! Or I'll kick you in the face!" she screamed.

He lifted off his stomach, his eyes locked on her bright light. Her physical and mental shocks had worked.

"Touch my boot. Keep reaching for it as we crawl." She moved forward, aiming the light ahead.

He followed.

"Sing something," she ordered.

"W-what?"

"Anything." She launched into the chorus of "Live Like You Were Dying" by Tim McGraw.

"On a bull named Fu Manchu . . . ," he recited. His fingers briefly touched her boot before it moved forward. They fell into a rhythm with the lyrics and he kept his gaze on her boots. They quietly sang the song twice, hoarsely mouthing the words. He kept his mind blank, his arms and legs moving on autopilot. "I spent most of the next days looking at the X-rays—" She abruptly stopped singing.

Truman halted midlyric and looked past her.

A piece of plywood blocked their way.

"Did one of the supports fall?" Truman asked, as terror flared through his body again.

"It's the end."

Mercy shoved on the board and it didn't budge. Panic rocked through her.

This is how Truman felt through every foot of that tunnel.

She put all her strength into driving the heel of her hand at the lower corner of the board, and it moved.

Thank you, Lord.

She did it again and the board started to fall. She caught it and wiggled forward on her stomach, easing the board into a larger space. Fresh air rushed through the tunnel and Truman sighed in relief. He'd terrified her a few minutes ago, and she felt bad for screaming at him, but he'd needed to be shocked. She hadn't known how to get him out of the tunnel, but then she'd remembered how Rose would sing to a skittish horse or sheep. The animal would calm, and its focus would zero in on the singer. It was the only idea she'd had, and it'd worked.

Hang on, Rose. We're so close.

She gently let the board slide out of her hands to the floor a few feet below the tunnel opening and picked up her flashlight, scanning the room in front of her. The tunnel emptied into the basement. Stacks of bins and boxes crowded the low-ceilinged space. Elation ran through her. They'd made it into the house and might be only steps away from finding·Rose.

"Mercy?" Truman pleaded behind her.

She hustled the rest of the way out of the tunnel and turned to give him a hand. His face and shirt collar were drenched with sweat.

"How are your ribs?" she asked as he awkwardly stood.

"Distracting."

"Is that a good thing?"

"It was." He wiped his forehead. "Thank you. I didn't think I'd make it."

"You shouldn't have tried it."

"Doesn't matter. Let's find your sister."

"Listen." Mercy froze. "Do you hear that?"

"It sounds like two men yelling at each other."

They worked their way between the bins to the basement stairs and ascended the steps, wincing at every squeak. Mercy glanced at her phone. "No service."

"Not surprised."

They reached the door to the inside of the house, a faint light shining through the crack at the bottom, and listened. One voice was in the house and the other sounded as if it came from outdoors.

"That sounds like Levi!" Shock took her breath.

"How would he know to come here?"

"He probably heard from Eddie that we were going to check out Toby's story. If he'd left my parents' house at that point, he would have beat any law enforcement who responded when I called later for backup."

Or did he already know Craig would be here?

She gripped her weapon and slowly opened the door. It swung out into an area near the boarded-up back door of the home. Mercy swallowed hard, remembering her first tour of the old house. And the fly-covered body in the bed upstairs.

"This is none of your business, Levi!" Craig shouted from the floor above them.

It is Levi.

"It's all over, Craig," her brother yelled from outside. "You need to let Rose go."

"Your brother has to know we're here somewhere," Truman whispered. "He couldn't miss my Tahoe parked on the road."

"Fuck off, Levi!"

"I'm calling the police!"

"Go ahead! Your other sister already ran off with her tail between her legs. I'm sure she's rounding up every cop in the county to come here."

"You haven't done anything yet! Let Rose go before they have a reason to come in shooting."

Craig laughed. "You think they don't know I killed those preppers? They're going to fry me."

"They don't have proof," Levi argued. "But if you hurt Rose, they'll definitely know. Release her before it gets worse for you."

Craig hasn't said Rose is dead. Mercy drew strength from that. Rose's silence was almost worse than her screams. Almost.

"So you can back out on our deal?" Craig yelled.

"Our deal was that I didn't tell anyone that you were at my parents' house that night. I've kept my word."

Mercy winced. That wasn't quite true anymore.

"And my end of the deal was that I don't tell them where you buried the body. Sounds like we're still even."

"Hurting Rose will wipe out our deal," Levi shouted.

Craig laughed. "Oh, she's already been hurt."

Levi was silent. Mercy could imagine his rage. *Hurt, not dead.* "We need to get upstairs," she whispered. "He'll be distracted talking to Levi."

Truman nodded, and she led the way to the stairs. She stepped on the edge of each stair, close to the wall, praying they didn't creak. The direction of Craig's voice told her he was in the room overlooking the front yard. The one with the boarded-up window with the slit for spying on visitors. Where he'd shot Truman.

Does Craig really believe we left?

She glanced back at Truman. He'd recovered from his trip through the tunnel, but he hunched his right shoulder in a way that told her his ribs were in pain. His knees and hands were as muddy as hers, and she assumed she was covered with the same layer of powdered earth. He looked as if he'd been caught in a dirt storm.

They reached the top of the stairs and turned toward the boarded-up window room, where Craig continued his conversation with Levi. They paused before reaching the open door.

"If you've hurt Rose, I'll tell them you confessed the prepper murders to me."

Mercy recognized the escalation in Levi's tone; he was nearing a breaking point.

"Sounds like you'll be ratting me out then," Craig hollered. "I can't have that!"

"Where's Rose?" Truman whispered. Mercy glanced down the hall. Every door was open. Was Rose locked up somewhere else?

A whimper made the hair on her arms raise. *Rose is in the room with him.*

Truman nodded; he'd heard it too.

"Goddamn you, Craig!" Levi shouted.

A shot was fired from outside, and the sound of wood splintering came from the room.

Her weapon leading, Mercy ducked her head around the door frame and saw Craig lunge toward the boarded window—which now had a fresh bullet hole—and fire back at her brother. Rose was at his feet, naked, curled up in a fetal position, blood staining the old carpet beneath her. *His back is to us.* She nodded at Truman, took a deep breath, and they both stepped into the doorway.

Craig leaned against the boarded-up window, firing at Levi.

Rose raised her head, nearly unrecognizable through a layer of blood. "Mercy?"

In a split second, Mercy realized Rose's face was covered with cuts.

Craig spun around, his gun pointed at her and Truman.

Mercy emptied her magazine as Truman did the same, and her ears rang from the rapid gunfire.

Craig collapsed, and Truman dashed to Rose as Mercy lowered her gun, rattled by the sight of the bleeding man on the floor.

It's over.

She's alive.

Rose sat up and leaned on Truman as Mercy rushed to the window. "Levi, don't fire! Craig's down!" she shouted before she peered through the slit.

Her brother was on the ground. Motionless.

Mercy couldn't breathe; she stood glued to the window, willing her brother to get up. *"Levi!"* she screamed. She couldn't move away.

"Mercy!" Truman said sharply.

She turned, adrenaline racing. "Levi's not moving! I have to get to him!"

Truman had put his thin jacket on Rose, and she batted away his hands as he tried to check her bloody wounds. "I'm fine," Rose insisted. He turned his attention to Craig. He pulled off his shirt and pressed it against the puddle of blood on his chest.

Mercy tore out of the room.

Craig's eyes opened, meeting Truman's gaze.

"Hold on," Truman ordered. "Help's coming."

"Fuck you," Craig muttered, coughing.

"Yeah, well, I love you too," Truman said, pressing harder on the shirt he'd balled up against Craig's wounds. It grew wet beneath his fingers.

"You were always such an ass," Craig mumbled. "Always doin' the goddamned right thing." Foaming blood came out of his mouth as he coughed.

Too much blood.

Rose's hand touched Truman's shoulder, and she reached out for Craig with the other. Her fingertips danced across his chest, noting the blood and holes. She touched his mouth, felt the red foam, and pulled back.

"It's not good," she whispered.

"You're not gonna save me this time, Truman." Blood flowed from Craig's mouth, and he went still.

"Craig!" Truman shook his shoulder. The man's gaze was unfocused.

"He's gone," Rose said softly. "It was too much."

Truman sat back, his soaked shirt wet in his hand, staring at the dead man.

What could I have done differently?

FORTY-ONE

Mercy fought with the locks on Ned's front door, her fingers fumbling, and finally flung open the door and launched herself down the steps. *"Levi!"*

Her brother was sprawled in the dirt, blood flowing from the side of his neck.

She slid to the ground, ripped off her jacket, and pressed it on the wound. She could feel the pulse of the blood as it left his body.

Craig had hit an artery.

How can I put a tourniquet on a neck?

Levi opened his eyes. "Rose?"

Mercy leaned closer. "She's going to be fine." *I hope.*

"Good. Should have told you about Craig earlier."

"You weren't sure."

"I wondered." He held her gaze. "I missed you. I'm glad you're back."

She smiled at him with shaking lips. "Me too."

"Take care of Kaylie for me. Keep her mother away."

Ice flooded Mercy's veins. *"Don't talk like that."* She pressed harder against his neck.

"Not Pearl," he whispered. "Not Mom. *You.*"

She swallowed hard. His words were so faint. The pulsations under her fingertips grew farther apart.

Sirens sounded. County deputies.

"You're going to be just fine," she pleaded. *He can't leave me now. I just got him back.*

"Tell her I love her."

"Tell her yourself!"

"Kaylie," he whispered. His eyes closed, and he took a shuddering half breath.

Mercy stared at her brother's body, ignoring the car doors that slammed in the driveway.

This isn't happening.

FORTY-TWO

Three days later

Mercy hated funerals.

She'd been to only two in her lifetime, but this third one would be filed in her memory forever. She watched them lower Levi's casket and gave up trying to hold in her tears. All day she'd held them in, trying to be strong for the rest of her family, but the finality of watching her brother disappear below the earth was too much. She looked up, past the mourners and acres of trees. Familiar white mountain peaks stood against the blue sky, and the dusty dry smell of the pines soothed her.

Central Oregon was still her home; her roots here were deeper than she'd realized. The fifteen-year absence seemed to dissolve, and she drew strength from the physical beauty around her.

Rose's grip on her hand tightened.

She was the reason Mercy had tried so hard to be stoic. Rose had suffered at the hands of her kidnapper *and* lost her brother, yet Rose was the one who'd shown strength. Scabs had formed over the long slashes on Rose's face, chest, and arms. Remnants of how Craig had made her scream . . . to torment Mercy.

It'd worked. She heard Rose's screams in her dreams every night.

The wounds were superficial. Rose might have some scarring, but every time Mercy looked at her sister, Craig Rafferty came to the forefront of her thoughts. Rose didn't care about the scabs; she held up her head. Men stared at her injuries. Children backed away. Women teared up. Rose ignored their reactions and offered support and thanks to everyone who talked to her about Levi.

"It's about Levi today," she'd told Mercy. "Marks on my face don't matter."

At the house Mercy had seen her gently trace the marks on her cheeks, her expression blank. Then she'd touched her stomach, a look of wonder on her face.

Mercy had begged her to get the morning-after pill.

Rose refused.

"I won't do that," she said. "If there's a baby, I want it."

"But Rose," Mercy started, a dozen reasons crowding her mind. *The child of a rapist. What will you tell the child? Will another man take on that child one day?* Then she realized that if anyone could handle the situation, it was her sister. Her heart was enormous, and she possessed a true gift of forgiveness.

Even blind, she was more resolute than Mercy.

Rose didn't know if she was pregnant. But her introspective expression told Mercy she hoped she was.

Their second big conversation had been about the death of Kenny, the first attacker.

They and Truman had agreed to keep it quiet. The only two other people who had known about Kenny were dead.

The police had found Jennifer's and Gwen's prom pictures in Craig's apartment. They'd also found his fingerprints on the stolen weapons at Owlie Lake. In her interview, Rose had stated that Craig had told her he'd killed the preppers and the two girls. Craig Rafferty would probably take all the blame for what both men had done.

It'd been enough to start the wrapping up of the cases and offer healing to long-grieving families.

David Aguirre started a final prayer over Levi's grave. Around her, heads bowed. Mercy stared at the gaping hole and struggled to pull up more memories of her brother. *Why did I let fifteen years go by?* His final moments in the dirt outside the Fahey home haunted her, and she hated that they would be a prominent memory for the rest of her life.

Around her everyone stood, and she stiffly moved to her feet, feeling decades older. Placing Rose's hand on her arm, she followed her siblings and parents out of the first row of seats, blindly walking behind Pearl. Her family started to form a receiving line, and Mercy begged off, transferring Rose's hand to Pearl and escaping to stand under a towering ponderosa pine between old gravestones fifty feet away. Her father still wouldn't look her in the eye, but her mother had assured her he didn't fully blame her for Levi's death. Mercy had been stunned at her mother's words. *Blaming me is an option?*

She carried her own minor guilt over Levi's death, but she hadn't placed him outside that house, and she wasn't the one who had hid the identity of a possible killer for fifteen years. She, Truman, and Rose had agreed not to share Levi's involvement with Craig. There was no gain for anyone in knowing what her brother had done.

The distance between her and her father might never be bridged. Her mother was coming around, but only as far as she was comfortable under her husband's watchful eye. Pearl was similar, acting stiff around Mercy when her husband was present. Owen wouldn't let his family acknowledge her, and Rose had admitted he was angry about Levi's death.

I don't care how my family feels. Not much, anyway.

She inhaled the baked scent of the pines, refusing to feel shame that she couldn't stand in a line and listen to the mourners spout their banalities.

Today is about Levi. I said my good-bye.

She'd come to terms with what Levi had done to her and Rose. She hadn't forgiven him. Yet. But she refused to harbor any hatred. What was done was done. Allowing anger to fester against her dead brother would only hurt her.

In a few weeks she'd ask a few people to share happy memories of her brother. Just not today.

"Aunt Mercy?" Kaylie appeared beside her. "I don't want to stand in that line."

The sight of her niece lifted her spirits. Levi was always present in Kaylie's face and in her gestures. The more time Mercy spent with the teen, the more she saw the young Levi she remembered. It was comforting.

Two days ago Mercy told Kaylie her name had been the last word on Levi's lips. The girl had fallen apart at the revelation, but Mercy had known it would comfort her later.

Now Mercy put an arm around her shoulders. "I can't do it either. I think it's okay if we stand back here and watch." Kaylie's mother hadn't attended, and Mercy's heart hurt for the teenager.

So alone.

"Your daddy loved you very much," Mercy whispered, knowing the girl had heard the phrase a thousand times in the last few days. Mercy's mother had brought Kaylie to stay in her home and fussed over her in a way Mercy suspected the teen had never experienced.

"I know," Kaylie said. She took a deep breath. "I have a big favor to ask you."

"Anything."

"I want to come live with you in Portland."

Mercy started. *That* she hadn't expected. Levi's last request rang in her head, and she shut it away. She hadn't told anyone what he'd asked of her. "You have another year of school left. You should finish it here. Grandma and Aunt Pearl will take good care of you." Her voice shook.

Kaylie shook her head. "They don't get me. It's always just been my dad and me. I don't know how to fit in with a family."

"Oh, Kaylie—"

"You don't have to make up your mind yet," she said quickly. "Think about it. I clean up after myself and I don't need to be entertained."

Can I take on a teenager?

She pulled the girl tight to her side, remembering how abandoned she'd felt as a teenager. She wouldn't let that happen to Kaylie.

But she had her own life to straighten out first.

"Trust me," Mercy said. "I won't leave you alone. But I have some things to do, and then I'll tell you what I decide."

Kaylie looked her in the eye. "Promise?"

"Absolutely."

Truman watched Mercy hug her niece as he waited his turn in the receiving line.

He wanted to skip it and escape like Mercy, but the chief of police had a duty. He took his turn, shaking hands, hugging the women and repeating his "I'm sorry for your loss" line until he felt blue in the face. He shook the last hand and stepped away.

"Hey, Truman." Mike Bevins fell into step with him, and he stopped to shake another hand.

No escape yet.

"I know this is the wrong time to bring it up, but I'm hearing some rumors and I thought I'd run them by you."

"What'd you hear?" Truman asked cautiously. He'd been interviewed several times about the shooting at Ned Fahey's home, but the public still asked him questions.

Mike looked down at his boots. "Did Craig really say that he killed those men because he wanted to be next in line for my father's business?" His shoulders slumped.

Truman took a breath. "Yeah, he told Rose that. That was news to you?"

"In a way." Mike finally met his gaze. "He was always a half step behind me, you know? Craig wasn't a talker, but when he did, he often asked about my future plans and encouraged me to move to Portland and start teaching those survival classes. I didn't realize it was because he wanted me out of the way."

"Is your father here?" Truman asked.

"No. His health has taken a turn for the worse."

"I'm sorry, Mike. What are you going to do?"

Mike turned to look at the receiving line, where Owen Kilpatrick stood next to his father. "For now I'm going to be what my father needs me to be. But I won't let it rule my life."

"You could do both. Run the ranch and teach."

"I know," he said. "But I'd hoped for a clean break." His blue eyes met Truman's. "There will be some changes at the ranch when my father dies. There are some aspects of his philosophy that I don't care to continue."

No more preparing for the end of the world at the Bevins ranch?

Truman wondered how the loss of that pillar would rock the rest of the town. "Good luck. I'm here if you need me." He held out his hand.

Mike was solemn as he took the hand. "I know. Thank you, Truman." He left to join a circle of men waiting for him. Truman watched him go, wondering how heavily those men leaned on Mike Bevins. They might have a few changes coming.

Mercy was now alone under the pine, and he headed in her direction. He'd been sitting two rows behind her at the service, watching as she held Rose's hand and feeling oddly disconnected. He and Mercy had been together almost nonstop since the shooting. He liked it that way.

He approached, admiring her green eyes that'd watched him walk across the graveyard. Her mouth turned up in a smile as he got closer, and he was stunned at how attracted he was to her. They still hadn't spoken about their situation.

Do we have a situation?

They did. But neither of them had been ready to address it. Instead they'd been silent, leaning on each other as she grieved, rarely leaving each other's side. He'd wanted to show he would always be there when needed. Even though there'd been no words, he'd seen the understanding dawn in her eyes. He'd spotted the knowing looks from her mother and the other women in town: Truman Daly was off the market.

He'd known it for a while, but Mercy was just catching on.

He held out his hand as he approached, and she took it.

"Can you get me out of here?" she asked.

"Where to?"

"I want to climb a mountain."

It wasn't really a mountain, Mercy admitted. But the hike up the peak behind Owlie Lake was exactly what she needed.

She and Truman spent the next two hours hunting for bones.

They found nothing.

On a rock overlooking the vast view, they finally took a break.

"I guess we'll never know the location of Kenny's body," Mercy said, turning her face up to soak in the sun.

"Or his last name," Truman said. "I've searched missing person records in the western half of the United States, but short of asking Mike Bevins for employment records from fifteen years ago, I don't know what else to do."

"Both of the guilty parties have paid the price."

"I agree."

"Thank you for keeping my and Rose's secret."

He shrugged. "Does it go against my grain? Yes. But more people will be hurt if I speak up. Especially now." He took her hand. "I don't mind doing this for you."

She squeezed his hand and studied his eyes. He was sincere. An old weight slowly lifted from her shoulders, one she'd been carrying for a long time. Was it because Craig was dead? Or from confiding in Truman? Now he carried half her burden.

"What will you do with Jefferson's house?" she asked.

"I'll hang on to it for now. I'm not ready to sell."

"You had your uncle's killer in your hands at the Fahey house."

"I did," Truman admitted. "Looking back, I'm proud I didn't simply watch him bleed to death. I suspect if I'd had time to think about it, I might have let it happen."

"That's not who you are," Mercy stated.

"No, it's not," he agreed. "I've changed my mind about a few things over the past week. I even want to take a closer look at my uncle's backup power system and water supply. Maybe there's a tiny bit of sense in being prepared in case of an emergency."

She punched him lightly on the upper arm and he winced. "Watch the ribs!"

"I forgot. Sorry." She leaned closer and pressed her lips on his, loving the heady rush that ran through her at the touch of his skin. There'd been several intimate moments over the last few days. Enough to make her question her future. He'd become important to her, and now her heart was vulnerable. A feeling she hadn't experienced in years.

But she wasn't scared. It felt good.

"When do you go back to Portland?" he finally asked. The question had been floating over both their heads for three days. Her case was done. She'd requested a week's leave, which had been immediately granted, but its end was near.

"Saturday."

"I'll come visit the following weekend. The drive isn't that bad."

"It'll begin to suck if we're doing it several times a month," she pointed out.

"It's worth it."

"Jeff told me his Bend office got a budget approval to let him bring on three more agents." She waited for his reaction.

Truman froze. "Are you serious?" His smile started to widen. "What will you do about that?"

"I've already applied." The joy on his face made her heart happy. "But there's a catch."

"What? I don't care. Just name it." He took both her hands and pulled her up to stand on the rock, where he hugged her tight.

"Kaylie might be living with me."

"That's fantastic. She needs a home and you're perfect for her."

"You think so?" *Is he joking?* "I know nothing about raising a teen."

"Weren't you a teenage girl?"

"Well, yes, but my situation—"

"Then you have more experience than half the population." He grinned at her. "You'll do great. You'll be good for each other."

"I think I might buy a house in Bend." She looked at their view of the spreading valley. "I need this. I need the wide-open skies and less gray rain. I need to look up and see a long row of white mountains. It speaks to my soul. I'd forgotten until I came back." She met his gaze. "I want to be closer to you . . . see what develops." She whispered the last word.

"Just don't ask me to inspect your crawl space." His grin made her heart beat faster.

"Never! I swear on my life I'll never force you into a small space."

"Then we have a deal."

He swung her into a dramatic dip and kissed her again.

Acknowledgments

In 2014 I was on a plane to Thrillerfest in NYC. My third book, *Buried*, had been nominated for a Thriller Award, and an editor from a different publishing house had reached out to me, saying she loved my work and wanted to know if I'd be interested in writing something for their house. I agreed to meet her in NYC, and on that plane ride I had a moment of terror as I realized I didn't have a concept to pitch. Ideas are difficult for me. I'm not that writer who has so many ideas she doesn't know where to start. I stress and moan to come up with every single one. I whipped out my notebook on the plane and started brainstorming. Mercy Kilpatrick was born at thirty-five thousand feet, and that editor was enchanted with my concept.

Long story short: I asked my agent to first officially offer the idea to my current publishing house. My editor loved the concept, and I was relieved because I adore my Montlake team and there's no one I'd rather have publish my books. They took a chance on me when no other house would and are the coolest, most innovative people on the planet. This is my tenth novel with them, and I look forward to the next ten.

Ten books? How did that happen so fast?

Thank you to Special Agents Devinney and Gluesenkamp for answering all my questions. Maybe I need to write an FBI duo with those names. Thank you to Charlotte Herscher for her editing expertise. Thank you to my agent, Meg Ruley, who has been an enthusiastic Mercy fan from day one.

My last book was dedicated to my espresso maker. This book is 100 percent caffeine free, so I hope my readers still enjoy it.

ABOUT THE AUTHOR

Photo © 2016 Rebekah Jule Photography

Inspired by classic female heroines such as Nancy Drew, Trixie Belden, and Laura Ingalls Wilder, Kendra Elliot has always been a voracious reader. Now a *Wall Street Journal* bestselling author, Kendra is a three-time winner of the Daphne du Maurier Award for best Romantic Mystery/Suspense. She was also an International Thriller Writers finalist for Best Paperback Original and a *Romantic Times* finalist for best Romantic Suspense.

Kendra was born and raised in the rainy Pacific Northwest, where she still lives with her husband and three daughters, though she's looking forward to the day when she can live in flip-flops. To learn more about the author and her work and to connect with her, visit www.KendraElliot.com.